ABOUT PETER RIMMER

Peter Rimmer was born in London, England, and grew up in the south of the city where he went to school. After the Second World War, aged eighteen, he joined the Royal Air Force, reaching the rank of Pilot Officer before he was nineteen. At the end of his National Service, he sailed for Africa to grow tobacco in what was then Rhodesia, now Zimbabwe.

The years went by and Peter found himself in Johannesburg where he established an insurance brokering company. Over 2% of the companies listed on the Johannesburg Stock Exchange were clients of Rimmer Associates. He opened branches in the United States of America, Australia and Hong Kong and travelled extensively between them.

Having lived a reclusive life on his beloved smallholding in Knysna, South Africa, for over 25 years, Peter passed away in July 2018. He has left an enormous legacy of unpublished work for his family to release over the coming years, and not only they but also his readers from around the world will sorely miss him. Peter Rimmer was 81 years old.

ALSO BY PETER RIMMER

~

LEOPARDS NEVER CHANGE THEIR SPOTS

ELEVENTH BOOK IN THE BRIGANDSHAW CHRONICLES

PETER RIMMER

PART 1

AUGUST 1979 – LET THE GAMES BEGIN

1

The high velocity bullet penetrated the windowpane above Randall Crookshank's head sending him to the floor of his father's lounge and making up his mind. His FN rifle was against the wall under the light switch ten feet away making him crawl across the carpet on all fours, looking up at the switch at a level above the windowsill. The cat, covered in shards of glass, had not moved, but the dogs on the lawn inside the security fence had begun to bark, an aggressive bark telling Randall the terrorists were not far from the farmhouse. Getting his hand up to the light switch, his head below the level of the windowsill, he turned on the outside floodlights sending light through the high fence into the bush turning night into day. With his gun in his hand, he crawled to the window, smashed one of the panes of glass with the barrel and fired into the night, short, automatic bursts. With the gun and two spare magazines he crawled across the floor to the Agric-Alert where he broadcast the attack on the farm through the police radio. From the direction of the manager's house Randall heard firing.

"This is Randall Crookshank. World's View is under attack. I am alone in the main house. Vince Ranger is firing from the manager's house behind me. The floodlights are on. The dogs are barking hysterically. The terrs must be close to the house."

"Be with you inside ten minutes, Randall. Are you all right?"

"I'm getting out of the house in case they fire a rocket-propelled grenade. I returned fire. Is that Clay Barry?"

"I'm coming myself. If you're getting out, switch off the floodlights."

"I thought the war was meant to be more or less over?"

"Nothing's ever over, Randall."

"I'm out of here. Right out of here. Right out of Rhodesia. I want a life."

"Keep your chin up. You're probably better inside the house in the corridor between the bedrooms."

"Do I leave the lights on?"

"That's your choice. They'll be getting out by now to get into the bush before we can circle the farm. If they haven't fired RPGs by now they likely won't. Where's your father and stepmother?"

"With their kids on holiday at Lake Kariba. They left me in charge of the house."

Cowering in the dark corridor, sitting on the stone floor cradling his rifle, Randall waited. He could feel his heartbeat, his mind in turmoil just below the point of panic, his life about to end at the age of twenty-one before it had even started. Outside the dogs had stopped barking. There was silence: August in Rhodesia was cold at night quieting the insects and amphibians. Far away an owl called. Not a sound came from the workers' compound a mile behind the grading sheds and tobacco barns at the end of the drive that led up to the farmhouse on its hill. Randall waited, the minutes passing without incident giving him hope.

"I'm still a virgin," he whispered to himself. "I can't die now."

One of the dogs barked, sending the pit of his stomach sick with fright. He could hear the grandfather clock ticking from the lounge. The quarter hour chimed. Straining his ears for the sound of help from the police coming from the village of Centenary or Vince Ranger from the manager's house, he bent over the gun, his mind and body petrified. Something pushed at his side making him cry out in the dark and his hand thrashed back, hitting a dog. The flap in the door at the end of the corridor let the dogs and cats in and out of the house after the servants locked up at night to go back to their compound and their families. The dog was nuzzling him. Randall was not sure in the dark which one of the four Alsatians had come into the house. He hugged the dog as it licked his face. They sat together on the floor giving each other comfort, making Randall think of the cat covered in shards of glass on the windowsill in the lounge, hoping she was still alive. The distant sound of a truck engine made his hope ride up, the cold shakes in his body subsiding. The sound quickly grew nearer along the main tarred road from Centenary. Randall heard the police vehicle turn off the road onto the farm road that would take it through the barns and up the hill to the house. But his hope was shattered by a powerful explosion.

"A fucking landmine," shouted Randall, jumping up.

The dog followed him down the corridor as he ran to the backdoor. The key hung inside on the handle on a piece of string. Fumbling, Randall opened the backdoor and ran into the night, his gun at the ready. Vince Ranger was running out of the manager's house fifty yards up in front of him.

"The bloody shot was to make me call the police on the radio," shouted Randall.

"Probably. You unlock the gate, I'll get the truck."

"Better walk, Vince."

"You're right. Where's your torch?"

"In the house."

"Get it. Bring the dogs. Who did you speak to?"

"The member-in-charge. Clay Barry."

"Someone's alive. I can hear their voices. Shit, the truck's starting up again. Must have come in an anti-mines vehicle with the V-shaped armour plate riding up from the road. Sends the blast up on either side of the vehicle. I'll open the gate. You hang onto the dogs. Did that shot hit anything?"

"A windowpane. I think it killed one of the cats with a flying shard of glass. It was sleeping on the windowsill. I thought the bush war was over with that agreement they're meant to be signing soon in London."

"They haven't finalised a date for the ceasefire. Mugabe and his army generals are meeting in Mozambique. Here come the police. It's all over, Randall."

"You're bloody right it is. I'm getting out. There's no future for us whites, however many agreements. I'm going to England to get a life. London. London's the place."

"What are you going to do for a living?"

"Who knows? I'll find out when I get there. I've never been outside of

Africa on my own. Dad will give me a ticket and some spending money. He part-owns a block of flats in Chelsea with one of his girlfriends he met after my mother was killed. Before he married Bergit. He'd got the money out of the country before sanctions and exchange control. We should all get out of the country, except my father won't leave the farm."

"I thought you wanted to be a tobacco farmer?"

"Not after tonight, Vince. Frightened the holy shit out of me. Here they come. I'll try and hold onto the dogs. Can a dog set off a landmine? It may not be just the one. Don't want to kill one of the dogs."

"When are you going?"

"Tomorrow if I could. Dad, Bergit and the kids come back to the farm on Thursday. That far I can wait. I'll go visit my mother's grave on the Zambezi escarpment. Then I'm out of here. What about you, Vince? I thought you were going back to England and I would be farm manager in a couple of years."

"I'm too old to start another career. Who knows? Mugabe may make a success of the country and we'll all live happily ever after."

"Do you believe in fairy stories?"

"Sometimes you have to."

"You got the key to the gate?"

"In my pocket."

"Their headlights are still on. Don't need the torch. The tyres are shredded. You can hear the sound of metal crunching on the gravel."

The gate in the high fence swung open letting the police inside the three-house compound. Vince Ranger locked the gate behind them. Both doors of the vehicle opened letting the police out onto the lawn.

"Are you all right, Mr Barry?"

"The blast buggered up the tyres but we're still driving. Shook us up. Sergeant Goodson banged his knee badly and can't walk properly. Glad to see you both. When's this bloody war going to be over?"

"Can you drive that thing back to the police station?"

"I hope so, Vince... Everyone deploy into the bush. Spread out at ten yard intervals. Randall, go turn out those bloody floodlights. Makes my men sitting targets."

"Yes, sir."

Inside the house, Randall turned off the lights, sending the surrounding bush into pitch darkness. There was no moon. Slowly the light of the stars brought pale light back into the garden. The cat was still sitting on the windowsill as if it were asleep. Randall touched the cat and it fell to the floor. When Randall bent down in the dark and picked it up he knew the cat was dead. Randall began to cry, cradling her. The cat's name was Lady and had been in his life for as long as Randall could remember. With his back to the wall under the window, one pane punctured by a bullet, another shattered by the barrel of his rifle, Randall sat crying, cradling his dead cat, his FN rifle next to him forgotten. He had never felt more lonely, soulless, empty, with no point to his life. When his mother had died, killed and eaten by a pride of lions, he was too young to remember, only the painting by Livy in the lounge reminding him he had once had a mother. The bullet through the window had made up his mind and the dead cat in his arms had made it certain. His love of Africa had gone.

"There's no point to it anymore, Lady. Tomorrow I'll bury you in the garden among the flowers. My poor pussycat."

When Randall got up from the floor the house and garden were empty. He was alone. The way he had been for most of his life. Later, he heard voices. The police vehicle started up again, disturbing the night. The police drove away. Inspector Clay Barry had called out his name, but Randall hadn't answered.

At first light, having not gone to bed knowing he wouldn't sleep, Randall buried the cat, his eyes unable to see as he dug the deep hole in the flowerbed under a msasa tree. The trees and circling flowerbeds dotted the lawn. The *simby* sounded from the compound calling the labourers to work. Life on the farm was going on as if nothing had happened in the night. With his cat buried, Randall walked to the garage and drove out the truck. Vince was down at the barns, supervising the gang.

"Where you going, Randall?"

"To see my mother."

Slowly for an hour Randall drove through the Centenary block until he came to the Zambezi escarpment, the road dropping steeply down into the valley. Every year since she had died, his father had taken Randall and his brother Phillip to see their mother. The grave was off the road not far from where she had died, most of her eaten by the lions. On her grave stood a crude wooden cross fashioned by his father with the words 'Go well, my darling' burned into the wood.

"Goodbye, Mother. I won't be visiting you again. I'm going to England. To where you and Dad came from. I'll always think of you here. Please look after yourself. They killed my cat."

When he stood up, leaving a single rose on her grave, he could see the Zambezi River far away down below in the valley. He was no longer crying. It was over. All of it. If his father didn't understand, it was his problem. He was going to get himself a life. Too much uncertainty and no one knowing if the whites in Africa had a future had got to him, making him want to run away. Whatever problems he found in England could not be worse than what was going on in Rhodesia. He'd miss the sun, the smell of the bush and the cry of the fish eagles as they soared high in the sky. He'd miss his father and Bergit, Phillip and his half-brother Craig and his half-sister Myra. But that couldn't be helped. The bullet through the window had only just missed his head. Sick with emptiness, Randall got back into the truck, fired the engine, turned round on the mostly unused dirt road and drove back to the farm.

ON THE THURSDAY RANDALL told his father he had made up his mind.

"I wondered when this was going to come." His father was standing looking out of the window, running his finger round the neat round hole made by the terrorist's bullet.

"Sergeant Goodson broke his knee cap. You know he's the brother of Josiah Makoni, Mugabe's general. There's talk Josiah may be the one to end up running the country and not Robert Mugabe... You want some money, Randall? Phillip is going through Rhodes University so it's right you should have your share. I can buy you the plane ticket with Rhodesian currency. Your Uncle Paul runs my affairs in London now Livy Johnston is living in the Lake District. She's Livy Gainsborough now. Got herself married. I'll give you a letter to Paul."

"You're not mad at me?"

"How could I be, Randall? I left England when I was your age after my National Service in the Royal Navy. There wasn't much going for any of us youngsters in England after the war. A bit like Rhodesia now. You go and see what you can find. You have your whole life in front of you. The kids will miss you most."

"You won't miss me, Dad?" smiled Randall.

"Of course I will. You'll always be in my mind. We each have to make our own lives. I came to Rhodesia in pursuit of a Crown Land farm they were offering to ex-British servicemen. It was an adventure for me. England will be an adventure for you, it will be so different to life on an African farm. When do you want to go?"

"Pretty quickly. That bullet over my head frightened the crap out of me."

"If it doesn't work for you, come back. There's a big world out there. You've only got one life. Go and use it. In many ways I envy you. Travel the world. Not just to England. You're young, good-looking according to what I've heard from some of the ladies, and you're healthy. Go for it, son. I'll follow your journey if you write to me regularly. Maybe that's my only condition. You let me know how you are, what you are doing, what you are thinking. Can you do that for me? How much do you think you'll need in England?"

"I'm going to pay my own way. Find some kind of a job. I want to make something of my life."

"Good for you, Randall. Your grandmother told me I could have anything I wanted in the world if I earned it myself. She said spending other people's money wasn't nearly as much fun as spending your own... Our poor cat. Sleeping on the windowsill as usual. You loved that cat. Well, this is going to be a wrench. Better get on with it. I'll go phone the travel agent."

"I already did. All they want is a cheque."

"Give me the amount and I'll do it now. Tell me something. Why are we always in such a hurry when we are young?"

"In case we miss something."

When Randall walked through the lounge ten minutes later with the cheque in his pocket, his mother's eyes followed him from her portrait painted by Livy Johnston.

"Isn't that a bit weird, her name changing to Gainsborough? Wasn't he a famous British portrait painter?"

"The man she married had the surname of Gainsborough. Just a coincidence. They say Livy will become just as famous as Gainsborough one day. I can never remember that painter's first name. Why do artists have to die before they get famous? Seems rather pointless for the artist."

"Did you love her, Dad?"

"She wouldn't live in Africa. Saw what I didn't want to see. So often we only see what we want to see. They were friends, Carmen and Livy. There was another girl called Candy. Stayed together in a house in the Avenues."

"Do you regret marrying my mother and not Livy?"

As Randall spoke his stepmother had come into the room.

"Of course he doesn't. He wouldn't have had you and Phillip. So you're leaving us?"

"Yes, Aunty Bergit."

"Give your stepmother a hug. I'll miss you."

"If I hadn't had my real mother I'd have chosen you. Thank you for bringing me up."

"When are you going?"

"Tomorrow. First thing tomorrow. Vince is going to drive me to the travel agent to pick up the ticket and then to the airport. Better to say goodbye to all of you here in case I blub at the airport. I'm going up to the cottage to pack."

With the dogs following, Randall walked up to the cottage where he lived as the assistant manager of World's View. From the veranda he looked out over the bush to the faraway hills. From every window the view was the same as if the house was on top of the world. He could hear Craig laughing with his sister down at the pool, their high treble voices ringing out over the African bush. He hadn't yet told them he was going. Phillip, he'd write to in South Africa. Excited and fearful, Randall began to pack. The dogs had gone off. He was on his own and would be for the rest of his life unless he met a girl on his travels.

"I wonder who you'll be?" he said to the half-empty suitcase.

Quietly at first, then louder, Randall began to sing a song he had heard many times on the radio: 'You're in my heart, you're in my soul, you're my best lover'. When he stopped singing Randall snapped shut the lid of his suitcase. Rod Stewart was a better singer, he told himself, even the words he had sung not quite right. He was ready to go.

In the morning, when the sun came up, with Vince Ranger driving the truck, they passed the hole in the driveway made by the landmine.

He had said goodbye to his family in the lounge in front of his mother's portrait. When he looked back from the door she was still looking at him, and Randall was sure she was smiling.

"Thanks for the lift, Vince."

"My pleasure, Randall. Have a good life."

He was free, happy and ready to start his journey. When he walked up the steps to the aircraft he didn't look back. Vince would be driving from the airport back into town and a beer in the bar at Meikles Hotel. He gave the uniformed man at the top of the steps his boarding pass.

"Good morning, sir. Welcome to South African Airways. Your seat is halfway down the aisle to the left. Have a pleasant journey."

There was music playing on the loudspeaker, people stuffing their hand luggage into the compartments above the seats. Most of them were smiling with anticipation.

"Sorry, my seat's the one by the window. You can have the window seat if you want or I can climb over you." She was pretty. Smiling at him. A girl his own age.

"Are you going on holiday to England?"

"Are you? I'm Randall."

"June. I'm going over to look for a job. I'm a bit nervous flying. Do you mind me taking the window seat?"

"I'd love you too."

"You're all happy and smiling."

"Do I look that excited? They say the plane's almost full. They fly to England full and come back half empty."

"Yes, I suppose they do. Rather sad. By the look of that suntan you live on a farm."

"In the Centenary. When the block was started in 1952 it was the hundredth anniversary of the birth of Cecil Rhodes. Hence the name Centenary... We were attacked the other night. The bullet drilled a hole in the window just above my head and killed my cat. Lady was sleeping on the windowsill. A shard of glass killed her. I buried her in the flowerbed."

"How terrible."

"It was. I loved that cat. Why I'm leaving Rhodesia. I'm going to remember that cat for the rest of my life."

Randall buckled his seatbelt for nothing better to do. He was no longer smiling. He hoped the girl could not see he was silently crying. When the plane finally took off he turned to look at the girl. She was looking out of the window.

Fourteen hours later they landed at Heathrow Airport, the main airport for London. When they had collected their luggage they said goodbye and parted.

"Thank you for making it such a nice journey, Randall."

"I enjoyed the company, June."

With the two pieces of luggage at his feet, having gone through customs and immigration, Randall looked around at the terminal building and all the milling people. Everyone but himself seemed to have a purpose. June had been met by friends and gone off laughing, himself forgotten in her excitement.

"Now what the hell do I do?" he asked himself. The money his father was going to give him would come from his Uncle Paul. In his pocket was a few pounds and US dollars his father kept in the farm safe. With a suitcase in each hand, Randall walked to the taxi rank.

"Where you want to go, cock?"

"Somewhere near Piccadilly Circus that's cheap. I need to rent a room."

"Do yourself a favour. Get on the train and get off at Piccadilly Circus. Taxis in London don't go cheap."

"Thanks for the advice."

"You're welcome."

"It's all a bit overwhelming."

"You'll get used to it."

Her name was June. Without a phone number he doubted he would ever see her again.

2

The traffic went round and round Piccadilly Circus, the statue of Eros in the middle of the roundabout. Randall stood bewildered, a suitcase on the pavement either side of him. There were buildings, their fronts covered with signs, most of them neon and flashing. Humping his luggage through the tube train system and up the long stairs from underground had made Randall wish he had spent some of his money on a taxi, a friendly driver taking him where he thought he wanted to go. Arriving on the doorstep of his Uncle Paul's house was out of the question, the poor relation down on his luck. The London policeman on the kerb across from Randall kept looking at him, the uniform of the Rhodesian police and the English police so different. At least it wasn't raining, he told himself to give himself courage. Everything around him was different, strange, and with so little money in his pocket, intimidating. Running away from his problems at home no longer seemed the bright idea he had dreamed of back on World's View. No one took the slightest notice of him, going about their business amid all the noise of the traffic and the bustle. The policeman was coming towards him making Randall pick up his suitcases with still no idea which direction to go in. An expression of Vince Ranger's came to him: 'You're wandering around like a lost fart in a haunted shit house'.

Randall had turned and was moving away when the policeman caught up with him.

"You lost, sonny?"

"You could say that."

"You from South Africa with those labels on your suitcase? South African Airways."

"Rhodesia, actually. I've just arrived from the airport."

"Where are you going?"

"That's the trouble. I don't really know. I want to rent a cheap room somewhere and park my suitcases."

"You won't find anything cheap in the West End. This is London theatreland. In the old days Soho was cheap."

"Where should I go to look for somewhere to stay?"

"You don't know anyone in London?"

"Not really. I have an uncle in Hyde Park but I don't know him. Came over as a kid with my father when he married his second wife. She was English."

"Hyde Park isn't far from here. He must be rich."

"I suppose so. When I'm settled, got myself some kind of job, then I'll visit them."

"What you do for a living?"

"I'm an assistant on a tobacco farm."

"Got any money?"

"A little. It's difficult to get foreign exchange in Rhodesia."

"Get into one of those taxis and go to Notting Hill Gate. It's a melting pot of people who come to England from the old colonies. You'll fit right in."

"Thank you kindly."

"You're welcome. Welcome to London. You got problems in Rhodesia." The policeman's words were a statement, not a question.

"You can say that again. A bullet came through the window of the lounge and killed my cat."

The man moved off. Randall watched the traffic, saw a taxi for hire and waved, his suitcases back on the ground. The taxi veered across the road and stopped in front of him.

"Do you know where I can find Notting Hill Gate?"

"I hope so, my china. Where you want in Notting Hill?"

"A cheap rooming house."

"The suitcases go in the side compartment. You get in the back. I got a relation in Notting Hill with a boarding house. Must be your lucky day. Not so cheap no more. But nothing's cheap no more in London."

THE FIRST FEW days with Mrs Salter were lonely. No one in the boarding house seemed to notice him, and there was no one he could go to for advice. The room was small, the carpet threadbare, with a small bed in a corner and one window looking onto the back yard and Mrs Salter's clothesline. Other than Mrs Salter there were only young men in her three-storey house. The top floor was more an attic, Randall's room the smallest of the three. Wedged in between two of the rooms was a bathroom that doubled as the toilet. Bursts of laughter from around and below him made him wish he was home on the farm, playing cards with Myra on the floor of the lounge, the cat purring next to him. Most of his money had gone to the landlady for the deposit and his first month's rent: Mrs Salter didn't play games when it came to collecting her money, an old woman as tough as old boots with a knowing look in her eye.

On the street, walking around, Randall saw a cross-section of people, a rich mixture of Jamaicans, Indians and Europeans, most of the Europeans not speaking English. The Jamaicans, being black, made Randall feel at home, bringing back memories of growing up with Moley and Happiness back on the farm. There had been so much for all of them before the war came along. Soon after the bush war started Moley had disappeared, his mother Primrose, Randall and Phillip's nanny, convinced her son had joined up with the terrorists. Randall himself had been called up to do his duty but soon afterwards was discharged for a medical condition he never liked to talk about. Now walking the streets of London, it was all so far away, a world apart in time and distance, a world of earth and trees as it had been for thousands of years before man built his cities of concrete and brick. Not only was Randall lonely, he was desperately homesick. 'Don't cry over spilt milk,' he kept telling himself. 'Get on with it.' At night, in his small, musty-smelling bed, he cried himself to sleep, wondering what would become of him, wondering what he had done to make life so turn on him. Randall had never believed a man could feel so lonely surrounded by so many people. Alone, walking the African bush, sometimes for days at a time, his rifle his source of food, he had never felt this lonely; the bush, the birds and the wild animals were his solace and company, killing a buck for his food his only regret. He had to do something: by the end of the month his money would run out and Mrs Salter would want her next month's rent.

The knock on his door brought him out of his reverie, the soft knock a sound of hope.

"You must be the new guy. Saw you come out of the bathroom. Are you also in the theatre? James Tomlin, at your service."

"Randall Crookshank. You want to come in? I can offer you a cup of tea."

"No booze?"

"I'm afraid not. Bit short of money. Fact is, I'm almost broke."

"Aren't we all... Mrs Salter was in the theatre in her younger days. Why she takes pity on us aspiring actors."

"Are you an actor? My goodness."

"I paint the sets always in hope. You learn, watching the professionals. Or so they say. Breaking into the London theatre is very difficult."

"I can imagine."

"Where are you from? You have an odd accent."

"Rhodesia."

"What's it like in Rhodesia?" The man had walked to the window to look down at Mrs Salter's washing on the line.

"They killed my cat."

"Who did?"

"The terrorists."

"How absolutely awful. Shall I put on the kettle? The best bit of Mrs Salter's boarding house is the gas ring in the corner so we can cook in our rooms... She always hangs out her washing when it's going to rain."

"Have you ever had a part in a play?"

"Only at school."

"Why do you want to be an actor?"

"Anything is better than spending my life in an office at a desk, pushing a pen. Anything, Randall. You mark my word. You got milk and sugar?"

"In the cupboard under the gas ring. The tea's in the packet next to the sugar."

"I suppose in Rhodesia you had servants to make the tea."

"I suppose we did."

They both laughed. Randall sat on the bed. James filled the kettle from the small sink where Randall cleaned his teeth, and sat on the only chair in the room.

They grinned at each other, Randall happy for the first time since saying goodbye to June at the airport.

"So, what can you tell me, Randall? In the old days people entertained each other by telling stories. They didn't have television and all this canned entertainment. Just each other. Must have been fun. Sitting round the fire in winter listening to storytellers. The new world has lost so much. Is your father English?"

"Yes. Went out to Rhodesia after the war when he'd finished his National Service in the Royal Navy. My mother was killed by lions when I was two and a half years old. She was English. I was told she was drunk and drove off into the bush on her own and ran out of petrol. A pride of lions attacked her as she tried to walk home. Dad's married again. Her brother Harry Wakefield is quite a famous newspaper reporter. Have you heard of him?"

"Not really. I don't read the newspapers. Just novels and plays. I can lose myself in a book for hours... That must have been a terrible shock."

"There's a painting of her in the lounge on the farm. Her eyes keep following you. The painter was Livy Johnston. She's famous in England. Have you heard of her?"

"No, I haven't."

"The kettle's nearly boiled. It boils quite quickly... Do you know how to make some money?"

"I wish I did. Painting sets isn't exactly a fulltime occupation. Once they're done they're done. Not like acting. In the old days we made tea in a teapot and covered it in a tea cosy to let it draw. Now we use teabags. Instant tea. Everyone is in such a hurry. Do you use teabags or teapots in Rhodesia?"

"Teapots, actually."

"So much better... You could get a job in a kitchen, I suppose. Washing dishes in a restaurant."

"How do you get the job?"

"Walk in and ask them. There are restaurants all over the place in London. The rich eat out most of the time. The old days of big houses and lots of servants came to an end when the war started according to my father. In his parents' house in Leatherhead the servants walked out in 1939. They were Austrians. They went back to Austria just after Hitler invaded… Now they eat in restaurants when they don't want to cook."

"How much do they pay for washing dishes?"

"You'll have to ask them… So, you don't have any money. That's a pity. Thought we could go for a pint."

"Have you got a job at the moment?"

"Not at the moment… Tell me more about yourself. I love learning about people. Tell me all about Rhodesia… Look, I was right. The moment Mrs Salter hangs her washing on the line it begins to rain."

"How do you dry your washing?"

"I take it to the launderette."

"I could afford a couple of pints, I suppose."

"That is good of you. Let's go."

"Don't you want to drink your tea?"

"How rude of me. Of course I do. Two pints of bitter will make me feel a whole lot better. Cheer me up. We'll go to the Leg of Mutton and Cauliflower."

"Do you know anyone in the pub?"

"All of them, Randall. It is Randall?"

"Randall Crookshank."

"The trick is to have enough money to buy the first round, Randall. Then you see what happens. Come on."

"You haven't had your tea."

The man had the door open and was out in the corridor. Randall got off the bed, his tea on the floor beside him. Then he followed. At least he had met someone. His wallet, with what was left of his money, was in his pocket. If he couldn't get a job washing dishes he would have to call on his Uncle Paul.

"Do they pay you at the end of the week or the month?"

"Every day if you ask them… Oliver, we're going for a drink," James shouted through a closed door. "His name is Randall."

"Coming!"

"You'll like Oliver, Randall. Landed a part in a play last week. By the end of the month he'll be rolling in money. Then we can bum off Oliver. We're all a bit bohemian in Notting Hill... Hello, Mrs Salter. Randall's taking us to the pub for a drink. It's beginning to rain. Your washing's going to get wet, I'm afraid."

James Tomlin took an umbrella out of the stand in the hall as they walked to the front door.

"You do have an umbrella, Randall?"

"We don't have umbrellas in Rhodesia. In the dry season it doesn't rain at all for six months. During the rains it's so heavy an umbrella wouldn't be much good."

"Then you'd better hide under mine... There you are, you see. It's always drizzling with rain in London. You'll get used to it."

Striding down the pavement under the plane trees, Oliver beside them, James Tomlin began to sing 'Singing in the Rain' dancing as he went, Oliver joining in, the umbrellas of little help. He was happy. He had company. It was all going to be just fine.

"Her name was June," Randall said, his thoughts miles away.

"Who was?"

"Oh, sorry, a girl I met on the aeroplane."

"Get under the umbrella. You're getting soaking wet."

"I would if you stopped dancing."

The sign caught Randall's eye. A leg of sheep with the fur torn off, the cauliflower white against the red of the meat. They went inside. All the girls knew Oliver, a tall, lightly built man against Randall's stockier stature. An actor on and off the stage, Oliver had a smile that was infectious. Without asking, a drink was put in Randall's hand. The girls were all young and fresh in their summer clothes. He had never seen so many girls. James and Oliver had their own pints of bitter, no one asking them to pay.

"Whoever bought me this drink I thank," said Oliver raising his glass. 'Down, down, down,' came the roar. Within seconds the pint glass was empty, everyone shouting their appreciation. Oliver, it seemed, was a favourite, accepted into the crowd. Randall smiled. The beer was flat and warm unlike the cold beers at home, not that it mattered.

"It's his new part," said James to Randall. "Juvenile lead. They all think he's going to be famous. When you have money or fame everyone wants to know you and be your friend."

"Where do all the girls come from?"

"London's full of young girls. They share flats. Sometimes nine in a three-bedroomed flat. Why they come to the pub in a gang."

"Who bought the drinks?"

"Graham. The one with the glasses. He's an investment banker or something. Comes here slumming it to chat up the girls. Throws his money around to impress."

"Do you know him?"

"He's not interested in me or you. Oliver's new part impresses him. With luck we'll go home drunk on his money."

"Shouldn't I buy him a drink?"

"Whatever for? He's loaded."

"In Rhodesia we always buy our round of drinks."

"Relax. This isn't Rhodesia."

Randall walked up to Graham, his conscience not letting him drink a stranger's beer for free.

"My name is Randall Crookshank. Thank you for the drink. My friend James said you paid for this round. Can I buy you a drink?"

"Same again," said Graham to the barman pointing at Randall and turning back to the girls.

After paying for the round Randall had less than a pound to his name. When they left, Graham went off with one of the girls in a taxi. Oliver had a girl on each arm. James had a girl. All the girls had a man except one.

"Do you have a room of your own? I'm Amanda."

"Randall. Randall Crookshank."

"Can I come back with you? My roommate wants the room to herself tonight."

"I don't have any booze or any money."

"Don't be silly."

When they got back to the room his cup of cold tea was still on the floor next to the bed. The girl took off her clothes and got into bed. She was drunk.

"There's room for two... What's the matter?"

"I'm not sure."

"You have a funny accent."

"I'm from Rhodesia."

"What are you doing in England?"

"They killed my cat. The terrorists killed my cat."

"You poor darling. Please get into the bed. I'm on the pill so don't you worry. This is London, Randall. Ships in the night. No complications. There's nothing better. Do you have a job?"

"No, I don't."

"Neither do I. Tomorrow you can spend all day telling me about your cat. What was her name?"

"Lady."

"I love cats. Please take off your clothes and get into bed... My goodness, that is a body. What a tan. Come here, lover. I'm going to eat you."

"It's wrong to take advantage of a girl who's been drinking. We all drank too much."

"Who cares? I like to have sex when I'm drunk."

Randall, shy and conscious of being a virgin, got into his bed next to a girl he had just met, turning his back to her, the girl's naked flesh touching his own. Randall was tense, not sure what he was meant to do.

"Have you done this before, Randall?"

"No, actually, I haven't. I didn't meet girls on the farm."

"Just leave it to Amanda. Oh, my goodness. Just wait till I tell the girls."

"Please don't... What do I do?"

"First you turn round... Oh, that's better. Much better... Much, much better... Don't stop... Please, please don't stop."

The last time they made love, the sun had come up, and pigeons were cooing from the rooftops. She was small, curvy, not conventionally beautiful but Randall was sure for the rest of his life he would never forget Amanda. She was his first. She had taken his virginity. For most of the morning they lay together and slept. When Randall got up and, still naked, walked to the window, Mrs Salter's washing was still on the line. Everything looked different. Everything felt different.

"I've got some bacon and eggs. You want some tea?"

"What I want most is you, Randall... Come back to bed and tell me all about yourself."

"When I've made some tea... Aren't you starving?"

"Only for you. Isn't it lucky we don't have to go to work?"

"I'm not sure. That round of drinks I bought last night almost cleaned me out of money. I'll have to go and see my Uncle Paul. Years ago, before sanctions were imposed on Rhodesia, my father invested in a block of flats in Chelsea. It's the only money my family have outside Rhodesia. My dad wrote his brother a letter for me to take to him. Do you know how to get to Hyde Park?"

"You go to Marble Arch and get off the Tube. Do you have enough money for the fare?"

"I think so."

"Then we'll go right now and visit your Uncle Paul."

"He'll be at his office, I suppose."

"Then we'll eat the bacon and eggs, go back to bed and make love, then we'll go visit your relatives. How does that sound?"

"Will you really come with me? You see, I don't really know them. I ran away from Rhodesia in a funk. If Uncle Paul won't lend me some money I'll get a job in a restaurant washing dishes. Never done the washing up in my life. Silas does the washing up on World's View."

"Who's Silas?"

"He's the cook boy. He's a man, of course, not a boy. I always thought it was rude to call a man a boy. Old colonial habits die hard. In the beginning it didn't matter what we called the servants because they couldn't understand our English. I liked Silas. Spent a lot of time as a boy talking to Silas in the kitchen."

"But how did you talk to him if he can't speak English?"

"I speak Shona. Fluently. Grew up with my nanny's kids, Moley and Happiness. My first language was Shona. It's a beautiful language. Very descriptive. We sat round the pool and swam together, Primrose looking after me and Phillip as well as her kids. Phillip's my elder brother. He's at Rhodes University in South Africa reading history. Dad says a history degree won't do him much good as men never learn from their mistakes. He's good at sport. Tennis and cricket."

"Why have they got such strange English names?"

"My father's favourite character in *The Wind and the Willows* was Moley, so he gave the name to the young boy. Primrose was happy to have a daughter. So she called her Happiness. They all have Shona names, of course, but all like to be called by an English name... The washing must be dry. Mrs Salter is taking it in."

"Will she mind me staying the night?"

"Both Oliver and James brought girls back last night... Moley went off and joined the terrorists. He'd call himself a freedom fighter. Life is so complicated. Now, instead of being friends, we could end up shooting at each other."

"Are you glad you got out?"

"I try not to think about it. It's not easy to give up the only home you have ever known. Friends and family. Most of all I'm going to miss the bush. England is so small. Everyone living on top of each other."

"You didn't mind being on top of me last night." Amanda was laughing, a rough throaty chuckle.

"That was different."

"Did you like it, Randall?"

"It was the best experience of my life."

From down below, Mrs Salter looked up, saw him standing in the window, and waved.

"Luckily she can only see the top of me."

"Who are you talking about now?"

"Mrs Salter. She waved."

Amanda got out of bed and stood naked next to Randall and waved down at Mrs Salter who gave them a smile.

"She was in the theatre before buying this boarding house."

"Then she understands. Did it herself. Why seeing us up here makes her smile."

"You think her generation did this sort of thing?"

"Every generation does when you get down to it. We're more open. We don't mind if other people see what we're doing... Now I'm hungry. Where's the frying pan?"

"In that cupboard under the gas ring next to the toaster."

"If Uncle Paul lives in Hyde Park he must be rich."

"I suppose so. I never thought about it."

"How many flats does your father own in Chelsea?"

"Twenty-eight in partnership with Livy."

"My goodness. Have you any idea what they're worth?"

"Not a clue."

"A bloody fortune. What's your father doing living in Africa with all that money in London?"

"He loves Africa, Amanda. We all do. That's the trouble. Some of the blacks want to get rid of us whites and we don't want to go. Gets into your blood: the open spaces, smell of the bush, living with wild animals."

THEY FOUND the four-storey townhouse without any difficulty. It was too early for his Uncle Paul to be home from the office so they decided to walk to Hyde Park. In the park Amanda held his hand. They were lovers among the strollers in the park. At Speakers' Corner a well-dressed man was standing on a wooden box ranting against the inequities of capitalism. No one was taking the slightest bit of notice, happy in the summer afternoon among the green of the trees. Neither of them talked. From the surrounding streets came the constant sound of traffic, the smell of exhaust fumes part of the air. At half past six they walked back to the house. The house had the biggest front door Randall had ever seen with a big brass knocker. There was a bell button on the side of the door. Randall, who disliked imposing himself on other people, couldn't make up his mind. Reaching up he lifted the knocker and let it fall, the sound of brass on brass resounding inside. They waited up on the steps, Randall turning round to look back over the low wrought-iron gate towards the park and its green trees across the road. The door opened, making Randall turn round. Amanda had stood back down a step leaving him alone. A very old woman with white hair was peering at him.

"You should ring the bell, young man. The knocker is an ornament."

"I'm so sorry. I wasn't sure whether to lift the knocker or ring the bell."

The old woman was now smiling up at him.

"You're much bigger than I expected from the photographs, Randall. Your father phoned. We've been expecting you. Well, come in."

"Are you my grandmother?"

"Of course I am... Come in, come in. The first thing is to give you some money. Jeremy explained how difficult it is to get money out of Rhodesia. What would we all do without money?"

An hour later, with a hundred pounds in his pocket, Randall left his uncle's house, all of it strange. His uncle, his aunt and his cousins had not been at home.

"I can't believe she's my grandmother."

"One of the links in the chain, Randall. It's how it works."

"Should I have given her a hug?"

"Who knows?"

"It was all a bit embarrassing. As if all I had come for was money."

"Wasn't it?"

"I suppose so. She never came to Rhodesia. Didn't like flying."

"Works both ways. Next time, give them a ring and make an appointment."

"What are you laughing at?"

"People. Give it time if you want to get to know them. A hundred quid is better than a slap in the belly with a wet fish. On the way back we can get my things. I need a nice long soak in your bath. Tomorrow's Saturday. Market day on the Portobello Road. Place is full of urban hippies looking for cheap food. You wait till afternoon when the stalls are selling it off cheap. We'll make a big curry and have a party. Buy a keg of beer and invite my friends. Then you can decide if you want to work for your uncle and do what you are told... To pay for the food and beer you put a bowl on the table. Those who can afford it throw in some money. Better than people bringing a bottle. Much cheaper than going to the Leg of Mutton. So, there's your choice, Randall. Joining your rich relatives and putting on a suit or living with the swinging hippies, living hand to mouth, laughing a lot and enjoying yourself while you're still young... This time we'll walk back through Hyde Park, down Green Park to Piccadilly."

"That's where it started, in Piccadilly. When I first arrived off the plane."

"If Mrs Salter wants a bit more rent, so what?"

"Exactly."

Running down the path through the trees, full of excitement, Randall did a skip and a jump.

"This is what life's all about. Do you believe in luck, Amanda?"

"Only serendipity. The happy accidents of life."

"So you're moving in?"

"Of course I am. Two can live as cheap as one. We're young and free.

What more can you want in life? Live for today and tomorrow takes care of itself."

"That house was a bit stuffy."

"You can say that again. Once a month, on Sunday, you can go visit your grandmother and behave yourself."

"Maybe we'd better not tell Mrs Salter. There are only young men in the house. A room's a room however many stay in it. How much stuff have you got?"

"Since I left home in a hurry, not very much."

"What happened?"

"You don't want to know. The usual family quarrel. I wanted my freedom. Dad wouldn't let go... Let's sit on the bench. I'm not used to all this running."

FROM SOLITUDE TO chaos in less than a week. They bought the food in the Portobello market and two pots for the curry, the spices from an Indian shop in Notting Hill. The kegs of beer, Randall had carried back on his shoulder in the morning. Amanda had told her friends when she collected her things. By nine o'clock on Saturday night the room was full of people, Amanda's curry simmering on the single gas ring, the rice already cooked by James Tomlin in his room. All the bedroom doors at the top of Mrs Salter's house were open, the guests moving freely between the rooms. Oliver Manningford, always the diplomat, had invited Mrs Salter for a 'damn fine curry' and a glass of beer and to listen to classical music, getting the harp, with its heavy base, with difficulty up the flights of stairs. Everyone knew to bring their own plates, cutlery and drinking mug, the rest provided by Randall and Amanda, half his uncle's money already spent.

The last time Randall had seen so many people at a party had been at the Centenary Club after a farmers' meeting. The guitar player, sitting cross-legged on the floor, had begun the music, a soft, sweet sound that mingled with the sound of many voices. Only when the girl sat behind the harp, her hands held out on both sides of the big instrument, did the guests stop talking, the perfect sounds stopping them, making them turn round, bringing smiles to their faces. The girl and the music were beautiful. Mrs Salter, who had not been sure of her house's invasion, was smiling, the long faraway look of memory painted on her face. Amanda, in tight jeans and a tighter white top, stood ladling out her curry. On the table, next to the two barrels of beer, sat the metal bowl overflowing with money. Most of the people, plates of food in hand, pints of beer by their sides, sat on the threadbare carpet, crossed-legged and happy. Some, who didn't drink beer, had brought their own, drinking the spirits out of the bottles.

At eleven o'clock, replete with food and music, Mrs Salter had gone down to her small flat in the basement. The music changed from classical to modern, the guitar and harp strings mingling with the girl's voice. Randall watched his guests get up off the floor and sway to the music, couples wrapped around each other, no room to dance. There was no amplifier for the guitar, no microphone for the singer. Not once did Randall see anyone put their hand into the kitty. The music stopped at one o'clock out of respect for the neighbours. Both the curry and rice pots were empty. When the last guests left, the kegs of beer were empty, the money bowl still not touched. When Randall and Amanda counted out the money on the bed there was one hundred and six pounds, over double what Randall had spent. All the plates and cutlery had gone, only empty bottles left standing under the sink.

"So, what you think of that, Randall? Not bad business."

"You just made us fifty quid."

"Good, so we don't have to work next week."

"Did you expect them to leave that much money in the tip bowl?"

"It varies."

"You've done this before?"

"If I had the inclination, I'd get myself a restaurant and turn it into a business but it wouldn't be the same."

"Where did those musicians come from?"

"The Royal Academy of Music. They're students."

"Shouldn't they get some of this money?"

"That's up to you. They found what they wanted. They had an audience. They were happy."

"You know who they are?"

"Of course, Randall. I know everyone… Let's go to bed. Payment time. For both of us. So, it's not so bad me moving in? We'll call ourselves a laid-back couple. How does that sound?"

"You make a fine curry."

"I should do. My parents met in India. My father was in the Indian Civil. My mother came out from England on the 'fishing fleet': the not-so-fortunate young women in England who couldn't find suitable husbands. There was a shortage of single women among the British community in India. A bit like what you've told me about Rhodesia."

"I know nothing about you, Amanda."

"Let's keep it that way. Life's a lot less complicated. Let the picture of me build in your mind the way you want it. We start with a clean slate. What we are is what we see in each other without all the background clutter, all the mistakes of the past... They really did like my curry. At the end I caught James Tomlin with his finger in the bottom of the pot and licking his fingers."

"What do you all do for a living?"

"This and that. Most of them are aspiring artists: musicians, painters, photographers, a couple of unpublished writers. To most of them money is secondary. They want to create something tangible and not just make money. Making lots of money, getting rich, is so boring. Did your grandmother look happy in that great big house all on her own? Can you imagine what that house in Hyde Park must be worth? If I had that kind of money I'd have a place far away from everyone in the countryside. What's the point of money in a city if you have to work so hard. Likely, your uncle and his wife are working twelve hours a day to keep that grand house."

"How about a six-thousand-acre farm in Rhodesia?"

"Sounds good to me if people behaved themselves. There wasn't one animal in your grandmother's house. Not even a parrot. The place was perfect and sterile. You think anyone has ever played that grand piano?"

"Uncle Paul plays the piano. Dad says in his youth he played piano in a jazz band. Played with Benjie Appleton in 101 Oxford Street."

"I don't believe it!"

"Never judge a book by its cover. Uncle Paul is quite hip."

"Then what's he doing in that great big house?"

"Impressing his clients, I suppose. How business is done in the big city."

"Have you ever been to a classical concert?"

"Not yet. There are lots of things I haven't done. Why I came to

England, apart from not wishing to get myself killed. That night they shot at the house and blew up the police truck with a landmine, I was terrified of dying a virgin."

"Well, you don't have to worry about that anymore... Were you really a virgin?"

"Cross my heart."

"You learn quick. Let's get into bed. We'll clean up the mess in the morning. There's a lot I can show you in London that doesn't cost a fortune. We'll do a circuit of the art galleries. Buy cheap last-minute tickets to the theatre and sit in the gods. Stand in the well of the auditorium at the Albert Hall and listen to the Proms. Libraries and museums. All the old buildings like the Tower of London and St Pauls. All that wonderful English history. There's more to England than pop music. There's a rich, old culture that makes us proud to be British. That's what we've got to find for you, Randall. Not the Leg of Mutton and Cauliflower and getting drunk. There's a rich tapestry in London and I'm going to show it all to you, lover... Now, how does that look?"

"You're beautiful naked, Amanda."

Gently, slowly, Randall took her into his arms, never so happy, never so excited by the future. With the lights out they cuddled, skin on skin, the smell of food and beer still in the room, far away the sound of the London traffic. Tired, well fed, a little drunk, they went to sleep, waking with the dawn breaking through the open window, only then making passionate love.

Later, both of them naked, they fried eggs and bacon and ate sitting among the debris left by the party, both of them hungry for food and each other. There was no washing on the line down below, just Mrs Salter's marmalade cat digging a hole in the flowerbed. Both of them watched, holding each other by the hand.

"Life is so good," whispered Amanda.

Instead of getting dressed they got back into the small bed, pulling up the sheets. Soon, they were sound asleep and deep in their dreams, both of them smiling. When Randall woke it was to the sound of church bells calling the faithful to matins.

After Randall made the tea, which they drank in bed, he ran the bath. Oliver and James had gone out. The house was quiet, the peaceful quiet of a Sunday morning. Together they got into the bath sitting at opposite ends, their naked legs entwined, lying back, soaking in the hot water. Neither of them spoke. They were too content, so happy to be with each other. Slowly, the water grew cold, neither of them caring. Amanda soaped his foot, washing gently between the toes making him aroused.

"It's a mathematical impossibility facing each other in a tub, Randall."

"We could try."

"You're insatiable... What do you want to do today? Outside the sun is shining. In England you take advantage whenever the sun shines. Does the sun shine a lot in Rhodesia?"

"All the time. On Sundays we sit round the pool and have a *braai*."

"What's a *braai*?"

"A barbecue. A cook out. Grilled meat over the hot coals of a fire. Cold beers in ice-cold glasses from the fridge. Lots and lots of salads."

"How many of you are there?"

"My dad, my stepmother, Phillip my brother. Myra and Craig, my half-sister and half-brother. We were all so happy until the bush war started. Always under the threat of attack. Took all the fun out of it... Where's the nearest park for us to walk?"

"Holland Park. We can take a picnic. My mother always makes boiled eggs for a picnic. We can buy some fresh bread. Make the best of a summer's day... What was your cat called?"

"Lady. She was such a lady. I loved that cat."

"I love you for loving the cat."

"It's gone down again."

"You want me to wash your toes again? Let's get out and get dressed. There will be a concert in the park."

"What kind of concert?"

"Classical mostly. Light classical. Music in the park. You sit on the lawns and eat your picnic listening to beautiful music."

"Do you want to be an artist?"

"I would love to. Just I don't have any talent other than loving what I hear and what I see. Oliver has talent. One day Oliver Manningford will be famous. He has that charismatic charm that catches everyone's attention. For me, I'll just be part of the audience. An appreciator of the arts. Not a bad way to be. Last night's harp music still plays in my mind.

And you, Randall. Would you like to be an artist? Maybe a writer. Think of all the storylines you have been through in Rhodesia."

"The trick is knowing how to tell a story. I wouldn't know where to begin."

"At the beginning. It would be some kind of catharsis for all you've been through. Your cat. Your mother. The loss of your home. I can't imagine how terrible it must have been for you to lose your mother to the lions."

"And the loss of my country. My bloodline may be English but I'm a Rhodesian. An African. I was too young to remember my mother, God bless her soul."

"Will you go home?"

"Not at the moment."

"When the war is over – and my father said all wars, however bad, are eventually over – would you take me to Rhodesia and show me your country? All those wild animals. All that open space."

"Would you come with me?"

"Of course I would. Africa. I never thought of Africa and being in the sun. We would be so happy together. A holiday to remember... Come on. We'd better get out of the tub... Is Africa very beautiful?"

"More beautiful than you could ever imagine. We could watch the weaver birds making their nests in the spring. When the male weaver makes the nest, if the female doesn't think it's strong enough she tears it apart and makes him start all over again."

"So she should. Her babies wouldn't be safe. They'd fall out of the nest."

"They're mostly yellow. Bright yellow. And sing to each other. When twenty or thirty weaver birds are in the same tree singing to each other it's the most beautiful music... You've let the plug out."

"Of course I have. Come on. Picnic in the park. With luck we'll find a bird to watch up in the trees."

It took them an hour to clean up the mess, boil the eggs and make ham sandwiches from the bread Randall bought from the corner shop. There was no thermos flask so they couldn't take any tea. They put their lunch in Amanda's shopping bag and left the room. There was still no sign of Oliver or James.

The sun was warm outside making them both feel happy as they walked down the road taking turns to carry the cloth bag. On this rare summer's day everyone they passed was smiling, the young, the old and the children. They left the Tube at Holland Park station and walked across into the park, following the convergence of people to the bandstand under the trees. The concert had not yet started, no sign of the players. They found a spot and sat on the grass, surrounded by people. Most of the people were sitting, some eating their picnics. A couple close to them smiled. The couple were young, a rug spread under them on the grass. People with dogs on leashes were walking the paths. Randall cracked open the shell of a hardboiled egg, added a sprinkle of salt and gave it to Amanda. She took a slow, sensual bite of the egg while she looked into his eyes.

A big man got up onto the bandstand carrying a cello in a case, opened the case and took out the instrument. Within minutes the small stage was full of musicians. A violin player tried her instrument, followed by one of the trumpeters. Amanda was sensually stroking the palm of his hand, making Randall aroused as she intended. The conductor came out and stood in front of the players, raising his baton. The music began, spreading the sounds of the orchestra through the park and the trees. A dog barked. Amanda closed her eyes listening to the music. With her eyes closed Randall thought her even more beautiful. For an hour the music played, neither of them moving from their place on the grass. Amanda had lain outstretched on her back to listen to the music. At three o'clock, after a second session of music, the orchestra packed up and the players walked away with their instruments, leaving a void in the park. Again they could hear the traffic from the road that ran next to the park, London continuing its business, the music forgotten. Their food had all been eaten. Neither of them had known the names of the composers of the music.

"It must be so wonderful to be a composer and leave the world so much. It doesn't matter who they were, Randall, it's the music they leave behind that is far more important than themselves. I met a composer once. He wasn't famous. Probably never will be. He said once he had emptied his mind of music onto a sheet of paper it was gone from him forever. No longer his. When another musician played his music it belonged to the musician and the people listening. He was happy to let his music go. Can you imagine how much joy Mozart has given to millions of people who go through their lives listening to every note of his music?"

"You're a romantic, Amanda. Didn't do Mozart any good. He still died young and was buried in a pauper's grave."

"But he left us all his music. No one could pay him for that. The tip-bowl would never be big enough. There is no amount of money that could ever compare to his music... You want to walk slowly home to Notting Hill Gate? We have the rest of the day to enjoy together. A nice walk will be good for us... Did you see that pigeon?"

"There were lots of them. We have pigeons in Rhodesia. Not quite the same but pigeons. The other birds in the trees I didn't know what they were. Do you know all the birds?"

"Every one of them. I grew up in the country. When my parents came back from India at independence in '47 my father went into business. He bought a house on two acres in Surrey with the money he had saved in India. Said the train journey up to London every day was worth it if he could live in the country. He was very old-fashioned was my father. From another age when England ruled the greatest empire the world had ever known. Of course that's all gone now. We're just another little country like Switzerland. It was all very grand and formal in his day. Everyone knew their place. He was a lot older than my mother and I was the last in the family: my mother was in her forties when I was born; quite a surprise. I was brought up by a father with a Victorian mentality who believed children should be seen and not heard. He was very strict with us children. Why in the end I fell out with him. By the time I was eighteen he was already looking for a suitable husband for me. All the other girls were suitably married living boring, suburban lives and scraping for every penny to send their kids to boarding school. Father said we all had to speak the Queen's English properly. He despised the common people. Looked down his nose at anyone with a provincial accent. I could never understand what bloody difference it made if you both understood what you were saying to each other. It is what you say that counts, not how you pronounce the words. He came from another world where the father ruled his family with a rod of iron. He was the master of the house. Backchat solicited a frigid stare or a clip round the ear if it came from one of the boys. He never praised any of us, no matter how well we did. In many ways it was what pushed the boys to become so successful, looking for father's approval. If he did think anything of us he never said so. My poor mother. I suppose getting married was the only favour he did for her. Mother says if she hadn't gone out to India on the boat she'd have ended up an old maid like her two cousins. They never married. Still live with each other. They were left just enough money by their parents to live in genteel poverty, spending their sad lives keeping up appearances. Those two old girls never approved of me that much I'm certain. Neither did Father. So I walked out of the house. And here I am."

"How long ago?"

"Nearly a year, Randall. A wonderful year. The best year of my life. If I ever make anything of my life in the eyes of my father at least I will have done some living. Have something to look back on. Something to have made life worth living. If you're not getting any fun out of life, what difference does it make if you live in a palace? I'd rather live in one small room with a gorgeous boyfriend, making friends and throwing parties."

"Do you ever go and visit them?"

"Not for a year. After the big row I was told not to come back again. I was shown the door in every sense of the word."

"What happened?"

"I was caught. The only thing I did wrong was get caught. We thought they had gone out. Father caught us on the couch."

"Ouch."

"Sometimes, what seems to be the worst moment of your life turns out to be the best. I got my freedom. To live, you have to have your freedom... Did you know, I stitched that rose on this shopping bag in needlepoint when I was sixteen. All very refined. That was to be my kind of life. A dutiful daughter followed by a dutiful wife and a dutiful mother. All boring, Randall. Just plain boring. Victorian England was boring. All of it. All they did was keep up appearances. Thank God England isn't like that anymore. You've got to be happy. No, I haven't been home. Don't think I ever will. Why did he bother to have children if he didn't like them?"

"How many kids are there in the family?"

"Six of us."

"He must have liked something to produce so many kids... When you come from a happy family you're inclined to take it for granted. I love my brothers and sister, my father, and Bergit my stepmother who never treated any of us differently. We love each other and get on together. If it weren't for the bush war everything would have been perfect. When Dad retired he was going to live on the farm and hand the running of World's View over to me. I had it all worked out... I was going to find a nice Rhodesian girl, preferably a farmer's daughter who had grown up on a farm, and have some children. I never wanted anything other than to live on the farm. We have a boat on Lake Kariba where we go fishing for tiger fish. Now that's some fishing. They fight real good. A day on the lake in the cooler weather of winter is perfect. We take a big cool box full of ice and beers. Fishing rod in one hand and a beer in the other. What more could a man want? When they flooded the lake after the big dam was built the trees died in the water, their tops sticking out as they calcified, making the perfect haven for the bream. You could fish for bream on the water and watch the elephant a few yards away on shore. At dusk many animals come down to the water to drink. They're all wild, not like seeing them in a zoo. We were part of them. Part of the animals. Then we'd sail back to Caribbea Bay where the *Seagull* is moored and where we spent the night in the hotel. There was a round bar looking out on the lake. Far away you could see the shore of Zambia. Rhodesia is such a small community we know nearly everyone. With the war raging there aren't many tourists. Then we drove back the next day in convoy with an army escort. Even with the war it was wonderful. Everyone protecting each other. Everyone in the same boat... Why are you smiling, Amanda?"

"Everyone in the same boat. Isn't that a pun?"

"I suppose it is... They never shot at the convoys. We were too strong for them. You know what they call the ones who leave Rhodesia? 'When we's.' 'When we were in Rhodesia.' We can never get the place out of our minds. Some people say we were all too happy. That that kind of happiness had to come to an end. It was all too good to be true. Some people outside Rhodesia even want us to fail."

"They're likely jealous. They do say all good things come to an end, Randall. The secret is to get as much out of it while you can. It's far worse to look back and see you had nothing. Like my mother's poor cousins. Two old ladies who have shrivelled up, the sap of life sucked out of them. You got your memories. Memories last a lifetime. On our holiday when the war is over we'll go out on your Lake Kariba. I know how to fish. My brothers taught me. You put a worm on the hook at the end of a line and hang it in the water... Isn't the sun hot?"

"We wear big, wide-brimmed hats to keep the sun off our necks and faces. In the summer during the day it's too hot on the lake, the sun's reflection on the water sears the eyes. Then we fish at sunrise and sunset."

"You had it all worked out."

"We thought so. Turned out we were wrong. Chances are those who hang on will lose everything"

"Except their good memories."

"Except our memories... It's so strange walking on concrete. Hard under the feet. The bushveld is far nicer under the feet."

"There you go, 'when we'."

"There I go. Thanks for listening. Now, tell me more about yourself, Amanda. I want to know all about you."

"I'll bet they don't have classical music concerts in the bushveld."

"Only when the birds sing... You want an ice cream? There's a man over there with a cart selling ice cream cones."

They walked on down the streets of London, the ice cream eaten and forgotten, just the two of them in a sea of other people. No one looked at them. No one cared. Everyone was absorbed with themselves.

"You know where you're going, Amanda?"

"Of course I do, not that it matters. In London if you get lost you go underground, study the map of the Tube lines, change trains a couple of times and come up where you want to... Now that's what I've been looking for. A good old-fashioned English fish and chip shop. None of this American culture of hamburgers. Come on."

When they came into the fading sunlight they carried their food in yesterday's newspaper. The chips were oily, the fish deep fried.

"Doesn't taste like Kariba bream. You gut the fish and put it straight on the fire. *Braaied* fish over the hot coals from a woodfire. Nothing tastes better."

"Yes, when we."

"How far are we from the room?"

"Ten minutes. Fish and chips out of an old newspaper is so British. There's salt in that twist of greaseproof paper. This is what I call living.

We can sit on that bench and watch the people go by while we eat our supper. It's been a lovely day, Randall. Thank you."

"Shouldn't it be me thanking you?... The twilight is so long in England. In Africa it's all over in half an hour... Now what are you smiling at?"

"You're at it again. Talking about Africa... You think we could smuggle a double bed up to the room without Mrs Salter seeing us? We could get a wooden frame cheap in the secondhand market. Get another single mattress. Might as well make ourselves comfortable."

The room was quiet and growing dark when they climbed to the top of the three flights of stairs. From his room they could hear Oliver shouting at someone. When they closed their door they could still hear the heated conversation. Then silence. Soon after came a tap on their door.

"Heard you come in. Where've you been all day? James has gone out. I've been on my own all day long."

"Who were you shouting at, Oliver?"

"No one. I was reading my part."

"Then who was answering?"

"I was. I change my accent when I'm reading for the other person. You got to get into a part to make yourself believable. I see you've cleaned up the mess. Was there anything over? Oh, well. You'd better come to my room for tea. You look flushed, Amanda."

"We've been walking. All the way back from the concert in the park... What's the new play about?"

"The usual light comedy. The producer says that if you want a play to be successful you must never make the audience think. They want to be entertained. Go home feeling good, empathising with the story. Douglas says real life is bad enough without repeating it onstage. In the play, the characters all live happily ever after, their love eternal."

"Then what was the row just about?" asked Randall. "Your characters were fighting."

"That was the villain. The old boyfriend. The much older man with all the money. This play is about the love not the money. I've never been quite sure myself. Money and all its comfort can last a whole lot longer than love. We all like to think that love prevails."

"Sounds wonderful. Have you got milk?"

"I don't think so."

"Then I'll make the tea."

"You mind if I go get the script? Maybe you two could read the other parts. Being two people all at once is a bit difficult. I've got extra copies of the play."

"We're getting a double bed."

"Good for you. Just make sure Mrs Salter doesn't see you bringing it in. She's old-fashioned. In her youth a girl was a virgin until the day she was married."

"Do you believe it?"

"It's what the old people say."

"What's the play called?"

"*Ode to Youth*. You can come and see it if you want."

"Nice title. Should bring in the crowds. How's your leading lady?"

"She's gorgeous. Of course, until the shows over it's strictly professional. Then we shall see. Can I help you by putting on the kettle?"

Playing the gorgeous lady Amanda was surprisingly good, reading her lines without making a mistake. Randall drank his tea and watched them, hoping Oliver's coming on to his girl was only part of the play. All the girls liked Oliver.

"You should audition for a part in a play, Amanda."

"You old flatterer. I know you too well. What do you want, Oliver?"

"Another cup of tea. We open in two weeks' time at the Theatre Royal Haymarket. My first big part. Lots of lovely money."

"So you'll be moving out of Mrs Salter's boarding house?"

"Let's see how long we run. The public can be fickle. The play could fold after a couple of nights. All depends on the critics. If they like me I can try and get into television and make myself famous. You want to read some more lines, Amanda?"

"Not really... Will you help us carry up the double bed? It'll just go nicely in the corner... Do you want to be famous, Oliver?"

"Of course I do. Who doesn't? I'm twenty-six. If I don't make my mark by the time I'm thirty I'll be finished. Looking for a barman's job. No good to anyone."

"The girls will still love you."

"Not if you're old and poor. James has never had a break. Why he's painting sets and living in a garret. What are you going to do with the rest of your life, Randall?"

"I have absolutely no idea anymore."

"But you did."

"The only thing I aspired to was running World's View, making the farm prosperous for everyone. This year I introduced the people's maize to augment the labourers' wages. Up till then the labourers on the farm worked small plots close to the river and their huts. Now we plough the land, plant the seed properly with good fertiliser and let the families tend their own lines of maize, weeding and reaping the crop. They sell the excess they can't eat to the Grain Marketing Board and get a bonus. We take their excess cobs, put them through the machine and bag the grain. Everybody wins. Why Rhodesia is known as the breadbasket of Africa, we export so much produce. The old peasant way of growing maize gets two bags to the acre if they are lucky. Our way we get forty. You got to have good management if you want to farm properly. Knowledge of modern farming."

"I'll stick to acting. Don't think I'd know how to grow a carrot. Grew up in the city. I like to get my food from the supermarket all nicely packaged. I don't like to think my meat was once a live animal... You going back to Africa?"

"Not unless we come to terms with each other, which is most unlikely. At the moment we're the boss. The agreement the British are looking to forge at Lancaster House here in London calls for a one-man-one-vote election. Either Nkomo or Mugabe will win. Then we are at the black man's mercy. Once your power goes, you should go, according to Clay Barry. He's our local member-in-charge. The local police chief. I'll have to find a career for myself in England and go back to Africa for a holiday. It won't be the same but there's no point moaning about it. What you lose on the swings, you gain on the roundabouts. Isn't that right, Amanda?"

"You got any money, Randall?" asked Oliver.

"A bit."

"Let's get ourselves a drink in the pub."

"Why ever not? You only live once. If that bullet had been a bit lower I wouldn't be here now enjoying your company. Having fun. Getting a life. I'll worry about making money when I have to. Come on. Let's go. A perfect end to a perfect day."

"Wouldn't making them think make a better play?" asked Amanda.

"It might make a better play but it wouldn't make better money," answered Oliver. "In the end it's all about making money whatever else we like to say. All you need is fresh air and love is a load of bullshit."

"I think you're wrong. Without fresh air and love, money is worthless."

3

With the help of Oliver and James they smuggled the big bed up the stairs on the following Saturday when Mrs Salter was doing her weekly shopping, the old lady quite predictable. James got stuck halfway up the stairs trying to turn the corner, the bed almost tipping over the old banisters. They all had the giggles. The bed frame with the two single mattresses and the new big duvet looked grand. Amanda had found herself a temporary job as a waitress through her temp agency leaving Randall on his own in the evenings to think. He was happy, making his thinking easy. The money they had made from the party was slipping away. By the time of Oliver's opening night, Randall was almost broke. The Theatre Royal was full, mostly through complimentary tickets. In the front row sat the stony-faced critics wielding their power, at the back Amanda, Randall and James all hoping their best for Oliver. By the end of the first act the play was flat as a pancake. The second act, with Oliver doing his shouting bit, brought the play alive, the older man getting his comeuppance. By the end of the second act, with Oliver and the gorgeous leading lady making their characters lovingly believable, the atmosphere in the audience had changed. The older, rich character had been the problem. By the end of the last act the audience was laughing at the smallest jokes, everyone smiling, everyone feeling good with themselves. There were seven curtain calls. Happy for Oliver, they went home, leaving Oliver, the star, to enjoy the after-show party while the players waited for the early editions of the morning newspapers. When Oliver came home at seven o'clock in the morning he was drunk with excitement, pounding up the stairs to his room.

"The crits loved it. They bloody loved it. I'm made."

He was not alone. Amanda and Randall listened from their double bed.

"It's the gorgeous girl," said Amanda. "We're going to lose Oliver. He'll now move up in the world. Have different friends."

"You sound disappointed."

"There's a twinge of jealousy in all of us."

"Yes, I suppose there is. Mrs Salter won't have any difficulty letting his room. What did you think of the play?"

"Knowing Oliver made it more difficult... You think you could get a television? If he's going to be on the telly it's the only way we'll be able to keep up with him. It's James I feel sorry for. The two of them have been friends for years. Now Oliver Manningford, famous actor, will be out of his reach. We must be especially nice to James. He'll be feeling flat. Inadequate. They are both the same age. You think James might get a break?"

"We all get a break if we try hard enough. The more times you try, the better your luck. I'm going to have to get myself some kind of job. Either that or go and see my Uncle Paul."

"You didn't leave them your address?"

"No I didn't."

"Try the agency. Say you were a waiter in Rhodesia. They'll never be able to check your references. You'll make a balls-up the first few times but you'll get the hang of it. The trick is to be nice and smiley to people. Then they tip. You chat up the man who's paying, never the woman... Oliver has gone all quiet. Didn't take him long to break his rule. They really did look in love on the stage. Life is now mirroring fiction. She's very pretty."

Turning over, Amanda tried to go back to sleep leaving Randall lying on his back and thinking: a waiter in a small London restaurant was a long way away from a six-thousand-acre estate in Rhodesia. Then he smiled. With the Lancaster House Agreement the war would be over.

That was something. They could all get on with their lives whoever was running the country. Try to understand each other and not keep to themselves. Hopefully for the better. With the top of the house quiet as a grave, Randall drifted off. The back of Amanda's foot was rubbing his leg. He was happy.

In the morning Randall wrote a long letter to his father and took it to the post office not knowing how many stamps to put on the envelope for Rhodesia. If he had had a phone he would have phoned. Dad and Bergit worried about him. The letter was chatty but held no mention of Amanda. He said he had seen his grandmother but not his Uncle Paul. There was no mention of money or the war in Rhodesia. The letter had made Randall think of his cat buried in the flowerbed. He said he was getting along fine which was what they wanted to know. After paying for the postage he had one pound left in his pocket. Finding the temp agency from Amanda's instructions was easy. He had gone alone so as not to incriminate Amanda in his lie. The reception was full of people. On the way he had got a haircut to make himself presentable, carefully asking the old Greek hairdresser how much a short back and sides cost before sitting in the chair... A harassed middle-aged woman was behind the only desk. The floor was bare wooden boards in an old building at the back of Soho, close to the West End and all the London restaurants. What Randall didn't know was that his Rhodesian accent sounded upper-class, which caused her to raise her eyebrows.

"You want a job as a waiter?"

"Yes, please," he said politely.

"Do you have any experience?"

"I have lots of experience in restaurants," said Randall, not quite answering her question. Many times he had eaten in the Meikles main restaurant in Salisbury when he went into town from the farm with his family. He knew all the waiters by name, all of them black, all of them friends.

"Standing up or sitting down?" The old girl obviously wasn't stupid, making Randall blush.

"Mostly sitting down. But I saw how they worked."

"Where are you from? You're not English. How old are you?"

"I'm twenty-one, madam. From Rhodesia. There's a bit of bother in Rhodesia at the moment. Why I'm over here. They killed my cat."

"Who did?"

"The terrorists. If you give me a job I'll listen well and concentrate hard."

"Who sent you here?"

"Amanda."

"What's her surname?"

"Hanscombe. Amanda Hanscombe."

"Little Amanda. She's good. How well do you know her?"

"Quite well, actually."

"Where does she come from?"

"I don't know, really. We met a couple of weeks ago. We know each other now, not in our pasts."

The woman was grinning as she handed Randall a form.

"Are you entitled to work in England?"

"My mother and father were born in England. My grandfather died at Dunkirk."

"Fill in the form over there and come back to me."

"Thank you very much."

When he filled in the form he found he was lucky. There was a shortage of waiters in London who spoke good English. Most of the people in the reception were foreigners with little English.

"The Tandoori restaurant is in Greek Street. It's an Indian restaurant. Don't drop any plates. To begin with, carry two at a time. Don't line them up your arm. You can report to them now."

"How much do they pay?"

"Two pounds a night. Your real money comes in the tips. They take ten per cent for collecting your tips. I take ten per cent of everything you earn. Most of the tips go on the bill and are paid by credit card. Be honest with me and the Tandoori and I'll give you more jobs. Enjoy yourself, Randall. When are you seeing Amanda again?"

"Tonight."

"She owes me ten per cent of her tips she took in cash."

"I'll tell her. Thank you so much. You've been such a help. Greek Street, you say. I'll find it. Do I need a uniform?"

"Go just as you are. Nice haircut. Did he put a basin over your head and cut round the rim?" The old girl had a nice smile.

With the address in his pocket, Randall prepared to leave the threadbare office. He had a job. His first job if he didn't count working on the farm for his father.

"I'll be careful with your ten per cent of the tips. What's your name, may I ask?"

"Sarah Rankin. I own the agency. Doesn't look much but we're busy. Good luck to you, Randall. Sorry about the cat. I love cats. Why I gave you the job. What was the cat's name?"

"Lady. I called her Lady. Buried her in the flowerbed in the garden. I loved that cat."

"Life never was easy."

The woman had given him a piece of paper with his name on it, the name of the restaurant and clear directions to the Tandoori. Randall decided to walk and not use his last few pennies on a taxi as London was no longer overwhelming. In his mind was Wilson the waiter at Meikles, handing out the menus, each of them at the table giving their orders, Wilson always remembering. Randall decided he would write down the orders and number the chairs at the table on a piece of paper so he would know where to bring the food. His father had said that in life, whatever he did, it was better to have a system if he wanted to get it right. By the end of his first evening, eleven o'clock at night and exhausted from running around and concentrating, he had earned ten pounds and change in tips. Off the Tube at Notting Hill Gate, he ran down the road in sheer excitement. When he burst into their room, Amanda was home, both of them smiling.

"So? You got a job. How much did you make?"

"Ten quid in tips. Ten bloody quid! There's more money being a part-time waiter than getting a regular job in the City."

"Didn't I tell you? How's Sarah Rankin?"

"She's damn efficient."

"Why she makes money. So, did you drop anything?"

"Not as much as a spoon."

"Where you working?"

"The Tandoori in Greek Street. The owner's from the Punjab. Both of us from the old British colonies. Hit it off straight away. The poor man's homesick for the old British Raj. Had trouble trying to understand his Indian accent. He's a Moslem. After independence in 1947, his family fled India into Pakistan. Problems from the end of the empire are not limited to Rhodesia. Deepak, that's his name. No idea how to spell it. Deepak offered me a permanent job."

"Did you take it?"

"Of course I did. Even with Sarah's ten per cent we'll be rich... You have a good day?"

"Eleven pounds, twelve shillings and sixpence. When you see Sarah about becoming a permanent, tell her I owe her some tip money. Come to bed. We can lie on our backs with our hands behind our heads and dream of the future, a great, bright future with lots of lovely spending money. Oh, Randall. Isn't life wonderful?"

ON THE SUNDAY morning in September, ten days after Randall began his job at the Tandoori restaurant with the weather beginning to get cold, a knock came on their door while they were still in bed.

"Come in, Oliver," called Amanda. "The door's not locked."

Nothing happened. Randall got out of bed, pulling on his pants.

"You think it's Mrs Salter?" he whispered. "Get under the duvet... And don't giggle."

By the time he opened the door, his shirt was half buttoned, his feet still bare.

"Good morning, Randall," said his Uncle Paul. "Mind if I come in? Your father phoned with your address."

"I can pay back the hundred pounds at the end of the month."

"Don't be silly. How are you? Why didn't you come back to see us?... Hello. My name is Paul Crookshank. I'm this reprobate's uncle."

"I'm Amanda."

"Hello, Amanda. I'm sorry to have called so early. Well, you know how it is. So, you two know each other. Nice little room. The old lady downstairs told me where to find you both. We had a long chat. She was in theatre in the old days when I was playing clarinet in a jazz band. It's amazing how little the world really changes. I had a room in Holland Park much like this."

"She knows I live here?"

"Oh, yes. Shouldn't she know? Any chance of a cup of tea?"

"We didn't tell her, Uncle Paul, in case she kicked us out."

"So, what are you doing, Randall? Apart from living with a beautiful young girl?"

"Serving tables in an Indian restaurant."

"Making any money?"

"More than enough to live on."

"And here I am thinking you would need a job. How foolish of me. For a moment I'd forgotten you are a Crookshank. Your grandmother is pining to see you again. Will you both come to lunch?... Well, there you are, you see. Why don't I go and stand on the landing while Amanda gets dressed and you can put on some socks. You do have some tea? I suppose playing in a jazz band or serving tables isn't much different when you're in your twenties. Some of the best days of my life. No responsibilities. The whole of life ahead. Welcome to your ancestral home, Randall. Someone said if you ever get bored with London you're bored with life. Roast lamb I think it is. With mint sauce fresh from our little back garden. Must be the only edible herb grown in the centre of London. You know my wife's father came from Rhodesia. But of course you do. How your father got to Rhodesia. Harry Brigandshaw and his father, Sebastian Brigandshaw, are legends in Rhodesia. My children's great-grandfather was one of the first elephant hunters in Rhodesia. Before it was even called Rhodesia. Maybe I'll go downstairs and chat to Mrs Salter while you two get dressed. We get on like a house on fire. Why don't you come downstairs when you're both ready? Better idea. Much better idea. She's all on her own, poor old girl. I said I'd seen her on the stage. What's the name of the restaurant? Not that it matters."

"How's my father?"

"I told him to come back to England. Not that it made any difference. Africa is in his blood. There's going to be a ceasefire any minute. Well, we all have to go through life. Jeremy chose a life in Africa. I stayed in boring old England and sat behind a desk to make my money. Not that your father doesn't have money in England. That block of flats in Chelsea where I invested the farm profits before they brought in Rhodesian exchange control is now worth a small fortune. You always have to spread your investments to limit the risk... I'll be downstairs. Well, that wasn't so difficult. I came in the car. Your grandmother and Beth are waiting. My kids are both on their travels. You know how it is. Children only look forward. When you get older you spend more time looking back. If you want to start a career you can join my company, Randall. More of a conglomerate, I suppose. We sort of grew and diversified over the years. We have strong links in America with Beth's cousin, Tinus Oosthuizen. Look, I'll tell you everything over lunch."

The door closed, leaving them alone.

"Well, at least we don't have to worry about Mrs Salter anymore," said Amanda. "Roast lamb and mint sauce. Sounds absolutely delicious. A good old-fashioned Sunday lunch with the family. He's nice. Talks a lot but he's nice. How quick everything changes." She was thinking of Oliver Manningford, playing to packed houses, his whole life turned upside down. "Do you want a career, Randall?"

"Let's stay with waiting tables and see how it goes. We're having fun. That's what I want. There's plenty of time in the future to be serious. You think my uncle will mind if we bring James Tomlin along for lunch? With Oliver now the big actor he doesn't smile so much."

"You think he really saw her on the stage?"

"Who knows?... Right. That's me dressed. I'll go and ask my uncle if I can invite James. Are you working tonight?"

"Not tonight."

"The Tandoori is closed on a Sunday. My one free night of the week. One of these days you should go and see your family and surprise them."

"Do you think we should?"

"By now I'm sure your father will have forgiven you. I miss my own family. Never thought I'd miss them so much. Whatever else we find, we only have family that really cares about us."

"What about friends?"

"Friends come and go... James will enjoy a good lunch."

"When's Oliver moving out?"

"At the end of the month."

Downstairs he could hear them talking in Mrs Salter's basement flat, both of them animated as they talked of the past. There was a stairwell from outside the front door down into the basement. Randall tapped on the open window.

"Sorry to interrupt, Mrs Salter. Uncle Paul, do you mind if I invite my friend James Tomlin to lunch?"

"That's perfect. Didn't know till I got here you would be bringing a girlfriend. Another man will make up the numbers for lunch. There's plenty of roast lamb. Beth always cooks too many vegetables when she does the cooking on Sundays."

"I'll go and ask him. Amanda is still getting dressed."

Mrs Salter was looking at him with a knowing smile, her tongue just poking the inside of her cheek.

"Take all the time you need. Mrs Salter and I are enjoying a chat and a cup of tea. She knows Tinus Oosthuizen's wife. The film actress, Genevieve. It's such a small world. She was in a West End show with Genevieve. Off you go and invite your friend."

In the street in front of the house stood a new and well-polished Jaguar, standing out from the smaller and older cars of Notting Hill Gate. His uncle was rich, no doubt about it. Smiling, Randall went inside the house, up the three flights of stairs and knocked on the door of James Tomlin's room.

"You're invited to lunch at my uncle's house. Roast lamb. All the trimmings."

"You seen Oliver?"

"Not for a couple of days. Will you come?"

"I'd be delighted. Can I come like this?"

"My uncle used to play the clarinet in a jazz band."

"I thought he was rich."

"He is. You want to see what's parked outside."

When they drove away from the house, Mrs Salter standing out on the pavement to see them off, Randall sat in the front seat next to the driver, Amanda and James in the back. Amanda had put on her best clothes and was wearing lipstick.

"Tinus Oosthuizen is an Afrikaans name. What's he doing in America?"

"All part of the Brigandshaw legacy. We're all tied to the Brigandshaws, Randall. Me through Beth, who was Harry Brigandshaw's only daughter, your father through my father-in-law's suggestion to go to Africa and apply for a Crown Land farm after he left the Royal Navy. After the war, the Rhodesian government encouraged ex-British officers to go out to Rhodesia. The British needed tobacco they could pay for in pounds sterling as they were short of American dollars. We British had mortgaged ourselves to our necks to the Americans to fight the war. In those days the tax on cigarettes and pipe tobacco paid for the new British health service. What we now call the NHS. Your father had done his National Service just after the war. But I'm digressing from your question, Randall... Aren't the plane trees beautiful in this part of London?... Now, where was I? Oh yes, Tinus Oosthuizen, who runs the Brigandshaw family business in America as I run it in England. His grandfather, also Tinus, introduced Sebastian Brigandshaw, Beth's grandfather, to elephant hunting in the latter part of the nineteenth century. Ivory was worth a fortune if you had enough of it. Together, under licence from King Lobengula of the Matabele, to whom they paid a substantial royalty, they amassed a fortune by hunting elephant for their ivory. Central Africa was teeming with elephant. There were great migrations of elephant in those days, mile upon mile of them head to tail. Why Sebastian called the family farm Elephant Walk before he was killed by the Great Elephant. Seb's daughter married Tinus's son, Barend, the man in America's father. Does that answer your question?"

"Most adequately. So the first Tinus was an Afrikaner?"

"He was. He was hanged by the British during the Anglo-Boer war for treason. He went out with the Boers to fight the British. As a Cape Afrikaner, which was where he came from before hunting in the bushveld of Matabeleland, he was British. The Cape was a British colony. So they hanged him for treason."

"How awful."

"It was. Especially for the Oosthuizens and the Brigandshaws."

"I hate wars."

"So do we all, Randall, if we have any sense. But it's all part of Darwinian survival. People fight to survive. Survival of the fittest. The behaviour of the human race isn't exactly pretty, I'm afraid. If we don't get our own way we pick up a gun. All part of the human condition. What can you do? And if someone comes at you with a gun you pick up a gun to defend yourself... That Mrs Salter is full of stories. A very interesting lady."

"You should have invited her to lunch."

"I would have done. I was thinking of you two. If the two of you get away with it in the same room I thought it better not to rub it in. She must have been a very beautiful woman in her day."

"I thought you said you'd seen her on the stage?"

"It's the way you do things, Randall. You meet an author, you tell him you've read his book. You say you can't remember the title if he asks you. Anyway, I might have done. I saw a lot of shows in those days. Can't remember all the players… I hope you are all hungry. So, tell me, James. What do you do for a living?"

"I build and paint the sets hoping one day I'll become an actor like our friend Oliver Manningford. Thank you so much for inviting me. Roast lamb is my favourite."

"I hope you like Donna St Clair. She's my wife's niece. You remember Donna, Randall? You were both three or was it four years old when she spent a long holiday on World's View with her mother; the then Livy Johnston before she briefly married Frank St Clair, Beth's half-brother. Turned out Harry Brigandshaw wasn't his father. Harry had been away in Rhodesia when his wife met up with her childhood sweetheart, the Honourable Barnaby St Clair. His father had the title of Lord, hence Barnaby's Honourable. Barnaby's elder brother inherited the title. So there you have it. Donna was so excited to hear you were in England, Randall. Ever since you visited your grandmother she's been hoping to see you."

"Her mother painted the portrait of my mother that hangs in the lounge at World's View."

"That's right. She's now Mrs Gainsborough. No relation to the painter. They all live in the Lake District where Livy paints. Donna is down for the weekend visiting friends in London. Your father's phone call from Rhodesia giving us your address came just at the right time. Donna said you were such friends as children. You'll like her, James. She's very beautiful. Outstandingly beautiful."

"What does she do?"

"She's just finished art school. Don't ask me which one. The trouble is, most artists find it difficult to make a living."

"Don't tell me," said James from the backseat. "A friend of mine at RADA – that's the Royal Academy of Dramatic Art – was told by his mime teacher that after five years of leaving RADA only two per cent of the students are still in the theatre. Is she a painter like her mother?"

"Hopes to be. She'd be better off finding a nice boy with a good financial future, getting married and having children… Why are you pulling a face, Amanda? I can see you in the rear-view mirror. Now you are blushing. I'm so sorry. When you are young, money doesn't seem important. Only when you get older do you find it means everything. Terribly unfortunate but you can't get away from it. What do you think, Randall?"

"Can I leave answering the question for a couple of years? Little Donna. Haven't thought of her in a long while."

"Here we are, everybody. Home sweet home. There she is standing on the top of the steps. Must have been watching for us out of the window."

As the car stopped at the kerb, Randall looked up to where he had been standing with Amanda when he knocked at the door on his first visit bringing out his grandmother. Instead of his grandmother he was now looking at the most beautiful girl he had ever seen.

PART 2

SEPTEMBER TO NOVEMBER 1979 – FOREVER
IS NOW

*A*manda, never one to worry, felt the cold shaft of fear burst her comfort zone. Randall's jaw had dropped, his eyes widening as he looked at the girl on the steps. Having lost his virginity it was time for him to move on like the rest of them. She was no longer the centre of his attention. James Tomlin was also looking at the girl, both of them gobsmacked. The girl was beautiful, way out of Amanda's league. Her life had always gone in stages, short, exciting bursts and then nothing. She could only hope the girl on the steps wouldn't be interested in a boy with a waiter's job and a family farm in Rhodesia that was rapidly disintegrating, a boy without a future in the competitive world.

They went up the stairs, everyone talking. Inside the house Amanda could smell the roast lamb cooking, making her mouth water. She had no claim on Randall. What happened, happened. There had never been any point in worrying. If the girl became a problem she would introduce her to Oliver Manningford who was always interested in a girl with a title in the family. It quickly turned out the girl's father was loaded, making Amanda relax. They were childhood friends, nothing in the present. The girl's aunt was pleasant, the food as good as it got. In the dining room where they sat down to lunch at a sumptuous table, the contrast to their room in Notting Hill Gate was hilarious. Amanda sat quietly eating her lunch while she listened. James, by the look of him also not sure what he had got himself into, said nothing: the talk was all about the Crookshank family in England and Africa; the Brigandshaw family; the St Clair family. It turned out that after the death of Harry Brigandshaw his widow, Tina, had married her childhood sweetheart, Tina being from the wrong side of the tracks. Donna was happy to tell everyone her great-grandfather had been the stationmaster at Corfe Castle, the village close to the St Clair estate at Purbeck that had been in the St Clair family for centuries. Her father Frank St Clair was rich, stinking rich like his father the honourable Barnaby St Clair. While Amanda ate and sipped from her wine in the fancy cut-crystal glass, the family names and their history flowed around her. Halfway through lunch, Randall, sitting next to Donna and across the table, gave her a smile of understanding, making Amanda reach out under the table with her foot. They touched, shoe against shoe, the warmth of comfort flowing back into her soul. Amanda raised her glass to Randall, both of them happy. Donna saw the look.

"Oh, how silly of me," she said, "I thought you were with James."

"Not if you count the fact that Randall and I are living together. We both work for the same temp agency. Both of us wait tables. We have a room together in a boarding house in Notting Hill Gate."

"How nice for both of you."

"It is. Very nice."

"You didn't waste much time, Randall. How long have you been in England?"

"No, he didn't. You should come over, Donna. You're out of Art School. We're all in the arts or trying to be. Every up and coming artist or actor waits tables. But you would know that."

Smiling, knowing it was always best to face a challenge, Amanda went back to enjoying her lunch. Donna, sensibly, had started up a conversation with James. Beth Crookshank, the one-time Beth Brigandshaw, talked of her two children. Granny Crookshank talked about her late husband, Randall's grandfather. Donna talked about her mother, the famous painter. It was a family Sunday lunch.

After lunch, they all trooped into the lounge where Paul Crookshank, Randall's uncle, sat down at a grand piano and played them what he called a Chopin nocturne, playing it well. It seemed he played classical music on a piano as well as he played jazz on a clarinet.

And then it was over, the danger gone with it. The uncle dropped them outside Mrs Salter's house, not coming in. Amanda was back in her comfort zone.

"Are you going to see your uncle in his office?" she asked Randall.

"Probably. Best to keep all the options open. What a lovely lunch."

"You have nice relations."

"Next time it's your turn, Amanda. When we visit your parents."

"She fancies you."

"Who does?"

"Don't look coy – Donna. You're a good-looking boy. She perked up when your uncle asked you to call at his office... Let's take a nap. The one thing I like to do after a heavy Sunday lunch is take a nap. You mind if we leave you, James?"

"Thanks for thinking of me. Haven't had a good meal like that for ages. You think Donna would go out with me, Randall?"

"Why don't you ask her?"

"Yes, I suppose I could. Thanks again. See you soon."

They watched James go into his room and close the door. Life went on. It always did. In their double bed, well fed, drowsy from the red wine, they turned over, bare bottom to bare bottom, and went to sleep. When they woke it was dark. They made love. Then went back to sleep, the rhythm of her perfect life returning.

The next day, Randall made nine pounds in tips, Amanda making eleven. Amanda smiled to herself remembering Oliver Manningford's favourite expression when he got what he wanted: 'It's not all bad.' And it wasn't. There was no phone in the room so no one could call them. If the beautiful Donna wanted to contact Randall she would have to come round, which Amanda doubted she would do. With a bit of luck, the competition had gone home to her mother in the Lake District to paint. Oliver was right. It wasn't all bad. The trick, she had found, was to enjoy what she had when she had it and let tomorrow, with its pain and sorrow, take care of itself. There was no point in worrying. There never had been.

"Why don't we get a cat?" she said to Randall the following morning.

"Where would it do its business? Can't get down from the window to the garden."

"Hadn't thought of that."

"When you lose something that is precious like Lady, it's difficult to replace them. You're a kind person, Amanda. Have I told you that?"

"What are you reading?"

"Howard Spring. *I Met a Lady*. The title caught my attention when I went to the local library."

"What's it about?"

"Love, Amanda. It's all about love. Families that love each other."

"Do they have a cat?"

"Not so far. He paints lovely pictures with words."

"Can I read it after you?"

"Of course you can. That's what you and I are about. Sharing things."

"Can I make you a cup of tea?"

"I'd love a cup of tea... You really think I could write a book about Rhodesia? Would anyone outside of Rhodesia want to read it? Most of the whites are leaving the country. The ceasefire is now going to be at the end of the year. The parties will be haggling over whatever details they agree to at Lancaster House, they always do. I read in the *Telegraph* the election is going to be next February. Mugabe and Nkomo will sweep it, of course. Smith and his Rhodesian Front have been guaranteed some of the seats in Parliament to bring some stability to the changeover from white rule to black."

"They'll read it if the story is good enough and you write it as fiction. If the people are real and they love each other. People are much the same wherever their lives are set. You should do some writing. I'd love to read what you say. Get to know you better. How you feel and how you see the world."

"I'm a bit young to write a novel."

"Got to start somewhere. Practice makes perfect. All you need is a pen and some paper. You could write at that table under the window. We'll have something other than our daily lives to talk about. Bring us closer."

"You know, I think I will. Wouldn't it be a hoot if I got a book published? Where do I start?"

"At the beginning... Didn't you tell me you were born in the back of a truck in a storm when the rivers came up and your father couldn't get your mother all the way to hospital? That you were delivered by your father. Now that's a good start. One hell of a start. Just don't begin by saying it was a dark and stormy night... What are you laughing at?"

"You, Amanda. You're so full of enthusiasm. It's wonderful. Most people are moaning about something. They're negative. You're always positive. I like it."

"Thank you, kind sir."

Amanda was glad he had dropped the subject of beautiful Donna. Even if she had not dropped the damn girl from her mind.

"You can write during the day when it's quiet. I can read while you are writing. Oliver has stopped reading his lines out loud. Not that he's around. You think he's living with the gorgeous girl? Probably. Poor old James. He's got an audition at the end of the week. We must keep our fingers crossed for him. Wouldn't it be wonderful if James got the part? Two famous actors and a famous writer straight out of the same garret."

"You mustn't call Mrs Salter's rooms a garret if we are at the top of the house. She'd be offended, poor old girl... Would we be as happy if we were famous?"

"Probably not. It's the idea that appeals more than the practice. The dream."

"What's your dream, Amanda?"

"I'm still working on it."

"But you have one?"

"Oh, yes. We all have a dream. Why it's called a dream as a dream never comes. Something like it maybe. Something that looks like it but isn't. A dream is beautiful. Reality often isn't."

"Will you tell me your dream?"

"When you write me a book. That's what I want. 'This book is dedicated to Amanda.'"

"Is that your dream?"

"Sort of, Randall. Sort of... Two for tea. How does that sound?... Why are they waiting so long before they stop shooting each other?"

"That's how it is. They go on shooting until they get what they want. Why wars are started. The politicians start the wars but rarely fight them themselves. They send young boys in their name or the name of the struggle to kill each other. I don't think they care about anything other than themselves. They just say it's all for the people but it isn't. Both sides are just the same. Horrible. Why I ran away."

"I'm glad you did or we wouldn't have met each other, Randall. Good things do come out of the bad. You know, your suntan is beginning to fade. When the war is over in Rhodesia we'll go and find the sun. Just the two of us."

"You're a romantic."

"Nothing wrong with that."

She had her own dream and it was terribly simple. She wanted to be happy. Get married. Have a family. Live happily ever after. 'If I ever write my own book,' she said to herself, 'I'd better keep that out of the ending.' In Amanda's mind, life was a lot more simple than people made it out to be. All that pursuit of unlimited wealth. Paying fortunes for objects that had no value other than showing them off. Bigger cars. Bigger houses. More and more money. One headlong pursuit of materialism. Her mother had dozens of pairs of shoes and never wore half of them. Happiness. That was her dream. Being happy.

"I want to be happy, Randall. That's my dream. Make other people happy. You think I'm naïve?"

"I hope not. No one's making anyone happy in Rhodesia. That much I'm sure of. When's his audition?"

"Friday morning at Drury Lane."

"Why don't we go along? Give him some moral support. The best part about waiting tables is having the day to ourselves. I like the night shift. Let's forget the tea and go for a walk. Outside the sun is shining. A good walk makes me feel good."

"Come on."

Hand in hand they walked from the house. The plane trees were beginning to shed their leaves in the prelude to autumn. They began to run. Hand in hand. Both of them laughing.

THEY WENT to the audition on their own, not wishing to spook James. The first person they saw, sitting in the front row of the auditorium, was Oliver Manningford, a solid phalanx of people seated around him. Amanda smiled, Oliver raising his right hand with his fingers crossed. Randall found them seats four rows behind Oliver. Oliver had turned back to talk to his friends. The fact that Oliver had come to help his old friend made

Amanda feel good. She picked up Randall's left hand and crossed his first two fingers. The audition got under way. The stage was big and cold, no sound of any music; hard feet on hard boards resounded in the mostly empty old theatre. Amanda remembered the pulse and vibrancy that rose to the rafters when her father had taken the family to see *Hello, Dolly!*. Amanda was ten years old. It was a week before the horror that changed her life and destroyed the normal relationship with her parents. William, the boy who had lived next door to them all Amanda's life, was also ten years old. Some called him Bill. Some called him Willie which was quite appropriate given the circumstance. Amanda always called him William. William Drake. Her best friend. Her only friend... A small man with beautiful hands was directing the audition from the stage. Amanda had no idea what the play was about. Or whether it was another grand musical in the tradition of *Hello, Dolly!*. The girl up on the stage being auditioned was so bad it was embarrassing. The girl stopped in the middle, burst into tears and ran off into the wings, Amanda feeling sorry for her. The pressure was enormous. One of London's most famous theatres. Her worry for James mounted. Randall squeezed her hand.

"You were much better when you read for Oliver," he whispered. "Here he comes. Oh poor James. I couldn't stand up there on my own for all the tea in China. Did you ever want to be an actress?"

"Not once that I remember. My mother called me inadequate which deflated any ambition I might have had. 'You're inadequate, Amanda. Please pipe down and listen to what other people are saying.' Once a week. Regular as clockwork. My father also had the habit of putting me down... Are your fingers still crossed?"

"So hard they're hurting."

James was surprisingly confident, the small man with the beautiful hands applauding when James had finished.

"That's more like it," said the man. "Next!"

Two hours later they were still in the theatre. Oliver had gone soon after James had left the stage, disappearing backstage, up a side flight of stairs. He had the confidence and look of a man knowing where he was going. There had been no sign of James after his audition.

"You think he saw us, Amanda?"

"I don't think so. He saw Oliver the moment he stepped onto the stage. Let's go home. We'll hear later if he got the part. That man only clapped twice through the whole audition."

"Wouldn't it be wonderful? I got such a warm feeling when I saw Oliver. That's what friends are for. Gave James his confidence."

"Five years of friendship."

By the time they went to work at their respective restaurants there was still no sign of James. Amanda's night was quiet, she served only two tables. She went home at ten, a pound in her pocket, only one of her tables leaving a tip. If James was in his room she could not hear him. And there she was, a one-pound waitress all on her own, no sign of Randall, wondering what might have happened with her and William if her father had not caught them behind the raspberry bushes at the top of the garden. At twenty-three she still thought back to him, to the happy years of her childhood mucking around with William in the garden. Theirs was the big old house, William's the small new one built too close to the fence. Her father had tried to buy the strip of land when it came on the market, missing his chance. When the Drake house went up he resented the closeness of where it was built. There had been an argument soon after Amanda had been born. Right from the start they had tried to stop her making friends with William, never inviting him into the house. Her mother said William was common, whatever that was meant to mean. To Amanda, the much younger last of her parents' children, he was unique. Anything but common. A rarity she had never replaced and now doubted she ever would. William had been her soul mate, Randall her lover. There was a difference. Looking back, her sexual awareness had developed earlier than William's, her curiosity with it. It had all been her fault.

"Take off your trousers, William. I want to have a look. You can have a look at mine."

"What do you want to have a look at, Amanda?"

"Your willie. You're different. You're a boy. I'm a girl. I don't have a willie. Please, William. I just want to look."

"It doesn't seem right."

So they showed each other their differences, Amanda curious, William not really interested.

"What are you kids doing? William, get off my property and never come back. You're disgusting. I never want you to ever see Amanda again.

If you ever speak to her again I'll go to your parents and tell them what you have been doing. It's disgusting."

"I'm sorry, Mr Hanscombe. I didn't know we were doing anything wrong. Amanda said we were different down there and we wanted to look."

"Disgusting. Get out! Now!"

Amanda, waiting in the quiet room for Randall to come back from his shift at the Tandoori restaurant, could still hear her father's words: the indignation, the righteousness, the revenge for the house next door built too close to their home. She had watched her only friend walk from her life. Nothing she could do about it. She had not even cried, the horror so great, the loss so devastating. And so it had been. They had lived next door, waving from the windows at each other, smiling, but never speaking. Neither of the families so much as spoke to each other again.

When Randall quietly let himself into their room she was sitting on the side of the bed, her head in her hands.

"What on earth is the matter, Amanda?" He sounded alarmed.

"Nothing, Randall. I was just thinking. About something that happened to me a long time ago... Why are people so nasty to each other?"

"I don't know. You want to tell me about it?"

"Not now, Randall. It all sounds so silly now."

"Did you eat at the restaurant?"

"We were quiet."

"So were we."

Being caught on the couch making love was nothing in comparison to being caught behind the raspberry bushes with William. At twenty-two she could do what she liked. At ten she could do nothing.

That night, for the first time, they did not make love. Amanda lay awake thinking of William. Would they too have become lovers? Would they have married? Had children? Lived a normal family life, soul mates and lovers, husband and wife, mother and father till the light of life left one of them? Who knows what might have been? Twice she heard James cough from his room. There was no sound from Randall. The distant noise of London went on; the traffic, the sound of a car horn. It was dark in the room, a faint smell of gas from the gas ring where they did their cooking in the alcove from when Randall had made some tea. When she slept she dreamed of William, both of them being chased by a monster.

In the warm light of morning, with the sun streaming into their room, her feeling of despondency had gone. She was cuddled up to Randall as close as she could get. He was still sound asleep. Then it came, making her realise why she had woken: James Tomlin was singing, happy as a lark.

"What the hell's that?" said Randall, sitting up in his bed.

"It's James. Must have got the part. I'm going to knock on his door."

"Better put some clothes on."

Throwing back the sheets on her side of the bed, Amanda pulled on the clothes she had left on the floor the previous night. Barefoot she went to the door, opened it and listened. The singing had stopped only to start again. He could sing, could James. No doubt about it... She walked across the landing and banged hard on the door.

"Did you get the part?"

"Of course I did. Why do you think I'm singing?"

"Open the door... That's better. James, you are naked. Stark, bollock naked."

"And you are beautiful, Amanda. Did I wake Randall?"

"You woke the whole bloody house but it doesn't matter. Oh, James. I'm so happy for you. A part at Drury Lane! You're going to be famous. So is Randall. He's going to write a book."

"Go back to sleep!" came a shout from Oliver. "Well done my old friend. Wonderful news. Now let me go back to sleep."

"Get up, you old bastard, and come and celebrate."

"I'm not alone."

"Neither am I anymore. I have a job. A proper part. No longer on the fringe. I think I'm going to burst with excitement."

"Please don't, old boy. Makes one hell of a mess... So, you're now a West End actor," said Oliver opening his door across the landing. He was also naked, the gorgeous girl giggling from her vantage point tucked up in his bed.

The two men shook hands.

"Well done, old boy," said Oliver. "I knew you would make it."

"Thanks for coming to the audition."

"My pleasure... When did he tell you?"

"Right at the end when everyone had gone. He'd told me to wait."

"How big's the part?"

"Big enough. Now the hard work begins. I'm going to concentrate so damn hard to get it right. You only get one big break in life. This is mine."

"Put some clothes on. Both of you. I'm going back to bed."

Feeling a little sad, even a little envious, Amanda went back to her room, took off her clothes and got into bed. Randall had turned over and gone back to sleep. She could hear Oliver and James still talking to each other, both of them excited. She had opened the window to let in some air, waving at Mrs Salter down below in the garden. She felt flat, let down. Everyone else was winning. Most of the flatness had come from thinking of William, of what might have been. She tried to tell herself she was being silly. The secret of life was to enjoy the present, never to dwell on the past. What might have been with William could just as easily have turned out a disaster. Life was fickle. So were people. Think positive, Amanda, she told herself... The sound of the traffic was louder now the window was open. She began to drift, her thoughts merging, no longer coherent. Both James and Oliver were singing. Then she fell into sleep.

A WEEK LATER, a few pounds richer, her ten per cent paid to Sarah Rankin, Randall gave her the first handwritten pages of his novel to read. There were twenty of them, easy to read with surprisingly few corrections.

"I'm going for a walk while you read. If it's rubbish throw it in the wastepaper basket and don't say a word. I'll understand."

"Take your raincoat and the umbrella. It's going to rain."

With the foolscap pages in her hand, sitting up in bed, the door to their room closed, Amanda knew it was a fragile moment in their relationship. A make or break. A watershed. If it was as bad as the girl at the audition she would have to throw it in the bin and hurt his feelings. Writers wrote about their own experiences. He would have opened himself up. Made himself vulnerable. If it was good, really good, she would be left feeling inadequate. All she had for him was her body. Maybe her friendship. There wasn't much more. A temp waitress in a string of restaurants wasn't much to show anyone... Amanda picked up the pages. The heading was simple:

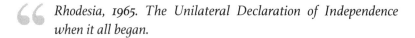

> *Rhodesia, 1965. The Unilateral Declaration of Independence when it all began.*

Two hours later, when Randall, dripping wet from the rain, came back from his walk she was lying back against the pillows, the pages of his book on top of the duvet next to her.

"What's the matter, Amanda? You've got that faraway look again. Did you read it?"

"Oh, yes... I want to correct some of your spellings and punctuation... It's a whole different world in Africa. Colonial Africa. The last gasp of the British Empire. You were all so different. Your lives so real. Everything seemed to matter. Here, nothing much matters except the size of the tip. Father never talked about India the way you talk about Rhodesia. You must all so love the place. Coming to England must have broken your heart. You write it as fiction but it's all so beautifully real."

He was smiling at her.

"My heart is quite good thanks to you. So you don't want to throw it in the wastepaper basket?"

"Whether publishers will like it I'm not sure. You're telling the white man's side of the story. The bleeding British liberals think of you as the oppressors. You colonials are the bad guys. The good guys are the leaders of the black revolution. Most publishers would want a writer to champion the underdog's story. Greater mass appeal. All the publishers are interested in is selling as many copies as possible."

"Probably. But it's not how I see Rhodesia. I'm trying not to write politics. I want to write about people. Politics is always changing depending on who's getting what: Communism against Capitalism and what people think they will get out of it. Look, I'm only twenty-one. What do I know about the rights and wrongs of government? I want to tell the story. My story. Our story. The only one I know. The question I want you to answer truthfully before I carry on writing is whether you are enjoying my story, despite the bad spellings and punctuation. Can you see the pictures I'm trying to bring to you with words? Can you see the bush and the animals? Hear the call of the birds? Have empathy with the people I'm trying to write about?... I'm sorry. Throw the bloody lot away. Writing the Rhodesian story was a bad idea. Too many memories. Now I've lost everything: Rhodesia and the story of Rhodesia."

"Let's decide that when you finish the book. Publishers' perspectives can change. People's opinions on who are the good people change. If the new black government makes a mess of it you won't look so bad."

"You think I should go on?"

"Right to the end."

"The end, of course, is Mugabe."

"Oh, there'll be life after Mugabe."

"So you are serious?"

"I've had a lot of spare time during the days. I don't have money to spend on entertainment so I go to the library. Reading is my only true hobby. Books, books and books, and any left-over newspaper I don't have to buy. Quite often people eat alone in the restaurants. People in London on business. They bring a newspaper to read and leave it behind. Sometimes news magazines. I'm a magpie. I pick them up, take them home and read them the next day. Why I'm telling you, Randall, this stuff is good."

"Except for the spelling and punctuation."

"That's technical. Anyone can spell and punctuate but not everyone can write a book. When it's finished we'll borrow a typewriter and I'll type it out for you. Correct the spelling mistakes. Tighten up the punctuation to make it read easier."

"Can you type?"

"Of course I can. Most girls can type. The one job for girls in plenty is that of a typist or secretary. My dear father made me do two years at secretarial college after I left school."

"So why didn't you get a job as a secretary?"

"Boring, boring. I prefer waiting tables where you meet all sorts of people from all over the world. Not be a slave to some self-opinionated boss, bound to his whims and a desk. At least when I bring them coffee to a table they say thank you and afterwards leave me a tip. It was another of my arguments with my father. Why I don't go home. They've always got something to criticise. If I tell them I'm working as a waitress they'll flip."

"There must be something else you could do."

"You tell me. You couldn't find anything. You need a degree or some training. But most of all you have to want to do something that isn't just for the sake of making money. Anyway, girls don't have a career. They have babies. How it works... Go and hang up your raincoat. You're dripping wet. Winter's coming. Welcome to England."

Carefully, Amanda put together the twenty pages and handed them back to Randall. Her heart was heavy with mixed emotions. Happy for Randall but somehow envious. She was going to be a typist but for the sake of companionship and not for money. Maybe that was better, the two years of mostly boring college not completely wasted.

"So you really don't want to go visit your parents?"

"No, Randall, I don't. What I do want to visit is Rhodesia."

"They're always looking for secretaries in Rhodesia." He was smiling at her, his raincoat on a hook in the corner.

"Shut up and go write your book."

She watched him sit down at his desk, pick up a pen and begin to read back the two pages he had written the previous day. He was quiet, hunched over and lost to her, gone back to another world. After an hour she made some tea and put a cup by his side. Randall, lost in his fictional world, didn't notice. Quietly she put on her coat and went out of the room. There was no one around. Outside in the street it had stopped raining. The sun was shining. Amanda went for a walk. A long walk with herself and her thoughts.

2

A month later, in the middle of a cold and wet October, the postman slipped the invitation to the Livy Johnston retrospective through the letter box in Mrs Salter's front door. James brought the fancy envelope up the three flights of stairs and knocked on their door.

"Hello, James. Come in. Randall's finished writing. When's the opening night?"

"Next month we hope. We want to open before Christmas. Looks like an invitation. It's addressed to Randall Crookshank and Amanda. Afternoon, Randall. This came for you both in the afternoon post. How's it going? You making tea? Wouldn't say no to some tea. I've heard of the Nouvelle Galerie. Run by a French American. Very upmarket. The Nouvelle Galerie is emblazoned on the envelope."

Smiling, Amanda took the invitation, leaving the two men to talk. She slit open the big envelope, her smile disappearing. Donna St Clair had written a note bringing back to Amanda the cold fear of feminine competition.

My mother's having a retrospective, Randall. You must come. She'd love to see you and hear the news of your father. They were lovers, you know. My father will also be at the opening

night. Along with my mother's husband. Jeanne Pétain, the owner of the gallery, is an old friend of mum's. Please come. Can't wait to see you again.

"So, who's it from, Amanda?"

"Your childhood friend Donna. Her mother's having a retrospective. We're invited. You'll have to take a night off. So will I. Wouldn't miss it for anything."

"Now what's the matter?"

"She's after you! That's what's the matter. Read for yourself."

"Don't be silly, Amanda. I'm not after Donna. I'm happily living with you... Let me have a look... My word, that is a fancy invitation. You know Livy Johnston painted the portrait of my mother that hangs in the lounge at World's View. Before any of them married they lived in the same house in Salisbury. My dad's old girlfriend Livy Johnston and my mother. Lucky Dad married my mother or I wouldn't be here. It's just an invitation. Should be fun. Next Saturday. That's a bugger. Saturdays are big nights at the Tandoori. Lots of lovely tips. Don't look so glum. She's not after me. Her father's rich and from the aristocracy. She wouldn't look at a penniless Rhodesian. We were just childhood friends."

"There'll be free booze and snacks," said James. "Sounds good to me. Never turn your nose up to free booze."

"My dad and Livy own a block of flats together in Chelsea. My Uncle Paul put the deal together. He was trying to persuade my father to get out of Rhodesia and sell World's View. That was before sanctions and exchange control. Lucky for me and Phillip he didn't. I'll ask Deepak for the night off. Ask Sarah Rankin to send a temp. Be nice to meet some new people, don't you think, Amanda? Get a different perspective of London. Chelsea! Very snooty from what I've heard."

"If your father owns part of a block of flats in snooty Chelsea your family are not exactly penniless. How many flats?"

"Twenty-eight, I think Dad said, James. They bought it years ago at a time when property in Chelsea wasn't so expensive. A big mortgage, paid off by the rental from the tenants."

"That was good foresight."

"Lucky you," piped in Amanda.

"It's nothing to do with me, Amanda. It belongs to Livy Johnston, the now Mrs Gainsborough, and my father."

"Have it your way. I just think she's after you."

"Nonsense. Anyway, what the hell does it matter? I'm not interested in Donna. We're having a fight over nothing. Why don't you come along, James? These art exhibitions are open to everyone. One big promotion. She'll love to hear you're opening in a play at Drury Lane. I'd ask Oliver if he wasn't working two shows on Saturday. When's he moving out from Mrs Salter's? He was meant to be going at the end of the month."

"He's not. Doesn't want to show off or miss his old friends."

"Good for Oliver. So, you'll come?"

"I'd be delighted."

"You can ask her to your opening night."

Amanda, furious with herself for making it an argument, picked up the day's writing on the desk in front of the window and began to read, the pen in her teeth. Twice she corrected the punctuation, once the spelling. She was back in his world. Back in Rhodesia, Donna forgotten... When she had finished she got up from the table. The window that looked down into Mrs Salter's garden was closed against the rain, the raindrops tapping the glass panes. Down below the garden was bleak, the clothesline empty. Amanda shivered, as if someone had walked over her grave.

"How does it sound?" asked Randall from right behind, making her jump.

"You're on track but it needs more pace or you'll lose the reader's attention. Got to keep making them turn the pages. Switch to telling the story from Edward's point of view. Give it more depth. Oh, and you need more description of where they are physically. Paint the scene for the reader in words. In the next couple of pages something big has got to happen."

"You should write your own book, Amanda."

"I would if I had a story. My parents have lived a boring life worrying about appearances, my father only interested in making more money. Your father did so much. Dug a farm out of the African bush. You can see a farm. You can't see money in a bank account. Or a business that sits in an office. Why rich people in England like to flash their money to show what they've got. All about impressing other people which I find boring... Africa is exciting."

"Sometimes too exciting and not for the right reasons. I'll think about what you've said. Build up the tempo. Thanks. I really need your help. Don't know what I'd do without you. You're my muse."

"What a lovely thing to say. Thank you, Randall. Now I'd better do the typing. You two go on talking."

"When are you going to show it to a publisher?" asked James.

"I wouldn't know where to start."

"I'll talk to Oliver. Put out some feelers for you. What you need is a literary agent. One who doesn't think the British Empire was a sin. I hope you are going to bring in the good work of the missionaries."

"Hadn't thought of it. Never met a missionary. Neither has Dad. Or if he did he never talked about it. That's a good idea."

"You're welcome. Why don't we go next door while Amanda is typing? You want to go to the pub tonight?"

"We're both working."

"You know work is the curse of the drinking classes."

The door closed, leaving her alone, the fancy invitation resting on the corner of the desk in front of her. For a moment, Amanda wanted to tear it up, obliterate any presence of Donna. Suppressing her innate worry, she kept looking at the typewriter... A girl knew. A girl knew when it was coming. She could feel it in her soul. She didn't have enough to hold him. In her past relationships, once they had both had enough of the sex, they drifted apart, both of them looking for somebody else. Sex, in Amanda's experience, never held them... Deliberately obliterating the thoughts in her mind, she began to type.

ON THE FIRST Saturday in November, two days before Guy Fawkes Night, the restaurant was packed. Amanda had never been so busy.

"Amanda Hanscombe. I don't believe it. What on earth are you doing waiting tables? Don't you remember me? I was your next door neighbour, William Drake."

"Well, this is a surprise... What are you ordering?"

"Can we talk?"

"Not at the moment, William. As you can see we are ever so slightly busy. It's the start of the Christmas season. What brings you up to London? Still living at home?"

"Not anymore. I live with Kelvin. Kelvin, meet my old friend Amanda. We were inseparable as children, weren't we, Amanda? Until we got caught. My goodness, I can still see your father's face. After that, Kelvin, we were never allowed to speak to each other again. We were ten years old. Where it all started, I suppose. Now, what are you going to have? Kelvin and I are going to the theatre. We so love the theatre, don't we, Kelvin? Kelvin's a dress designer. A very good one. So am I. We're both going to be famous, Amanda. What a surprise seeing you. So, what are you doing with your life? I'll have the prawn cocktail and a little glass of wine. We never have more than one glass of wine when we go to the theatre. It's a play. A serious play. Well, my goodness. What a surprise. I'll have the rump steak to follow. Medium rare. With a nice salad. Have to watch the figure."

Amanda, her eyes popping, went back with their order to the kitchen, the humour building up inside of her: the one and only love of her life. The irony was too delicious.

"What are you laughing at Amanda?"

"Life. Just life. Two prawn cocktails and two rump steaks. Medium rare. For the first time in my life I find out my father's nastiness did me a favour."

Only when Amanda got home did she think whether the horror of being caught behind the raspberry bushes had permanently frightened William away from women. When Randall came back half an hour later she was sitting on the bed feeling empty and miserable. Randall sat down next to her, putting his arm round her shoulder.

"You want to tell me what's going on?"

"I met him tonight... You want to hear a horrible story?"

"Of course I do. I like stories. Even horrible stories. What writers look for are stories they can use. Weave into their plot."

"Please don't use this one. It's about me."

"Tell me. It's always better to get it out of the system."

When she finished telling Randall she was crying uncontrollably.

"It was all my fault, Randall. I ruined his life. He'll never have a family. Never be a father. All because I wanted to look at his willie. For God's sake stop laughing. It's not funny."

"I think it is. Anyway, who's to say he won't be happy? Maybe he and Kelvin will be lifetime partners. Happy as Larry... Who the hell was Larry?... That's better. Got to see the funny side of life. The trick is never to take life too seriously. You know what? The day after tomorrow is Guy Fawkes Day. We'll take the night off. Say we're sick. Watch some fireworks. Go to the theatre... What do you think?"

"That you're wonderful, Randall. Just wonderful. Please hold me tight."

"There's only one snag. Where do we find a firework display in the centre of London?"

"I have no idea."

"Neither do I. The biggest bang should be in London. Didn't Guy Fawkes try and blow up the Houses of Parliament in Westminster? They did teach us English history in Rhodesia. Didn't I tell you my brother Phillip has a degree in history from Rhodes University in South Africa? Not that it's done him any good. Can't make a career out of history. Now he wants to start a safari company and live in the bush. All that money our dad spent on his university education completely wasted according to our father. At least Phillip had the experience of varsity. Expanded his mind. Made him think. I read somewhere that education is not about what you learn but about teaching you how to think. On second thoughts, I don't think I want to meet your father. You were ten years old for God's sake. You were curious. If people weren't curious we'd never learn anything new. It wasn't as though either of you were doing anything. You were just looking. So, did you find out where William and Kelvin are living? Just because they're gay doesn't mean we can't all be friends. Never met a couple of gays before. Or if I have they never mentioned it."

"No I didn't."

"Maybe he'll come back to the restaurant again. You can't alter your childhood friendship. That will always stay with you. Did you make any money tonight?"

"Pots of it."

"So did I. Let's go to bed. I'm dog-tired standing on my feet all night. Waiting tables is damned hard work."

"Don't tell me. Back and forth. Back and forth... You want to make love?"

"Of course I do. I'm not that tired. Good sex and then a good sleep. Nothing better... Isn't that gallery invitation for some time this week? I warned Deepak."

"Saturday night. I'll remind James. Two nights off in one week. Aren't we getting lazy?... So you don't think my curiosity ruined a man's normal life?"

"You do what you have to do. It's built into you. You don't just become a homosexual. It's built into you at birth. Different strokes for different folks. Don't worry yourself about it."

"I often wondered what would have happened if we hadn't been caught, whether we would have ended up together."

"You can put that one to rest."

"Please stop giggling."

"I'll try to. It's a bit like me and Donna. We were just kids. Kids make friends not lovers. You think it's going to snow on Christmas Day? A white Christmas. I've always imagined a white Christmas from all the Christmas cards we got from England. In Rhodesia we spend Christmas Day round the pool. Put a sheep on the spit. Now that's something. Sheep on the spit. Takes hours to cook. My job was regularly turning the spit. What a lovely way to spend Christmas in the shade of the msasa trees. Now I'm getting nostalgic. Are we really going to Rhodesia when the war is over? I won't want to come back. Neither will you. Africa gets to you. It's so free. So much space. Far away from the crowd."

"Of course we're going... Thanks for listening to me, Randall."

He was smiling at her as they took off their clothes, both of them quickly getting into bed. There were three blankets on top of the duvet to keep them warm during the night. They began to make love, slowly, beautifully, building up the passion...

AT EIGHT O'CLOCK on the Saturday night, dressed to the nines and wearing make-up, Amanda walked arm-in-arm with Randall around the Nouvelle Galerie, both with glasses of white wine in their hands. In the middle of the room in the glass case was a stuffed pig on display that was meant to be some kind of art. They walked round the huge display in a mild state of the giggles.

"He's very famous," said a middle-aged woman next to them, disapprovingly. "You obviously don't understand modern art."

"It's a dead pig, poor thing," said Amanda. "Oh, well, it's better for the pig I suppose. Better than being eaten."

The woman walked away with her nose in the air, Amanda and Randall sipping their wine. Away from the pig display on the walls were paintings, all of them, so far as Amanda could see, painted by Livy Johnston.

"It brings in the crowds. Running an art gallery is all about marketing. Creating a buzz. Between you and me I can't see art in it either. My name is Jeanne Pétain. I'm the owner of the gallery. If you want to blame anyone for a dead pig in a glass case you can blame me. I don't wish to be rude, but did you receive an invitation? You both look a bit lost. Most of my patrons are old and rich. They think, correctly, art is a good investment: somewhere different to put their money. You see, money can vanish but not a beautiful Livy Johnston painting."

The woman had an American accent with a French undertone, a good-looking woman in her mid-fifties. Randall pulled the invitation from his jacket pocket and handed it to her. James Tomlin had drifted off from one painting to the other, seemingly happy with what he saw.

"I hope you don't mind, Mrs Pétain, but I asked along a friend who wasn't invited. We all live in the same boarding house. James is opening a play at the end of the month. Drury Lane. Do you know where I can find Donna? We met as small children in Rhodesia."

"Oh, I've heard about you, Randall. And it's Miss Pétain. In the end I never married. She and her mother went out to supper. They'll be back shortly. Enjoy yourselves... The things we do in the art business. I made Donna's mother famous in a way. Got people to buy her paintings when no one had heard of her. What's the name of the play?"

"*The Priest's Lover.*"

"Sounds interesting. Controversial. What sells theatre tickets. Enjoy your evening. When I see Donna I'll tell her you've arrived, Randall. She was expecting you earlier. She was waiting at the door most of the evening."

The woman walked away now joined by another couple, the couple old and stinking rich by the look of them. The mention of Donna lying in wait at the door had brought back Amanda's fear of losing Randall.

"Look at those over there," said Randall, pulling her by the hand. "Those are paintings of Africa. Oh, my goodness. Look at that. It's called *The Big River*. I know that river. Those trees. That's the Zambezi. Look. Here's another one of a beautiful black woman. *Princess*. There's a note under the painting. 'On loan from Josiah Makoni.' He's one of the terrorist leaders along with Robert Mugabe and Josiah Tongogara. I remember Dad telling me the story. Josiah Makoni's parents were at the funeral of Harry Brigandshaw in Salisbury when Livy Johnston saw Josiah's mother and painted this portrait soon after. This all makes me so homesick. All these paintings of Africa were done by Livy Johnston when she visited Dad in Rhodesia before I was born. They are all so real... James. Come over here. These were all painted when the artist was going out with my father."

"And when we first met each other. Hello, Randall. You're late. You probably won't remember my mother from all those years ago."

"Of course I do. Thank you so much for the invitation to your exhibition, Mrs Gainsborough. These paintings are all so wonderful. So real. I can almost smell the African bush. This is my friend Amanda. And our friend James. The only thing I don't understand is the dead pig in the case."

They were all smiling at each other, mother, daughter and Randall, Amanda left out of it: old friends with lives in common.

"How's your father?"

"Dad's just fine. It's the war that's scary."

"Isn't it nearly over?"

"We hope so. Do you know Josiah Makoni?"

"Very well. He was running the ZANU party in London before he became a freedom fighter in Rhodesia. Or what you and your father would call a terrorist. Life can be so complicated. The 'Princess' I painted was Josiah's mother. Her husband worked for Harry Brigandshaw on Elephant Walk all his life. Harry was your father's mentor giving him the impetus to go to Rhodesia. Fact is, Harry Brigandshaw paid for Josiah's education. I saw his mother's beautiful face and wanted to paint her. I gave the painting to Josiah years ago when he was living in London... Let me show you around. My husband stayed in the Lake District where we have a beautiful house that belonged to his mother. He says London is too much for him now. As you know, I'm divorced from Donna's father.

Come on, all of you. I'll show you around. Hopefully give you a thirst for the arts. Donna has so been looking forward to seeing you, Randall. You're just like your father. And just as good-looking. I believe you just met my old friend Jeanne Pétain. She's French. Lived in Brooklyn in New York. Lives get so mixed up together. Without Jeanne's help I would never have made the money to buy the block of flats with your father. One big family don't you see, Donna. Isn't my daughter gorgeous? Her father says she's the prettiest girl he's ever seen. Maybe Frank is a little prejudiced about his daughter. And there's another connection. Frank St Clair's aunty, Lucinda, was married to Harry Brigandshaw before she was murdered by Mervyn Braithwaite, Harry's old CO in the Royal Flying Corps. He was crazy. All the killing in the war had warped his mind. I've always said I would have been a novelist if I hadn't become a painter. There's so much story in people's lives."

"Randall's writing a book. About Rhodesia."

"Is he, Amanda? Now that is interesting. When it's finished, Randall, I would like to read it. Maybe help you find a publisher. We all need some help in the beginning. Making a living as an artist, whether a painter, writer or musician is never easy. Some of the best art in the world has been lost as it didn't make money. You've got to have a mentor or make a lot of noise to gain the public's attention. Famous people can sell their art however they made themselves famous."

Amanda saw Donna's mother was looking at the dead pig in the glass case while Donna was watching Randall, a sweet smile on her pretty face.

"You have to grab the media's attention, who grab the public's attention, who make the artist interesting so the public buy the art."

"Will someone buy that pig?" asked Amanda.

"They already have. For a great deal of money. You see, the artist has made himself famous... Let me show you around, Randall. Explain where I did some of my African paintings. Always, when I see them again, they bring back such wonderful memories. The sad part about selling a painting is losing it. It's gone. What was so much part of you has gone. Only when people who own them lend their paintings to a gallery for a retrospective like this will I see them again. It's like meeting old friends again. Very special old friends. If I'd been born with money I would never have wanted to part with any of my paintings. Does your father still have my painting of your mother, Randall?"

"It's in the lounge at World's View. All I have of my mother. Always her eyes follow me round the room giving me comfort. Phillip says without your painting we would never have known our mother. Thank you so much."

"That's a compliment I won't forget. Worth far more than all the media acclaim or all the money." She was smiling sympathetically at Randall, a sad, faraway look on her face. Donna was still smiling at Randall. "There's food laid out in the other room. This one of the elephant was painted in the Zambezi Valley. What memories. Africa is so beautiful but it's all so unstable. You are wise to have come to live in England. Much safer. We'll find a good publisher for your book and make you famous. How does that sound? Let the story of Rhodesia live on. Are you any good at writing, Randall?"

"I think so," said Amanda, getting herself in between Donna and Randall. "I do the typing. Correct the spelling and punctuation."

"I'm looking forward to reading it. Do you have a title?"

"I'm going to call it *The Tawny Wilderness*."

"Interesting. Yes. That's how it was. The colours so deep. So you both wait tables to make some money, Donna tells me. Most artists are poor. It's doing the art that counts, not the money. Until, of course, you want to buy a house and have a family. Then you have to be responsible and make real money... Enjoy your youth while you can. Build up your memories for more serious times. I did. Though I was lucky. I met Jeanne Pétain and she made me a lot of money. Hope you have the same luck, Randall. I really do. I envy you your youth and your freedom. Now, go and have a good go at the food."

With Donna in tow they made for the food. James had gone off again to look at the paintings. Amanda was hungry and needed another glass of wine. Donna had mostly ignored James, concentrating her attention on Randall.

"You know he's in a play at the Drury Lane theatre?" she said to Donna.

"Who, Amanda?"

"James."

The woman was going to be a problem. What to do was another problem. It was up to Randall. Nothing she could do about it.

In the room next door with the long table, Amanda picked up a plate and a fork and helped herself to supper, the fear in her stomach still rising, the rich man's beautiful daughter a mounting threat.

"You got enough, Amanda?"

"I hope so, Randall. I really hope so."

"What kind of an idiot pays money for a stuffed pig? Must have more money than sense. Can you imagine parking that thing in the middle of your lounge?"

"It sold for a quarter of a million pounds," said Donna.

"Shit. I'll tell Dad. We'll stuff all the pigs on the farm and ship them back to England. Not old Blackie of course. He's a bull. Best bull on the farm. I remember when he was born. No, we won't stuff Blackie. He's much too precious... This food is good... James. There you are. Grab a plate. Free food thanks to Donna. What can a couple of starving artists want more than free booze and free food? Quarter of a million pounds. Whoever bought it must be out of his fucking mind. Sorry, ladies. That one slipped out. Quarter of a million. I could live like a king for the rest of my life on half a million quid. Buy myself a place in Cornwall. Write books. Visit Africa whenever I wanted. Never have to worry a day in my life. Money. That's what money can do. It can buy your freedom. And some twerp used all that money to buy a glass case with a stuffed pig inside. The mind boggles... So, James. What do you think of the food?"

"The food is marvellous. And so are your mother's paintings, Donna."

"I'll never be as good as Mum. Don't have the talent. You can go to all the art schools in the world but if you don't have the talent it's all just technique. Mother's paintings are all so alive. So three-dimensional. They come at you out from the canvas. Mine are as flat as a pancake."

So it wasn't all wine and roses thought Amanda feeling better. Both good looks and talent would have really pissed her off.

"Maybe my children will have talent," said Donna. "They'll inherit the talent from their grandmother. They say it quite often misses a generation. So, what are you doing after this?"

"Going home," said Amanda sweetly. "But I'm sure James is free. He can tell you all about his part in the play. James is going to be a bigtime West End actor. Get into movies. Get on television. Aren't you, James?"

"If you say so, Amanda."

"Of course I do. Think positive. *The Priest's Lover* is going to be a howling success. Make you famous. Make you rich."

For the first time that evening Donna was looking at James, making Amanda feel less threatened.

"You want some more food, Randall? If we eat enough tonight we won't want any breakfast."

"You want some more wine?"

"Why not?"

With her hand under Randall's arm, she steered him nearer the food table leaving Donna and James in meaningful conversation. It had worked. The mention of money and fame had caught the girl's attention.

"You know, I think she likes him," said Randall.

"I hope so. James needs his confidence boosting... Now isn't that nice? All the bottles of wine on the table have had their corks pulled out."

For the first time since Donna came on the scene Amanda was feeling happy. Like Randall with his book, James needed encouragement. However good a writer or actor, they needed their confidence boosted, all part of the job of their girl. That was it, she thought. James needed a girl. When she looked up from filling their plates, James and Donna were still talking, both of them animated. She looked around at all the rich people in all their fine clothes and gave them a smile. She was feeling better. Much better. The panic had gone.

"You going to pass me my plate or stand there all day?"

"Sorry, Randall. You know, they really do look as though they like each other. How much longer are we staying?"

"We'll finish our food and go."

From small speakers in the corners of the ceiling classical music was playing, the piano concerto mingling pleasantly with the hum of human conversation. Everyone that came into the gallery first stopped and looked at the pig. So many of the older people looked bored, an evening out for something better to do.

"I want to go back to Africa one more time by looking at her paintings. You coming?"

"Why we came here."

Plate in hand, occasionally forking in a mouthful, chewing slowly as her mother had taught her, Amanda tried hard to understand the magic Randall found in the Livy Johnston paintings. For Amanda, she saw what she saw, none of the depth, the smell of the bush or the sound of the wind in the trees that so fascinated Randall. The woman called Princess was just another black face like so many others Amanda had seen on the streets of Notting Hill. By the time Randall had had his fill of the African paintings she had forked down all the food on her plate. Back at the table, she found her glass where she had left it, drank it down and turned to Randall.

"What now, my handsome knight?"

"The streets of London, the Tube, back home and into bed. Haven't felt so well fed since the night of the party when you cooked up your perfect curry."

"Home sounds good to me. I'm full as a boot."

There was no sign of James or Donna. Randall waved at Livy Johnston and the owner of the gallery, both of them deep in conversation. Amanda mouthed 'thank you' to both of them, not sure they had seen, wrapped her scarf round her throat and went out of the gallery into the Portobello Road. Outside it was bitterly cold. There was an old vendor out on the pavement selling jewellery from a barrow. An east wind had come up. The old man had a fire burning in a metal bucket with holes in its side. He was warming his hands.

"Goodnight," said Amanda, smiling at the old man. "Do you happen to know why it's called the Nouvelle Galerie when it's on the Portobello Road?"

"Been out here on the pavement since it started. Nearly thirty years ago. On exhibition nights like this they send me out a plate of food."

"You make any money?"

"On nights like this you got to believe it. People like them in there got more money than sense. My name's Stan."

"Is the jewellery real?"

"Don't be daft. I'm selling off a barrow. Trinkets for the wife, I tell 'em. You see the old men inside talking with the young girls? Them girls aren't their wives, they're aspiring artists. Course I tell 'em it's real. When they get home they got something for the wife, you see. Back when it started Nouvelle Galerie had a nice ring to it. Then they bought the building and tarted it up. You wanting to buy something?"

"We both wait tables, I'm afraid," said Randall.

"Here, have this one on Stan. Give it your girl. A little heart on a chain."

"How much is it, Stan? I got to pay you or I wouldn't feel right."

"Make it five quid... Where you from? You got a funny accent."

"Rhodesia."

"Livy went out to Rhodesia all them years ago. She was going to marry a bloke but didn't want to stay in Africa and he wouldn't come back to England."

"Here's your money. Lucky for me she didn't marry him. The man was my father."

"Well I'll be buggered."

"Goodnight, Stan."

"Look after yourselves."

When Amanda looked over her shoulder from down the street, the old man was hunched over the open fire still warming his hands at the coals.

"You didn't have to buy me anything."

"It'll be a talisman from a writer to his muse. Hell, it gets cold in England. I can't wait to get home."

When they reached their room, well fed and happy, they got straight into bed. Amanda had forgotten all about Donna. The chain with its small heart was now hanging round her neck. Her soft fingers were rubbing the heart, feeling its smoothness.

"Thank you, Randall," she whispered. "I'll keep it all my life."

"A stuffed pig. Quarter of a million pounds. Can you bloody believe it?"

With the lights out, no sound from the rooms of Oliver or James, she felt his first exploratory touch that would bring him into her, the silver heart just between her breasts. She felt Randall take the heart in his hand and touch it against her nipple.

3

Some days later, after a full week for both of them at their respective restaurants, Amanda heard a knock at their door. It was eleven o'clock on the Sunday morning. The church bells had just finished ringing for matins. They were both in bed, warm and content. It wasn't James or Oliver at the door as neither of them got up so early on a Sunday morning.

"You think it's Mrs Salter?... Who's there?" called Amanda.

"It's me. Your old friend William Drake."

"Hang on while I put some clothes on. Are you alone?"

"Took me a week to find out where you lived, Amanda. Can't you open the door? Don't you remember calling to each other from the second-floor windows? We weren't allowed to see each other, remember? We used to imitate the call of an owl to bring the other to the window, mine from the window on the landing, you from the family bathroom."

"Hang on, William. I don't sleep in pyjamas."

"It's cold out here. I went to the restaurant where you were working. They gave me the address of the temp agency. After I explained who I was a woman called Sarah Rankin gave me your address. You don't have a phone or I'd have warned you I was coming round."

Pulling on enough clothes to hide her body, Amanda went to the door and pulled it open.

"Good morning, William. This is a pleasant surprise. I've told Randall all about you. How we grew up so close. William, meet Randall, please get up. We've got a guest... You want some tea? Sorry I couldn't talk the other night. The busy season, you have to understand. You must have laid on the charm for Sarah to give out an address. She doesn't want another agency poaching her temps. Come on in so I can close the door. You make good money temping and it isn't so boring. If you don't like the owner of a restaurant you don't have to go back."

Amanda was trying not to laugh. Under the duvet Randall was struggling to pull on his pants. She filled the kettle from the small sink in the alcove, lit the gas and put the kettle on the gas ring. Outside it was raining. The rooftops looked wet and cold. A typical November morning in England.

"She's done it again. Mrs Salter has put her washing out in the rain... So, William, how are you? How are tricks?"

Just for fun she imitated the sound of an owl, two short hoots and one long. Randall got out from under the duvet wearing his trousers and walked across to William with his hand out. The two men shook hands.

"An old English custom we still use in Rhodesia. I'm a Rhodesian. Randall Crookshank. How do you do... They killed my cat. Why I'm here. Let me put on my shirt. Inside the room it isn't so cold. It was the terrorists. The shot came through the lounge window on World's View and a shard of glass killed the cat... There's a war on in Rhodesia if you haven't heard."

"Sorry. Not one to read newspapers or listen to the news on television. I find the news depressing, most of it... I want to make you some clothes, Amanda. Use you as one of our models."

"I'm not really pretty enough to be a model."

"You will be when I've finished dressing you. That's the art of a dress designer. Making the best of people. I make individual clothes. Some call it bespoke. You'll see. You'll be the prettiest waitress in London."

"Really! You'll make a dress for me?"

"Just for old times. Make up for what happened to us. That day still haunts me."

"Me too. It was the worst day of my life. Ruined everything... You take sugar?"

"Milk and two sugars. Don't you remember? No of course not, why should you?"

"At the age of ten, I doubt very much if I would."

"Well anyway, no one ever changes the way they drink tea. Or do they? My, this is cosy. And convenient. A little sink with hot and cold water: that must be a gas geyser over the sink. A gas ring to do the cooking. A nice big window. I suppose you all share a bathroom. Just right for the two of you and not too expensive. My word, you are organised, Amanda... So is Kelvin. I'm a mess when it comes to living. I do the washing up when I need a clean plate. Drives Kelvin insane. We have a little flat not much bigger than this in Knightsbridge if you know where that is, Randall. London's all much the same to me but in our business you need a good address. Very important for the customers. Our sewing room, as we like to call it, is part of the flat. Have you been to America? In America they call a flat an apartment. One day, when we are famous, Kelvin and I want to live in America."

"You must be doing well to live in Knightsbridge."

"Oh, we are. Very nicely, thank you... Isn't the kettle boiling? I did say two sugars?"

"And where is Kelvin?"

"Oh, he's still in bed. There's only one bedroom. One bed, actually. We're lovers... How are your parents, Amanda? Do you know our parents still haven't spoken to each other since your father caught us looking at each other behind the raspberry bushes? It was all so silly. As it turned out, it wouldn't have made the slightest difference you being a girl. What a hoot."

To Amanda's surprise, William waved his right hand from the wrist and gave out a high-pitched hoot just as Randall was pulling on his sweater. When Randall's head came through the sweater he was grinning, Amanda thinking what a pity Donna hadn't turned out a lesbian.

"I can just see the hat that will go with the outfit. Mostly I design and make the dresses while Kelvin does the hats. You have no idea what the right hat can do for a girl. Make her stand out in a crowd. That's what it's all about really. Making a girl stand out. Make people notice her. We all want to be noticed, Amanda. You see, that day when your father caught us was when it all started. I also wanted to look at your naked body so I could see how to dress you. I knew girls were different but I wanted to see. It's so important in dress design to start from the basics. Your poor father got the wrong end of the stick. People so often jump to the wrong conclusions. At ten, I already wanted to dress women. I think a soft shade of blue will suit you best. I've always wanted to dress you, Amanda, ever since we were kids."

"How are your parents?"

"Much the same. Dad still drinks too much and Mum still hates housework. The house is still a mess but who cares? They're happy, that's all that matters. Belinda is married. My sister has two kids. A boy and a girl. We don't see much of each other. But you remember that. I think she worked out I was a queer years ago. Doesn't worry my parents and that's all that matters... You'll need a nice full skirt to slim down your waist. You have such a lovely full bosom. We'll make the best of your bosom. Show it off so to speak. I'll leave the hat design to Kelvin. Dressing Amanda. At last my dream comes true... What are you laughing at?"

"Life. Just life. Come here, William, and give me a kiss. Just for old times' sake. Both of us had dreams. My dream was to kiss you."

"What a hoot."

The second high-pitched hoot had all three of them laughing, bringing a knock on the door.

"What's going on?" said James when Amanda opened the door.

"An old family reunion... Want some tea?"

"Never say no to tea... We're opening on Saturday."

"How wonderful, James."

"My stomach is all of a flutter. Did I tell you, I've invited Donna to the opening night? Here are your tickets. If you can't get off work I'll have to give them back. Have to have a full house at Drury Lane on opening night, don't we?"

"James Tomlin meet William Drake."

"How do you do?"

"So nice to meet you. An actor, by the sound of it. Drury Lane. My word. What's the play called?"

"*The Priest's Lover.*"

The third hoot from William had them all in stitches.

"I'd better get Oliver," said Randall. "Haven't laughed so much since before the war in Rhodesia when we all had something to laugh about... Oliver! Come on in here. We're going to have a party."

"Have you got any booze? It's Sunday so there isn't a show tonight. Can I bring the gorgeous lady? We've got some wine. What's the occasion, Randall?"

Oliver, half dressed, had opened the door and was standing in the doorway.

"A family reunion and James opening *The Priest's Lover* on Saturday. Meet William Drake, an old family friend of Amanda's. They grew up next door to each other. How is *Ode to Youth* going?"

"Still packing them in, Veronica's mostly the big attraction. They say we have this great chemistry together onstage... Veronica! Get dressed, darling. Randall and Amanda are having a party. You see it's not all bad. No, it's not all bad."

"Please close the door, Oliver," said Amanda. "It's freezing on the landing. The cold air's coming into the room."

"Back in a minute. Just what I feel like. A damn good party. Can we invite some of our friends? We'll tell them it's a bottle party and to bring some booze. The best party is always a spontaneous party. Spur of the moment."

"Please close the door."

"Back in a tick... Veronica, darling, please get on the phone and invite our friends... The new phone in my room is so convenient. Money. What you can do with money. Never stops surprising me. Never had much money as a kid, a bit of pocket money from Dad and that was it."

"Close the door!"

"I'll be back."

When the door was closed Amanda saw William was all excited.

"He's gorgeous," said William.

"Down, boy. So's his girlfriend."

"There's always a bit of gay in everyone."

"Don't you believe it, William. There's nothing gay about our Oliver. I'm the only girl in London Oliver hasn't taken to bed."

"You got to be kidding. The naughty boy. And I thought it was just us gays who were promiscuous. Not that I am. I love my Kelvin. But it never does any harm to look... He's positively gorgeous. Can I ask him to phone my Kelvin? Wouldn't want Kelvin to miss all this. The real theatre crowd.

Two famous actors and one famous actress. Oh, this is all so exciting. If I dressed Veronica West every celebrity in London would be knocking down my door. All that lovely publicity. It is Veronica West in the next room? I don't follow the news but I do follow the theatre. *Ode to Youth* is a smash hit. Oh, my goodness. Isn't this exciting?"

"And you won't forget me in all your excitement."

"Of course not, Amanda. I've wanted to make you a dress since we were ten years old... The West End theatre. That's the place for a dress designer. Can we open the bar? I'll tell Kelvin to bring some lovely wine. We both do love our wine. Kelvin knows all the best vintages."

"Drink your tea, William."

"Of course. Always finish what you are doing... Drury Lane. *Ode to Youth*. The mind boggles, ducky. Positively boggles. What a day. You know what you and I should do, Amanda? We should go down to Great Bookham and reintroduce our parents. What a hoot. All of us can go. When your father sees me with Kelvin it'll make everything right. Unless he's homophobic and then he'll throw me out of the house. What a hoot. You can't spend all those years not talking to your neighbour. I'm sure Randall would love to meet your lovely parents. How about next Sunday? Or we can surprise them at Christmas. It's so lovely to see you again, Amanda. You don't think Oliver will mind my using his phone?"

"Why don't you ask him? It's the room directly opposite."

"How old is Veronica West? She must be a whole lot older than Oliver. Not that it matters. I remember my mother talking about a show years ago. Where I first heard her name. It's much easier to hide a person's age when they're up on the stage."

"She plays a young girl in *Ode to Youth*."

"So you see what I mean. Fame, Amanda. That's what you need. And talent. You got to have talent up on the stage or it doesn't work... There you are. An empty teacup. Now we can all have a little drinky."

"Kelvin. Don't forget Kelvin."

"Of course not. I'll be back. Don't go away."

When the door closed behind William, Amanda looked at Randall, both of them laughing.

"He's hilarious," said Randall. "Have you met Veronica?"

"Not up close... We can't go to the opening on Saturday, James. Sarah Rankin will kill me. She's always short of temps on Saturday nights. It was only a week or so ago that we took a Saturday off. Sometimes you can't take advantage of the people who pay you."

"Why don't we give our tickets to William and Kelvin?" said Randall. "Sounds right up their street. James told me the plot. The priest gives up his calling to be with his young lover. Gives up his God. It's a tragedy. As far as I know it's the first openly gay play in London's West End. Isn't that right, James? The world is changing, Amanda. Not long ago you went to jail for practising homosexuality. Now it's quite the thing."

"So James, you are playing the part of a gay?"

"I'm the priest's lover."

"What a hoot, if you'll excuse me stealing William's favourite expression. How do you know how to act like a gay?"

"You watch people like William carefully. You get into the part."

"What happens to them in the play? The priest and his lover?"

"They kill themselves. The priest has forsaken God. Said that God had made him as he was and God had forsaken him. That he can't live without my character. He can't live without the comfort of God. So they make a pact and take poison. A bit like Shakespeare's Romeo and Juliet... You can give William your tickets. Maybe I can get you tickets to an afternoon show when you're not working. If you want to see the play that is. And if it doesn't sink on the opening night. And yes, Veronica is a lot older than Oliver. A bit like me and the priest. Life never works out the way it was meant to be... I'm going to get some beers from my room."

"You won't mind if we're not there on Saturday?"

"I will if the play folds on its opening night. But it's a good script, so it shouldn't."

"Tell Donna I said hello," said Randall. "Don't forget."

"I won't. She's bringing her mother to the première."

Amanda watched Randall clear his writing desk, put the manuscript in the small drawer, lock the drawer and put the key in his pocket. The typewriter was in the cupboard where she kept it. With a white tablecloth placed over the desk, they were ready for the party. Outside, the sun was coming through, a wind blowing Mrs Salter's washing. For the first time since he started the book, Randall was not going to do his daily writing. She would have to wait for the next instalment of what Randall said was a fictional story, something that Amanda doubted. So far as she understood the truth of Randall's life, what she read in his book sounded much like his personal story. The main character was born between two flooding rivers in the back of a truck during a storm when the character's father was driving his pregnant wife to hospital. The mother, like Randall's, was a drunk who got lost in the bush and was killed by a pride of lions, the black nanny doing the job of bringing up the children: two of them, just like Randall and Phillip. Not that it mattered to Amanda, the truth of the story. The nanny in the book had two children, Happiness the girl and Moley the boy. The children mixed freely, become close-knit friends until the white boys are sent to all-white schools and the children find out they are different. Moley, in the part Amanda had read in bed before William Drake came calling, had just joined the liberation struggle. The two boyhood friends were now enemies, the wrench in their friendship as painful as the war. It made Amanda smile. They had both been torn apart from a perfectly normal childhood friendship by other people's bigotry. Her from William, wanting to innocently look at her body, and Randall's character, who Amanda suspected was Randall, from his friends because they looked different. And when William showed her father he was gay all hell would let loose – bully for bigotry. The world, she thought as she tidied the room, was indeed strange.

"How long's it going to be before you finish the book?"

"Not long. It's running fast at the moment. Two thousand words yesterday. How did you like what you read this morning?"

"I sympathise with the main character for losing his childhood friends. It all sounds very similar to me and William but for different reasons."

"What different reasons?" asked James as he opened their door, walking across the room and putting six beers on the desk. "Oliver's still phoning. William's chatting to Veronica. Good idea putting a cloth on the desk. Can't have the genius upset by stains on his writing desk. How's it going, Randall? You want a beer? Just look at that. Outside the sun is shining. Mrs Salter is going to win... Cheers, old boy. To happy times. Thanks for your friendship. Both of you. Makes a man feel good having friends."

Within an hour people were arriving, all of them young, all of them happy. The men brought bottles, the girls plastic containers filled with food. Amanda emptied the contents of the containers onto plates and put the plates out on the desk. Randall had put out the glasses and a pile of plates, with forks next to them. Oliver had brought across his battery-operated record player which was playing in the corner by the sink on a stool, the music from *West Side Story*. This time there were no musicians from the Royal Academy of Music. Most of the partygoers were in theatre; Kelvin, when he arrived, in his element, as was William. The party began to swing, the noise increasing. Oliver, always the diplomat, went downstairs and invited Mrs Salter to come up. When she came she sat in a comfortable chair, a glass of wine in her hand, and smiled, happy that everyone else was young and happy. She had a faraway look on her face as if she remembered, a naughty, faraway look that said to Amanda without using words that Mrs Salter had been there many times before. For a moment, Amanda saw the young girl behind the old woman's face.

"You had a good life didn't you, Mrs Salter?"

"You can bet on it... I love being with young people, Amanda. They have so much energy. So much zest. You go and enjoy yourself. I'm happy just where I am."

Amanda walked across the room to stand behind Randall who was listening to Veronica West surrounded by a group of people. William was right, the woman was much older than Amanda first thought, ten or fifteen years older than Oliver. Amanda put her arms round Randall from the back, squeezing him, her mouth close to his ear.

"I'm so happy, Randall. I'm just so happy. You can catch up with the writing tomorrow. I'll be as quiet as a mouse. I promise... She's a lovely lady."

"She's famous."

"I was talking about Mrs Salter. She's sitting in the corner so enjoying herself. There'd be a book in Mrs Salter if you could get her to tell her story. You'll need something to write when we've finished *The Tawny Wilderness*. Older people love to tell their story. Brings it all back to them. Why she's sitting there looking so happy. We remind her of her youth... I suppose Veronica has a smart flat of her own. Wonder why they both don't live there instead of one room in an attic?"

"You'd best ask Oliver. Here he's in control. If he moved in with Veronica West people might think he was using her. Here they both get what they want without any complications."

"Why are you so clever, Randall?"

"Because I'm Rhodesian. We're all smart in Rhodesia... Of course I'm just kidding."

"Then how did you end up in a war?"

"Don't ask me... You know, William is right. We should go visit your parents."

"It's perfect as it is. Please don't spoil it."

"Why should we? They're your parents. William mentioned it again. You know something? I really think those two love each other. The same way a man loves a woman, a woman loves a man. Just look at the way William is looking at Kelvin. Tell me that isn't love."

"I love you, Randall. You think we could be together forever?"

"Forever is right now. That's how you've got to look at it. Forever in the moment. You see we're happy. Forever happy. We'll always have this moment. Forever... Here come some more people. Where are they all coming from? They'll never eat all the food. They're bringing so much of it... Enjoy the moment, Amanda. That's what life's all about."

"You call them Happiness and Moley in your book. Are they the same people you grew up with?"

"I couldn't think of better fictional names. It doesn't matter now for Happiness and Moley. They've lost their childhood names. They'll be known now by their African names. We were all so happy in those days. Why I want to capture it forever in a book."

"So we won't be together forever?"

"Who knows? Whoever knows?... For all I know it could have been Moley who fired that bullet through the window that killed my cat."

"Maybe he missed you deliberately?"

"Who knows? Whoever knows?... You want to dance? This is my favourite disco song. 'Saturday Night Fever'."

"Come on. Let's jive."

"It's a pity we didn't invite Donna for James."

Amanda gave him a wan smile as they faced each other.

"Who knows, Randall?... We should have put out a tip jar."

"Who needs a tip jar when we're both making money? Anyway, this time, they brought their own food and booze... Now look at that. Someone has got Mrs Salter on her feet. Just look at her dance!"

"If you want to see some real dancing look behind you at Kelvin and William. Together they make John Travolta look positively pedestrian."

PART 3

DECEMBER 1979 TO JANUARY 1980 – THE CHURCH BELLS ARE RINGING

1

*R*andall finished writing the book early in December, the day before they went down to Great Bookham with William and Kelvin to visit Amanda and William's parents. They drove down in William's new car with William driving. Randall was feeling empty, with nothing to write, the story finished. In the book he had moved past the coming ceasefire to the election of the new black government, Moley coming home in triumph, the main white character not so sure of his future. As they reached the village where William and Amanda had grown up, the two childhood friends were silent. Neither of them had told their parents they were coming.

"Don't you think we should turn the car round and go back to London, William?"

Amanda, sitting in the front passenger seat had turned to look right at William as she spoke.

"We've come this far so we're not turning back. Here's the turn. Agates Lane. Now doesn't that name bring back memories, Amanda? What do you think, Kelvin?"

"Very leafy except at this time of the year there aren't any leaves on the trees. So, explain to me how you are going to re-introduce the parents. It's so ridiculous, for God's sake. They're next door neighbours. And they really don't speak to each other?"

"Not for years. Not since her father caught us behind the raspberry bushes... Here we are, folks. Home sweet home. This is going to be fun."

"With luck my parents have gone away for Christmas," said Amanda, looking uncomfortable.

"What do you think, Randall?" asked William.

"That it all looked a much better idea when we were in London."

The car turned in at a gate, drove slowly up a driveway and parked in front of a large, two-storey house. Behind the house, on the other side, was a tall wooden fence, and close behind the fence a second house, newer than the first. There was a car parked in the driveway. The front door was opening. An old man and an old woman were coming out of the house. Amanda waved as she got out of William's car. The old woman was crying with happiness, the old man beaming his pleasure. Randall, breathing a sigh of relief, got out of the car. By the time he walked round the car, mother and daughter were hugging, making Randall feel better. So far, so good, he said to himself.

"Good morning, Mr Hanscombe. Remember me? William Drake from next door. I've brought Amanda with her boyfriend on a visit. That one is Randall, Amanda's live-in boyfriend. This is my live-in boyfriend, Kelvin. Happy Christmas. Do you mind if I go next door and bring round my parents? We all want to make friends again. How do you like your daughter's dress? I designed and made it for her. I'm a dress designer. In your day, I suppose, I would have been called a dressmaker... Long-time-no-see, Mr Hanscombe."

"Well, I'll be blowed. William Drake. Come in, my boy. Come in. Yes, of course you can bring round your parents. Happy Christmas to all of you... Just look at them. My wife is so happy to see our daughter. Thank you for bringing her, William."

"This is Randall Crookshank from Rhodesia. His family are tobacco farmers. And this is the love of my life, Kelvin Taylor. A dress designer called Taylor. What a hoot."

"Pleased to meet you both. I say, would you all like a drink? You can invite your parents over when we've all had a drink round the fire and got to know each other."

Randall, shaking his head, followed last into the big house. His father had always said it was better to confront a problem rather than run away from it. When the big front door was closed it was warm inside, and

Randall looked around. The young girl he had picked up outside the pub with no ulterior motive had turned out to be more than expected. Her parents were rich. Stinking rich by the look of it. As he followed the old man into the lounge where a log fire was cheerfully burning in the grate, Randall knew the ball game had changed. She was no longer just a temp waitress.

"So, what do you do, Randall?" asked the father.

"I'm a waiter in an Indian restaurant."

"Indian restaurant. Now that is interesting. Spent much of my life in India. Indian Civil, you understand... So, what are you going to do for a career?"

"I have absolutely no idea."

"Yes, well. So what would you care to drink? Rhodesian you say? Stopped at Mombasa in Kenya on my way home from India a couple of times. Difficult times, Randall. The empire's over. Gone. Out of the window. We all have to get used to it. So you've come back to live in good old England. Your family are English, I presume. Knew a Crookshank who went to school with my younger brother. Big shot in the city they tell me. Paul Crookshank was his name."

"He's my uncle."

"My word. What a small world... So, what are you drinking? Have a glass of whisky. I'm sure you drink whisky in Rhodesia. Frightfully colonial. Sundowners, I think you call it. Anyway, the war's over. They're sending out Christopher Soames to be the last British governor of Rhodesia. I think he's Winston Churchill's son-in-law. Quite appropriate... Did you have any trouble?"

"They killed my cat."

"Sorry to hear it... I'm sure your uncle will give you a proper job. Terrible job for Soames having to haul down the Union Jack for the last time in the last British colony in Africa, poor chap."

"I've just finished writing a book."

"Have you now? Well, that isn't exactly a proper job is it?... I was thinking of writing my memoirs... Just look at my wife and daughter. My goodness. Now they're both crying. Come and have a drink, my dear, before you have us all in tears. This really is a reunion. So Paul Crookshank is your uncle, Randall? My goodness. When he was at school all he ever wanted to do was play the piano. Just shows... I suppose you Rhodesians could call yourselves the last colonials. It's all over now. Not much for a young Englishman to do anymore these days. In my day you could join the Indian Civil or the Colonial Service. Get a posting anywhere in the world if you joined the Colonial Service: Malaya, Kenya, Hong Kong, Burma, you name it. The world mostly belonged to us British. Now we've shrunk back to this tiny island and the Americans have inherited the Anglo-Saxon Empire. In the end, history will merge them together, I suppose. There's still Hong Kong, of course, but most of Hong Kong is on a lease from the Chinese that's due to expire. Have to hand it back. Anyway, no one emigrated to Hong Kong like you chaps did to Rhodesia and made yourselves Rhodesians. All rather sad. Hundreds of years of British history slipping through our fingers... How does that one look, Randall? Now, my dear, what's my wife going to drink?"

"Isn't it a bit early?"

"Never too early when you've got an excuse. And Amanda, what are you having? I say, this is a pleasant surprise. We looked out of the morning-room window when we heard a car coming up the drive. Your mother saw you first, Amanda... Whisky all round?"

Randall, taking his drink, tried not to smile. The man was so nervous his hands were shaking. To put it simply, he told himself, Amanda had her father by the balls. When parents grew older they lost their power over their children. The tables were turned. When old parents wanted something from their kids they had to ask instead of demanding... Everyone in the room, including Kelvin, was given a whisky. William had gone off on his own to fetch his parents, not wanting to wait.

"According to the *Telegraph*, there's going to be a swift one-man-one-vote election and then Soames will hand over to Mugabe, probably in April. The longer the delay, the more likely the changeover will have problems. Ian Smith is committed and, as we say, an English gentleman's word is his bond. Smith's father was a Scot but that doesn't matter... So you got out, Randall. Very wise. There won't be any future for us British in Africa. Take a bit of time but in the end you'll all have to get out. As we got out of India and Malaya. No more rubber planters in Malaya. Or tea planters in Ceylon for that matter. Soon there won't be any tobacco growers in Rhodesia, I'm afraid. Anyway, with the Lancaster House Agreement now being implemented it should be a peaceful withdrawal.

Nothing we can do about it, I'm afraid. We British have lost our power. Lost it to the Americans. Has your father got any money in England, Randall?"

"He has, luckily. Most of our friends aren't so lucky."

"Yes, well, that is bad luck. They'll have to start all over again. Rather like I did. Gives a man a challenge. Something to do. Never does any good crying over spilt milk. Come here, Amanda. Let your father have a good look at you. My goodness, you have changed. A beautiful young lady I see before me."

"Thank you, Father. So you like my new dress?"

"Suits you perfectly," said her mother, letting Randall pull back and leave Amanda alone with her parents.

Twenty minutes later, when William came back with his parents, Randall was on his second drink. The old man was on his third. Trying to think of the present and not what was about to happen at home in Rhodesia, Randall listened to all the small talk between the long-separated next door neighbours. People made him laugh. One minute they were not saying a word and next they were gushing all over each other... So, he thought, by the time I go home it won't be Rhodesia anymore. Rhodesia will have been dumped on the garbage heap of history. Instead, they were going to call the country Zimbabwe, making Randall hope they would know how to run the place and not fight with each other over the spoils. It was a long way from fighting a liberation struggle, with the help of the Russians and Chinese, to running a country... Surrounded by so many people, Randall suddenly felt lonely. He wanted to go home. To see the sun. To hear the wild animals call from the bush at night. The screech of the crickets, the croak of the frogs on a hot African night. England, though part of his heritage, was strange to him. He was an African, not an Englishman. The wild call of Africa was in his blood, not the ordinariness of suburban England. His mind craved for the chance to be on his own, away from the crowd.

"What's the matter, Randall?" asked Amanda softly, breaking away from her parents. "Why are you crying?"

"I'm so damn homesick. Sorry. Am I really crying?"

"Just a little moisture in the corners of your eyes. It was all my father's talk about the end of the British Empire."

"And now I've finished writing the book. It's all over. Rhodesia and the story of Rhodesia... And I can't spend the rest of my life waiting tables."

"Of course you won't. You're going to publish your book and make a fortune. You'll see. All you have to do is think positive."

"Thanks, Mandy. You don't mind my calling you Mandy?"

"You call me what you like if it makes you happy."

"I've decided I prefer Mandy."

"Then Mandy it is. They called me Mandy at school. I like it... So, Mother dear, what's for lunch?"

"You think that literary agent of Oliver's is going to like my book?"

"Of course he is. Stop worrying. Have another drink... So, Mum, what are we eating?"

"Your father is going to take all of us to the Running Horses at Mickleham. I'll be driving the car. One small whisky is quite enough for me, Amanda."

"We have to drive back to London this afternoon. Both of us are working tonight."

"When are you going to get a proper job?"

Randall, standing behind the mother, smiled at Amanda and shrugged his shoulders: everything changed and everything stayed the same. It made him want to laugh. Anyway, he thought, they were all talking to each other. The trip had not been wasted.

THE MAN'S name was Frederick Ponsonby. Not Fred or Freddie or Ponsonby-Smythe. Plain, simple Frederick Ponsonby, a man in his forties, bald, bespectacled and wise, a personal friend of a personal friend of Veronica West, the gorgeous lady. Randall had submitted the manuscript of *The Tawny Wilderness* to Frederick Ponsonby, literary agent, the day after James Tomlin's play folded at Drury Lane. Amanda's typescript of the book had been sent by mail. Soon after, at Oliver's insistence, Veronica had phoned the man to make sure he was reading the book, saying she would phone again on the Monday to see what he thought. Veronica's fame had worked, the man asking Randall through Veronica to call at his dingy little office off Shaftesbury Avenue.

"Well, yes, I rather thought so," said the man from behind his desk, the neatly typed manuscript in front of him. "You're a bit young to be writing a book. From my experience in literature a writer has to reach forty before he has something to say. So, how is Veronica West? She is such a celebrity. I was honoured to receive her phone call. I've seen her so many times on the stage. My goodness, fancy a young man like you knowing Veronica West personally. I did hear somewhere she has a predilection for young men. Nothing wrong with it, you understand."

"So, Mr Ponsonby, what did you think of my book on Rhodesia?"

"Quite frankly, not much. If you'd written Moley's story, the glorious struggle of the downtrodden black man, it would have had reader appeal. No one's interested in the demise of a family of rich, white, privately schooled people with their noses stuck up in the air. The media in England, as it is in America, is very liberal. So are all the critics. Even if they liked the story, which I must say has a lot in it, they'd say it was dreadful because they don't like your colonial supremacy politics. You're a hundred years out of date, Mr Crookshank. Books extolling the virtue of the British Empire are so politically incorrect."

"So it's no damn good?"

"I wouldn't say that. It's just not publishable. It would never get the attention we need from the media to make it sell. A book has to sell, Mr Crookshank."

"You can call me Randall."

"There has to be a handle on the story to get all that lovely free publicity. The public only read what they are told to read by the newspapers and television. Can you imagine a television or radio show wanting to interview a young, white Rhodesian author about how the whites in Rhodesia stole the land of the black man? I don't think so. You have to be practical, Mr Crookshank. From where we look in England the hero is Robert Mugabe or Josiah Makoni, not Ian Douglas Smith. Oh, heavens, no. To put it mildly, you got the wrong end of the stick. Quite a shame. You write well. For a moment and quite unwillingly, you understand, I quite liked your leading character. Especially when they killed his cat."

"So you won't be submitting the book to publishers?"

"Don't be ridiculous... Please give my best regards to Miss West. Tell her how much I admire her work. A phone call from Veronica West! I just couldn't believe it."

"So that's it?"

"I'm afraid so… Josiah Makoni. Now there's a fine man. I met him in London when he was raising money for the Zimbabwe African National Union, the party of Robert Mugabe. Now there are two fine international heroes. Bring me a book extolling their virtues instead of some plundering colonial Englishmen and I'll find you a publisher without the slightest difficulty. It's all marketing, Mr Crookshank. It's all in the marketing. I would suggest that before you waste your time writing another book you work out beforehand what sells. You must be on the side of right, not on the side of wrong."

Wondering what the hell he was going to do with the rest of his life, carrying the useless manuscript, Randall left the man's office. He had been rejected; himself, his book and the life of his whole damn family. When he got back to the room, Amanda had left a note saying she had gone shopping. Feeling sick in his gut, Randall went out of the room onto the cold landing and knocked on James's door.

"You better come in, Randall. You don't look so good. So the bugger didn't like your book? Oh, well, we've got something in common. They didn't like my play either. The critics raved about it but no one was interested in the trials and tribulations of a couple of gays."

"Do you want to go to the pub? I've never felt more like wanting to get drunk, rat-arsed drunk. James, old friend, let's go down to the Leg of Mutton and Cauliflower and drown our sorrows."

"Spoken like a man… Randall, why is life so difficult? Go get your overcoat. It's cold outside."

The first two beers went down in mournful silence, both of them feeling sorry for themselves. The bar where they were sitting was empty. One old man was sitting at a table nursing a pint of beer, making it go as far as possible. Randall didn't even have the energy to smile. The man looked screaming bored, his eyes blank, his mind in neutral. The next drink they had was a double whisky, the beers having done them no good. The old man still had an inch of beer in the bottom of his glass. The whiskies were neat; no ice, soda or water. They looked at each other, both feeling utterly miserable, picked up their glasses and drank. The strong whisky burnt Randall's throat, followed by a jolt to his head as the whisky circulated. A glow had come up from his stomach. He felt better.

"Shit, this stuff's strong, Randall. I normally only drink wine or beer. Never neat spirits. Got a kick like a mule."

It was four o'clock in the afternoon by the clock between the brandy bottles on the shelf behind the bar. The old man had not touched what was left in his glass, making Randall feel sorry for him instead of himself. He smiled at the old man without any response.

"You want another one of those, James?"

"Bring it on, brother. We said we were going to get drunk. Thank goodness the pubs in England don't close after lunch anymore... You got enough money for double whiskies?"

"When the money's gone it's gone."

"All I managed to do with the money from *The Priest's Lover* was pay off my debts."

"What are you going to do now?"

"Anything that comes. Paint sets. Get a bit part in television. Back to living hand to mouth. For a moment out there I thought I was going to make it. Be a big shot like Oliver and Veronica West with everyone after me."

"You had some good crits in the papers. That should help."

"Thanks for trying to make me feel better... You going to write another book?"

"Don't be ridiculous... It was like having a bucket of cold water thrown over my head. The thought of having to wait table tonight and be polite to people is plain horrible... Someone wrote the only advantage of having money was not having to be polite to people. Now I understand what he meant. All that bullshit I go through in pursuit of a tip makes me want to vomit... To better days, James. Down the hatch."

"You two had better go easy," said the barman.

"Can you do me a favour, George or whatever your name is?" said Randall. "Please send that old man at the table a pint of beer on me."

"He can only afford one beer."

"I can see that. And make it another two pints of draught for me and my friend. You're right. That's enough oomph from the whisky. We're drowning our sorrows. Both our dreams just went down the toilet."

The barman walked away to pull the pints, showing not the slightest bit of interest in their troubles.

"You think those critics who liked me were gay, Randall?"

"Probably. Certainly liberal. Mr Frederick Ponsonby, literary agent, says the entire media is liberal."

"He's talking shit... You want me to read your book?"

"What for? I never saw your play."

"I'd forgotten that... Why do some people talk so much shit?"

"They do when it suits them. He was just making excuses. It's my book that's a load of crap... Have you seen Donna?"

"Not recently. People go off you when you don't succeed."

"She's not like that."

"I was generalising... The old man's grinning at you. Please turn around. You've made his day."

"At least I've made someone's day."

The old man raised his new pint of beer, a broad smile on his face. The old beer glass was now standing empty on the table. Randall raised his glass. He felt better. And it wasn't just the whisky.

"I'm not going to work tonight. I'm going to use their pay phone. Tell Deepak. He can phone Sarah Rankin for a temp. Can't face people tonight. Keep my seat. Don't go away."

"I don't think either of us is going anywhere these days. First they kill your cat. Then they throw out your book."

"I've still got Amanda. She'll understand. If it gets much worse I'll have to go and see my Uncle Paul. Get a proper job. What Amanda's mother said to her. 'When are you getting a proper job?' Some day both of us are going to have to face reality... Can you imagine pushing a pen for the rest of your life?"

"You were pushing a pen at your desk."

"Ah, but that was different. When I was writing, I wasn't sitting at my desk. I was far away in the happy times in Rhodesia where I want to be. Not in cold old London feeling rejected... I'll go and phone Deepak. Make him pissed off. Better than working drunk... When I was deep in the book I wasn't conscious of writing. I was literally out of my mind. Far away. Living the lives of the characters in my book."

The sharp argument with Deepak, the owner of the Tandoori restaurant, came as a surprise. They had made friends, two expatriates far away from their homes after the collapse of the Raj in India, which had led to partition and all its violence, and the collapse of colonialism in Rhodesia. Randall thought they had something in common.

"If you don't want to work when you are meant to work, Randall, don't bother coming back again. We're fully booked tonight. It's two weeks before Christmas. All those tourists in London don't you remember?"

"You can phone Sarah Rankin."

"Do you know what time it is?... You sound drunk."

"They rejected my book."

"Go away, Randall. I haven't got time for this. I'm trying to run a business."

"I'm sorry."

"It's too late to be sorry."

Problems always compounded themselves, thought Randall, putting the phone back on its hook in the small open booth. He stood for a moment not knowing quite what to think. If he had gone to work drunk he would have tipped a plate of food over someone. Feeling guilty, he walked across to the bar. The old man smiled at him as he passed.

"I just got fired, James."

"Oh, happy days... Your temp agency will find you another job."

"Not after Deepak has finished with me. I'd forgotten it was Christmas. I wasn't thinking of my boss. And I'm too drunk to go and make it up to him... Life sucks."

"You'd better not go home until Amanda has gone to work. It's fine when you both get drunk together. But when one is drunk and the other sober it gets ugly. Let's finish this beer and have another whisky."

"You two go easy on the whisky."

Randall, about to give the barman backchat, felt a hand on his arm. James leaned close to him and whispered: "First rule in a bar. Never argue with the barman, old boy. Golden rule. Done it a few times. They throw you out on your neck. When you get the next whisky, give him a big, fat tip. Usually works."

The two double whiskies drunk quickly after the beers had them slurring their words, Randall unable to control the working of his tongue.

"No wonder Deepak fired me," he giggled. "We'd better stick to beers. The place is beginning to fill up, James. Let's go sit at a table. We won't be so conspicuous... Look at that. The old man has drunk his beer... You want another one, old man?... Mr Barman. Another one here for my friend."

When they went home they were both supporting each other. They parted on the landing, fumbling with the keys to their rooms.

"Good night, Randall. Just remember, not every day is a rejection. Thanks for the drinks. You look after yourself."

Inside his room, Randall fell on the bed. The room was cold and empty. Quickly, fully clothed, he fell into a drunken sleep. In his dream they were all laughing at him, making a fool of him, sneering at a loser. He woke from his nightmare sometime before Amanda returned from her work, taking off his clothes in the dark and getting under the duvet. When she came home and turned on the light Randall pretended he was fast asleep. When the light went out and Amanda got into bed he lay there wide awake. There was nothing to look forward to anymore. For either of them.

When Randall finally fell asleep the morning light was showing through the crack in the curtains. On his desk, where he had thrown it before going with James to the pub, was his rejected manuscript. He even thought of getting out of bed and hiding it from Amanda. His mouth felt dry and tasted like the bottom of a parrot cage. Amanda was smiling in her sleep. Then she woke, smiling into his eyes.

"Don't look so worried, darling. It's what you and I think of the book that matters. Not some literary agent."

"I got fired last night."

"What happened?"

"James and I went to the pub to drown our sorrows."

"Did you succeed?"

"We staggered home arm in arm singing a song. Deepak, when I phoned him, told me to go and get stuffed after I suggested he get a temp from Sarah. She'll never give me another job... So, you must have seen the manuscript on the desk."

"Did you see the letter downstairs from my parents?"

"I didn't look at the mail under the door. What was in it?"

"An invitation to spend Christmas with them in Great Bookham."

"Are we going?"

"It'll give you a chance to get to know my father."

"The dream's over, Amanda. Living penniless at the top of a house with actors, trying to be a writer. It's over. I'm going to see my uncle... When do we go down to your family?"

"Christmas Eve."

"You think your father will let me make a phone call to my parents in Rhodesia? I can pay him for the call."

"Don't be silly. And what's this Amanda business? I thought you were calling me Mandy."

"I've changed my mind. I met a girl called Amanda. Amanda was my muse. By calling you Mandy I got my book rejected."

"You're superstitious!"

"Just a little... I've had enough of wheedling tips out of people."

"Do you want to ask your uncle for a job?"

"What I want is to go home. Take us both to Rhodesia. But like publishing my book, that dream is over. Got to face reality... I've got the most terrible hangover."

"Poor darling. Go back to sleep."

"Is it raining outside?"

"Probably."

With her arms round him from the back, and feeling comfortable for the first time since his book was rejected, Randall began to doze, going from consciousness to sleep and the world of his dreams. In his dream he was back in Rhodesia where the sun was shining. They were all sitting round the pool. He was a child. Moley and Happiness, Phillip and himself were sitting in the shade of the msasa tree at the feet of Primrose, Moley and Happiness's mother, Randall and Phillip's nanny, all of them happy.

When Randall woke, Amanda was putting down a cup of tea for him beside the bed. His hangover had gone. He felt better.

*U*ncle Paul's executive suite was on the twentieth floor of Brigandshaw House in Billiter Street, as far away from playing clarinet in a jazz band as Randall could imagine. He had made the appointment for ten o'clock in the morning, arriving at the reception desk five minutes early, his father's words clear in his mind: 'Five minutes early for an appointment, five minutes late for a dinner party.' The receptionist took his name. Feeling insignificant, Randall sat in the middle of a row of chairs in front of reception, one of three people waiting for their appointments. All the doors to the executive offices were firmly closed. On the wall opposite, next to the lift, in big letters, were the names of all the companies in the Brigandshaw Limited Group, or BLG as the company was called on the London Stock Exchange. Four of the subsidiary companies were separately listed on the exchange. Randall had done his homework... By quarter past ten he was still sitting on his chair feeling uncomfortable. He was broke, jobless and rejected. Life sucked. The other two people, a middle-aged man and a young woman, had gone into their meetings. Randall was alone, staring at the receptionist, an old woman with horn-rimmed glasses, the archetype of a battleaxe. On the walls of the big reception area were original paintings. Everything he looked at was expensive. The furthest office door opened down the corridor behind reception, and two men came out followed by

Randall's uncle. The men's suits looked expensive. As they passed the line of chairs, Randall could smell one of the men's cologne. Uncle Paul took them to the lift and pressed the button. When the lift opened, the three men shook hands, Uncle Paul holding back the door. The door closed on the two men.

"Let's go to my office, Randall. How are you? Today's been hectic... Mrs Walker, can you bring us some tea?... Sorry to keep you waiting. We did the deal which is all that mattered. A new development near Canary Wharf. Those gentlemen are going to be our partners, helping to fund the project."

Feeling like he felt as a schoolboy going into the headmaster's study, Randall followed his uncle into his office, a room four times the size of the room Randall shared with Amanda. At the far end was a large desk, to the right a long table with upholstered chairs along either side. Underfoot, Randall trod a thick, plush carpet. On the wall, overlooking the mahogany table, was the smiling portrait of a man.

"Where are you spending Christmas, Randall?"

"With Amanda's parents in Great Bookham. Her dad's younger brother went to school with you."

"What was his name?"

"I don't know. Amanda's surname is Hanscombe."

"Froggy Hanscombe! Well, I'll be blowed. Haven't seen Froggy for years... Is your relationship with Amanda getting serious? You're a bit young to settle down. So, you've given up waiting tables. Your grandmother will be happy."

"I got fired."

"Did you now?"

"My book was rejected. James and I got drunk. His play has folded."

"What book, Randall?"

"I wrote a novel on Rhodesia. More of a novelette, I suppose. Not quite eighty thousand words. The literary agent said I'd got the wrong end of the stick. I was telling our story and not the black man's."

"I'm impressed you wrote a full-length book. There's a gene in the family that makes some of us want to be artists. Performing artists like myself on clarinet and piano. Creative artists who want to write books like yourself. Did you have fun writing the book? What did you call it? Can I have a look?"

"It was the most rewarding experience of my life. I called it *The Tawny Wilderness*. Now it's been rejected, I'm too embarrassed to let people read it."

"So you want a job?"

"Something like that."

"You can grow tobacco, wait tables and write a book."

"That's about it, Uncle Paul."

"We need trainee project managers. You'll have to start right at the bottom. No favouritism just because we share the same name, you understand. You can start on the seventh of January. It's a Monday. Thanks for coming to see us... Thank you, Mrs Walker. Put the tea tray on the board table. My nephew is coming to work for us. Randall, be a good chap and pour the tea... So, when did you last speak to my brother?"

"I'm going to phone him from Mr Hanscombe's on Christmas Day."

"Froggy Hanscombe. I'll be blowed... Make mine one spoonful of sugar."

"Who's the man in the portrait?"

"That's Harry Brigandshaw, our founder. Cost the company a fortune. I commissioned Livy Johnston to do the painting for us. Must be ten years ago. She wanted to do it for nothing but we wouldn't hear of it. Probably worth ten times what we paid for it. She's famous, our Livy. Anyway, it kept the money and the portrait in the family. Didn't she do one of your mother? Long after we are dead, and this fancy office and the fancy building are forgotten, people will still be admiring Livy's paintings. Sad part is, for every Livy Johnston there are thousands of unrecognised artists who never get out to the public. She can thank Jeanne Pétain for getting her paintings out. So don't take your book rejection to heart. You're not the only one with an unpublished manuscript. Write another one. Practice makes perfect. We all go through our trials and tribulations to get anywhere. It's the way of life. When they knock you down, you get up again... And there's one condition, Randall. If you ever get drunk again when you are meant to be working, you'll be out on your neck. Is that understood?"

"Yes, sir."

"I liked your honesty... You'd better go. I'm behind schedule. Come and see your grandmother before Christmas."

"So I just arrive here on the seventh of January?"

"That's about it. Welcome to BLG. How much do you expect to be paid?"

"Probably nothing until I know what I'm doing."

"We all have to invest in each other. How does four thousand pounds a year sound to you? I'll review it in June."

"Sounds wonderful."

"And in August you can take a holiday and go see your father. He'll be missing you, Randall. When kids grow up they have their own lives to live but they still shouldn't forget their parents. If you buckle down to the job, I'll pay your airfare."

"Amanda wants to come with me."

"Eight months is a long time in a relationship when you are twenty-one years old... Froggy Hanscombe! I'll be blowed... Can you see your way out? Oh, and buy yourself a suit."

Wondering if the job interview would have gone so well if it hadn't been his uncle, Randall tried a smile at Mrs Walker as he stood waiting by the lift. There were four lifts that served the building. One of the lift doors slid open.

"Thank you for the tea, Mrs Walker."

"You're welcome."

Not sure if he had enough money to buy himself a suit, Randall walked into the lift, pressed the ground floor button and waited. A new life he was not sure about had begun. Outside the building it was cold, his overcoat welcome, something he had never worn in Rhodesia. In Rhodesia he had never even owned a raincoat. It only rained from November to March and when it came down a raincoat wasn't much good to anyone. In the lands, like the labour force, he wore an oilskin with a big, wide-brimmed hat, to keep the rain from his face. He had decided to walk through the city to the Bank tube station and make his way home. He was bored, the thought of sitting in an office making him unhappy. He passed a men's shop selling suits and stopped to look in the window. 'You can only ask,' he said to himself, opening the door to the shop.

"Would ten pounds be enough deposit to get myself a suit? I've just landed myself a job with BLG. They're a listed company."

"I'm aware of that, sir. Do you have a reference?"

"You can phone my uncle's receptionist. A Mrs Walker. My uncle owns the business. He told me to buy myself a suit. I start on the seventh of January."

"I think that could be arranged. Do you have the company's telephone number? Everything here is off-the-peg. Go and see what you like. I'll be with you in a moment."

Randall wrote down the company's phone number, gave it to the man and went to look at the suits, rack after rack of them, all of them dark.

"Do you know your size?"

"I have no idea. Never owned a suit in my life."

"I should think you are a medium. I'll measure you in a moment."

Sorting through the racks, Randall watched the man finish his phone call. Then he smiled, the salesman's smile of expectancy. He was walking across with a tape-measure hung round his neck.

Ten minutes later Randall was walking out of the shop wearing his suit, his overcoat open, his old brown shoes incongruous under the dark legs of the new trousers, his old clothes in a large plastic bag with the shop's name on the outside. He'd have to buy himself a new pair of shoes to go with his suit. There were people walking the pavement all dressed in their suits and overcoats. He was part of the crowd, no longer away from them. It began to drizzle, making Randall button up his coat.

Randall got off the Tube at Holland Park station to walk in the park before going home to tell Amanda he had got himself a job. He should have been happy but he wasn't. In the park, the trees had no leaves, all of them were stark. The sky was grey, low over his head. A pigeon, cold like himself, was looking at him out of a tree. It looked as miserable as Randall felt. Above everything else, at that moment, he wanted to go home... Picking up speed, he walked out of the park on the road towards Notting Hill Gate.

When he let himself into the boarding house it felt as cold as charity. There was no sign of Mrs Salter or anyone else. Plodding up the three flights of stairs he let himself into his room. The room was warm, Amanda sitting in the comfortable chair reading her book.

"Why are you looking so miserable, Randall?"

"I got a job."

"That's good, isn't it?"

"I'm not sure. It's all so permanent. Like my new dark suit. Put down a ten pound deposit. They all want to give you credit when you have a job."

"How much they paying you?"

"Don't you want to know what kind of job it is?"

"Not really. One clerical job is much the same as the next."

"Three thousand pounds a year. If I'm good, they'll pay my fare to Rhodesia to see the family."

"That's not bad."

"It's horrible. Nine to five. Monday to Friday. The same old journey day after day. Same old desk."

"So what are you going to be doing?"

"Trainee project manager."

"Sounds grand... I dig the suit. Cheer up, Randall. The sky hasn't fallen."

"In the park, I thought it had. Went for a walk in the park. No one does any exercise in London."

"Whatever for? Anyway, it's raining. You want me to make you a sandwich?... You should try another agent or go direct to a publisher. It can't hurt. No point in leaving the manuscript on the desk. The poor thing looks lonely. So, when do you start?"

"Seventh of January. It's a Monday... It's not going to be so much fun me working during the day and you working at night."

"You want me to get a proper job!"

"It wouldn't hurt."

"We'd end up just like the rest of them."

"One of us has, Amanda. At least we could be together in the evenings. It's going to be lonely every evening on my own."

"A bloody secretary. It's too horrible to think about."

"Your mother and father would be so impressed. With both of us. We would have both conformed. In their eyes, become normal people."

"Poor old Randall. You really are screwed. Come here, lover. It'll all work out. Life goes on. It always does. Until the day we die."

"The very thought of a normal urban life makes me want to vomit."

"It's not much different to what you've been doing. We still live in one room in London."

"Not when I'm writing. Then I'm back in the African bush."

"I know what you mean. Even reading a book takes you out of your daily routine. At least you'll have a monthly income. The shops will give you a credit rating. You'll be able to buy expensive things you can't really afford so you'll never be able to get off the treadmill. It's all part of the modern system, the money going round in a circle. We'll be able to buy ourselves a house in the suburbs in a year or two with a thirty-year mortgage, get married, have children and pay off everything with a credit card."

"You've got to be kidding!"

"You don't ever want to get married?"

"What I don't want, Amanda, is to saddle myself with a thirty-year mortgage and live in a rabbit hutch with a chicken run for a garden. Instead of borrowing more money on my future salary I'm going to save for your airfare to Rhodesia. At least I'll have something to look forward to. I want to show you Africa. The kind of life that's worth living. In England, for most of the day, you can only see the wall in front of you... What are you reading?"

"It's a translation from the French. By the same chap who once said, among other things, 'hell is other people'. What do you think of that, Randall? He and his girlfriend were what we now call hippies, living in Paris. Why the splurge on the back cover caught my eye in the library. It's all a bit like us. Can you believe it, his girlfriend is a novelist."

"Who's the author?"

"Jean-Paul Sartre... You can read it when I'm finished... We all grow up, Randall. If we didn't, life as we know it would have disintegrated years ago. Our parents went through it. So did their parents. Just hard to imagine it. A bit like trying to imagine our parents having sex. We always put that thought out of our mind but, when you come to think of it, if they hadn't made love neither of us would be here talking to each other. None of us are much different to the animals. Survival and procreation is what life's all about. And if that includes a thirty-year mortgage, so be it."

"Do you know, that's remarkably intelligent of you."

"It's not me. It's in all the books I read. I'm a bookworm during the day when it's raining outside and there's nothing much to do."

"Better than television."

"Probably. But that's an idea now you've got some money."

"That's the start of the slippery slide into ordinariness. That's my point, Amanda. I don't want to be ordinary. Lead an ordinary, boring life."

"Next you'll be smoking pot."

"Better than television."

JAMES TOMLIN GOT his part in a television sitcom three days before Randall and Amanda took the train down to Great Bookham. The television producer was a gay man who had seen James in the play at Drury Lane and liked what he saw.

They walked from the station to Agates Lane. There was snow in patches of white and black sludge by the side of the road. Some of the houses with their small front gardens had white patches of melting snow on their lawns. The cold wind was in Randall's face making his eyes water. It was Christmas Eve with miniature plastic Christmas trees in the front windows of the houses that Randall could see from the road. The Christmas lights were twinkling among the decorations, a promise of warmth and good cheer. It was half past three in the afternoon and the light was beginning to fade. They were holding hands, Randall unable to feel her skin through the gloves. By the time they turned into the driveway and walked up to the big, glass-fronted door his feet were cold, making him stamp them on the path as they waited for someone to answer the bell. Next door, William and Kelvin had already arrived at the Drakes, having driven down the previous day. Amanda had had to work that night making them take the train. Through the front door, Randall could see a big Christmas tree, a genuine fir tree, covered in twinkling decorations that reflected the fairy lights. Amanda was about to ring the bell for the second time when her mother walked through into the big hallway and passed in front of the tree, smiling as she walked towards them. When the door opened a warm draught of air washed over Randall's face.

"Come in. Come in. Happy Christmas, darling. It's so wonderful to see you. How are you, Randall?"

"Happy Christmas, Mrs Hanscombe."

"Randall's got a job in his uncle's office in the City."

"How wonderful," said Mr Hanscombe coming through into the hall.

"My uncle remembers your brother."

"Does he now?... Come in. What would we do in England without central heating? The new gas central heating makes all the difference. Give me your bags. You should have phoned me from the station and I'd have collected you in the car. A bit of snow for Christmas. Not exactly a white Christmas but never mind... A job, by jove. Much better than being a waiter... Bit early for a drink... Some tea, I should think. So, this must be your first Christmas in England. Have you heard from your family in Rhodesia?"

"Not yet. You see, we don't have a phone. I was wondering..."

"Of course, dear boy. There's a phone in my study whenever you want to use it. Not like the old days when you had to book a long distance call. Now you just dial the number. I remember in India it was quite a performance speaking to my parents in England. They gave you three minutes. Then the telephone operator cut you off."

"We still have a party line on the farm in Rhodesia. The line is often engaged. You have to keep dialling until the line is free and the neighbours have stopped talking."

"Bit primitive."

"We have a radio alarm system to the neighbours and the police in the event of a terr attack."

"Terr attack?"

"Terrorist, sir."

"Of course. There's been a war in Rhodesia. You must be so enjoying the peace and quiet of England."

"Not much quiet."

"No, I suppose not in London. Have some tea by the fire before you use the phone."

"I'd like to pay you for the call."

"Don't be ridiculous... Happy Christmas, Randall."

"Happy Christmas, Mr Hanscombe."

"I want to hear all about your job. With a bit of luck, our Amanda will be next to get a proper job. Her mother worries about her. You have to have some permanence in life. That wonderful feeling of security. Temporary jobs are fine for a while but they don't get you anywhere. If you work hard, and with your uncle owning the business, you can get right to the top. Does he have any children in the business?"

"My cousin Henry is in the army. Went to Sandhurst Military

Academy. My cousin Deborah is married. She's a housewife with two kids. Don't know either of them."

"Well, that really is splendid. You'll get the top job when your uncle retires. Probably why he wanted to employ you. Always better to keep it in the family. You can trust your family. Outsiders are inclined to have their own agendas. Father to son. Father to son, I say. I have two boys in my business, so I know what I'm talking about. Import-export. I started it when I left the Indian Civil Service, when we handed India back to the Indians. All my old contacts. There's a great deal of trade between Britain and India. We got into India through trade in the first place. The East India Company, long before India became part of the British Empire. They may not be part of the empire anymore but trade goes on, my goodness. Trade is what it is all about in the end. Nothing better than a family business... Now isn't that just perfect? Our housekeeper, Mrs Reed, with the tea... Thank you, Mrs Reed. We'll take tea in the sitting room next to the fire... Some things never change, Randall. Of course we're not as big as BLG. We're not quoted on the stock exchange. I prefer to keep our family affairs a little more private. There are so many disclosures with a public company. And all that worry about a share price. Outside shareholders are only interested in their dividend and the price of their shares. They don't have any interest in the long-term prosperity of the company. The boys want me to do an Initial Public Offering, or an IPO as they say on the stock exchanges. We'd all get rather rich if the flotation is successful but we'd lose some of our control of the company. We'll see... Isn't that fire lovely? What Christmas in England is all about. A big Christmas tree from out of the garden and a big fire in the grate. You can leave your overcoat on the stand in the hall next to the Christmas tree... Now, Amanda, come here and let me look at you. Happy Christmas, my youngest daughter. Happy Christmas. Sadly your brothers and sisters are having their Christmases with their own families. They've promised to visit their mother and father on Boxing Day. Have you done any more modelling for William Drake? They're coming over on Boxing Day for drinks with everybody."

Randall, having left his overcoat in the hall, feeling out of it, stood next to the fireplace drinking the cup of tea Mrs Hanscombe had poured for him. All the talk of family had made him feel homesick.

"Why don't I leave you alone to talk to your daughter while I try and make my phone call, Mrs Hanscombe? I'm sure you have lots to talk about to Amanda. Mother-daughter talk."

"I'll show you my husband's study... Oh, I've been so looking forward to Christmas. A big job with a public company. Now isn't that something?"

"It's not very big at the moment. Not very big at all."

"Everything starts small, Randall. Like relationships. And how are you getting along with our daughter?"

"We have a lot in common."

"I do so hope you will have a lot more in common with Amanda. You're a good influence on her, Randall. Because of you all that nonsense with the Drakes next door is over. They would never have come on their own... Isn't Christmas exciting? I do so love Christmas. Don't you?"

"Yes, Mrs Hanscombe. It's my favourite time of the year."

Following the mother to a room off the hall, a comfortable den, small, lined with books, a desk and a phone, Randall found himself alone, the door discreetly closed for him. He picked up the phone, listened to the dialling tone for a moment and dialled the long number for home. As Randall had expected, the number was engaged. The trick was to keep dialling, to get in between the neighbours using the phone. Opposite the desk was a small fireplace, the red glow of the coal fire smiling at Randall where he sat at the desk. The room was well used and friendly. Mr Hanscombe must have been in his study when Amanda rang the bell. There were business papers stacked neatly on the right of the desk. On the desk in front of Randall was an open book face down nearest to the fire. Next to the fire was an old, leather armchair. The old man had been reading when the doorbell rang, got up and left his book on the desk. From where Randall sat the book was upside down. Randall dialled the number for World's View and it rang. His hopes rose.

"The Crookshank residence. Mr Phillip Crookshank speaking. How can I help you?"

"Phillip, you old scoundrel. What are you doing at home? Do you always have to answer the bloody phone like some nineteenth-century butler?"

"Randall! Where are you?"

"In London. Or more exactly, in a place called Great Bookham. How are you?"

"Happy the bloody war is over. What's this place you're in?"

"My girlfriend's parents' house."

"You have a girlfriend!"

"We live together in a London boarding house... Can I speak to Dad? I don't want to use the father's phone too much. Don't have a phone in the boarding house."

"Dad!" shouted Phillip all the way from Rhodesia. "It's Randall. He's on the phone. Come quickly. He's using someone else's phone... Have you heard about Josiah Tongogara?"

"Other than he's the head of the Zimbabwe African National Liberation Army and grew up on the farm owned by Ian Smith's parents, that's all I've heard about him."

"He's dead. Killed in Mozambique on his way back to Rhodesia in a car accident. Here's Dad."

"Hey, Randall, son. How the hell are you? And no one here thinks it was an accident. Josiah Makoni was also in the vehicle. They're both dead. A bit ironic, don't you think? Sergeant Goodson thinks it was Mugabe wanting to eliminate the opposition. Had a long talk with Clay Barry at the police station. Goodson says the accident was in the middle of nowhere and it's far too much of a coincidence. He and Josiah Makoni both have the same father, but you remember that. All grew up on Elephant Walk, Harry Brigandshaw's farm. And all that money Harry put into educating Josiah Makoni at school and university ended in a car accident in the bush."

"Do you think it was an accident? Does it affect the peace agreement?"

"When are you coming home?"

"Uncle Paul has given me a job at BLG."

"Doesn't surprise me. Henry went into the army instead of joining BLG. So, how are you?"

"Can't talk long. I borrowed a phone. Happy Christmas, Dad. It's been snowing where I am in a place called Great Bookham. Never seen snow before I got to England. It's a terrible climate. Cold, and it rains most of the time."

"You know the old saying, Randall. If Britain had had a decent climate we would never have had an empire. Everyone would have stayed at home. So when are you coming to visit us?"

"Uncle Paul says if I buckle down to the job he'll pay my airfare to Rhodesia in the summer holidays... So you think Robert Mugabe killed his top general and one of his top political commissars?"

"Looks like it, if you don't believe in coincidences. Whatever happens, there's still going to be shit in Rhodesia. Or Zimbabwe as Mugabe is going to call it. Thugs rarely stop being thugs, even when they win. But we'll see. Anything is better than war... The new crop looks good."

"How's Vince Ranger? Is he coming back to live in England?"

"Not anymore. We'll soldier on. Rather apt, don't you think? Whoever knows what's going to happen in life? At least we all got through the bush war in one piece."

"What's Phillip going to do? He can't still be running a safari company with his fancy degree in history."

"Oh yes he is. With peace in the country the tourists will come back again in big numbers. Your stepmother is shouting to give you her love."

"Happy Christmas to all of you, Dad."

"Happy Christmas, Randall. When you see Paul, give him my best. What are you going to be doing?"

"Trainee project manager. I'll write you a long letter. Got to go. Can't use someone else's phone when it's long distance. Hopefully see you in August. I'm staying with Amanda. I told you about Amanda in my letters."

"Is she nice?"

"She's wonderful."

"Then wish her a happy Christmas from all of us at World's View."

"Give Vince my best."

"Will do. Thanks for the call."

Putting down the phone, the connection to his family broken, Randall sat staring at the fire in the grate, feeling a mixture of regret and happiness, hope and loss, not knowing anymore what he wanted to do with himself. He would have to tell Donna St Clair about Josiah Makoni, who would tell her mother who had painted Josiah's mother, the portrait *Princess* he had looked at at Livy Johnston's retrospective at the Nouvelle Galerie. What a waste, he thought. For all of them. That beautiful face he had admired so much in the gallery had now lost her son. All he had lost was his cat... Turning the book round on the desk, Randall read the title.

Mr Hanscombe had been reading Gibbon's *Decline and Fall of the Roman Empire*. It made Randall forget about himself for a moment and smile. How appropriate, he said to himself. He hoped Lord Soames, the son-in-law of Winston Churchill, enjoyed lowering the Union Jack in Rhodesia. Everything had a start. Everything had an end. The Roman Empire and the British.

"You'd better make the best of it in England, old cock," he said to the book on the desk in front of him. "If they've started to kill each other there can't be a future in Africa. What a bugger. One big bugger-up after another."

Turning the book round to the same position where he had found it, Randall got up from behind the desk. He looked at the fire behind its fireguard and smiled. "You're right, Oliver Manningford. It's not all bad. You just got to make the best of it."

Going round the desk to the door, Randall looked back at the bookcase that covered the one wall. Opening the door, he turned off the light, leaving the room in a red glow of warmth from the grate. Quietly, he closed the door and walked back through the hall, past the Christmas tree. He could hear the low voices of the family talking in the sitting room. Again quietly, he opened the door, closing it behind himself. Amanda's face lit up when she saw him.

"Did you get through?"

"Yes, I did. Thank you, Mr Hanscombe."

"How's everything in Africa?"

"Much the same as usual."

"How about a drink?"

"I wouldn't say no. I really wouldn't say no."

"Problems at home?"

"Not for us this time. They say Robert Mugabe has just killed his top general, though he'll say it was an accident. A car accident."

"Can I offer you a beer or a whisky?"

"A beer please, sir... The tobacco crop is all right. That's something."

With his mind in Rhodesia and his body in Great Bookham, Randall took a drink of his beer. Phillip had made him laugh, World's View being anything but an English anachronism for those born in the country. Maybe together, if it all came right, they could run a safari company. That would be something. Living in the bush. Telling stories to wide-eyed tourists round the campfire. Living the kind of life he loved... Forcing himself back to the world of reality, he listened to their conversation. One minute the old man had been throwing his daughter out of the house for bonking on the couch. Now the tables had turned, mother and father were gushing all over her. Despite the snow outside, the bottle of beer wasn't cold enough. A beer, wherever you drank it, had to be cold. For the first time since leaving the train station his feet were warm. They were talking about the family, all trying so hard to be friendly. Randall moved away closer to the fire, putting his glass of warm beer on the mantelpiece. What struck Randall most was so much wealth with so little purpose. Two rich old people living a lonely life, their kids all left, the family nest a place full of echoes. Randall wondered how William Drake was doing next door. Whether his parents were doing any better. At least at home, Phillip was back and their half-brother and sister, Craig and Myra, were still living at home making a family. He would have liked to speak to Craig and Myra had there been time. Maybe he could have talked for half an hour and the Hanscombes would not have cared.

"Something wrong with the beer, Randall?"

"No, sir. Nothing. It's very nice."

"You look far away. I know what it's like to miss a country. I often think of my days in India. More as I get older. Those were the wonderful days of my youth. Oh, I know what it is. The beer isn't cold enough for you Rhodesians. Have a whisky. With ice. Sit yourself down by the fire. Make yourself comfortable."

"Never waste a beer, sir. The beer is fine."

The old man walked away again, back to his daughter. He wasn't as bad as they thought. Picking up the beer glass he drank down the beer and sat down in a comfortable chair. When he looked up again Mr Hanscombe was standing in front of him, offering him a crystal glass with ice clinking inside.

"Try this one."

"Thank you, Mr Hanscombe."

"My pleasure. If you want to talk about Rhodesia I'm happy to listen."

"Not much to talk about anymore. It's all over. All over as far as we are concerned. Didn't India change for the Anglo-Saxons once the country got its independence?"

"Yes, but not necessarily for the worse. All of this around you came out of India. We have all prospered. That's the beauty of trade. Enjoy your whisky. There's roast duck for supper. With orange sauce. One of Mrs Reed's specialities. A nice bottle of red wine. How does that sound?... Happy Christmas."

"Happy Christmas, Mr Hanscombe."

They slept in separate beds that night, something they had not done since they met each other. There was a wind outside brushing the branch of a tree against the window in Randall's solitary bedroom, not a comforting sound, the strange tapping in the dark of the night sounding creepy. Randall pulled the bedclothes up to his chin and tried to make himself feel comfortable, missing the warm soft body he had grown used to lying next to him. It was not all sex; comfort was a part of it, making him feel less alone. Randall lay on his back thinking. The roast duck had been good, the stilted conversation in the dining room when the parents tried to include him not so pleasant. The old man had tried to find common ground between British India and Rhodesia, the world of Colonial India in the 1920s sounding to Randall as distant as the moon. On Boxing Day the rest of the family would be arriving leaving Randall less conspicuous. Under the table Amanda had felt the inside of his thigh making the situation more difficult. It was tricky to talk across the table to a man when the man's daughter was stroking his crotch.

The sudden bang on the window made him jump up in the bed. It was like someone trying to get in. There were stories of ghosts in England Randall had read in books. His father had said it was all about ancestors. Africa, where none of Randall's ancestors had died, left his father free from ghosts. The blacks in Africa always talked of the ancestors. It was part of their culture and their religion. The ancestors looked after you if you were good and punished you if you were bad. The constant taps had Randall thinking his own ancestors had found him and were trying to tell him something. It was pitch dark outside, not a trace of light in the room. Maybe the house was haunted. Too much food at dinner had given him indigestion. Part of him wanted to get up and make sure it was the tree branch tapping the window. Randall lay in bed, the fear too great to let him move. Inside, the house was silent. Quiet as a tomb. Randall, his mind in a state of terror, tried his best to think of his home in Africa. A violent storm in Africa made him comfortable, knowing every part of what was happening. Apart from the war and the threat of a terrorist attack, he had never felt so uncomfortable as he did at this moment. There was no point in turning on the bedside light as it would not show him what was happening outside. He would have to get up from his bed.

Somehow, eventually, he must have dropped off because when he woke in the dark there was more of the tapping, this time coming from his door. The fear screeched up inside of him, his whole gut in a state of twisted turmoil, the fear greater than the terrorist bullet that had penetrated the window.

"Who's there?" he squeaked.

"Mrs Reed with your morning tea. May I come in?"

"Of course. I'm so sorry. What time is it?"

"Seven o'clock in the morning. Did you sleep well?"

"I think I did. This place is spooky."

"It's an old house."

"Is there a tree outside the window?"

"I don't think so. I'll leave the tea tray by the side of the bed. Breakfast will be in the dining room at half past eight."

"Thank you, Mrs Reed."

When the housekeeper had come into the room she had turned on the light and opened the curtains.

"Shall I leave the light on? We don't want you going back to sleep and letting your tea go cold."

"Are you sure there isn't a tree just outside the window?"

"Quite sure. I'll leave you to enjoy your tea. Happy Christmas."

"Happy Christmas."

With the light still on, the tea by his side, Randall's heart kept pounding. She was right. As far as the overhead light showed, there was no tree outside the window.

By the time Randall had finished the tea from the small brown pot Mrs Reed had covered with a cosy, the light of dawn was showing through the big sash windows, challenging the overhead electric light. Randall could see through the window. There was nothing outside that was close enough to tap on his window. With the dawn, his fear from the night had gone.

"You must have been dreaming, you idiot." he said, getting dressed.

Carrying the tea tray, Randall went downstairs. Amanda and her parents were up. The breakfast, Randall could see through the open door of the dining room, was laid out on the long mahogany table.

"Did you sleep well?" asked Amanda.

"You feel like a walk?"

"Are you crazy? It's freezing outside. Happy Christmas... What's the matter?

"Someone was tapping on the outside of my window during the night. I thought it was a tree in the wind but there isn't one close enough."

"Probably the ghost, Randall," said Mr Hanscombe.

"Which ghost, Mr Hanscombe?"

"All old English houses have ghosts. It's part of the tradition, especially at Christmas. Happy Christmas. We'll be giving out the presents from under the Christmas tree after breakfast."

"But we didn't bring any presents."

"Most of the presents are for the grandchildren tomorrow."

"What was tapping on my window?"

"Sound does tricky things at night. It may have been the cracking of the water pipes. After hot baths, the old pipes contract in the cold. You want some breakfast? Good old English bacon and eggs. Do you eat bacon and eggs in Rhodesia?"

"Yes, we do. With pork sausages and fried tomatoes."

"Then you're in luck. Exactly what we have. You see, we're all English when it comes down to it... We're all going to church. Do you attend church in Rhodesia, Randall?"

"Not very often. The nearest church is over a hundred miles away... So you think it was a contracting pipe?"

"Something like that... It's an old Norman church. Eight hundred years old. Brings back the real meaning of Christmas. Church of England of course. You are Church of England, Randall?"

"Yes, I am. I was christened in the Salisbury Cathedral, according to my dad."

"Good for you."

"I'm sorry about the presents."

"You weren't expected to bring any presents. Bringing Amanda is all the Christmas present her mother and I expected."

"Then it wasn't a ghost?"

"Of course it wasn't."

Christmas Day went quite smoothly, everyone eating too much food. In the afternoon, old Mr Hanscombe fell asleep in front of the fire in the middle of a conversation. One minute he was talking, the next minute he was sound asleep, a fond look appearing on Mrs Hanscombe's face. The curtains were drawn, everyone comfortable in big armchairs. Wondering what he was expected to do, Randall kept looking at the fire, the flames burning bright. The overhead lights were out, a standard lamp behind the old man giving the only illumination. Mrs Reed had brought in the turkey with all the trimmings, wished them all a happy Christmas and retired, making Randall wonder what she did for her Christmas. Randall knew no more about Mrs Reed than when he had arrived. With luck by the time he went to bed he would have digested the food. Another night of ghosts was not Randall's idea of a happy Christmas. Next to fall asleep was Mrs Hanscombe. She had a sweet faraway look on her face. Randall's eyelids began to droop. The soft sounds from the fire were sending him to sleep. The ticking clock on the mantelpiece over the fire read ten past four. Randall dozed, half awake and half asleep. Amanda's eyes were closed, the house was quiet. When Randall again looked at the clock it read half past six. He was the only one awake. Mr Hanscombe, his mouth half open, was snoring, a line of dribble running down the side of his face. The old woman's glasses had fallen off her face onto her lap, the long cord to the glasses still around her neck. Randall felt extraordinarily comfortable.

When the rest of the family arrived before lunch the next day the peace and quiet was shattered. Mrs Reed was all of a flutter. The kids tore round the house screaming at each other. One of the boys had been given a water pistol for Christmas from under the tree. For some reason Mr Hanscombe had given Randall a book on the life of Mahatma Gandhi, not really his kind of reading. Randall preferred stories that drew him into the lives of the characters. He would have given the book to Deepak had he still been working at the Tandoori restaurant but then remembered Deepak was a Moslem and wouldn't be interested in Gandhi. Maybe a book on Cecil John Rhodes, the founder of Rhodesia, would have been more appropriate. Gandhi, so far as Randall remembered from school, had placed the first nail in the coffin of the

British Empire. Well, it was now all over, all the nails in place, so a book on Gandhi was probably quite appropriate, a reminder of how everything in Rhodesia had changed.

They left after lunch, after the visit of the Drake family, as Amanda had to work in the evening. One of the brothers drove them to the station.

"That went well," said Amanda. "So, lover, what do you think?"

"Your parents love you whatever they might have said. Tough love is often better than soft love. Equips us better for life."

"Where did you hear that crap?"

"In some crappy book."

"They've accepted you."

"I did rather think so."

"So what are we going to do?"

"Go home, get into our bed and make love."

3

Once they had you on the hook they reeled you in. Randall's happy-go-lucky carefree life serving tables was over. At the end of January, a month after he joined BLG, Mrs Walker, the old receptionist battleaxe from the twentieth floor, called Randall on the phone in his cubicle and summoned him to come up to his uncle's office. A better job description for Randall would have been office boy rather than trainee project manager. He was at everyone's beck and call, with some of them, including Mrs Walker, seeming to enjoy ordering around a man with the name of Crookshank, the same name as the managing director.

"Right away, Mr Crookshank. Right away."

The cubicle was just big enough for a desk making Randall move out sideways. There were rows and rows of identical cubicles, everyone head down and busy. At the end of the long room stood the lift shaft. Randall pressed the button. The third lift in the row of four opened. Randall selected the button for the executive suite on the twentieth floor, and the lift soared from the second floor to the top of the building in seconds, leaving Randall's stomach down on the ground. Wondering what he was wanted for, he stepped out of the lift. His first month's salary had been paid into his new bank account so being fired was likely not the problem.

"Good morning, Mrs Walker," said Randall to the old battleaxe, knowing an innocent smile and a little deference went a long way in BLG.

"You may go in. Last door at the end of the corridor. Knock before you enter."

"Thank you, Mrs Walker."

Randall marched down the executive corridor, knocked on the last door and waited like any dutiful employee, making him feel like a twerp. At his father's office next to the grading shed on the farm, Randall, like everyone else, just walked in. When the door opened, to Randall's surprise he was looking straight at his uncle.

"That was quick. If you do everything that fast you'll make us a fortune. Building a new complex is all about speed. Come in. How are you enjoying the new job? I've been getting very good reports of you, Randall."

Following his uncle into the enormous office, Randall had to smile. Of course they would give him a good report for running their errands: the boss was his uncle.

"Have you learnt anything this first month, Randall?"

"I am very good at making the tea."

"Good for you. It's important to start at the bottom. But that's not why I called you up to my office. To be any real good to us and yourself you have to have knowledge, which is why I want you to attend night school and get yourself a degree in economics. Part time, it will take you five years at the London School of Economics, the same period of your apprenticeship at BLG. You'll be twenty-seven when you graduate. I spoke to your father who agrees with me. The good luck is the education system in Rhodesia is based on the Oxford and Cambridge O level and A level system. Despite sanctions your school exam papers were marked in England. Your seven O levels and two A levels at Prince Edward School are good enough for university entrance. I'm surprised your father didn't send you to Rhodes University like your brother."

"I wanted to be a tobacco farmer. I could have gone to an agricultural college but there was a war on. Anyway, my dad knows more about growing tobacco than any professor or whatever they call them at college."

"A levels in maths and English. Unusual combination. Arts and science. We'll pay for your tuition fees, of course. So, here are the application forms. Be a good chap and fill them in right away and give them to Mrs Walker. How's Amanda? You can use the reception desk outside. Building a complex requires the best financial skills to extract the maximum profit. Business is all about maximising the profit. Oh, and your grandmother is still expecting you."

"How often must I attend night school?"

"Every night except Saturday, Sunday and public holidays. You have to work hard in this life to get on... Please close the door on your way out. You can tell Mrs Walker to send in my next appointment. They've been waiting while we had our little chat. Never stops. In business, it never stops I'm afraid. And the war is over in Rhodesia. Congratulations."

Feeling as if he'd been given a prison sentence, carrying the application forms, Randall left the office that doubled as a boardroom. As he went, he looked up at the portrait of Harry Brigandshaw smiling at him from over the board table. Harry Brigandshaw, the one-time Rhodesian farmer of Elephant Walk turned businessman, and wondered which job he preferred. If nothing else, it wouldn't matter anymore Amanda working at night. All they'd have now was the sleeping time together and not much spare time over weekends if Randall knew anything about university degrees. In order to get on in his future he was going to have to sacrifice the best years of his life. That sucks, he told himself as he closed the door. Really sucks.

"You can send them in, Mrs Walker. May I borrow a pen? I have some forms to fill in which you are to give back to my uncle."

When he went home that night it was dark. Not once had he seen the light of day. Above the cubicles were neon lights, everything artificial. He wanted to scream. Not that it would have made much difference with the noise of people and traffic all round him, every one of the faces blank in the street light that showed them their way, lemmings on the way to the Underground and the crowded tube trains that would take them home, most of them standing and holding on in the rush hour, packed tight like sardines in a tin. For Randall, used to the wide-open spaces of Africa, it was suffocating.

"Five more years of this and I'll go out of my fucking mind."

"Did you say something?"

"Sorry, lady. Please excuse my language."

The train lurched to a start and pushed him against the girl. They were so well wrapped up neither of them felt a thing.

"You have a funny accent."

"Yes, I do."

"I've seen you on the train before."

"Same time, same place every day."

"Where are you from?"

"Rhodesia. A farm in Rhodesia and I'm going out of my mind."

"Poor thing. I've only ever lived in London... Are you going back?"

"Not by the look of it. I got sandbagged by events."

They both got off at Notting Hill Gate, the young girl following. Randall quickened his pace. When he turned into the road that led to the boarding house and looked back, the girl had gone. Randall let himself in, looking down at the letters that had dropped inside on the floor through the letterbox. There was a letter from Rhodesia from his father, the handwriting quite distinctive. When he got upstairs with the letter his room was empty, Amanda having gone to work. There was a pot on the cold gas ring with a stew for his supper. The place was cold, the curtains still open. Amanda had left early or had forgotten to draw them. He had nothing to do, which made him think of the girl he had met on the train. Sitting back in the comfortable chair, Randall stared at the ceiling.

"Oh, Deepak, why did I get drunk and why did you fire me? I'm going to grow fat, old and rich and have bugger-all to look back on in my life. James! Oliver! Is there anyone at home? I'm dying of boredom."

"You want to go for a drink?" asked James as he opened the door. "You don't mind my barging in? What's the matter, Randall?"

"They've got my whole bloody life mapped out for me and it's boring. There's a letter here from my dad with my school certificates in it. They want me to go to night school. For five years. Can you imagine? Five years is a lifetime... Sorry, James. How's the sitcom coming along?"

"Very well, actually. It's like family."

"Wish I could say the same about BLG. They are like robots. I want a life, James. Office work isn't a life. It's just about making money. There's no fun. What's the point in life if you're not having fun? Let's go and get a drink. I don't care anymore."

"I don't have any money."

"I've got money, James. I've got money. It's all I've got. Only beers, mark you. None of that whisky. That's how I got into trouble last time... I met a girl on the train today."

"Are you sure you don't mind about the money?"

"It was my idea... Just look at this. There's enough chicken stew in this pot to feed an army. You want some supper?"

"I want a beer."

"Let's go. Haven't seen Oliver in a while."

"They're spending more time at her place. There's a girl in the cast I quite like. Is it raining outside?"

"Wasn't when I came in."

Three beers then they walked back home and shared the stew between them. Randall was so tired his eyelids were closing. James took his cue and went back to his room. There was still no sign of Amanda. When Randall woke to the alarm clock at six-thirty Amanda was fast asleep next to him. He had not heard her come in. Randall got up and went to the bathroom he shared with James and Oliver. There was no chance of it being occupied so early in the morning. When he left the boarding house to walk to the tube station it was still pitch dark outside except for the street lights. People all around him were scurrying towards the station. Again he saw the girl he had spoken to the previous night, and she gave him a smile. Randall smiled back and felt guilty. Before leaving the room he had not spoken to Amanda she was so fast asleep. Randall walked away from the girl up the platform and waited for the train. He was hungry, bored and needed his morning cup of tea.

The day went much the same as every day. When Randall got on the Notting Hill train the girl was there again. This time Randall avoided looking at her. All day Randall had achieved absolutely nothing. At home, Amanda had gone to work, his supper was waiting for him on the gas ring. Two pots this time, one with curry and the other with rice. Not even a note. The whole thing was ridiculous. Randall warmed the food and ate, the food as good as usual making Randall think he should tap his father for a loan backed by the block of flats in Chelsea and buy themselves a restaurant. It would all be a lot more fun. It was Friday night, usually a late night for Amanda, and he didn't have to work the next day, not that it made any difference. His application for entrance to the LSE night school had been sent in the mail, Randall hoping with his

Rhodesian education they would reject him. James had not come home from the studio and again there was no sign of Oliver. Going to the pub on his own was a no-no. He hated standing up at a bar alone looking like a social reject. He tried, after the food, to read a book but he couldn't concentrate. The girl on the train's face came back to him. The girl had a pretty face. By midnight he was still on his own, no sign of Amanda, no sound from James or Oliver. Randall got into bed, determined to stay awake. When he woke in the night Amanda was next to him, her arms round him. She was sound asleep. After lying awake wondering what his uncle had got him into he went back to sleep.

"Good morning, lover. You want some tea?"

"You up already?"

"It's ten o'clock in the morning, sleepy eyes. What did you do last night?"

"Nothing. Absolutely nothing... Come back to bed."

"Don't you want some tea?"

"We haven't spoken for a couple of days let alone made love. They want me to go to night school and get an economics degree. So it doesn't matter anymore you working at night. I'm screwed."

"You wish. I'll make some tea. Then we'll see. We have the whole day to ourselves. I don't have to be at work until seven and tomorrow's Sunday and I don't have to work. Why don't we go to church tomorrow? So often we hear the bells and do nothing about it. I loved going to church on Christmas Day. It made me feel so comfortable with myself. At peace with the world... My mother and father will be impressed. A degree in economics. Where are you going for classes?"

"London School of Economics. If I get in. Why don't we buy ourselves a restaurant? My father might be persuaded to lend us the money."

"Don't be silly. We're far too young to own a restaurant. We barely know how to wait the tables let alone do the buying, cooking and running the books. We'd go bankrupt in a week. Anyway, no one would come to a restaurant owned by a twenty-two-year-old. Young people get take-aways. They don't sit down at a restaurant."

"Then we could buy a take-away. Anything's better than what I'm doing. Five more years of this crap and I'll be out of my mind."

"Or you'll be a productive citizen with a degree. You'll get used to it.

Everyone does. Anyway, I'm going to get myself an office job. Solve the problem. I love you, Randall. Don't you know that? We'll be fine. We have each other. What more can we want? Our life as bohemians is over. That part is gone... There. Have your tea."

"You coming back to bed?"

"Of course I am. It's been ages. The last time we didn't have sex of a night was at my mother's... So, what else can you tell me?"

Not sure whether he should have told Amanda he loved her, Randall sipped at his hot tea with its just right amount of sugar. Six months before, he had been a virgin straight out of the African bush. Everything was new to him. The job, having a girl, the life in London. Only when he had finished his tea and they made love did he feel like an old hand. He lay back in bed afterwards, his hands behind his head smiling at the ceiling. It wasn't all bad. Oliver was right. The idea of going to church came back to him, reminding him of his mother and the day he was confirmed into the Church of England. The old man who had given him his confirmation classes was retired as vicar of Avondale, a small parish at the end of the long road from the farm into Salisbury. At school, one of Randall's O levels had been scripture knowledge, both the Old and New Testaments. At their last meeting before the confirmation service in Salisbury Cathedral Randall had been emotional. He was fifteen years old.

"Will I see my mother again when I go to heaven?" he had asked. "She was killed by lions when I was very little."

"I'm not sure, Randall. I'd like to say I was but I'm not sure."

"Then there isn't an afterlife?"

"I'm not sure. I'd be lying to you if I said I was. It's all about faith. We have to have faith in the Bible or life doesn't have any meaning or any purpose. God will answer your question when you die. Have faith, Randall."

"But you said you're not sure."

"I'm an old man. Facing the end of my life. At this time of life you're never sure of anything."

Ever since, Randall had not been sure either. But the old man had been right. If there wasn't the chance of something more important to go to, his own small life had no purpose.

"What are you thinking, Randall, staring at the ceiling?"

"My mother. My birth mother, not Bergit. Do you think we go to heaven?"

"Only if we behave ourselves... I was thinking. If we're both working during the day we can go to the theatre, a rock concert, a classical concert. We'll be able to spend our money on all the lovely things that are available in London. We'll be real urbanites instead of bohemians. Won't that be lovely? We'll have money to spend. Once a week. Saturday night. Make all your hard work worthwhile. There's a whole big exciting world out there if you have money."

"Do you think I'll see my mother again when I die?"

"Of course you will, silly. It says so in the Bible. And tomorrow we'll go to church and thank God for all our blessings."

"I love you, Amanda."

"I'm glad to hear it. You want another cup of tea?"

"I wouldn't mind. There's something about lying in bed drinking tea that is so thoroughly decadent."

"If you have the right company."

"That goes without saying."

The next morning, properly dressed, Randall in his suit, Amanda in one of the dresses made for her by William Drake, they followed the sound of the church bells until they found the church, neither sure of its denomination. The church was half empty. They sat at the back while the rest of the worshippers were up at the front near the pulpit. The service had already started, the choir singing, the congregation going along. It made both of them feel much better. When the service ended they slipped out unobtrusively and walked back to their room. They were holding hands. They were happy. Randall's only problem was the doubt the vicar of Avondale had left in his mind. Often, Randall wished the man had not been so honest, had not passed his doubts onto Randall.

"That was lovely, Randall. We must do it again. Going to church makes me feel a much better person."

"Why don't we go to a restaurant for lunch?"

"Why not? We'll find one that does a traditional Sunday roast. What's the point in having money if you don't enjoy it?"

"Can we go like this?"

"I don't see why not. Dressed as we are we could go to Buckingham Palace. Take lunch with the Queen."

A week later, when he was enrolled at the LSE for his night classes, the new drudgery starting for Randall on the Monday, his life worked out by other people, by a rare miracle he found a seat on the train. It was a Friday and they were going to the theatre. Amanda, never one to delay when she had made up her mind, had told Sarah Rankin she was finished as a temporary waitress. An employment agency had three interviews for secretarial jobs lined up for the Monday. Resigned to his fate in an office, Randall sat back ignoring the stare of a middle-aged lady who expected him to get up and give her his seat. Amanda had bought the tickets to the theatre, Randall having no idea what they were seeing. He was tired, happy the boring week was over. And on Sunday, he had made up his mind to visit his grandmother and give her a surprise.

"I've been reading all about Rhodesia."

Startled out of his reverie, Randall turned to look at the speaker. Next to him, smiling sweetly, was the girl.

"I'm sorry?"

"Don't you remember me? I asked about your funny accent and you said you were from Rhodesia. We both live in Notting Hill Gate. My name is Judy, Judy Collins. There was a book in the library called *Anatomy of a Rebel*. All about Ian Smith who unilaterally declared Rhodesia independent from the British in 1965. What a life it must have been as a British colonial in Africa. Where are you from in Rhodesia?"

"Randall. Randall Crookshank. I grew up on a farm in the Centenary. A tobacco farm."

"Wasn't that where the war started?"

"They say so. There were incidents earlier in other parts of the country but it really started not far from our farm."

"Were you ever attacked?"

"Yes. Why I'm here. They killed my cat."

"You poor thing... You're not married or anything?"

"I share a room with a girl. In Rhodesia they call it living in sin."

"Well, you know my name if you break up, Randall. I see you most days coming or going to work. I'd love to hear more about Rhodesia from someone who lived there. It sounds so exciting. So different. How old are you, Randall?"

"I'm twenty-two. I turned twenty-two last month."

"Now isn't that a coincidence? So am I. And how old is your girlfriend?"

"She's twenty-four this year."

"Is she pretty?"

"I think so."

"And how did you meet?"

"Coming out of the Leg of Mutton and Cauliflower."

"We go there sometimes. That's another coincidence. Well, you've obviously found out about swinging London."

As she spoke, the girl had unbuttoned her overcoat, pulling it open, exposing for Randall two large, firm breasts under a tight white sweater, making Randall's hormones stand up and scream as the girl deliberately moved in a way that pushed out her nipples. Randall looked away, trying to think of Amanda. When he looked back the girl was still smiling, knowing she had sunk in the hook. Carefully, methodically the girl buttoned up her coat as she looked at him. For the rest of the train journey they looked straight ahead, the middle-aged woman who wanted his seat still giving him nasty glares. When they got off the train the girl walked beside him, neither saying a word, until Randall turned into his road.

"Goodnight, Randall. My goodness, we're almost neighbours. See you again on the train."

When Randall turned she was walking on down the main road. Even through the overcoat he could see the movement of her bottom. He let himself into the house and walked up the three flights of stairs. Amanda was waiting, already dressed for the theatre. Randall walked across the room and took her into his arms, giving her a hug.

"What was all that about, lover?"

"You... What are we going to see?"

"A comedy called *Just the Ticket*. You want to go now?"

"Why not? There'll be a pub near the theatre."

"How was your day?"

"Bloody awful as usual but now I'm happy... You think we could make love before we go out?"

"I've just finished tarting myself up. You'll have to wait until we get back. What's got into you?"

"Nothing, Amanda. You're right. Can't ruin the make-up. Let's go."

"Oh, and William is showing his spring collection and wants me to join the rest of the models. Not all ramp models have to be skinny and tall."

"Is he paying you?"

"Says I can have the clothes. That when he's truly famous he'll pay me a fee."

"My goodness. My girlfriend is a model. We really are coming up in the world. On Sunday, I'm going to make a surprise visit to my grandmother. Want to come along?"

"You mind if I take a rain check? I want to put all my school certificates and my secretarial college diploma together and think about my job interviews. Be prepared. You know the old boy scout motto. She won't want to see me. She'll want to talk to her grandson. What time do you want to go?"

"Late afternoon. I won't be long. How long can it take to talk to my grandmother? I barely know the woman. How is William?"

"Much the same. His mannerisms are so gay it's absolutely gorgeous. The way he waves his hands. And it's not all affectation, it's just the way he is. And they truly love each other. The world really has changed… Come on. I feel like that drink before we go into the theatre. You think we will be able to find a pub?"

"There's always a nearby pub in London."

RANDALL ARRIVED at the home of his uncle to see his grandmother soon after five o'clock on the Sunday. The Friday night had come and gone, no big event. The silly comedy had made Randall and Amanda laugh with the rest of them. By the time they got home they had forgotten what it was all about. Walking up the steps to the big front door, with his back to Hyde Park, Randall rang the doorbell, this time ignoring the brass knocker. He waited. He was about to turn round and leave when the door opened.

"Come in, Randall. This is a nice surprise. Your grandmother will be thrilled. Haven't spoken to you in the office for a couple of days. Come on in. It's freezing cold outside. We really do have the worst climate in the world. You'll stay to dinner of course. We have guests from America.

Barend and Hayley are my wife's cousins. Never know if it's first cousins once removed or second cousins. Come on in. Beth's first cousin, Tinus Oosthuizen, is their father. All part of the Harry Brigandshaw legacy. They'll love to meet someone from Africa. Their grandfather and great-grandfather were true blood Afrikaners. The Oosthuizens and the Brigandshaws have been tied up together for nearly a century... Isn't that right, Barend? Meet my nephew Randall from Africa, the ancestral home of the Oosthuizens. And this is Hayley. They are both visiting BLG on business from our New York office. Or, as Barend would say, visiting their London office. Our cross shareholding is somewhat complicated. What a pleasant surprise. Hang your coat here in the hall... Mother! It's your grandson, Randall."

Overwhelmed, Randall shook the woman's hand and then the man's. They were both in their thirties with broad American accents. The girl reminded Randall of someone he had seen in the movies. Too old for Randall, he could still see she was a beautiful woman.

"Rhodesia, Randall," said the man. "I want to hear about Rhodesia. Where my roots are. My grandmother was Harry Brigandshaw's sister. When my grandfather was killed, Harry took my father under his wing."

"Was your mother the film actress, Genevieve?"

"You got it. The lives of the Brigandshaws, the Oosthuizens and the St Clairs have woven in and out of each other for a hundred years. My mother was the natural daughter of Merlin St Clair. You know Donna St Clair, of course. She's also a cousin. We're all having a dinner party."

"Hello, Randall. Where's Amanda?"

"Hello, Donna. She's at home. Just dropped in to say hi to my grandmother."

"Come here and give your grandmother a hug. You'll stay to supper. It's a bit of a family reunion. Have you heard from your father? On the phone he seems a lot happier now the war is over. He thinks Robert Mugabe will win the February election in a landslide. Just look at you after six months in London. Paul's been keeping me up to date. All sounds wonderful. I'm so proud of you."

Not quite sure if he didn't want to turn round and make a run for it, Randall followed them through the big house into the lounge where a fire was burning in the grate.

"So, you'll stay for dinner?"

"Of course, Uncle Paul. You're the boss."

"I'd forgotten that. Well, why don't we open the bar? A bit early but who cares? So, how was your week at the office?"

"Most enjoyable."

"I'm so glad you're having a good time."

Deliberately, Randall had not looked at his uncle when he lied. It never paid to tell the big boss the last week in the office had bored him out of his skull. Even the mention of Rhodesia had his whole mind pining for Africa. But life was as it was. He had to make the best of it.

"So, nephew, what will it be?"

"A beer if you please."

"Ice-cold beer it will be. I know how you chaps drink your beer in Africa. Will Amanda be all right if you stay for supper? You don't have a phone or you could phone her."

"She'll understand."

"Call it business. British and American business."

"I actually came to see Grandmother."

"Of course you did... One cold beer coming up."

He had the hundred pounds in his pocket his grandmother had given him when he first arrived in London, not sure if she would take it the wrong way if he gave it back to her. He hated owing people anything. Donna and the man called Barend seemed to have a thing going for each other the way they exchanged looks. Randall smiled. Amanda would have liked to watch them, knocking out any thought that Donna was after him. As he looked at them flirting with each other, the tight sweater and the big boobs in the train came back to him. Across the room his grandmother was looking at him fondly, making Randall think the old girl must be lonely. For Randall it was all a bit difficult working for the family which was why he had not come round. Anyway, he could never think of anything to say. Amanda had been right. It was just a link in the chain going far back into history and the men and women who lived in the caves. Donna had a satisfied look on her face as she listened to the American talk. Looking from Barend to Donna, Randall was sure they were lovers. Randall kept quiet and listened to the conversation that flowed between Uncle Paul and the two Americans, most of it business.

Later, when they all trooped into the dining room where he had first sat for lunch with Amanda and James Tomlin, they were still talking business, all of it going straight over Randall's head. It was all about something called 'leveraged buyouts', Barend telling Uncle Paul he had found an American company in pharmaceuticals whose shares on the New York stock exchange were grossly underpriced. The trick, so far as Randall could follow, was to put up a dollar of BLG money, borrow another thirty-three from the bank, buy the company at the current low share value and break it up into its component companies and sell those companies individually. By putting up the one dollar of their own money they would turn it into ten, no one in BLG having to know anything about pharmaceuticals. In six months of buying and selling, BLG would make themselves millions, making Randall wonder how the whole exercise could be true or ethical or even legal. All through the dinner he and his grandmother smiled at each other. If what Randall heard at the table was going to be part of his course at the London School of Economics he was going to end up with a permanent headache. What was the point of running a business that manipulated other people's money, he asked himself. Where, in Randall's view of life, was the satisfaction in milking other people, apart from getting the money and spending it extravagantly on things you didn't need or really want in the first place? Having a farm, watching the crops grow gave Randall a deep satisfaction. Just making piles of money for the sake of showing it off was beyond Randall's comprehension. All the talk of money had Donna St Clair's attention, making Randall look at the girl differently. And if money was the only purpose in their life he had it all wrong.

At the first opportunity after supper, using Amanda at home on her own as the excuse, Randall said it was time for him to go. His grandmother saw him to the door where he took his overcoat off the stand and put it on.

"All that talk of money is boring, Randall. You didn't say much."

"Do you want your hundred pounds back, Grandmother? I have it in my pocket. I'm sorry I haven't come round earlier... Why are you tearful?"

"It's the thought that counts so much more than the money. If you think that way about other people's property you'll go a long way in life, Randall Crookshank."

"Why don't you catch a taxi one Sunday and come to our room? Amanda is a wonderful cook. That way we'd have a chance to get to know each other without all the other people around. We're going to get a phone. Then we can call you instead of my coming round uninvited... Goodnight, Grandmother."

"Did you understand what they were talking about?"

"Not a word of it."

"Neither did I."

When he got home Amanda was in hysterics.

"You know what time it is, Randall?"

"Not really. They had some cousins visiting from America who work for BLG Inc. Uncle Paul invited me to dinner. When are we going to get a phone? When the boss invites you to dinner you can't tell him you don't want to stay. Donna St Clair was there."

"So that's why you stayed. I should have known."

"By the look of it, she's screwing the cousin, Barend Oosthuizen. He's rich and she likes the sound of his money."

"Are you sure?"

"She barely said a word to me all night... My grandmother is lonely. When we get the phone in I'm going to invite her to Sunday lunch. I told her you were a wonderful cook."

"Are you sure Donna wasn't after you?"

"Absolutely certain. So you don't mind my grandmother coming to lunch?"

"If she doesn't mind slumming it."

"I have a feeling she'll really enjoy herself. I want to know more about my family. It will be fun. I read somewhere you are only the sum of your ancestors. Shit, I've got to go to work tomorrow and you've got your interviews. Let's go to bed. Have you ever heard of a leveraged buyout?"

"What on earth are you talking about?... I was so worried. I thought something had happened to you. England's not the safe place it used to be. There are so many immigrants. People who aren't English. Many of them poor. When people are poor they do things to survive."

"I'm an immigrant, Amanda."

"Don't be silly. Apart from the accent you're as English as I am. You want some cocoa before we go to bed? It'll help you sleep. Your overcoat is wet. It must be raining outside. Take it off and give me a hug... I'm so happy you're home, Randall."

When they went to bed and made love the problem of staying out late had evaporated, the sex having calmed both of them down. They heard James Tomlin come home from the television studio. Shortly after, Oliver Manningford came back with Veronica West, the two of them giggling about something. When their door closed there was silence, the top-floor attic quiet, only the rumbling sound of traffic lulling Randall to sleep. The curtains were drawn and everything around him was familiar, making him comfortable. He was home with his girl.

"Are you asleep, Amanda?"

"Go to sleep, Randall. I have interviews in the morning... Do you ever think of other girls when you make love to me?"

"Of course not. Goodnight, Amanda."

"Goodnight, lover."

She snuggled up to him, naked body against naked body. Randall, happy, content, drifted into sleep.

PART 4

FEBRUARY TO SEPTEMBER 1980 – ON THE
BANKS OF THE ZAMBEZI RIVER

1

---

*A*manda's job interview went well. Typing Randall's book had brought her up to speed. The man was in his late thirties, as much interested in Amanda as he was in her typing, the diploma and her school certificates. Men never changed. It was what you looked like that counted. Deliberately, Amanda had left the top two buttons of her dress undone, leaning forward at the start of the interview to give him a view down her front. It worked, his eyes suddenly riveted. He had given her a tape, told her to go to the small office next door and type out what she heard on the tape. After fifteen minutes of typing, with the help of the earphones and the foot pedal that stopped and started the tape, Amanda took back what she had typed. The man read through the first paragraph and smiled.

"If you want the job you can start right now. My last secretary has gone off to have her first baby and isn't coming back to work. Here are the financial details."

The man turned round a piece of paper and pushed it towards her. One job being as good or bad as the other, Amanda accepted. At two thousand pounds a year she would be earning half Randall's wage, though the hours and perks of time off and holidays were much the same.

"I've just one problem. My boyfriend is a Rhodesian and wants to visit his family in August. By then I won't have earned sufficient leave. We want to go for a month. Is there any chance of some unpaid leave?"

"I go away for the month of August. You'd have little to do on your own. I'm sure something can be arranged."

"So that's it?"

"You can go back to your new office and finish typing my tape. Welcome to Home and General Insurance, Amanda Hanscombe. I hope you'll be happy with us. These days, most of the girls applying for jobs as secretaries haven't been to secretarial college."

The man had a slight, twisted smile on the left side of his face. Amanda, getting up, flashed him again.

"Can I use the phone and cancel my next two appointments?"

"Provided you don't call Rhodesia you can use the phone whenever you want. Who did you work for before?"

"I didn't. This is my first secretarial job."

"My goodness."

Smiling sweetly, Amanda walked into her new office. Men were so easily manipulated, she wanted to laugh. And there she was. The routine had already begun. With the two salaries they'd have enough money to get themselves a flat. Even get married. Within a year they'd be a staid old couple like the rest of them. At lunchtime she'd be able to go and see Sarah Rankin at the temp agency, pay her the ten per cent of the cash tips from the previous week and give her the news. Whoever knows what happens in life? If the man next door came onto her heavily she'd end up out of her job and back waiting tables. 'Never burn your boats,' she said to herself as she sat back down in front of her new typewriter, connected up the Dictaphone and started typing.

The telephone came in the next week followed by the television. The privacy of the room no longer belonged to them. The TV blared, people phoned. Amanda found herself more interested in the television than having a conversation with Randall. They had bought a second comfortable chair so they could both sit in front of the screen. The TV went on when the first one got home, turned off when they got into bed. Within a week Amanda talked mostly about what she had seen on television, her world inside the screen, no longer in the room. They forgot about going to the theatre. With the new money, Amanda bought television dinners after buying a microwave. James stopped coming into their room when they didn't turn off the TV and have a normal conversation. With TV dinners, potato crisps and no exercise Amanda began putting on weight. During the week, when Randall was at night school, she sat comfortably in front of the television and stuffed her face. Sex dropped from every night to three times a week, Randall exhausted from work and studying economics, their lives in a rut, everything concentrated on Randall's future. Feeling broody, Amanda thought of not taking her contraceptive pill and getting herself pregnant. They needed the two salaries for a flat so the idea quickly evaporated.

"When are we going to move into our flat, Randall?" she asked when Randall came home, the programme she was watching beginning to bore her.

"When we come back from Rhodesia. We need to save for your airfare and a nice bit of spending money to enjoy ourselves. I want to rent us a four-wheel-drive camper with a tent on the roof and go on safari."

"You can't drive with a tent on the roof, silly."

"It folds down onto the roof of the Land Rover when you break camp. It's safer from the animals sleeping on top of the vehicle. We don't want to spend the whole month on the farm. I want to show you the country... Barend Oosthuizen is over again from America. I told him we were flying out in August and going on safari. He wants to come too and bring Donna. It's always better to drive in the bush with two vehicles in case one of them breaks down. You can't exactly phone a tow truck to come and pull you out of the Zambezi Valley. Wouldn't be bad for my career. He's got pots of money so hiring another vehicle won't be a problem. I wouldn't mind going to America."

"I thought what you really wanted was to go back to Africa."

"What I want and what I can have are two different things, Amanda. Would you mind if Donna came on our holiday?"

"Not if she's screwing him... You want some potato crisps? Once I start a packet I can't stop until I finish it. In half an hour we can watch James. Why doesn't he drop in anymore? That's the trouble with people when they get famous. They forget their old friends."

"He says he has enough of television at work. Can I turn it off?"

"Why, Randall? James will be on soon. Have a crisp."

That night, after making love, Amanda looked at the packet and realised that she had forgotten to take her pill that morning. She was getting sloppy. As Randall rolled over to go to sleep she worked out the dates on her fingers. She was all right. Her period was due in three days. Lazily, content, she rolled over and went to sleep.

The weeks went by, neither of them bothering about looking for a flat. They were stuck in a rut. Winter changed to spring, followed by summer, and Mrs Salter's clothes on the line below their window began drying much quicker. Except for the wedding rings they were a staid old married couple. Randall had booked and paid for their passage to Rhodesia. Barend Oosthuizen had scheduled his flight from New York to London to give him three days in the London office before flying with them to Rhodesia with Donna. Barend and Donna would be travelling first class. Apart from spending their money on worthless luxuries the trip to Africa was all they had to look forward to.

By the time they were all walking into Heathrow Airport, saying goodbye to Barend and Donna as the American and his girlfriend parted for the first-class lounge, Amanda had put on twenty pounds in weight, her bottom tight in her jeans. Barend and Donna were holding hands, which made Amanda happy as Randall was showing no sexual interest in the girl. Donna was radiant, even more beautiful than the first day Amanda had seen her outside the Hyde Park house, a sight that had made Amanda panic. For the past few weeks, Randall had had a faraway look in his eyes, their sex life having deteriorated. Deliberately, Amanda had stopped taking the pill. She was nearing her mid-twenties, the break-even years, when all young girls required better clothes and more expensive make-up to maintain their pull over men. Their first anniversary, of when she moved into his room the night they met outside the Leg of Mutton and Cauliflower, had been on the previous Tuesday.

"You know today is the anniversary of when we first met?"

"My word, time does fly... So, we're off to Rhodesia on Saturday."

"Don't they call it Zimbabwe now?"

"Yes, I suppose they do."

"Don't you want to celebrate?"

"It's no big deal, Amanda. Not as though we got married and it's our wedding anniversary."

"Why are you home so late? Don't your classes finish at half past eight?"

"My tutor and I went for a drink."

"What's his name?"

"Payne."

"His first name?"

"I have no idea."

"Just you and the tutor?"

"Something like that."

"What was the name of the pub?"

"Is this a bloody inquisition? We had a couple of drinks... Are you all packed and ready for Saturday? I can't wait to see my family. See the farm. It's the dry season. No rain and not so hot. At night we'll sleep under blankets on the farm. Dad's so excited. Spoke to him today from the office. August in Rhodesia is the best month of the year. The seed beds go in next month so there isn't much work on the farm. Tobacco farming is highly seasonal. During the reaping season we get up before dawn and work until dark. Sometimes after dark, filling the barns by the headlights from the truck."

An hour later, the memory of the argument still fresh in her mind, having gone through customs and immigration, they boarded the plane.

"What's the matter, Amanda?"

"Nothing. Let's enjoy ourselves. We're on holiday. Do you still love me?"

"Of course I do... Those are our seats over there. You can have the one next to the window. I can't believe I'm finally going home."

When they took off, Amanda sitting next to the window, looking out as the big plane came off the tarmac and rose into the sky, Amanda was smiling. Her period was late. All these years she had been as regular as clockwork. By the time they reached their cruising height, feeling content, Amanda fell asleep on Randall's shoulder. When she woke an air hostess was standing at the end of their row of seats with a drinks trolley.

"What time is it, Randall?"

"Twelve o'clock. They're going to be serving lunch soon. Want a drink? You fell asleep."

"Didn't sleep much last night with all the excitement."

"I know how it is. What are you going to have?"

"A soft drink."

"They've got Appletiser. You'll like it. I'm going to have a Castle. In Rhodesia, it's Castle or Lion Lager. A man gets used to his beer."

"I've got something to tell you, Randall. But I'm going to wait until we get to the farm."

IF THERE WAS one thing Randall hated it was being left hanging. When Amanda said she had something to tell him it was not usually good news. Especially when she kept it from him. Girls, when they wanted to, could be so frustrating. The beer, nice and cold, was going down well. Randall looked at his watch and made the calculation. In nine hours they would be landing at Jan Smuts airport in Johannesburg where the four of them would be changing planes for the two-hour flight to Salisbury. There was no first class on the Air Zimbabwe flight so they would all be sitting together on the old Viscount. Flying in the turbo-prop aircraft always made Randall feel comfortable, the sight of the four propellers going round and round somehow more reassuring than a jet engine. He wondered what Amanda had to tell him. Ever since putting him on the hook of wanting to know what she had to say, she had been holding her stomach, softly feeling her tummy with both hands. After Randall's second cold Castle she was still doing it, a sweet smile of contentment on her face. When he looked at her she just smiled, the kind of smile that said she knew something, the look giving Randall a sharp jab of panic deep down in his stomach. She saw the panic in his eyes and smiled right into his eyes. Realisation dawned on Randall: the girl was pregnant, the hand gestures telling him more than any words. He was caught. The trap had been set, the jaws of the trap landing right round his balls. He was twenty-two. Lived in one rented room. Had little or no knowledge of the job he was meant to be doing. And for all intents and purposes had no property and no money. First he was trapped by his uncle. Now Amanda had him by the balls. His life was over before it had started. For the rest of his life he was going to be providing for other people, working his fingers to the bone in a job and a lifestyle he hated. Never before in his life had Randall wanted to run so fast so far. He hated responsibility and now they had got him.

White as a sheet, his heart pounding, he turned and looked at Amanda. He wanted to ask her and couldn't, the words stuck in his throat. When they got back from the trip he was going to tell her about Judy Collins, the girl he had met on the train. There had never been drinks with Payne the tutor, he had been with Judy. He'd ambushed her off the train on his way back from the LSE weeks ago, having told her one morning in the rush hour why she no longer saw him going home each evening. Randall and Amanda were no longer the laid-back couple, their bohemian lifestyle shattered by regular jobs and all the conventions that went with them. When they were together they sat in front of the television. Instead of talking, they sat staring at the screen with its mindless programmes, and fed themselves with packets of peanuts and crisps. When they did make love it was brief and mechanical. Judy was fresh, interesting, making love with a passion, the same passion that had once been his and Amanda's, the bohemian laid-back couple. He had been unfaithful and now he was going to well and truly pay for it for the rest of his life. Of course, if she was pregnant he would have to marry her. What about the kid? What about what people would say if he ran away from a pregnant girlfriend? Randall wanted to stand up and scream. He couldn't look at her. He looked away and over the passenger next to him, a little old lady. The air hostess, coming back with the trolley, smiled at him. She was young and pretty, her eyes when she looked at Randall full of mischief. Amanda put her hand on his knee and gave it a squeeze, making him certain. She was pregnant, no doubt in his mind about it.

"I'm going for a pee," he said, putting his beer on Amanda's pull-down table and climbing round the old lady. "I'm so sorry to disturb you. The beer has gone straight through me, I'm afraid." The old girl said nothing.

He almost ran up the aisle and into the loo. In the toilet he stared in the mirror to see if he looked any different. The same old Randall looked back at him. Then it came to him, making him smile, a big, wide smile that stared back at him. He was going to be a father. Another person, a person that would belong to him for as long as he lived, was coming into his world. By the time he had finished his pee the feeling of panic had washed away, a whole new world in front of him. He walked back to his seat slowly, looking over the heads of the passengers, passing the pretty air hostess and turning sideways to pass with his back to her, not wanting to look at her face. By the time the kid grew up he would still be young and able to have fun, not like some men who fathered their kids in their forties. Again, the old lady pulled back her knees, letting Randall get into his seat. Amanda was looking out of the small, round porthole of a window as Randall picked up his beer and let down the small table in front of him. The old lady was looking at him.

"Does that feel better, young man? You really were in a hurry."

"Much better, thank you."

When the lunch came, Randall ate his chicken with relish. After lunch it was his turn to take a nap, drifting off into the world of his dreams. In the dream he was chased by a lion, Randall climbing straight to the top of a tree. After looking disappointed the lion walked away into the bush. After the sleep, Randall read the book he had brought on the plane with him, a book of short stories by Ernest Hemingway, most of them set in Africa, making Randall wish he could make his own book read as easily as Hemingway's. By the time they were close to Johannesburg in South Africa he had finished the book.

"That one kept you enthralled," said Amanda.

"It did, didn't it? Welcome to Africa, Amanda. We're beginning our descent."

"How long have we got on the ground?"

"An hour and a half and we're off again. How was your flight?"

"Perfect."

"So was mine. I can't believe I'm coming home."

"Would you stay if your father asked you?"

"Let's cross that bridge when we get to it. You and I have a lot to talk about. Phillip's meeting us at the airport in Salisbury with the safari truck, big enough for all of us and the luggage."

"Will everyone be at the airport?"

"Probably. We'll have time to drive straight back to the farm. During the war they built a tarred road that was meant to be safe from landmines. Now the drive takes a couple of hours."

"What time will it be in Salisbury?"

"Seven o'clock in the evening. It'll be dark. There won't be any traffic at that time of night. All you have to watch for are animals straying onto the road. How are you feeling?"

"Just fine. Why are you asking?"

"Just wondering. Flying can upset the tummy... You know what I want to do?"

"What's that, Randall?"

"I want to write a book of short stories like Hemingway."

"When are you going to find the time to write?"

"During the weekends. There's always time when you really want to do something."

"I'll have to turn off the television."

"And take the phone off the hook. Short stories are easier to sell. You can sell them to magazines. We'll need the money. Of course, if we were to stay in Zimbabwe I'd have all the time in the world to write. We'd be able to go back to being the laid-back couple. None of the pressure."

"I don't know whether I want to live in Africa. Everything is so uncertain."

"Life's uncertain wherever you are. England wasn't too certain during the war. Look what happened to my grandfather. He went down at Dunkirk on the *Seagull*. You never know. You pay your money and take your chances. So long as you are happy it doesn't matter, Amanda. Happiness. That's what life should be about. Not worrying about what's going to happen to you in the future. You can get run over by a bus or killed by a pride of lions like my poor mother... You'll see Livy Johnston's painting of my mother in the lounge at World's View. They lived in the same boarding house in Salisbury when they were young and having fun. There were three of them: my mother Carmen, Livy and Candy. They were all naughty girls from the bits I picked up from my father. Donna will be interested to see her mother's painting."

"Are they coming up to the farm or staying in a hotel in Salisbury until we all go on safari?"

"We'll have to ask them... Fasten your seatbelt, Amanda. We're about to land."

"I've got butterflies in my stomach."

"So have I. I feel so happy I just might burst."

"What are you so happy about suddenly?"

"Life. Life and all its wonders."

"Did you have a nice flight?" asked the old lady next to him.

"A wonderful flight when I come to think of it."

"My son is meeting me at the airport with my grandchildren."

"Enjoy your holiday."

"Oh, it's going to be more than a holiday. I'm going to live with them."

The smooth descent and landing had both of them staring out of the window, both Randall and Amanda deep in their thoughts. When the seatbelt light went off, Randall stood up and took their hand luggage from the overhead compartment. The old lady pointed to her luggage and Randall brought it down for her onto the seat. Like old friends who would never meet again they parted, Randall holding back, waiting for the aisle to empty.

"There's never any point being the first off the plane. You still have to wait for the luggage. Anyway, we're changing planes so there's time to waste. They'll put our luggage on the Salisbury flight for us so we'll have nothing much to do... Come on... Look, there's Donna and Barend waiting for us... How was your flight? Welcome to Africa. A Barend Oosthuizen with an American accent, Barend. That should make the South Africans have a giggle. Did your father teach you any Afrikaans?"

"Not a word. I'm an American. Nothing else. An American from the state of New York. I'm proud of my heritage. But I'm more proud of being an American... Will they transfer the luggage safely?"

"Of course they will. South Africa is one of the most efficient countries in the world."

"You want to find a bar in the airport and all have a drink?"

"Why not? But first, I'm going to walk round the concourse and stretch my legs."

As they walked through the open door into the building, Randall saw the old lady being greeted by her grandchildren, the old girl full of smiles. Watching them made Randall happy. Maybe one day in a distant future he'd be greeted by his own grandchildren at an airport, everyone happy, everyone smiling.

"There's a bar over there, Randall. When you've had your walk come and join us."

AMANDA WATCHED the back of Randall for a moment wondering why he wanted to go for a walk in a crowded airport.

"You guys go on into the bar. I want to find a chemist. I'll join you in a minute."

"Are you all right with all those bags?"

"There's not much in them, Barend. Typical man leaving me with the bags. Can I put them on your trolley? Are you allowed to wheel a trolley into the bar?"

"I can try."

Amanda found a pharmacy next to the bookshop, not sure what to do. A man was standing behind the counter.

"Excuse me, do you have a pregnancy test kit?"

The man smiled, found what she was looking for and gave it to Amanda.

"How soon after conception does the colour change to blue?"

"All in the instructions. That'll be one rand and twenty-seven cents."

"I can give you a pound."

"And I'll give you your change."

"Keep the change. We're in transit to Zimbabwe."

"I'll put it in the Animal Welfare box."

Back in the bar, Barend had found them a table, the trolley with the hand luggage standing next to him. She sat down, surprised at the way the man was looking at her. There was still no sign of Randall.

"The flight's on time. We board in an hour. Did you get what you want?"

"I think so."

"This place isn't exactly O'Hare or Kennedy but it's busy. Johannesburg is the financial capital of South Africa. Started as a mining camp for the gold mines back in the nineteenth century. My father fed me books on South Africa. The Oosthuizens first got to Africa from Europe in the seventeenth century not long after Van Riebeeck. He was South Africa's equivalent of Christopher Columbus. You want something to drink, Amanda? The one thing I hate about air travel is sitting around airports."

"How was first class? Is it worth paying so much extra?"

"Not really. Force of habit. In the big world of American finance they expect an executive to fly first class. They wouldn't want to do business with a man who travels tourist. So much of doing business is image. What you look like. What car you drive. What kind of house you live in. The fact the car's on finance and the house has a mortgage they can't see. Everything back in the States is about appearances. Makes the buyer feel comfortable he's dealing with a man of substance. All a load of bullshit but it works. So, you want a drink?"

"Not really."

If Amanda didn't know better, with Donna sitting next to him, she could have sworn the big American was trying to chat her up. Men! They were so predictable. Donna was smiling at her and didn't seem to notice. For a moment, Amanda was tempted to go into the toilet by following the sign at the end of the bar, and find out if she really was pregnant. She was about to get up when Randall came into the bar. For an hour, thinking of the pregnancy test in her bag, Amanda listened to their chit-chat, no one saying anything important. The public address system came on, announcing their flight was boarding. They all got up, this time Randall pushing the cart. Before they went through to board the small aircraft, they each picked up their hand luggage. There were two seats on either side of the aisle, the men giving the girls the window seats. On the way up the steps of the aircraft, Barend had again come onto her. It made her feel good. More confident. When Randall chatted to Donna she would not feel so vulnerable: confidence was a girl's best friend. Part of her wanted to know. Part of her didn't want to find out, not if the test proved negative. There was still a chance her period would start. The excitement of leaving England on a long journey might have upset her metabolism. Life was full of hope and disappointment. Better she wait, she told herself. Give it another couple of days. Twice she felt inside her handbag where the test kit was hiding.

The plane droned on. The aircraft had taken off without Amanda realising, she was so deep in her thoughts. It was going to be a girl. A girl to give her comfort for the rest of her life, part of each other, unlike her childhood best friends from school that had grown up and quickly parted, men friends being more important to them than girls. A daughter would be permanent.

All she could see down below the wing of the plane was mile after mile of bush. There was a river meandering through the savannah. No towns or villages. No sign of mankind. It was all new and strange to Amanda after the south of England where housing estate followed housing estate and village followed village, everything small and compact, everything built on top of each other. Randall had a faraway look of longing on his face when she looked back from the window. He didn't seem to notice her looking at him, he was so engrossed with what he was seeing out of the window. Across the small aisle, Donna had gone to sleep, Barend smiling at her with that same look he had given her in the bar. Men always roamed, whatever you did for them, which was why she so much wanted a child, to give her a feeling of permanence, something that would bind her to Randall for the rest of their lives, a common bond that could never be broken. For a moment, a flash of the office and her boss came into her mind. She didn't like the office or her boss but the job was all part of her security. With rents so high in London, if they wanted a future, both of them had to have jobs. Life in one room surrounded by actors and artists was only fine up to a point, that kind of life having no future. She had had enough of drifting from restaurant to restaurant serving people at tables. She had tried out all the different types of men. Maybe not a New York executive but that would have to be one trophy she wasn't going to get. Instead, she would help Randall become her London executive by keeping his nose to the grindstone and giving him financial backup until he passed his economics examination and moved up the ladder in BLG. She would make herself irreplaceable, so much a part of his life that he would never be able to do without her, however many Donnas came across his sights. And the key was in her stomach: a daughter for both of them to give their lives a permanence and reason.

By the time the aircraft came into land at Salisbury airport, she was more determined than ever to make a success out of life, to have a husband and family, a real purpose, something more than a day-to-day existence.

"Here we are, Amanda. Home sweet home. I can't wait to get off the plane and smell the bush again... Come on. This time I'm going to be first off the plane."

"What's the hurry, Randall?"

"I want to stamp both my feet on the African soil at the same time... What you got in your handbag? All through the flight you've been fiddling inside your bag."

"Was I? I wonder why?... You think your father will like me?"

"Of course he will... Come on. The seatbelt light's gone off and they're opening the door up front. You mind if I go first?"

"Make a run for it, lover. I'll be right behind you."

. . .

HE WAS HOME. Despite meeting Amanda, and all the fun he had had in London with James and Oliver, he had never been truly happy in England. Happiness for Randall was where his roots came from and his roots had been planted in Africa, whatever the colour of his skin or whether they wanted to call him a Rhodesian or a Zimbabwean. He was down the steps like a shot out of a gun, almost tripping. At the bottom, he did what he had promised himself and jumped up with both feet, stamping them back down together on the ground. A black man in overalls was standing at the bottom of the steps, a smile on his face.

"Glad to be home?"

"You can say that again. No place like home. Thank God the war is over."

"The struggle is over thanks to Mr Mugabe."

Feeling uncomfortable, Randall turned to look back up at the plane disgorging its passengers. Whatever the future, his country had changed. Amanda came through the aircraft door and stood on the steps. When she saw him down below she waved. Randall waved back. Barend came out next followed by Donna, all of them carrying their hand luggage. The airport attendant had walked away when Randall turned round again. The baggage door of the aircraft was now open. Torn between waiting for them and running through to see his family, Randall impatiently waited, his whole body bursting with pent-up excitement.

"Did you jump up and down?"

"Of course I did. Let me carry your hand luggage."

"The air smells different. A warm, dry smell you don't get in England."

"Hasn't rained for months. The rains will only come in November. The main rain's in December. So, what do you think?"

"The airport building is so small."

"Barend – do you feel anything? The old ancestral pull?"

"Not a thing, buddy. You think they'll be waiting for us or do we take a cab to a hotel? Back in the States the man in the travel agency said Meikles was the place to stay. Booked us a room just in case. Always have backup, Randall. Remember that in business. However good plan A looks, always have a plan B."

With the rest of the passengers they trooped across the tarmac and into the terminal building. Randall showed the girl his Rhodesian passport at immigration.

"Welcome home, sir."

"Thank you. It's good to be home."

Randall walked away. Across the room, where they waited for their heavy luggage, the glass sliding doors to the terminal exit were shut. People waiting for the disembarking passengers were pushing up against the other side of the heavy plate glass. Randall saw Phillip and waved. On either side of him stood Myra and Craig. Behind the nearly grown-up children stood his father and Bergit, the whole family grinning like Cheshire cats. Craig had grown. At fifteen, he was nearly as tall as his half-brother Phillip. Myra at thirteen, looked more like a woman than a girl. Randall pointed to his hand luggage and made a gesture. Then he bowed from the waist, Phillip copying his gesture.

Ten minutes later, the man he had seen at the bottom of the steps drove the tractor towing the luggage trailer up to the building. The luggage was taken off and brought into the building.

Randall and Amanda, their luggage now on a trolley, pushed towards the green light that said 'nothing to declare'. A sliding door opened. Quickly, Phillip was shaking his hand.

"You remember Donna St Clair? She was a little girl back then. This is Barend Oosthuizen. And this is my Amanda... Everyone, meet my family... Hello, Dad, it's good to be home."

A babble of conversation ensued. All bits and pieces, no one really finishing what they were trying to say. His father had hold of his luggage trolley, pushing it across the road into the car park. The sun was shining. A truck was waiting for them. On top, at the front of the roof rack, were a pile of spare tyres. A tarpaulin covered a mound of goods on the rest of the roof, the ropes over the tarpaulin pulled tight. On the side, a rack ran round the vehicle with spare cans of petrol. The whole outside of the truck was covered in dust. Their luggage was put inside through a double backdoor. Further inside were rows of seats, big windows on either side of the vehicle. To Randall it was more of a bus than a truck. Everyone piled in, Phillip taking the wheel, Randall sitting next to his brother.

"We built the body onto the chassis of an old Bedford truck. Cost a bloody fortune but it's worth it. My intention is to take overland tours right up Africa. The last great adventure on earth. We're nearly finished with the second vehicle."

"Isn't it dangerous, all the coups and plots that go on in the new Africa?"

"Part of the marketing. A lot of youngsters in the developed world are jaded. They want some excitement. We're going to give it to them. We're an island unto ourselves. Everything we need is on this truck. Unless the engine blows up or the chassis breaks we can fix anything. We'll drive the two vehicles in convoy so we have backup if one of the trucks breaks down in the bush and we can't fix it."

"What does a history major know about fixing trucks?"

"My partner's a mechanic. Trained with Mercedes in Germany. Did you see that winch on the front? You could pull a tank with that winch."

"What's all this got to do with your fancy degree in history? I thought you were going to be a school teacher and go on playing your cricket."

"There's not much future in the new Zimbabwe for a white schoolteacher. Teachers are all going to be black. With so many whites leaving there's a new joke doing the rounds. In the old days, before the bush war, tourists came to Rhodesia to see the Zimbabwe ruins that so far the archaeologists haven't been able to date as they're so old. Now they're saying that in a few years' time they'll be coming to Zimbabwe to see the Rhodesia ruins. But who knows? Under the Lancaster House Agreement there's a power sharing consensus that keeps Smith and his Rhodesian Front party in parliament as a minority for ten years. Mugabe has retained Peter Walls to run the new Zimbabwe army while he integrates his own guerrilla forces into the old Rhodesian army. We'll see. So, what do you think of my business plan?"

"I think you're nuts."

"So does Dad. We'll see. If we disappear into darkest Africa and never come back then you'll all know it didn't work."

"All the way up Africa?"

"All the way to the shores of the Mediterranean, right across the Sahara desert."

"Didn't you learn anything at Rhodes University?"

"Not much... How about a singalong, everyone? The prodigal son is home. How about 'We're on the Road Again'. Myra, make your mother sing. She's got the best voice of the lot of us. Barend, can you sing?

Donna? Come on, all of you. Take us two hours to get to the farm. Let's all sing our hearts out."

THEY WERE SOON OUT of Salisbury, the big lights of the truck probing the road ahead. There were no lights on either side, but a pale moon showed Amanda the African bush far into the distance. She was no good at singing so she mouthed the words. Both her mother and father said she sang out of tune. Barend was enjoying himself, the big man singing at the top of his voice. She was seated next to Randall's stepmother. Randall had introduced her as Bergit, not Mother. Behind them sat the father, a typical Englishman who had been to a good boarding school, his face dry and tanned from all his years in the African sun. When she turned round to look down the back of the bus and check her luggage he smiled at her, a nice, friendly smile of welcome. Amanda gave him a knowing smile, thinking of the man's granddaughter beginning to grow inside her stomach. The young daughter gave her a not so friendly look. A look that said get off my property. The girl, unlike the young brother next to her, wasn't singing. Amanda thought it must be strange for Randall to have a half-brother and sister, the same father but different mothers, making them always that bit different.

At the airport, before they all piled into the bus, the American had excused himself to make a phone call from the pay phone outside the terminal building. He had said he wanted to cancel his hotel booking at Meikles, not wanting to lose his deposit. The thought of a man so apparently rich wanting to save his deposit had made her smile. Or was it just good manners so someone else could have their room? Or just the right way to do business? Amanda's mother had used the phrase 'waste not, want not' throughout Amanda's upbringing. It was engraved on Amanda's mind. The American's mother, Genevieve the famous actress, had been English before they all lived in America. Maybe she had taught her American son the same simple wisdom that had likewise been passed down from her mother. It was all about upbringing. She would have to remember all those home truths and pass them onto her daughter. Like the one that said 'charity begins at home'. All about looking after one's own family first, not splashily giving away money to charity just to impress one's friends. Maybe the man wasn't trying to chat her up, just trying to be friendly. Americans were much more open than the British. They were different. Their culture was different. In England, it was rude to make a big display: 'Never be loud, Amanda. It's vulgar. And never show off.'...

She had stopped mouthing the words of the song, deep in her thoughts. Life was going to be different now she was about to become a mother. Maybe many of her mother's annoying habits had been right and good for her. Had given her the knowledge to get through life based on the best principles of a good upbringing. She was glad she and Randall had followed the bells and found the church. They would go there again when they got home. Unknowingly, she had opened her small handbag and was feeling inside, her fingers touching the pregnancy kit, making her smile. Then she smiled at the back of Randall's head: he was so enjoying being with his brother, making Amanda wonder what their mother would have been like had she lived.

"You're not singing, Amanda."

"You wouldn't want me to, Mrs Crookshank. I sing out of tune. Always have."

"Call me Bergit."

"Isn't Bergit a German name?"

"I was called after a German woman whose husband saved my father's life before the Second World War. My father was in Berlin on assignment for the newspaper when he was abducted by the Nazis. The von Liebermans had been friends of Harry Brigandshaw after Harry shot down Klaus von Lieberman in the First World War. In those days, the small planes could land in a field. Harry landed next to the wrecked plane and pulled out the German, saving his life before the plane burst into flames. My brother Harry is named after Harry Brigandshaw. So, no. I am not a German. I just have a German name."

"This Harry Brigandshaw had an enormous influence on so many people."

"Without Harry, none of us in this bus would be together. Our common link is Harry Brigandshaw. In about ten minutes we'll be driving past Elephant Walk, the farm his father, Sebastian Brigandshaw, built up with Barend's great-grandfather. Elephant Walk was eventually sold to Anglo-US Incorporated. It's now a big citrus estate all under irrigation, an idea started by Harry."

"There's a portrait of him in Paul Crookshank's office in BLG that Randall says looks down over the board table. It was painted by Donna's mother."

"Like the portrait of Carmen you'll see in the lounge at World's View. They say Harry was one of the very few truly good men. An extraordinary legacy. The men people think are good mostly lied and cheated to win their fame. They're called politicians. Or men hiding as priests... I'll tell you when we're passing through Elephant Walk. In the moonlight, you'll see all the rows of orange trees spreading up over the hills... Are you going to marry Randall?"

"I hope so. We've lived together for a year. Since the first night we met, we've never been parted."

"That's lovely... What have you got in your bag?"

"A pregnancy test kit."

"Have you used it?"

"Not yet."

"I wish you luck. Does Randall know?"

"Not yet."

"He's very young to have the responsibility of being a father. He's been a loner for much of his life. I tried to be a mother to him but he never let me close. It was always Randall and Phillip. Phillip and Randall. Look at them. If the farm hadn't been attacked that night, Randall would never have left Rhodesia... Are you two close?"

"I think so. A year can seem a long time when you are living it but it's not. I have a lot more experience of life than Randall brought up on an African farm. No wonder he and Phillip are so close. I'm two years older than Randall. Girls mature quicker than men."

"Do you know much about him?"

"As a matter of fact I do. When we were both waiting tables to make a living, Randall wrote a book. We only worked at night and our bedsitter was quiet during the day. When he'd finished writing, I typed up the pages. He called the book *The Tawny Wilderness*. Said it was fiction. I'm sure the main character was Randall. The character he called Edward was born in the back of a truck like Randall. There's a black man called Moley in the book. I think I know as much about Randall from reading his book as he knows himself."

"What happened to it?"

"We gave it to an agent. The agent said it was told from a white perspective and wouldn't sell. That readers want to empathise with the oppressed blacks in this country, not with the whites who stole their land."

"There... Look out of the window. You can see the even line of the orange trees by the light of the moon. That's where Harry's father, the elephant hunter, first put down his roots. Gave up his hunting and settled down to farm. Back then, there was nothing here. Just bush and wild animals. No one owned the land. There were a few African villages near the rivers with patches of land they cultivated. They were itinerant. Cattle and goats. When the grazing was gone they moved on, leaving their pole and mud houses to the elements. There were less than half a million in the whole of what is now called Zimbabwe. No one stole the land from anyone. It was there. Unused. Waiting for someone to farm... But yes, I can see where that agent was coming from. British colonialism was wrong. Bringing what we brought with us to Africa was probably wrong. Our culture – our language. What we like to call the rule of law. Only history will tell... So they rejected his book. Was it any good?"

"I think so. Especially at the end when they kill Edward's cat. But then I'm biased. I'm the author's lover. For a brief moment, we thought we would be able to make enough money from his writing to continue our lives as bohemians, surrounded by actors and artists. But life isn't that easy. We had to come down to earth. And when Randall got fired from his restaurant job for getting drunk one night and not pitching up – it was the day his book was rejected – he got himself what everyone calls a 'proper job'. And here we are. Me, a secretary, Randall doing his apprenticeship with BLG and going to night school. I suppose we both grew up."

"How sad for you."

"It was... Still is. But we all have to face reality in the end. And reality is making a living that will last. You can't make a future waiting tables."

"Did he bring the book with him?"

"You'll have to ask him. That book's a touchy subject... So, this is where Harry Brigandshaw's father brought civilisation to this part of the world."

"Something like that. Whether our civilisation is a curse they are about to find out."

"What do you think?"

"Give me a hut by a river with a couple of cows anytime. Why I was happy to get away from our so-called civilised ways and live on a farm in the bush with Jeremy. Maybe we will have to face the facts a bit like you, Amanda. What you want from life and what you get are not often the same."

"Would you go back to England?"

"If I had to. Mostly, you do what you have to do in life. It's not your decision. Myra and Craig might enjoy an urban life. All that sex and drugs and rock and roll... Look, they've stopped singing. You see, life does have its occasional blessings." She was smiling, a slight twist at the corner of her mouth.

"You sing beautifully."

"Thank you, Amanda... Do you love him?"

"I think so."

"Does he love you?"

"I hope so."

"People say they love a person when they want to be loved. It's how it goes... Just look at all those orange trees under the pale light of the moon."

"It goes on and on."

"That's right. When the English do something they do it properly. Twenty-four thousand acres under fruit trees irrigated from the Mazoe dam. It was Harry Brigandshaw's dream. Damming the river and using the water before it ran from river to river and out to the sea. Acres and acres of prosperity for everyone. They crush the oranges and export the juice giving jobs to thousands of people. The oil is extracted from the skins of the oranges and sold to the cosmetic industry. All of it sustainable year after year, not a drop of water wasted as they drip-irrigate directly onto the roots of the trees. All of it Harry's dream of perfect efficiency that made a better life for everyone."

"Will it continue under Mugabe?"

"Who knows? There are rumblings of taking the land from the whites and giving it to the blacks and making Britain pay the farmers compensation, bringing into Zimbabwe a large amount of foreign currency. Makes good populist politics. What the war was fought about, according to Mugabe. Getting back the land. Jeremy thinks that if white management and expertise is taken out of the equation, Zimbabwe agriculture will collapse. That places like this will revert to subsistence farming and the country's economy will disintegrate. The whole farming infrastructure will collapse: the roads will degenerate, the agriculture research stations will disappear without the trained extension officers who call and advise the farmers, the supply of fertiliser and insecticides will dry up, to say nothing of finance from the banks to grow the crops without privately owned farms to put up as security for the loans. Jeremy says the system is so intricate, the web of continuity so important, that you break one link and the whole farming industry will fall apart. Personally, I think the blacks would have been a lot better down by the river in their grass huts if we British hadn't come anywhere near them. There would have been far fewer of them living much shorter lives but they would have been happy. Idealistic, of course. There's always some predator trying to interrupt your life. If it isn't a marauding tribe looking to steal your cattle, it's the wild animals. Maybe we are all wild animals. Maybe you can never find a place in life to live in peace and quiet. Like Mugabe's Shona, who were conquered by the Zulu tribe of Matabele that had come up from South Africa, we white farmers will lose everything. Why Jeremy hedged his bets and bought a block of flats in Chelsea with Donna's mother. But it will never be the same however much money we might have in England. Nothing can replace the beauty and lifestyle of World's View. You'll see, Amanda. Living in the African bush with people you love is the perfect way of life. Not too many people to get on your nerves. Now we have the invasion of so many television programmes, my children don't think so. They want the glamour of life in England or America. The good life shown to them by glamorised television. All the excitement. We all think we want what we haven't got and are never satisfied. They call it human nature, always wanting more. Always running from pillar to post. Never to be satisfied. I find it sad, really. And then, when you've got what you think you want, someone comes along and takes it away from you. Now isn't that ironical? Nowadays, I enjoy each day to the full and let tomorrow take care of itself. As individuals, there is usually little we can do about it, anyway."

They lapsed into silence, Amanda not knowing what to say. The bus had gone quiet bringing to Amanda the sounds of the engine and the tyres on the road.

"How much further is it?" she asked Bergit.

"About an hour. Are you hungry? I put a nice big picnic basket on the bus before we left the farm. Silas is the best cook in the world. Been with us ever since Jeremy started farming on World's View. Ever since he built the house."

"Does Silas live in the house?"

"No. He has a hut down by the river in the African compound. There's wives and so many children I lost count. Myra and Craig made pigs of themselves on the way into town. There's still some left."

"Thank you. I ate on the plane. I've been putting on weight recently. A girl has to look after herself or it can get away from you. Putting on weight is easy. Getting rid of it is the problem."

Listening to the woman's problems made Amanda think life was a permanent struggle however you looked at it. Her eyes were closing, her mind lulled by the rhythm of the tyres on the road. Once, the headlights showed her a herd of cows on the other side of the fence that protected the road. Her mind was drifting comfortably into sleep and into her dream... Her dream was all about a little girl who was hers, only the two of them in a strange world of animals and trees. They were so happy alone. The colour of the sky was a soft orange. All round them they heard the gurgle of water from a river. Everything was beautiful. They ran, hand in hand, down to the edge of the river, both of them laughing. Just as they were about to run into the water she woke, the gears of the bus changing down, the vehicle slowing as they turned off the tarred road, bumping over the gravel. On either side of the bus, tall and stark, were lines of gum trees in darkness, the light of the moon unable to penetrate to the level of the passing bus.

"We've arrived, Amanda. Did you sleep well? Welcome to World's View."

"What are those tall brick buildings?"

"Tobacco barns. Where we cure the tobacco."

There was a light on the end of one of the barns. Amanda looked at her watch that said eight o'clock.

"What's the right time, Bergit? My watch is still on British summertime."

"Just gone nine o'clock."

The bus drove past the farm buildings and up a gravel road towards a long bungalow up on a hill. There was one light on in the front of the house. The bus stopped at a security fence and Phillip got out and opened the gate, while Randall, now in the driving seat, drove the bus through the open gate, Phillip closing and locking it before climbing back into the bus followed by a pack of excited dogs that jumped all over Myra and Craig before running up and down inside. Randall parked below the house. From Amanda's seat, she could see forever in the moonlight to a distant range of mountains. Phillip had gone into the house and was turning on the lights. Suddenly, a row of floodlights, that ran between the trees on the well-cut lawn, flooded the trees and the security fence showing Amanda a closed area inside the lawn with a swimming pool inside a fence. With the bus engine silent, Amanda could hear the screech of the crickets and the croak of the frogs. The big, almost full moon was right above the house. The dogs, now out of the vehicle, were chasing each other in and out of the trees. An old black man was standing waiting up on the veranda that ran along the front of the house at the top of some steps. One of the Alsatian dogs caught up with Randall and jumped all over him, licking his face. Randall was laughing. Amanda followed everyone up to the house, clutching her handbag. Inside, they went into a big room with a fireplace at one end, a log fire burning in the grate. On one wall, away from a long dining room table, was the portrait of a young woman, whose eyes followed Amanda as she went up to look. There were big sofas and easy chairs nearer the big fireplace.

"That's my mother," said Randall, coming up and standing beside her. "Hello, Mum. I've been away. How have you been?"

"You talk to her?"

"All my life... So, what do you think?" He had looked away from the portrait of his mother to look around at the room.

"It's big. Everything is big."

"It's chilly at this time of the year. Let's go stand by the fire. Silas has put out the drinks and a cold buffet supper if you're hungry."

"I'm overwhelmed, Randall. All this in the middle of nowhere. A typical Englishman's home. It's awesome."

"Never thought of it that way. It's my home... Let's go over there and I'll show you the bullet hole in the window that killed my cat. Dad says he's never going to replace the glass. Wants it to stay as it is to remind us.

My cat was on that windowsill. The bullet smashed into the wall right over there, after splintering bits of glass. You want some food? Fresh mangos right off the farm. Kariba bream that Dad caught on the lake last week. Farm chicken. Everything is fresh off the farm. You'd better have a drink first. The family won't stay up for long. Dad gets up with the dawn from years of habit. He's usually asleep at this time of night. We'll have to see. Right there is the bullet hole. Drilled a hole and didn't break the rest of the glass. A shard flew down and caught my cat. The hole is so small you can't even poke your finger through it."

"Poor, Randall. You're crying."

"Of course I am."

When Amanda turned round, Donna was standing in front of her mother's portrait of Carmen, studying it carefully. With Randall, she walked back to stand in front of the painting with Donna. Barend and Randall's father were in deep conversation, helping themselves to food at the table, each filling a plate. Myra and Craig were already eating their food.

"I will never be half as good as my mother. Your mother's face, Randall, is so much alive. A photograph can never do that. You are so lucky to have it. They were good friends, my mother and Carmen. The three naughty girls. Livy, Carmen and Candy. Mum says being young and single was the best time of her life. Free as a bird in colonial Africa just before the end of the empire. She said they caught the very last gasp of empire before the corpse expired."

"Didn't she enjoy having you?" Amanda had turned from the portrait to look at Donna.

"Oh, we're like two peas in a pod when we're together. I just wish I could paint like my mother."

"Maybe you will one day."

"Not in a million years. You can't teach people that kind of talent. You're either born with it or you're not."

"But you're her daughter."

"And my father's daughter. Somewhere in between I missed out on the spark of genius. You going to get some food? Look at Barend. He couldn't pile more on that plate if he tried."

"Do you remember this house?"

"Of course I do, Randall. The same way I will always remember you.

That holiday is one of the best memories of my childhood. Very young and very innocent. Your mother was very beautiful, looking at my mother's painting. I just so wish I could paint like that."

"Randall, old cock. Are you going to have a beer with your brother?"

"Why not? It's so good to be home."

"She really was a beautiful woman, our mother. She's always in my heart."

"And mine, Phillip... Amanda, want a beer? Let's celebrate. There's nothing much going on at this time of year on the farm. We'll just have to keep Dad awake. So, here we are. Back home on the farm. Donna, what you going to have? Silas has stuck the beer bottles in a bucket of ice. What would we all do without Silas, may I ask? So, beers all round? When in Rome do as the Romans. Everyone for a cold Castle?"

The kids had put on some music, blocking out the sounds of Africa that Amanda found so fascinating. Someone had turned off the floodlights. Their whole world had moved inside. Amanda stood back with her glass of cold beer to look around the room where Randall's life had so nearly ended. She couldn't imagine that once, not long ago, all round them had been the threat of terrorism. Everything looked so normal, more like her parents' home in Great Bookham than the African farm she had expected. There were no trophies on the walls of dead animals. No animal skins on the floor. Bergit had closed the curtains leaving nothing to remind Amanda she was deep in the African bush. The music was familiar, the same music she played on the radio in England when Randall was at night school and she sat alone in their room.

"What are you looking so puzzled about?"

"It's so much like home, Randall. So much like England."

"Of course it is. We're English, despite the fact Phillip and I and the kids were born in Rhodesia. We moved England to America. We moved it to Australia and New Zealand. We created pockets of England in Africa, little bits of the First World, surrounded by the Third World. But wherever we were in the empire we were still British. Maybe that was our mistake in India and Africa. We never assimilated with the local population who are in the majority, unlike America where the indigenous Red Indians were outnumbered by the flood of immigrant Europeans. Probably why we'll have to go. The English are a strictly homogeneous people. They don't like to intermarry. Dad tells a story of one of his school friends who wanted to marry an Italian. The man's mother freaked. 'An Italian!' If he'd wanted to marry an alien she couldn't have been more amazed. In those days the British only married the British. They called it good breeding. Sounds so old fashioned when you talk about it now. Now in England you can marry who you like and nobody gives a damn. It's a global world. Everyone flowing backwards and forwards. From all around the world people are trading with each other. It's a global village and what you see here is likely a total anachronism that will soon be forgotten. For better or worse. The blacks have taken back their own lives and why shouldn't they? They want their own lives, not somebody else's."

"I told Bergit you had written a book. Did you bring it?"

"I want her to read it. It's in my suitcase. If she thinks it's any good she might ask me to show it to her brother. He's a journalist with lots of writing connections. You've got to know people to get published. Without Oliver Manningford we would never have got an agent to look at it. How the system works... You hungry? Let's get some food. Just look at Dad. He really does want to sleep. Can barely keep his eyes open."

"The dogs are barking outside!"

"They do that. You get to know what they're barking at. That's just fun. They're excited I'm back. You know dogs and cats can love us as much as we love our cats and dogs. Some people love their horses... Get a plate. Let's eat. I'm starving."

"Did you love all the other cats I've seen like the one that was killed?"

"No. She was special. There are special loves in life."

"Am I one of your special loves, Randall?"

"Of course you are."

"Would you ever be unfaithful to me?"

"Would you be unfaithful to me? We never know what's going to happen in our lives. I'd be a liar if I said anything otherwise."

"Who is she, Randall? You weren't with your tutor, were you?"

"No, I wasn't. But that's all over now."

"I'm pregnant."

"I know you are. You've been rubbing your stomach ever since we left Heathrow. Are you certain?"

"I have a test kit in my handbag."

"So that's what was in your bag."

"What was her name?"

"It doesn't matter. What does matter is me not lying to you. We must never lie to each other, Amanda. Will you promise me?... And please don't cry. My father's looking at you. I was a virgin. You weren't. So what's different? What's right is it's all over. I'm not going to ask you the names of your previous lovers. How many were there?"

"I'm not going to tell you."

"That's my point. So please dry your eyes. I can't wait for the test to tell me I'm going to be a father. I'm so excited I'm ready to burst."

"You really are something, Randall Crookshank."

"So are you, Amanda Hanscombe... Are we all right?"

"Of course we are."

"That's my girl."

The sickness at the thought of Randall sleeping with another woman behind her back wouldn't go away. If she hadn't been far away from home and possibly pregnant she would have stormed out of the room. Gone away. Found another life to live, a life that in the end would have most likely turned out like the one she was having. She had slept with many men before she bumped into Randall, many of whom had been unfaithful to their girlfriends making her a part of their deceit and often the trigger. Most of the one-night stands she couldn't even remember their names. A night in the sack with a stranger. What better fun when you were single and young? Randall was probably right. It took two to tango. But it hurt, deep in the gut of her stomach, a lurching, twisting feeling that would not go away. But the evening went on. She drank some of her beer and followed Randall to the food table and picked up a plate, everything outwardly normal. When she looked up from the plate she had filled with food, the eyes of the woman in the portrait were smiling at her, the grandmother of Amanda's daughter who would soon be coming into the twisted world where no one had any control over what was happening. She would go with the flow. Accept life as it came. Enjoy what she could. People were people and that wouldn't change... While Amanda was deep in her own thoughts, the not-so-wicked stepmother came up to them.

"I've put you and Randall in the same bedroom. Donna and Barend I've given separate rooms. It's your old bedroom, Randall. We've moved in an extra bed. You can push them together if it makes you more comfortable. How's the food?"

"Lovely, thank you, Bergit."

"Are you two all right? You seem to have gone quiet. You had a long journey. Go to bed when you're tired. Silas has put the suitcases in your rooms. Don't stand on ceremony. It must all be overwhelming for you, Amanda. So, Randall, Amanda tells me you've written a book. Did you bring it with you? Can I read it? You know I come from a family of journalists. My late father and brother. I know good writing when I see it. Part of my upbringing. If I hadn't come to Africa and married Jeremy I would have ended up in journalism in one form or another. In life, you use your family contacts to get on."

"It's in my suitcase."

"If it's any good I could do an edit and could give it to my brother to read when you get back to London. He's still at the *Daily Mirror*. I'll give you his phone number and you can both go and see him."

"If it's no good will you tell me?"

"What are stepmothers for? Enjoy your food. You can all stay up for as long as you like. You and Phillip have a lot to natter about. Jeremy and I are going to bed. See you in the morning… I like the title, Randall. *The Tawny Wilderness*. It's nice."

"I was hoping you would read it for me. But please tell me the truth."

Amanda watched the stepmother walk away, the father passing them to follow her.

"Goodnight, Randall. See you in the morning."

"Goodnight, Dad. Thanks for coming to the airport."

"My pleasure."

"Sleep tight."

Barend and Donna were sitting together on a sofa in front of the log fire. Myra and Craig had gone outside to play with the dogs. They were alone, standing at the table eating their food with forks.

"So, what's her name?"

"Judy Collins. She picked me up on the train."

"Does she live close to us?"

"Pretty close. Please, Amanda. Let's leave it. I promise it's over. When are you going to test if you're pregnant?"

"So it wasn't just once?"

"It was just that one night."

"Now you are lying."

"Sometimes a small lie is better than a big truth. The woman ambushed me. She found out I was coming home late from night school. She catches the same train in the morning... You know what? When I've eaten this food I'm going to bed. All that travelling takes it out of you. Let's leave the subject alone. Forever. We can find out tonight if you are definitely pregnant. If you are, we can get married in that church we found following the bells. If they'll marry us. Or we can go to the registry office if it's going to take too long."

"So you want to marry me?"

"Of course I do. Our son has to have two parents to bring him up."

"It's going to be a girl... I'm so scared the test will be negative."

"Let's go and find out. No time like the present. I'll go and say goodnight to Barend and Donna."

"I'm still furious with you, Randall."

"I'm young. Stupid. Sometimes I do things without thinking. I'm sorry, Amanda. We've got a whole life ahead of us. Not everything will be smooth. My father's marriage to my mother was tumultuous. My mother was an alcoholic. How she got herself killed... Phillip, old boy. You mind if we go to bed? I don't like eating too much before bedtime or it gives me nightmares. Thanks for picking us up at the airport. We'll catch up with everything tomorrow."

"Glad you are home."

"So am I. Tell the kids goodnight for me. Hell, haven't they grown? Myra's going to be a knockout. You'll soon have to keep an eye on the male predators."

"I know what you two are going to get up to. I'm jealous."

"Find your own girlfriend."

"Not so easy in Africa. Anyone who can is leaving the country. Especially the young girls."

"They say nothing ever changes. Goodnight, old boy."

"Goodnight to both of you. And pleasant dreams."

Amanda watched Randall walk across to the fireplace and wish Barend and Donna a goodnight. They all looked up to where she was standing alone. Amanda smiled, her stomach still in turmoil, the thought of Judy Collins, whoever the bitch was, churning round in her mind, tearing at her insides. Randall came back across the room after a last look at the bullet hole in the window. He bent down and stroked a cat asleep on one of the chairs. They went through a door at the end of the lounge cum dining room which led into a long corridor. Randall opened one of the doors off the corridor.

"That end door leads out to Silas's kitchen. At least the bloody Agri-Alert has gone. It was under the wall telephone next to the dining room table."

"I'm just going to read the instructions of the kit... Oh, it says it needs to be done in the morning. Well I am happier about that as I wouldn't sleep if it's negative. You want to help me push the beds together?"

"We could sleep in the one single bed like we did when you first moved in. It all seems so long ago. Now Oliver is famous and James is on television. They've done so well the both of them. I'll miss them both if we move into a flat."

"Let's push them together. I want a good sleep after that flight. I don't think Mrs Salter will want a screaming baby in her house. Or Oliver and James. Our baby would keep them awake."

"I suppose so. I don't know much about babies. Don't worry about the light. There's a fly screen over the window. During the war I pushed the bed up under the window to make it more difficult for a terr to get a shot at me from outside the fence."

"It must have been frightening."

"It was for everybody."

"So, this was where you grew up?"

"Yes, it was. From teddy bears to FN rifles. I slept with the loaded gun next to my bed. It all seems so pointless when you look back at it. All wars are pointless. What was the point of my grandfather losing his life at Dunkirk when we're now all such good friends with the Germans? Politicians make wars. People suffer in them... Now, does that look better? The sheets and blankets are just big enough to cover both beds."

"Everything is so terribly quiet. At first I heard crickets and frogs."

"They don't make so much noise at night in the winter. That flight really has taken it out of me."

"Me too. I really am tired. You can turn off the light when you're ready. Goodnight, lover."

"Goodnight, Amanda."

2

When Randall woke in the morning, not a blink, not a dream, Amanda was standing next to the bed with what looked like a plastic stick in her hand. Her hand was steady as a rock. She was smiling, her eyes bright. Outside in the garden the birds were singing to each other, among the birdsong the distinct sound of the grey lourie making its 'go away' call. Randall, his eyes still full of sleep, smiled up at Amanda.

"That bird call is so much Africa. We call the louries the 'Go Away' bird."

"It's blue. I'm pregnant."

"I gathered that. That sweet smile on your face."

"I can't drink alcohol anymore."

"Of course not. Get back into bed. By the sound of the birds, the dawn has only just broken. It feels so good to be home. Maybe we could have the baby in Zimbabwe and I could go back to farming. It's not a bad place to grow up on a farm."

"But she wouldn't have a future."

"He wouldn't have a future."

"It's going to be a girl."

"It's going to be a boy."

Impulsively, Randall jumped out of bed and hugged Amanda.

"I'm just so damn happy, Amanda. You have no idea."

"Why didn't you make love to me last night?"

"I was thinking of the baby."

"You idiot. You can make love to me right up to the time she's born."

"Won't that be difficult at the end?"

"You have to be inventive. And stop giggling. You've got to be serious. We're going to be parents."

"You're quite sure?"

"Absolutely bloody certain. I tested three times. Each time it went blue. It's a whole new life for us. Forever, you and I will be bound together in our child."

"Are we going to tell everyone?"

"Why ever not? We'll tell them at breakfast. You think your 'Go Away' bird is trying to tell us something? Warning us. Telling us to go back to England."

"Probably."

"So you don't want to stay?"

"Of course I do. It's just I can't put our son through what I went through. There's no future for us whites in Africa. There never was. We were living in a fool's paradise. No, we'll go back to England and I'll just dream about Africa for the rest of my life."

"So, when does the safari begin?"

"It's begun. We'll ask Phillip if he'll take us into the bush in his new bus. We don't have to hire two Land Rovers. I'm sure Barend will be happy to pay Phillip the going rate. I've got a brother in the safari business. Got to keep it in the family. We can go up to Lake Kariba. Drive down the bottom of the lake to the Victoria Falls. Visit Botswana and the Okavango Delta. I've got a month to show you Africa. It may be our last holiday for a long time. Our last bit of freedom. We're going to enjoy it. When we're really old, we'll tell our grandchildren all about our African safari. By then, who knows, there may not be any wild animals in Africa the way the human population is exploding. It's a once in a lifetime opportunity. Now, Mother, get back into our improvised bed. Father wants some more sleep. And he wants something else."

"Are you going to make love to me?"

"Come here and find out."

Giggling, they fell into each other's arms, Randall hoping Judy

Collins had now been forgotten. He would have to be careful never to speak to her again on the train. As he made love to his future wife, all he could see in his mind were Judy's big boobs, the nipples protruding, the sound of her voice as she reached her climax. Only then did Randall climax. Thankfully, they both went back to sleep.

RANDALL WOKE with Amanda pulling his arm, trying to get him out of bed.

"Get up, lover. We're going to tell your family. We can have a bath together. Your stepmother won't mind."

By the time Randall came out of the bath the feeling of euphoria at being a father had been replaced by the fear of responsibility. Instead of hating his job at BLG and going to night school as an imposition he would have to concentrate, no room anymore for failure. From now on in his life he had to be a winner. Make money. Compete in the world that only respected people with money. He would have to make himself hungry for success. While he dressed in his old room he was thinking of Barend Oosthuizen and the opportunity of making a good impression on a director of BLG America. His whole reason for bringing the man on holiday had changed.

When he opened the bedroom door he could smell the breakfast cooking, making him hungry.

"You'd better tell them the news, Randall."

"That's what husbands are for, Amanda. Taking responsibility. Come on. That smell of bacon and eggs has made me hungry... I can smell the coffee. Did you know Americans drink more coffee than tea?"

"No, I didn't."

"Well you know now... What are we going to call him?"

"We're going to call her Carmen after your mother."

"That's so sweet of you."

Laughing, holding hands, they walked down the corridor away from Silas's kitchen and into the living room. On the veranda, Silas had laid the breakfast table. Barend Oosthuizen was looking out over the brick wall that ran the length of the veranda, the veranda running out to the right of the living room. From the veranda the view to the far mountains, now purple in the morning, was spectacular, giving the farm its name.

"Good morning, Barend. Hope you slept well. One of these days I'd love to visit your office in America. London and New York. That's where all the big deals are done. I can't wait to get through my apprenticeship, get my degree in economics and sink my teeth into business. Isn't the view wonderful? World's View. That's what Dad called it. Makes you feel the whole world is there in front of you."

"So you don't want to come home now the war is over and grow tobacco?"

"Don't be silly, Barend. I want much more than that out of life. The real life is in the big cities not stuck out on a farm. Where are the rest of them?"

"Took the dogs for a walk. I got up with the sun. I've had my long walk. Found a dam across a shallow ravine. Your farm is so beautiful. No wonder my ancestors loved Africa. Dad's always talking about his days on Elephant Walk... Here they come. Your stepmother must have told Silas when she wanted breakfast."

"Now I've seen Phillip's small bus, why don't we hire him for our trip instead of finding vehicles in Salisbury?"

"Suits me. Keep it in the family. So, you really want to be a businessman?"

"Oh yes I do. I'm going to make money. Lots and lots of money... Phillip. Good morning. We're going to hire you, old boy, to show us the country. Take us on our safari."

"That's wonderful."

"Just tell us what you charge."

"Don't be ridiculous. My partner, Jacques, will help me do the driving. We'll treat it as a test run while they're finishing the second vehicle... How long have you got?"

"Got to be back in London in the second week of September. How about you, Barend?"

"Two weeks and then I'm back to the States."

"There's an airport at Victoria Falls to make your connection. On the way through Salisbury we can check your flights with the travel agent... Good morning, Dad. Amanda and I have something to tell you. We're getting married. Amanda is pregnant. You are going to be a grandfather... Don't look so shocked. We can handle it."

"You're so young."

"That's the beauty of it. We're going to call her Carmen if the baby is a girl. So, everyone, isn't that exciting? A new generation of Crookshanks... That breakfast really looks good. I'm starving."

"Where are you getting married?"

"In London. We want to use our time in Zimbabwe to go on safari. It'll be our last chance for years... Barend, can I help you to some coffee? Why are you smiling, Bergit?"

"Amanda told me in the truck. And where's the book?"

"I'll go and get it... How does that look, Barend? I know you Americans like your coffee... On the way up to the lake, Barend can check his flights back to America."

"Instead of going round to Kariba through Salisbury, how about we go over the escarpment and down into the Zambezi Valley direct from the farm? We can visit our mother's grave on the way and give her your news. Vic Falls can check Barend's flights."

"We're going to pay you, Phillip."

"We'll argue about that later. Jacques can drive up to the farm tomorrow. Well, well. I'm going to be an uncle. Oh, and Vince Ranger says hi. He's working on a tractor down at the sheds."

"Are any of the farmers leaving?"

"Quite a few. They're going to Australia. Getting whatever money they can out of the backdoor. The club's not quite the same. They say there isn't much incentive to stay in Africa anymore. The old British Empire is dead and buried. Australia is happy to import their farming skills. How it goes. One door shuts and another door opens. That's right isn't it Barend? You're all happy in America?"

"Couldn't be happier."

"It's an American world. The Russians aren't going to last much longer. At least we all speak English."

"You know what they call some of us back in the States? WASPS. White, Anglo-Saxon, Protestants."

"Maybe, one day", said Jeremy Crookshank, looking at his sons, "the world will look back on it not as the British Empire but the Anglo-Saxon Empire, with the centre of power now having shifted from London to Washington. There were two centres of power at the end of the Roman Empire. Rome and Constantinople. History repeating itself. Whoever knows... Everyone. Enjoy your breakfasts... So, I'm going to be a grandfather. I'll be blowed. Makes me feel old, Randall. Each generation comes and goes. The progression of life. Everything changes and everything stays the same. I'll drive up with you as far as your mother's grave. Would you mind my doing that, Bergit?"

"Of course I wouldn't. While you're away I'll read your book, Randall. Tell you what I think of it when you return to the farm. On the way back you can drop Barend and Donna at Victoria Falls for their flight to Johannesburg and onto America. You can relax with us on World's View before you both have to fly back to London. It's a big responsibility becoming a father. Come here and give me a hug."

"Can we come on safari, Phillip?" asked Myra.

"Not this time. You and Craig have got to stay on the farm and look after your mother and father. Anyway, you have to go back to school next month."

"I hate school."

Randall, looking around the table at his family, had a surge of wellbeing flow through his mind. Apart from all the new responsibility he had never felt happier.

"Myra, please pass me the butter. Don't worry about school. We all hated school... Bacon, eggs, sausages and fried tomatoes. What else could a man possibly want?... And Dad, stop grinning at me."

"It's just so good to have you home."

ON THE FOLLOWING day the two boys and their father stood in front of Carmen's grave, close to where the lions had killed her. Nearby a waterfall fell over the escarpment far down into the Zambezi Valley. For Randall, it was the most peaceful place on earth. A wooden cross made in the farm workshop by his father stood over the simple grave. On the cross, burned into the wood, were the words 'Go well, my darling'. Barend, Donna and Amanda had stayed back in the bus with Jacques, Phillip's partner. All three men were choked, their heads bowed. Randall lifted up his head to look down the small river in front of them that ran its course out over the escarpment to drop thousands of feet down into the Zambezi Valley. Far, far away in the shimmering heat he could see the great river meandering. Back at the bus they parted, Randall watching his father get into the farm truck and drive back down the fateful road that had been the death of his mother. Ahead lay the winding gravel road that led down into the valley. Phillip got up into the driver's seat, turned on the engine and put the bus into bottom gear.

"We're off on the first safari of Crookshank Safaris' new bus, Jacques. You think it will get us where we want to go?"

"Of course it will. You have my personal guarantee, Phillip."

"That's reassuring. Here goes." The two partners were grinning at each other.

Amanda was holding Randall's hand as the bus ground its way down the road having reached out for it when he got back into the bus, neither of them speaking. To their right, the veil of water was flowing out into space, the sun making a rainbow out of the falling water. Far out in front, a pair of fish eagles were circling on the thermals pushed up by the heat from the valley floor. The further they dropped the hotter it grew in the bus. The minutes ran by as Phillip drove them down the winding road, no one in the bus talking, all of them awed by the spectacle. At the bottom, the bus levelled out. To their right there was no sign of falling water, all of it lace as it dropped gently on the tops of the trees. As far as they could see were animals: elephant, impala, buffalo and three giraffes, their imperious heads turned to the sound of the bus with a look of wise disapproval. Instead of running away, the animals took no notice of them. Three long hours later they reached the Zambezi River where Phillip stopped the vehicle. The river was flowing strongly, an island thick with trees in the stream of the river, a crocodile basking on its shore, the bulging eyes watching them as Randall got out of the bus and looked around him.

"We'll drive closer to Mana Pools and camp for the night," said Phillip. "There's a spot I know high on the bank where the hippo won't be able to get at us. Are you any good at pitching a tent, Barend?"

"Never pitched a tent in my life."

"When we stop, I'll drop a line in the water and see if I can catch our supper. There's nothing in this world better to eat than a Zambezi River bream cooked over an open fire. We've got plenty of cold beers in the freezer box. Jacques hooked it up to the generator through the battery. Bream and a cold beer. You'll think you're in heaven. Did everyone take their anti-malaria pills as I told them? The nets will keep the mosquitoes off you at night. If you keep in the smoke round the campfire they won't bother you. Just everyone remember: this place is wild. The animals are wild. We're the intruders. Both Jacques and I have loaded rifles and we know how to use them. Keep your wits about you. And you won't be doing any swimming in the river however inviting it looks. You'll never get this experience anywhere else in the world outside of Africa. Just us, the river, the veld and the animals. This is paradise on earth. So, who wants a beer? In these parts we drink straight from the bottle, Donna and Amanda. Keeps the beer colder. So, what do you British and Americans think of our Africa?"

"It's all just so beautiful," said Donna. "I've brought my paints and a collapsible easel. Later, I'm going to paint what I see and take all this back home with me. Make my mother envious. Do you feel anything from the past of your family, Barend? Any great stirrings? Longings to live in Africa?"

"You're a romantic, Donna. Artists are romantics. No, I'm quite happy in New York. I like where I live."

"You're lucky. I could fall in love with this Africa. So much space. Wow. Just look at it all. The trees, the animals, mile upon mile of savannah and running through it all, dark and powerful, one of the great rivers of the world."

The American, to Randall's amusement, was clicking away with his camera, the typical tourist who had been to so many places he needed pictures to remind him later where he had been. In his mind, the thought of his stepmother reading his book kept intruding. When they all trooped back into the bush, the crocodile was still watching from its island in the stream. With all his new responsibility he was finished as a writer whatever Bergit thought of his book, an artist's life too precarious to provide for his family. A lost feeling swept over Randall, a mix of the book and his mother. There was a road of sorts running along back from the river, used in the war by the police and army to stop the terrorists infiltrating across the river and valley, up the escarpment and into the Centenary. Most of the valley was a hunting concession for the richest of tourists who paid fortunes to kill the animals, or cull them as it was politely called in the tourist brochures. Intermittently, there were African villages, pole and dagga huts with roofs made of grass and river reeds; among the huts a few scrawny chickens and goats. Apart from killing the wild animals there wasn't a way to make money in the Zambezi Valley.

Between the hunting concessions they passed through old gates and broken down barbed wire fences, all abandoned for the duration of the bush war, Randall wondering if the old white owners would again be starting up their hunting businesses now it was safe for tourists. It was hard for Randall to imagine anyone in their right mind wanting to kill a lion or an elephant for the pleasure of killing and putting the dead head of a lion with its pelt on the floor of some high-rise apartment in London or Manhattan just to show off to their friends, to remind them of their power and their wealth. Would Barend want a dead lion on his living room floor? It made Randall wonder. In the years ahead in the corporate world would he end up as cynical and detached from reality as the rest of them? Would what he saw out of the bus window fade from his mind, replaced by pictures on television, his world shrunk to the couch in his living room, making him question the purpose of a life living in a man-made world where everything was artificial? He was sweating even with the windows open.

"You'll have to put in air conditioning for the tourists, Phillip," he said to his brother.

"They'll miss the feeling of Africa."

"First, they'll want their home comforts. Am I right, Barend?"

"They'll want air conditioning in their tents. The rich want to see and not touch."

"You can't air condition a tent," said Jacques.

"Caught you there, buddy. How much further to making camp?"

"An hour. At this time of year it cools off once the sun goes down."

"It's really hot," said Amanda. "You think it will be all right for the baby? I don't want to have a miscarriage."

"He's half African. He'll survive. You should be here in October in the build-up to the rains. Then it's really suffocating."

"I'd hate it. Is it going to be as hot as this for the rest of the journey?"

"Aren't you enjoying yourself?"

"Of course I am. It's just too damn hot."

"Put one of Jacques's cold beers between your thighs."

"I need something to fan myself. The hottest day in an English summer isn't anywhere near as hot as this."

"Are you going to be okay?"

"I hope so."

"Here. Use my bush hat."

"It smells of sweat."

"Of course it does. It's just come off my sweaty head."

"When we stop you can get a bucket of water out of the river and tip it over my head. Why can't I swim?"

"You'll be eaten by crocodiles or snapped in half by a hippo."

"This is horrible."

Randall, horrified, watched Amanda begin to cry, having no idea what he could do for her. For the first time he realised how different they were.

"You all right back there?" called Phillip.

"We're fine," said Randall. "I'd forgotten how daunting Africa can be to a stranger. You and I take it for granted. To us this is all so normal. You'll get used to it, won't you, Amanda?"

"I hope so."

Behind the bus the dust trail, untouched by any wind, trailed far out behind, hanging on the air as they drove along, Randall hoping he had not landed himself with a problem. When Amanda heard the lions roar at night she was going to freak. This time Randall took Amanda's hand and gave it a squeeze.

Half an hour further down the road, passing through a thorn thicket, Phillip slowed the bus, buffalo on either side of them not ten feet away from the window. Amanda gripped his hand, digging her nails into the palm of his hand.

"I'm frightened, Randall."

"We're inside a bus and Phillip's got a gun."

"They're so close, so menacing the way they look at you. Tonight, I'm going to sleep in the bus."

"We'll have a big campfire and keep it stoked all night. The animals are frightened of fire."

"Are you sure? What are they?"

"Buffalo. Some say the buffalo is the most dangerous animal in the bush. Especially if you wound one of them. He'll wait for you to come back and charge out of the thicket. They've got memories like the elephants."

"I could never live in the wilds. Give me the noise of London's traffic any old time."

"People are far more dangerous than animals. They have so many ways of getting at you. Why the prisons in England are full. Man is the most horrible predator of them all. He kills for pleasure. Wild animals only kill for their food or to protect themselves. Why do you think in so-called civilised countries they put locks on all their doors?"

"You've had such a different life, Randall."

"You don't have to be black to be African... Let me get you that beer. By tomorrow you won't be so frightened. Being frightened of the unknown is a primal instinct. How we survived as a species."

The cool box, plugged into the cigarette lighter connection on the dashboard of the bus, was up at the front behind the driver's seat. Randall got up, letting go of Amanda's hand, and walked up the aisle.

"She's scared out of her wits," whispered Randall to Phillip. "I'm giving her a beer. It's all a bit sudden. One minute she's in London, next minute a buffalo's staring at her from the other side of the bloody window. The only thing we ever see in London on the other side of the window is Mrs Salter's washing, drying on the line. I hope we're not going to have a problem. She wants to sleep on the bus."

"We're nearly at the campsite. How are Donna and Barend back there?"

"They look happy enough. Amanda's a city girl. She's only ever seen cats and dogs and animals in a zoo. We take all this for granted... I like the cool box, Jacques. Great idea. Maybe just the one night here and then through to Kariba. You can put the bus on the ferry instead of driving to Vic Falls below the lake."

"She'll settle down. This is one of the best spots. It's really wild."

"That's what's freaking her."

"Women, old boy. They don't want the same as you and I."

"What do you know about women?"

"Go drink your beer and comfort your girl. First job when we stop is to collect firewood. Lots and lots of firewood. We'll make one bloody big bonfire to keep the animals away. One of us three will stay awake at night if she's worried. Stand guard with a loaded gun... You see that small hill over there by the riverside? That's where we're going to camp. While you and Jacques are collecting firewood I'll go fishing."

"You're an idle bastard, Phillip."

"I've been driving the bus for hours while you sit on your arse.

There's a case of whisky on board. Get her drunk. She won't feel a thing... Can you remember how to put up a tent?"

"Of course I can. I've only been in London a year... The trees are so much taller nearer the river."

"Their roots are in the water. I feel like one of those beers myself... Now look at that for a spot. We haul the shower bucket up into a tree and turn on the tap at the bottom of the hosepipe where there's a rose to sprinkle water slowly. We've thought of everything. I raided Dad's booze cupboard and Bergit's freezer. A couple of beers, a shot of whisky and she'll be singing like a bird."

"She doesn't think she should drink with the baby."

"Women. Maybe a celibate life in the bush isn't so bad after all. Once she tastes a cold beer she'll drink it. Then another. Then you ply her with the whisky. Trust me, Randall. I'm a professional tour guide, safari manager or whatever you want to call me. It's my job to give everyone a good time... Doesn't the river look beautiful?... Everyone, we've arrived. Two hours to dusk. Let's get organised."

An hour later three tents were up, the firewood collected and Phillip had caught six fish. The first beer drunk in the bus had calmed Amanda down. When Randall hauled the bucket of water up into the tree, Jacques having tossed the rope up over a bough, the hosepipe with its shower-rose just above his head, Amanda got out of the bus. With the sun going down it was cooler, helped by the closeness of the river.

"Come on. Stand underneath and I'll turn it on for you."

"What about my clothes?"

"They're soaked in sweat anyway. Get under the shower or I'll spank you."

"Have you seen any wild animals?"

"Only my girlfriend. Come on, Amanda. Get under the bloody shower... How does that feel?"

"Oh, that's good. It's not all bad, as Oliver would say. Get me another of those beers. This is divine... Just look at Phillip's fish."

"The calm water among the reeds is teeming with bream. You can put in a line without any bait and the fish will bite."

"Donna! Come and have a shower," said Amanda, her face turned up to the last of the water as the bucket drained out.

By the time the sun went down, blooding the few clouds in the sky, the red of the clouds reflected in the flowing river, the fire was lit, the fish gutted, folding tables and chairs put out and Jacques had prepared the salads. To Randall's relief, Amanda had got over her fright from the buffalo. Phillip, having made a second, smaller fire to cook his fish, was smiling. The dusk came quickly, sending the light from the bigger fire up into the riverine trees. Within half an hour their world had shrunk to their campsite round the fires, the smell of cooking fish making all of them hungry. Away from the light, among the trees, Randall could see the outline of the small bus. Against their chairs, to reassure the girls and Barend, Phillip and Jacques had propped their FN rifles. All Randall could hear was river-frogs and crickets. Later, as they ate their fish, the kerosene lamp in the middle of their table, far away Randall heard barking from a troop of baboons that were arguing with each other, the gruff shout of the elders, the shrill squealing of the children. Amanda took no notice.

"Are the mosquitoes worrying anyone?" asked Phillip. "They're not so bad in the dry season. We've hung mosquito nets in your tents. You ever felt anything like this before, Barend? Just us in a world of our own."

"New York seems a long way away."

"A different world. This is the real world. How it was meant to be. Us and nature… There's plenty of fruit to eat if you want dessert. How's the whisky going down? A cold shower. Ice in the whisky. What more could a man possibly want?"

"What was that sound far away?" asked Donna.

"Baboons having an argument. You know what they do if you camp under their favourite tree? They shit on you. Baboons have got a sense of humour. They're not too dissimilar to us. We're both the same animal, just from different branches of the same ancestry. Being in the bush for so long makes me realise we are not the all-powerful. We can talk. That's about the only difference between us and the monkeys. We just think we're better than everything else on the planet. The African bush humbles you. Makes you feel your own insignificance. Here, it's all real. We're just another animal eating our food we pulled out of the river."

"I'm going to paint the moment the sun comes up. What time are we leaving?"

"When you're ready. We can go, stay a day, stay forever. A man can survive on fish and meat. All my life I've envied the old lifestyle of our black friends. Now we've buggered it up for them. Shown them the comforts of modern civilisation, making people lazy, dependent on other people. Modern life has lost us our independence."

"Civilisation isn't so bad, Phillip," said Barend. "You're a romantic like Donna. The company of lots of different people can be exhilarating in New York. Theatre. Restaurants. The excitement of doing business. Business is a lot of fun if you do it right. And there's nothing wrong with home comforts. This around us now is beautiful. But at the end of the journey I know I'll be glad to be going home... This whisky is rather good. You mind if I have another one?"

"Help yourself. Good to have you here. Good to have you back, Randall. I've missed you."

"Don't get soppy and sentimental on me."

"Cheers, brother. You feeling better, Amanda?"

"I'm fine again. It was all a bit sudden. As Randall said, I'll get used to it. You sure this whisky won't hurt my baby? She's only very little."

The trick for Randall was to drink the whisky slowly: roll it around in his mouth; get the taste of it; then swallow. It made him feel mellow and comfortably lazy. He had poured Amanda's drink, putting in a small amount of whisky and filling the glass up with ice and water. The ice in the bottom of the cool box, below the beers, would last another day or two before it melted, the ice taken from his father's freezer on the farm. At the small village of Kariba on its hill above the Kariba Dam, they would be able to buy more ice from the bottle store, the thought making Randall smile as he savoured his ice-cold sip of whisky: maybe modern civilisation wasn't so bad after all. In life there were so many contradictions. Like Barend, Jacques and Phillip, his legs were stretched out now they had moved a little back from the table, all the fish eaten and finished. Amanda, her whisky glass back on the table, was sitting with both hands clasped over her stomach. She was smiling at him, the firelight reflecting in her eyes. A fish plopped out in the river making her look away from him, the fish making a gentle sound without any threat. There were no mosquitoes biting them, everything was peaceful.

Randall got up and threw more wood on the big fire, the cooking fire having gone out. Sparks flew up into the trees, competing with the fireflies that hovered above the long grass Jacques had cleared away around the fires. For a long while nobody spoke. Amanda picked up her glass and sipped at her whisky as content as she could be. The contours of their faces from the firelight and the hissing kerosene lamp made all of them look different... Something crashed away from the river into the trees and, no one, not even Amanda, took any notice as the sound of the retreating animal faded away. Donna had hooked her leg over Barend's, their canvas chairs facing each other, Donna's back to the river. The stars had come out showing Randall the silent flow of the big river, the stars in the heavens reflected in the dark of the flowing water. A buck barked from the opposite bank. On the other side of the Zambezi was Zambia that had once been Northern Rhodesia and part of the Federation of Rhodesia and Nyasaland, a country lost to the new black autonomy as each of the three countries gained their independence.

When his glass was empty, Randall got up, walked to the bus in the dark, found the cool box, filled his glass and walked back the thirty yards to the table where Phillip had left the bottle of whisky. With him he had brought Jacques's guitar.

"Phillip says you can play this thing, Jacques."

"Maybe later when I'm drunk. Now the night is too beautiful to interfere with."

"Can you sing?"

"I try. Once, after school, I thought I wanted to be a singer. Instead I became a mechanic. Shattered dreams. We all have them at some time in our lives. We all at stages want to be sportsmen or artists. Very few of us succeed. A man has to be practical... Barend, did you ever want to be an artist?"

"Not on your life. I've only ever wanted to do one thing in life and that was make money. The more money the better."

"There must be a point when you have made enough."

"Believe me, in America you never have enough money. There's always something bigger to spend it on. The richer you are the less you have to worry about in life. Money protects you. And those around you. Unless you had made a fortune out of your book, Randall, what was the point in writing it?"

"There is such a thing as satisfaction."

"Don't tell me. It's why I like making money. The reward in life is the money you make out of whatever you are doing. Money lasts. Money is security. Money is getting on in life so people can see you are successful."

"If you had liked reading my book, wouldn't I have been successful?"

"Yes, if a million other people had paid you for reading it."

"Good art lives forever. Money gets spent."

"It doesn't help the artist when he's dead."

"Neither does the money."

"Then spend and enjoy. You can't take it with you. Life is to be lived and the better you live the more you enjoy it. And that takes money... Can I have that whisky?"

Phillip got up, the gaslight showing Randall his brother's face which looked sad.

"I'll get the cool box so we don't have to walk to get the ice. You're probably right, Barend. It's all about money. If my safari business doesn't make money, Jacques and I will be out of jobs. Don't get up, Barend. You're the client."

"So you don't mind my paying you for the trip after all?"

"Of course I don't."

The American held out his glass. As Phillip walked to the bus for the cool box, Barend gave them all a deep, satisfied chuckle. Donna had moved her foot away and was looking at Randall, making Amanda take his hand. Jacques took up his guitar and began to play softly, picking the notes, the sound mingling with the night. Then he sang, the words of loss and longing flowing over Randall.

When Jacques had finished singing everyone stayed quiet. Phillip had replenished everyone's glasses. A cool breeze was coming to them across the water and an owl was hooting from the island in the stream, the trees where the owl was sitting dark among the twinkling stars reflected in the surface of the flowing river. The owl, it seemed, had liked the music. Jacques, imitating the hoot of the owl, answered the bird on its island. The owl hooted back. Jacques answered again.

"Who wrote the music?" asked Donna into the ongoing silence.

"I did... That bird thinks I'm a potential mate. Why she's calling back to me. In the bush, there's always a reason."

"The music was beautiful."

"Thank you, Donna."

"Maybe you should come to the States," said Barend, a smile on his face.

"And lose all this?... I don't think so... Cheers to you all. There's plenty more whisky for everyone. When you've had enough, you know your tents... What a beautiful night."

"You can't live without money," said Barend very softly. "And one day in Zimbabwe you whites may well come to understand that. And it will be painful. I'm glad my Afrikaans father came to America and gave me the chance to get what I've got. You got to have money. You got money, you got certainty. You got no money, you got nothing. Mark my words. All the way through a life it's money that counts. If I were running your business I'd make my overseas clients pay me overseas and only bring into Africa what I need to live on and run the business. So if this new guy Mugabe doesn't run the country properly and steals from it, you'll have somewhere to run. In the meantime, enjoy what you're doing. But take precautions. If you got money where you are running to, you can start all over again. But it's your life. Your business. I'm just making a suggestion. Don't let me dampen your spirits. Without entrepreneurs like you and Phillip, America wouldn't exist. You got a good business if you market it properly. I appreciate you taking me and Donna along. Please, play us some more of your music. This whisky is good. Life is good. The company is good. When I get home I'll remember tonight. For a long time. It's enabled me to feel close to my ancestors who lived in Africa for three hundred years... Jacques, what is your surname?"

"Oosthuizen. The same as yours."

"I'll be damned. We're probably cousins."

"Are you related to General Tinus Oosthuizen? He was hanged by the British for treason during the Anglo-Boer War. He was from the British Cape so when he joined the Boer army the British said it was treason."

"He was my great-grandfather."

"He was my great-grandfather's cousin... Now, isn't that amazing? I have a rich relation."

"You do indeed. Not as rich as I'd like to be but there's still plenty of time at thirty-four to make more and satisfy my thirst for money."

"It's been a long day, Barend," said Jacques. "Do you mind if I go to my tent? A good sleep and sweet dreams is the perfect end to a perfect day."

Jacques picked up his guitar and took it back to the bus. On the way back to his tent he picked up his gun.

"Don't worry. If there's any sound of a threat outside my tent I'll wake up instantly. After years in the bush during the war you get good at it. Danger penetrates sleep. Goodnight, ladies."

A wind had come up ruffling the trees giving the night a new sound. Jacques came back briefly to put wood on the fire before disappearing into the tent he was sharing with Phillip. Randall yawned. As much as he wanted to stay awake his eyes were closing, the camp bed with its mosquito net protection calling. Donna stood up and faced down to the river before looking up at the stars.

"There are three layers of stars. I've never seen anything like it before. The heavens are alive. It goes on forever. All those twinkling stars. When does the moon come up?... See you shortly, Barend. It's time for my bed. And I'm getting up with the sun to paint... Can we stay here tomorrow, Phillip? Why chase on like a busload of tourists when we've found one of the most beautiful places on earth. I want to savour it... Let it soak in. And hopefully capture on canvas some of its spirit... You think God is looking down on us tonight? It certainly feels like it. This is all so special. So perfect. It makes me so glad to have lived."

"I'll finish my whisky and join you," said Barend. He had got up from his chair and was looking down at the river.

"Aren't one of you going to stand guard?" asked Amanda.

"We'll all be standing guard for you, Amanda," said Phillip. "You'll be safe inside the tent with my brother... Do you want a gun, Randall? There's an extra one in the bus."

"Please, Randall. It will make me sleep better."

"One more whisky for both of us and I'll get the gun. I know where it is. So, Barend. It's all about money."

"I'm afraid it is."

"What a pity."

"The kid will appreciate it. You can make your own money, inherit it from your parents or you can marry it, but mostly money marries money. It doesn't much matter how you got it. When you qualify, Randall, come and visit me in the States and I'll show you how we make our money."

"I'd like that. That would be wonderful."

"It's not what you know but who you know most of the time. Add in some luck. Being in the right place at the right time. Seeing and not missing a good opportunity. Good old Harry Brigandshaw, the founder of BLG Inc and BLG Ltd. What would we have done without his opportunism?... You know where the last seed money came from? He had gone prospecting with my grandfather in what was then South West Africa, but they now call Namibia. Harry found a diamond so big they were not sure it was a diamond. When he got home to Elephant Walk he hid it in full sight by building it into the mantelpiece over the fire in the lounge. Only two people were told about the diamond: his son, who died in his Lancaster bomber over Berlin during the Second World War, and my father. My grandfather had been killed and Harry adopted my father, his nephew, and treated him like his son. My grandmother was Harry's sister. When Elephant Walk was sold to Anglo-US Incorporated after Harry Brigandshaw died, my father went out to Rhodesia and retrieved the diamond by cutting it out of the mantelpiece. By then it was black from all those years of smoke. He took it to Amsterdam and sold it for a fortune: Amsterdam is the diamond capital of the world. That diamond gave BLG the money it needed to grow and got us where we are now, both in England and in America... So you see, some of it's luck. If they hadn't found diamonds on the Skeleton Coast we wouldn't be the company we are today... And the other secret of money isn't just luck. The most difficult part is holding onto it. Investing it so it grows. And that's our job, Randall. You get your economics degree and learn the trade and you and I will have some fun together making piles of money. Real piles. So big you won't be able to see over it. How does that sound, Randall?"

"Sounds pretty perfect."

"Have another whisky with me."

"I don't mind if I do."

"Let the others go to bed. You and I can sit up and get to know each other. And that's the other thing in business. You got to know who you are doing business with so you can trust each other... Goodnight, Jacques, my cousin. There'll be many more nights on the trip to listen to your music. Donna, you go get your beauty sleep. Not that you need it, a beautiful girl like you. Young Randall and I will enjoy the night and the whisky. Don't often get time to relax. In New York, I'm always under pressure. When I get home, I'll be rested and relaxed and raring to go. I'll blow their heads off making so much money. To those who go for sleep, I say goodnight, sweet dreams and don't let the bugs bite... You better go get your gun, Randall, in case something bigger comes at us out of the night. I'll pour the whisky."

Tired, but not wishing to miss the opportunity to get on at BLG, Randall went back to the bus and retrieved the FN rifle, checking that it was loaded. With the gun slung over his shoulder, he went back to the fire.

"Stoke the fire before you go to bed," said Phillip. "Goodnight all."

WHEN RANDALL MANAGED to find his tent the moon had long come up and the whisky bottle was empty, the kerosene lamp having gone out from lack of paraffin. Nearly all the talking had come from Barend. Not as drunk as Barend, Randall piled the fire with wood. The fireflies had long gone. Sparks flew up to the night sky, briefly showing the high branches of the trees. He looked up and smiled at the heavens, the sickle moon now smiling at him from below the three layers of stars. When he got into the tent, Amanda was fast asleep. He laid the gun on the ground next to his camp bed, got under the net and lay down. Within seconds, Randall had gone from the world and was fast asleep in his dreams.

3

The sound of breaking branches brought Randall awake, his whole body tense as he listened. Amanda was still asleep. The firelight was still playing through the gauzed window of the tent. Without making any noise, he got his hand under the mosquito netting that hung over them from the centre pole of the tent and found the gun. He waited, his heart beating, up on one elbow, looking out of the tent. There was still plenty of wood on the fire: someone had stoked the fire while he was sleeping. Slowly the tension left his body, letting him relax and lie back on the bed. His hand let go of the gun as his thoughts drifted away into sleep... There was a time in his sleep when he heard voices outside the tent.

When Randall woke with the light he was not sure if the voices had been part of his dreams. Amanda was still asleep beside him, a blanket half pulled over her mostly naked body. There was no trace of a hangover, and Randall was thankful he had not drunk too much of the whisky. What he wanted more than anything else was a cup of tea. Then he remembered. In nine months' time he was going to become a father. He put his arm over Amanda's middle and gave her a cuddle, her soft skin smooth under his touch. He felt her body stir as she came awake, both of them still not moving.

"Good morning, lover. Where am I?"

"In a tent by the banks of the Zambezi River."

"Is that where I am?... What a gorgeous sleep. Was I dreaming or did we eat fish last night?"

"Right out of the river."

"It's all so wonderfully peaceful. What are the names of all those birds I hear singing?"

"The pretty sound is a black-headed oriole. The louder noise an ibis... You want some tea?"

"How long did you stay up for with Barend?"

"It was late. He likes talking. And he likes whisky."

"Did you do any good?"

"I hope so... Did you hear voices in the night?"

"I didn't blink... Are we going on or staying?"

"Depends on Donna. She's outside with her paints. I can see her through the window. The easel is under a tree right above the river. How long do painters paint?"

"How long do writers write?"

"Forever."

"You going to write another book?"

"If Bergit says *The Tawny Wilderness* is good I will... Ah, that's better. Phillip's put a kettle of water over the embers of last night's fire to make the tea."

"Is it going to be hot again?"

"I expect so. You can have showers all day. I'll haul as many buckets of river water up into the tree as you want. It's my job to look after you."

"Thank you, Randall. That is so sweet."

"Relax and enjoy. I'm going out to help my brother make the tea."

Randall stretched, opened the flap of the tent and walked out into the morning. Phillip was putting some slivers of wood under the kettle. As Randall walked across, the wood burst into flames.

"Good morning, Donna." For a brief moment she turned and smiled to him. "How's the tea coming along? Got to have tea. You sleep well, Phillip?"

"Never had trouble sleeping. Even during the war. You get used to anything... I want to show you something... And Donna apparently doesn't talk when she's painting. I don't think she's conscious of anything much other than the painting. Look at her. She's got the perfect spot high up on the bank. Did you know, if you don't pitch camp up a steep incline from the river, the hippo can charge at you right out of the water. A nice slope like that slows them down."

"I'm glad to hear it. Just don't mention it to Amanda."

"It's over here... You can see where the grass is flattened. The branch of that dead wood has been recently broken."

"What does it mean?"

"An elephant slept thirty yards from your tent last night."

"Good God! I woke to the sound of breaking branches. It must have been the elephant. Do elephant lie down at night?"

"Must do. That patch of flattened grass is the perfect match for an elephant on its side. I've never seen an elephant lie down before."

"I'll be buggered. If I'd known what it was I'd have shat myself... Have you looked at what she's painting?"

"Did you and Barend sit up late?... It's mostly the river. When she started there were buck drinking from the bank down in front of her. You can't really make out anything on the canvas. Barend's not up yet."

"What's for breakfast?... I'd love to be able to paint. Writing is different. Anyone can write a book... So, are we staying?"

"Looks like it... Good morning, Jacques. Why don't we three go get a swim in the river? The trick is for one of us to stand guard with a gun up on the bank where it's high. Fire a couple of shots into the water. Then two of us swim. An old trick I heard from a Selous Scout during the war. They lived in the bush for months sometimes without going back to base. How they caught so many of the infiltrators. The crocs keep away from the area around the impact of the bullet."

"You see any crocodiles?"

"None this morning. Then I'll catch us some fish. Fried fish for breakfast with fried tomatoes. We'll make a pan of chips... That whisky bottle is empty."

"Why he's still in his tent."

"We'll drive onto Kariba tomorrow."

Randall stood back from the fire and looked around, smiling at what he saw.

"I can't imagine a problem in the world right now... I like Donna's sunhat. Artists. They live in a world of their own."

"Is Barend serious about her?" asked Phillip quietly.

"Who knows? At his age, marriage is more like doing business. Everything is calculated. Nothing spontaneous. Young people fall in love. Older people work out what's in it for them. Or so I hear from my friend Oliver Manningford. Except that with Oliver you don't know if it's him talking or the play. When you're young, like me and Amanda, these things just happen naturally... The kettle's boiling. I can see the steam coming out of the spout. Won't the milk have gone off? You didn't put it in with the beers."

"Powdered milk. You get used to it."

"He drinks coffee."

"Instant coffee. We're in the bush."

"You better catch breakfast before we bang away at the river."

"When the guinea fowl go up to roost in the trees tonight Jacques is going to take out a couple. He's good at shooting them with a .22 pistol."

"Can't you just bang them over the head? Once they roost, they don't move. We've done it before on the farm."

"It's easier with a gun... Who's going to make the tea? Here comes your future bride. She's pretty, Randall."

"Thank you. I think so. One big pot of tea and let it stew next to the fire. What a life you're going to have running safaris. I envy you."

"Don't you like London?"

"There are too many people. I like people, don't get me wrong. But it's nice to get away from them and be on your own... You really think it was an elephant?"

"Can't think what else it could have been..."

"I'd better get some water for Amanda's shower. What a beautiful morning. It makes me want to sing with joy... If only I could sing."

"What the hell are you doing now, Randall?"

"Sitting down to take it all in. Sometimes you just have to stop still."

"Good to have you back, Randall."

"So much beauty. Look at them both... Amanda, come and sit next to me. It's a pity we can't all stay here for the rest of our lives and keep away from all the shit in the world... The sad part is that in the end it would catch up with us. James Tomlin says you can never stay out of the shit. He's an actor. In and out of work. Nothing ever lasts according to James. Now isn't that a pity? I'll remember this spot on the big river for the rest of my life. All of us and the river. None of us getting older. The river constantly flowing. I do hope Donna captures it. If she doesn't sell the painting she'll have all this with her for the rest of her life."

Quietly, without a word, Amanda took his hand. Phillip bent down to make the tea. Jacques had walked down to the water's edge. They sat and looked, the sun dappling them through the trees. Donna painted. There was still no sign of Barend. Randall knew he was happy. Knew what it was like to be truly happy. Neither of them wanted to move from where they sat.

When Barend, bleary-eyed, made his way out of his tent, the fish Phillip had caught in the river down in front of Donna was frying, the chips cooked, sliced tomatoes ready to go in the pan and a fish eagle was watching the river from a tree high above them, the crocodile back on the bank of the island in the stream. The sun was getting hot. Randall had filled the shower bucket ready to haul it up into the tree. Through the riverine trees that flanked the river, Randall could see the impala grazing peacefully. As Phillip put the tomatoes in the frying pan, the fish eagle swept down over the river, its claws trawling the surface of the water as it tracked its prey. When the big bird rose into the sky a fish was clutched in its talons. Randall lost sight of the bird behind the tall trees. Donna, caught by the sweep of the bird as it passed in front of her easel, had watched the flight of the bird.

"You want some breakfast, Donna?" called Randall.

"I'll be with you in a moment."

"How's it going?"

"I'm not sure. I'm never sure until it's finished. And that's the big problem. You never quite know when a painting is finished... Are we staying?"

"All day. And tomorrow if you want to... Good morning, Barend. Did you sleep well? Instant coffee, I'm afraid. The rest of us are English and only drink tea. What would the English have done without China? You know tea is a Chinese word... We finished the bottle."

"Feels like it. Why is drinking alcohol so pleasant at the time and so horrible the next morning? I hate hangovers. Any kind of coffee will do. A man I know from Texas pours himself a beer first thing in the morning into a big mug. Then he tops it up with cheap red wine and drinks it down. Swears by it. Says he's never had a hangover in his life."

"Not surprised. The bugger must have been permanently drunk."

"How's your hangover, Randall?"

"I'm fine. I enjoyed our time together. Learnt a lot... How many sugars?"

"Two big ones... So, how's it going up there Donna?"

"Come and see."

Randall watched the big man walk to where Donna was standing on the high bank above the river. In Barend's hand was his mug of coffee. To Randall's surprise, neither of them touched each other. Barend gave a cursory look at the canvas on the easel and looked down at the river.

"There's a crocodile over there on that island," he said, seeming surprised.

"It was there yesterday when we arrived," called Randall. "To the crocodile, we're the intruders."

"Shit. I ain't going in that damn river. That's one big bastard."

Randall smiled, sipping his tea, watching his brother take the chips out of the boiling fat. He was hungry. The fish looked good. The chips looked good.

"Can I get the plates, Phillip?" asked Amanda.

"They're in the back of the bus in the wicker basket. Bring the salt."

"You got any ketchup?" called Barend.

"And bring the bottle of tomato sauce. And Randall, stop doing nothing and help your future bride."

"Yes, sir."

"And bring the cutlery."

"At your command, brother."

"And be quick about it... You want a cold beer with your breakfast, Barend?"

"Why not?"

"And bring a cold beer, Randall."

"At your service, master."

They were both laughing. Randall put down his tea, took Amanda by the hand and walked to the back of the bus where he opened the double doors.

"Is he really going to drink a beer with his breakfast, Randall?"

"He's American. How do I know?... You take the tomato sauce and the salt. I'll bring the plates and the cutlery."

"What about his beer?"

"You take him the beer. He can be very useful to us when I'm qualified. Humour him. He's got a hangover. Must have drunk half a bottle of whisky. You want a shower before or after we eat?"

"After. I'm hungry... He's not in love with her."

"How do you know?"

"I can tell by looking at them together."

"What a shame for Donna. It makes all this pointless."

"Oh, I don't know. Not every relationship lasts forever... Fish and chips. Never thought I'd be eating fish and chips in the African bush. Fish and chips are so English."

"Should I write to your father and ask him for your hand in marriage?"

"That's a good idea. Then we can tell them after they get the letter that I'm pregnant. My shining knight in armour. Asking for my hand in marriage. It's so last century. When the baby is born, we can tell them it was premature if we tie the knot quick enough. I was thinking of a wedding in Great Bookham and not the bell-ringing church near to Mrs Salter's."

"If I make a formal request he'll want a formal wedding. Unless he tells me to go to hell. Maybe you should write them a letter and tell them you're pregnant. It's usually easier in the end to tell people the truth. Life is complicated enough as it is... You got the beer?"

When Randall finished laying the table for breakfast, Donna had stopped painting. A breeze was ruffling the trees and pushing at her easel where it stood alone up on the top of the riverbank. A broken branch of a tree floated past their camp, most of it submerged. Barend finished his beer straight out of the bottle and threw the empty into the river. The bottle floated downriver, the look of it making Randall annoyed. When they arrived at the river there had been no visible sign of man. Not a footprint. As Randall watched the bobbing bottle it sank.

"That one hit the spot," said Barend, pleased with himself.

They all sat round the table and ate their breakfast, no one else seeming to be worried about the tossed-away bottle. After breakfast Donna went back to her easel, the big sunhat protecting her from the sun. It was hot, the breeze having gone down as Randall pulled the shower bucket up into the tree. Amanda got under the shower in her pants and bra, turning on the small tap just above the hanging shower-rose, shouting with glee. When the bucket was empty, she stayed under the tree in the shade, not bothering with a towel. Barend had found himself another beer.

"Give me the bottle when you're finished."

"Oh, I'm sorry. I wasn't thinking. Back home we sling empty bottles in the trash can."

"We take the rubbish away with us."

"There's so much space. No one will see it."

"But we will."

The three men left Barend sitting in a canvas chair in the shade of a tree and went down to the river below where Donna was painting. Jacques fired his FN rifle twice into the river. Across on the island, the crocodile took no notice. With Jacques standing watching from the bank above, Phillip and Randall jumped into the river, Randall wondering whether a couple of metal bullets were any better than a glass bottle, the feel of the cold water on his body invigorating. On the high bank Amanda stood next to Donna looking down on them.

"Come out of the water, Randall. You're frightening me."

"My turn," called Jacques running down the slope in his shorts. Before Randall could get to the discarded gun to stand guard he heard the splash as Jacques jumped into the river. Phillip was still in the water. Watching patiently, Randall stood guard, the gun at the ready. Behind him, the small herd of impala had run away, the buck startled by the gun shots that had smacked into the river. The crocodile on its island, its big eyes bulging, had still not moved. When Jacques and Phillip came out of the water, Randall felt relieved. He walked back up to the camp, found the book he was reading in the bus and walked over to Amanda. She had put out an extra canvas chair next to where she was sitting. Donna was still painting. Barend had gone back into his tent, leaving the flaps wide open.

"Wasn't that a bit stupid, Randall?" asked Amanda as he sat down.

"Probably. Boys will be boys."

"You're going to be a father. You should think of that."

"I'm sorry... What are you doing?"

"Writing the letter to my parents telling them the news. Can we post a letter from Kariba? You can write your own letter and we can post them both at the same time."

"You don't wait around."

"No time like the present. And no more beer and whisky drinking for Amanda. We have to be responsible from now on, Randall."

"Can I drink beer?"

"You can get drunk. I'm carrying the baby."

"I was only kidding."

"You can use my writing paper when I'm finished."

"That's very kind of you."

"You frightened me, Randall. There's a crocodile right out there in front of you. It doesn't matter for Jacques and Phillip. They are not about to become fathers."

"I'll behave myself in future."

"You'd better... What are you reading?"

"It's by Wilbur Smith. Good stuff. The hero always wins. The women are always the most beautiful."

"Sounds my kind of book."

"You think she's liking it?"

"Who?"

"My stepmother. You think she's enjoying *The Tawny Wilderness*?'"

"Why shouldn't she be? It's a good book... Why is it so hot?"

"Because we're in Africa. In the tropics. The sun is shining."

"When I've finished this letter I'll take another shower. Please don't frighten me again, Randall."

"I'm sorry."

"That's better. Now give me a kiss and you can read your book."

Before Randall opened his book he sat thinking. Amanda had her head down writing the letter to her parents. She had placed a wooden board she had found in the bus for chopping vegetables and made a table out of it across the wooden arms of the chair so she could write. Ever since Amanda had told him she was pregnant he had tried to keep the picture of Judy Collins out of his mind. As he toyed with the book he was wondering what life with Judy would have been like. Whether he would have had to behave himself and be responsible. Not that it mattered. His life was now mapped out. He was going to get married to Amanda. He was going to be a father... With the thought of Judy's big boobs uppermost in his mind, Randall took up the book and tried to read. He was caught. Well and truly caught. There was no way out even if he wanted it. Within minutes, Wilbur Smith had taken him out of the world around him and into the story. He was completely absorbed.

When Randall looked up half an hour later the sun had moved round and was burning his arm. Amanda had gone, the chopping board and her box of writing paper on the ground next to her chair. Randall picked it all up and made himself comfortable, moving his chair away from the sun. On top of the writing paper was a ballpoint pen. Randall picked up the pen and began writing, starting with 'Dear Mr Hanscombe'. He was pleased with what he wrote. While he was working, Amanda had sat back in her chair watching him.

"Can I read what you've written?"

"Of course not. It's between me and your father. If he wants to show his daughter the letter afterwards that's his business."

"You talk a lot of crap."

"You know, when you are married to me I'm the master of the house. Little wives have to do what they're told. You will belong to me when you are Mrs Randall Crookshank. It's the whole point of this letter. You pass from your father's control into mine."

"He lost legal control of me when I turned twenty-one."

"Husbands are legally in control of their wives."

"The laws have changed, Randall. Women are independent. Married or otherwise."

"They never seem to say that in the divorce courts."

"We're not even married and you're talking about divorce."

"Under old English law I shall be allowed to spank you if you're naughty."

"You're giggling, Randall. I want to read that letter."

"Be my guest... You think he will let me marry you?"

"Of course he will. It's up to us, not up to my father. Now, shut up while I read."

"Yes, ma'am."

Smiling, Randall watched Amanda read through the letter.

"This is so old-fashioned, Randall. But it's lovely."

"Got to get off on the right foot... It's getting bloody hot again. My turn for the shower. Barend must be stinking hot in that tent."

"It's under the tree."

"I suppose so. You can shower after me. It's the perfect day for being lazy. For doing absolutely nothing... You think Oliver and James have missed us?"

"Good friends miss each other."

"I suppose so... Don't go away."

"Where the hell am I meant to go?... Are there really laws that make me your property? What about women's lib? Women's rights?"

"I was only kidding. When we're married you can go on doing exactly as you like."

"But I have to change my name."

"Or the kids get confused."

"Are we having more than one?"

"You and I are going to have a herd of them... I'll be buggered. Look at that. That crocodile on the island is walking down to the water for a swim. His mouth is wide open. Just look at those teeth. Did you know it's the tail of the crocodile that hits you first? The power in the tail knocks you cold. Then he eats you."

"Please, Randall."

"Sorry. When I've showered, I'll draw another bucket of water for you."

"But the crocodile is in the water!"

"Don't worry. I'll take my gun... And don't start reading my book until I've finished it."

"I'm going to enjoy being married to you. We have a good rapport."

"Would you like to live in Africa? Be the wife of a tobacco grower?"

"Not really. Africa is strange. I like what I'm used to. What is familiar. Anyway, you're all living under notice with the new government. Why would they want you all hanging around?"

"Because we know how to farm. How to make the best use of the land. The population has exploded since the white man arrived in this part of Africa. If we don't use the land productively we won't be able to feed everyone."

"They'll want to get rid of you once the new government gets established."

"Probably. Anyway, you're not going to be a farmer's wife. I'm going to make oodles of money like Barend. We'll have a pied-à-terre in the West End of London and an estate in the English countryside. And, of course, a summer house in the South of France."

"What's a pied-à-terre?"

"A temporary residence for when we want to go to the theatre or go to a concert. All those big rock concerts in the Wembley Stadium."

"By the time you make all that money we'll be too old for rock concerts."

"Then we'll go to the Albert Hall and listen to a symphony."

"Whoever listens to symphony concerts? It's so boring."

"Not when you're old. These days people get rich quickly. Barend's word for it is leverage. You buy something big with as little of your money as possible borrowing most of the purchase price from the bank, and when the price goes up, you sell, pay back the bank a pittance in interest and the profit is all yours. You use other people's money to get rich."

"And if the price goes down?"

"It won't according to Barend. The world economy is expanding. People have more money to spend. And since the time my father was born the world population has trebled. More people wanting more houses pushing up the prices. You got to take a risk to get rich. Once you're on the property and share ladder the sky's the limit."

"What's a share ladder?"

"Stocks and shares. You buy a piece of a company by buying some of its shares. When the company expands and it makes a bigger profit the value of the shares goes up. When it does, you borrow more money from the bank using the increased value as collateral and you make more money. Money makes money. You just got to know what you're doing. It's not hard work that makes money these days but knowing how to make money out of the system. You make money by using your brains, not by digging ditches. Brains not brawn. Throughout history it was never the workers who made the money. It was the thinkers."

"I don't understand a word of what you're talking about. What's collateral?"

Randall, not really knowing what he was talking about, walked to the shower tree and picked up the spare bucket before walking down to the river. He looked carefully before dipping the bucket in the water. What Barend had said as he drank the whisky round the big fire had got Randall excited. Getting rich sounded so easy. With a smug smile on his face he walked back to the tree, filled the shower bucket with its hose pipe attachment and hauled it all up into the tree. With no one looking he took off his clothes and turned on the spigot, the river water drenching his upturned face. Life was good. Life was going to get better. And living in England he would no longer have to worry about all the problems in Africa. When the new black government kicked the last of the whites out of the country he would be rich and far away.

The gunshot startled Randall back to reality. Everything went quiet. The few birds stopped singing. Randall pulled on his pants and trousers and walked out from the trees. Donna had stopped painting. Barend had his head out of the tent. There was no sign of Phillip or Jacques. They all waited, looking around. When Jacques appeared through the trees the carcase of a young impala was slung over his left shoulder. Phillip was carrying the gun.

"You want to help us skin the buck, Randall?"

"Wow. Venison for supper. My personal favourite. So no guinea fowl then?"

By the time Amanda had finished her shower, the skinned buck, minus its head and feet, was on a metal spit over the still-hot ashes of the previous night's fire.

Randall looked at his brother. "I thought they ran away when we went swimming, Phillip."

"There's so much game in the valley, you don't have to look far... Takes hours to cook. You got to keep turning the spit by changing the position of the pin on the ratchet."

"What's for lunch?"

"Randall, you have worms. You're always hungry. Cheese sandwiches with tomatoes and cucumber. The big meal's tonight. Baked potato in the ashes of the fire. A nice big salad. You can help make the sandwiches for lunch a little later. Just relax and enjoy yourselves."

When Randall got back to his book, Donna was painting. Barend had gone back into his tent, the meat was slowly cooking, Jacques was checking the engine under the open bonnet of the bus and Phillip was down at the river with his fishing rod. Far and wide the birds were singing as the sun moved through the sky. As the sun moved, Randall changed the position of their chairs. Lunch came and went. The day came and went. They sat round the fire, all of them eating too much of the venison. By eight o'clock they were tired and ready for bed. Once in bed, Randall lay comfortably with his hands behind his head.

"Goodnight, Amanda. That was the most beautiful day of my life."

"They're making love. I can hear them."

"That is naughty."

"Poor Jacques and Phillip. They must be so frustrated. Come here, lover. Let's end the perfect day making love."

Twenty minutes later they were both asleep under the mosquito net, the loaded gun lying on the other side of the net next to Randall.

Randall woke once, got out of bed without waking Amanda and went to the stack of wood next to the dying fire. When he had finished piling on the wood the fire was blazing again. Far away, barely within earshot, he heard the roar of a lion. Clouds partially obscured the sickle moon. The flow of the moonlit river was making a sound of its own. Randall looked up at the stars, smiled and went back into the tent. He climbed over the loaded gun as he got under the net. Amanda turned over but didn't wake up. When Randall woke again it was morning, the sun shining, a new day begun.

By eleven o'clock they had broken camp. Barend had said he needed the use of a telephone to call his office in America. By five o'clock they came out onto the main road between Salisbury and Chirundu, the bus turning left onto the tarred road that would take them to the small town of Kariba overlooking the Zambezi gorge and the wall of the Kariba Dam. When they arrived two hours later Barend made his phone call at the Kariba Breezes Hotel. They were back in civilisation. The magic had gone.

The next morning, Amanda posted their two letters to her mother and father at the post office. By the evening, the fifteen-seater bus was on the ferry to take them down the lake to the small town at the Victoria Falls. Barend was in a hurry. Something had gone wrong at the office.

When Barend and Donna caught the weekly flight from the Victoria Falls airport to Johannesburg the safari had lasted a week. The next morning they started the long road back to the farm through Bulawayo and Salisbury.

Myra and Craig were pleased to see them. The dogs went mad running and barking round the garden. By the time Randall's father came back from the lands, Jacques and Phillip had left in Jacques's car to drive back to Salisbury and supervise the finish of the second bus. Randall looked hopefully at his stepmother, not wanting to ask if she had read his book.

"It's a good book, Randall. But it won't sell. You're far too sympathetic to the white farmers. Too much colonialism. The world's gone past colonialism."

"So I wasted my time?"

"Yes, when it comes to publishing. If you'd castigated us whites and extolled the virtues of the downtrodden black man and his struggle for liberation from colonial rule you'd have likely found a publisher. Every newspaper in the world would have been happy to review your book and tell the public to read it. As it is, no one will touch it. Just as well you joined BLG and are going to night school. But it's a good book. Pity you told the wrong side of the story. Write another one. With a different story. And keep your eye on what will appeal to the media. Go talk to my brother Harry at the *Daily Mirror*. I'll ask him to read *The Tawny Wilderness* next time we talk on the phone. The pictures are vivid, Randall. Your characters are alive."

"I can't write and work for BLG."

"Probably not. But you've got to live. So has your family. The choices in life are few."

"So you think I can write?"

"You can write, that's for certain. Whether you can make enough money out of it for your family to live on is a whole different question."

"Thanks for reading it."

"My pleasure... The American went home?"

"Something happened in the office."

"It usually does. I watched my father go through the same problems. He always wanted to write a novel but never had the time."

"Maybe I could make a fortune and then write books."

"With a lot of money you could even get this one published."

"So it's all about money?"

"Afraid it is, Randall. Always was and always will be... Are you hungry?"

"Not at the moment."

"I'm sorry, Randall."

"So am I."

"Did Barend and Donna enjoy themselves?"

"Donna did. She spent most of her time painting. Barend got bored."

"It happens to business people on holiday. Their whole lives are wrapped up in business. It's all in their head. However far they travel the worry and tension won't go away. There's a lot of stress living in a big city like New York. London was the same. When you've got your own work responsibility you'll worry like Barend. It never goes away... I've written down my brother's phone number and address for when you get back to London... So the urgent summons back to New York was an excuse for Barend. Poor Donna. Men that age get quickly bored with everything, including their girlfriends. Why the man isn't married. So, you'll stay with us on the farm for the rest of your holiday, then it's back to the grindstone in good old England. I still miss England. Maybe one day we'll all be going home."

Randall, half listening to his stepmother, had walked across to look at the Livy Johnston portrait of his mother that had hung all his life on the wall in the lounge.

"She was a beautiful woman, Randall."

"Yes she was. Just a pity I never had a chance to get to know her."

"I did my best bringing up you and Phillip."

"You did more than your best, Bergit."

"Thank you, Randall. Can I have a hug?"

When they both dried their eyes they were laughing. Holding hands they walked out onto the veranda that looked out over the garden and the trees to the distant range of mountains. For a long time they stood looking at the view, neither of them speaking. Bergit broke the comfortable silence.

"The next book, Randall, should be about a pro-black white activist who helped the liberation struggle and got herself into all sorts of trouble. You as a writer must champion the cause. Become an activist yourself. My brother Harry will tell you what to do to get your name known. When your name is known as the champion of the good cause every publisher in London will be after you. An agent will auction your book. They'll be fighting over the book of a famous activist. That's how it's done. Otherwise it costs the publisher too much to promote you and your book. Famous people sell books. Unknowns, however good the work, are ignored. Publishers are only interested in money. You'll find it's the same in every business."

"Those kind of activists were selling out their own people and perpetuating the bush war. I'd hate to write about them."

"Depends what you want, Randall. Think of your writing as just another business. Go and see Harry. Talk to him. He'll guide you in the right direction."

"Are you worried about staying in Zimbabwe? Is Dad?"

"The biggest worry is next year's crop. Always was and always will be. That's farming. Will it rain or won't it."

"Irrigation has taken away some of that worry."

"There are always problems growing tobacco. You're well out of it."

"He still has his share in the Chelsea block of flats."

"That is comforting. It's my kids I worry about most. Are they going to have any future in Zimbabwe? I personally doubt it. So do all of us if we are honest with ourselves. The Rhodesians were eternal optimists."

"I'll be there if Myra and Craig come to England."

"Thank you, Randall. That's also comforting... So, what do you want? A cup of tea or a beer?"

"I think a beer."

"I'll join you with a cup of tea... We've missed you. All of us. Let's go get you that beer. When have you got to be back in London?"

"Two and a half weeks' time. On the tenth of September."

"Make the best of your stay. Who knows when you'll be able to come out again? Young kids tie you down... Here she comes. Randall's having a beer, Amanda."

"Not for me. I'm having a baby."

"Of course you are. You're going to make a wonderful mother. I'm so happy for you both."

PART 5

SEPTEMBER 1980 TO SEPTEMBER 1981 – THE
TORTURE OF LIFE

1

$\mathcal{D}$r Hickman confirmed Amanda was ten weeks pregnant the day after she got home. Randall had gone to work and was going to be home late from night school. The doctor's rooms were just round the corner making it easy for Amanda to call at his surgery on her way back from work. Everything at Home and General Insurance was much the same. Her boss of six months, Mr Pettigrew, had as usual looked down the front of her dress, making Amanda smile at the predictability of men. Lechers, like her boss, never changed. Ever since landing at Heathrow Airport the weather had been perfect, Amanda so happy to be home. In London there were no bugs to bite her, no sounds to frighten her and everyone did not carry a gun. She was glad Randall had enjoyed himself and hoped his love affair with Africa was finally over. Even the idea of living on the farm appalled Amanda. She was a town girl, not a country girl. How Randall's family lived in the middle of nowhere for so long all by themselves was beyond her comprehension. Oliver Manningford had made a big display of welcoming them home. There was a 'welcome home' sign at the top of the stairs. As their arrival had been in the middle of the morning both Oliver and James Tomlin were at home. Soon after they let themselves into the boarding house, Mrs Salter came up to their room with a home-baked cake, smiles of welcome all over her face.

As Amanda moved round the small, familiar room after getting back from the doctor she hugged herself, crossed hands over her shoulders, her mind full of happy thoughts. Diligently, she began to make them a stew for supper with the ingredients she had bought from the shops on her way home. Oliver was at the theatre and James was not back from his television studio. With the vegetables chopped, the onions and meat fried, she added the water and put it all in the pot to gently cook before strolling over to the window. On the roof opposite sat a pigeon. Below in the small garden, Mrs Salter's washing was out on the line. She could hear the London traffic. Everything was predictable and safe. With the stew simmering, Amanda sat down in a comfortable chair and turned on the television. After changing channels she found what she was looking for and sat back to enjoy. Next to her on the small table was a box of chocolates. She was pregnant, about to get married and she was home. "It's not all bad, Oliver," she said, picking out her favourite soft-centred mint chocolate and putting it into her mouth.

An hour and a half later, when Randall let himself in from his stint at night school, Amanda was absorbed in sweet romantic comedy and the box of chocolates next to her on the coffee table was empty.

"That smells good. I could eat a horse. How was your day, Amanda?"

"Dr Hickman says I'm ten weeks pregnant. And please don't eat a horse. The stew's ready whenever you want to eat. How was your first day back at the office?"

"Terrible. After being back on the farm, office work sucks."

"You mind if I watch the end of this movie?"

"Be my guest."

"Did you see her?"

"Please, Amanda. That is now all in the past."

"Did you see her this morning on the train?"

"I did. And I didn't speak to her... So, Dr Hickman said everything was fine?"

"He said everything was as it should be... Why don't you catch an earlier train?"

"Because when I got there the office wouldn't be open. Can we leave it alone?"

"That depends on you."

"Enjoy your movie. I'll help myself to some of this stew. It smells delicious."

"Just don't drip water from the lid on the floor."

"Did you eat all the chocolates?"

"Every one of them."

"They'll ruin your supper... Why didn't you buy two ready-made meals and put them in the microwave?"

"I wasn't thinking. Old habits die hard."

"I'm glad. You're the best stew maker I know."

By the time Amanda finished watching her movie, Randall had eaten his food and got into bed. The early nights on the farm had changed his time clock, Zimbabwe time only one hour ahead of England. Even before she had eaten, Randall was fast asleep. Amanda turned off the television when she finished her food, the stew pot almost empty, the earlier conversation with her mother coming back to her. At first she thought of waking Randall to tell him the news. The letter from Randall had arrived first, impressing Amanda's father, the old-world courtesy of Randall asking her father for her hand in marriage fitting perfectly with her father's old life in colonial India. She could imagine her father smiling after reading the letter. The second letter, arriving in Great Bookham from Kariba the day after, telling her parents she was pregnant, was not so successful. According to Amanda's mother the word 'slut' had slipped into her father's diatribe before he calmed down and made a pragmatic decision.

"You two, Amanda, will be married in the Guildford registry office as soon as your father can arrange it. Probably next Saturday. We presume neither of you are working on a Saturday morning. Your father and I will be the witnesses. Really, Amanda, what do you think our friends will think of us when you give birth six months after your wedding? They'll all think you had to get married."

"That was the idea, Mother. These days men have affairs. They never commit themselves. A girl has to look ahead and make some choices."

"You mean you got yourself pregnant deliberately! Really, Amanda... Does Randall know?"

"Of course he doesn't. He thinks it was an accident."

"I just don't know what has happened to your generation... Where are you going to live? You can't stay in one room with a baby. The world as I knew it growing up has fallen apart. With Randall's letter to your father we thought a boy growing up in Rhodesia had been given the same upbringing."

"You did bring me up, Mother. Maybe it's your generation that is to blame for bad habits."

"Don't be rude, Amanda... I'll talk to your father and see what can be done. You will both catch the train on Friday night."

"Will Father be able to arrange the wedding so quickly?"

"Your father can always arrange things quickly when it suits him. Do you two have any money?"

"Only what we earn. And we spend most of what we earn."

"So how are you going to pay for a baby? There are cots and baby clothes. A baby is expensive."

"We'll get by, Mother. Our generation is adaptable. Maybe Randall's father will give us some money."

"But his money is locked up in Zimbabwe!"

"He part-owns a block of flats in Chelsea."

"Does he now?... I'll speak with your father."

"Aren't you happy for me, Mother?"

"Of course I am. Just why couldn't you do things properly? You know perfectly well your father would have given you a church wedding with all of our friends invited. That lovely Norman church in Great Bookham. Really, Amanda, I just can't imagine the looks I am going to get from my friends when they add up the dates on their fingers. They won't say anything. They'll just look. That satisfied look."

"Then you'd better start adding up the months from wedding to birth of their children."

"I never thought of that. Mavis Cook's daughter gave birth quite soon after she was married. I'll check the dates. The wedding date will be in your father's appointment diary. George Hunter is the little boy's godfather. He'll know the birthday."

"That's the stuff, Mother. You catch up with the times. If you look back over our family history you'll probably find lots more surprises. My generation is more open. We don't hide what we've done. Give me a ring when Dad writes the time of the wedding into his diary."

"You're being rude again, Amanda."

"Most likely see you on Friday after work. It'll be late. Randall goes to night school on Fridays."

Smiling at the memory of the conversation, Amanda picked up a spoon, took the lid off the pot and finished the rest of the stew before undressing and getting into bed next to Randall and turning off the light. Confident she had everything under control, Amanda went to sleep.

LIKE MR PETTIGREW in the office her father was quite predictable. The wedding was arranged for eleven o'clock on the Saturday morning, no messing about. They caught the nine-ten from Waterloo Station on Friday, her father waiting for them at nine-forty-six at Bookham Station. The two men shook hands, Amanda watching them smugly. She was pregnant, neither of them able to do a damn thing about it.

"So, where are you going to live after you get married, Randall? I really enjoyed your letter. I appreciate good manners. You and I are going to get along well together. We have started off on the right foot with that letter. I'd ask you where you went to school if you'd grown up in England. The schools in Rhodesia won't mean anything to me."

"I suppose we will stay in our room at Mrs Salter's. She's a very sweet old lady. In her earlier days, she was in the theatre."

"I've given it some thought and have decided to buy you both a flat of your choosing as a wedding present. Three bedrooms should be enough... Property prices are going to go up in England so it will be a good investment for your futures."

"That's very kind of you, Mr Hanscombe. Won't three bedrooms be a bit big?"

"Not under the circumstances... Where would you like to buy your flat? You have both eaten? I'm normally in bed at this time of night. Amanda's mother and I retire to bed early. You do these things as you get older."

"I'm sorry to bring you out so late. Night school, you know. A father has to have a good education."

"Very commendable."

"Somewhere in the Notting Hill or Holland Park area. I've no idea of the price of flats. We wouldn't want to be far from our friends. That area can't be as expensive as Mayfair."

"How's your job going with your Uncle Paul at BLG?... Froggy and Crookshank. I'll be blowed. What a coincidence."

For Amanda, as she got into her father's car, it was only getting better. She was quite sure the idea of buying them a flat had come from her mother. Mentioning the flats in Chelsea, part-owned by the Crookshanks, had done the trick. 'Men!' she thought. 'They are just so easy to manipulate.'

When she got home and went to bed in her old room, Amanda burst out laughing. Randall had been shown to a separate room. Only once they were married, after the shotgun wedding, were they going to be allowed to sleep in the same room under her father's roof... With the father of her child sleeping down the corridor, Amanda snuggled up, turned over and went to sleep, not a care in the world.

AMANDA MARRIED the young man she had followed from the Leg of Mutton and Cauliflower three weeks before her twenty-fifth birthday, the cut-off day in Amanda's mind after which she would have been on the shelf, the prospect of a good marriage steadily declining. An old man with a grey beard officiated, everyone signing his papers. When she walked out of the Guildford registry office she was Mrs Amanda Crookshank. Her father looked relieved it was all over. September the twentieth, a date Amanda hoped to remember with pleasure for the rest of her life. As was expected from the father of the bride, her father took them all out to lunch. For some reason Amanda couldn't imagine she had worn a hat to the brief ceremony, 'will you have this man' still ringing in her head. The room was more like a doctor's reception than a place to get married: not a picture on the wall, not a flower, just nothing. Even the floor was bare of a carpet. As they trooped out of the plain room another, much older couple walked in. The lunch, despite a good bottle of French red wine, was strained, none of the joy and exuberance of a traditional wedding. Randall, very quiet, reminded Amanda of a deer caught in the headlights of a car, transfixed, unable to move. She put her foot under the table and rubbed the inside of his calf. Randall looked from her to her father, only half smiling. After lunch, they were driven to Guildford railway station, their overnight bags in the boot of her father's car. Randall had explained how much work he had to do on

Sundays to keep up with his studies at the London School of Economics. When the train for London pulled out of the station, Amanda's mother and father were still standing on the platform, both looking forlorn. It was over. Her new life began.

"What's the matter, Randall?"

"It doesn't feel any different."

"Why should it? We're the same people. We've just made our cohabitation legal. For the sake of the baby. You wouldn't have liked our child to be a bastard?"

"Of course not," Randall said quietly.

Even on a Saturday afternoon, the train carriage was half full of people. The rhythm of the wheels on the rails continued as both of them looked out of the window at the passing Surrey countryside: a few fields, small clusters of trees and villages.

"It all looks so damned different to Rhodesia," said Randall sharply, making the woman sitting opposite look up at him.

"It's a lovely summer's day. What's wrong with it?"

"It's not Africa. I'm homesick. We should have stayed on the farm and to hell with the consequences. You only get one life."

The woman looked from Randall to Amanda, making Amanda touch the new wedding band on her finger, giving it a twist. She still didn't have an engagement ring: maybe that would come later. After the brief, bitter exchange, Randall had gone back to looking out of the carriage window, the woman looking away. The train stopped at every station before ending its journey at Waterloo. They got off the train, Randall carrying their bags.

"It was all so clinical," said Randall. "We should have left your parents out of it and gone to the church with the bells. Invited our friends to a wedding party."

"We're getting a free flat out of it."

"That's so material... There's the Central line. Let's get home. If you weren't pregnant we could get drunk together. Anyway, here we are."

"We can go for a walk in Holland Park. We can go to the pub. You can drink."

"There's nothing more alarming than a sober drinking companion when you are drunk."

"James may be home. You two can go to the Leg of Mutton."

"Don't be silly. It's our wedding day... Why do I feel so hollow?"

"I'm sorry. You know my father. It was better to do what he said. He's old. You know he's a lot older than my mother. He was brought up under Victorian principles when children were seen and not heard. Daughters did what they were told by their parents. They certainly didn't have sex before they were married, let alone get pregnant. There were no free spirits in those days. You got a job, did what you were told by your seniors and worked your way up in the same company until your retirement and the pension you had worked your whole life for. Women didn't go out to work. They stayed at home looking after the house and the children. Lots and lots of children. Most Victorian parents had ten or more children. The man ruled the roost, everyone bowing to his command. That's how my father still thinks. He's from a different world. Can you imagine it?"

"Doesn't sound too bad to me... Sorry. Just kidding... Everything changes so quickly. That bullet through the window that killed my cat seems a whole lifetime away."

"When we buy our own flat we can get a cat. Kids love animals."

"I once heard of a cat sleeping on a baby's head and suffocating the baby. The baby was six weeks old."

"Then we'll wait until she's out of the cot... So what is it? A walk in the park? Be happy, Randall. We're married. We're going to be with each other for the rest of our lives. Isn't that wonderful? Never again are either of us going to be lonely."

THEY HAD NOT HAD enough money for two gold wedding rings, only the one for Amanda. In the train, with Judy watching him, Randall wished they had bought the second ring. Trying to ignore Judy Collins was like ignoring a time bomb that was about to explode. A month had gone by since the wedding and Randall felt shackled, caught on a chain. The lads in the office called being married like having a ball and chain tied round your ankle, the ones who were married. And every morning when Judy smiled at him it made it worse. With Amanda pregnant the thought of sex with her was somehow wrong. And she was putting on weight. All they did at home together was watch television and eat. Randall felt stifled. Stifled by a forced marriage, by England, by his job. Barend

Oosthuizen's idea of making piles of money had flown out of his mind. Every day he got up, had a bath, got dressed, went to the station, avoided eye contact with Judy Collins, got to work, sat at his desk, ate sandwiches for lunch from a tray brought to the office by a vendor, went to the LSE, went home, watched television and ate food, and went to bed. Despite all the idea of pots of money in the future there was no real purpose to his life. And then, to cap it all, they bought the flat and were going to move away from their friends. His life was boring, utterly, totally and completely boring, the same old mundane routine. Ever since getting back from Zimbabwe, Randall had felt miserable.

And to cap it all Amanda never seemed to notice. The days went by, Amanda's stomach grew fatter and Randall learnt all about the challenges and rewards of the free market system with all its plans and graphs that showed the brightest how to make money out of nothing. Randall's appointed mentor in the office, Pat Grimshaw, called it asset stripping: buying a company, having no allegiance to what they had bought, selling the good bits to competitors for a huge profit and dumping the rest. There were so many tricks for making money. Mostly, after buying a new company, BLG was out of it within a year. Nothing was permanent, everything for now, no care for the future or making a company organically grow with good management. So far as Randall could see in his ignorance it was all short term. On the rare occasion when he was called into his Uncle Paul's office, and Randall looked at the portrait of Harry Brigandshaw on the wall above the boardroom table, he wondered if the founder of the company would have agreed with what they were doing. The Rhodesian land had grown nothing when the likes of Harry Brigandshaw had moved onto it producing wealth by good husbandry that, if managed properly, would last for future generations. Nothing Randall ever saw in BLG was tangible, everything written in precise columns on sheets of white paper. As hard as Randall tried to be motivated by the thought of money, he couldn't get himself excited. He wanted satisfaction, not an entry on a piece of paper that mostly meant nothing to him. At the ripe old age of twenty-two he had hit a brick wall.

When he got off the train at Bank tube station, Judy Collins having got off three stops before, he wondered what had happened to the laid-back couple, the two happy bohemians, the fun they had waiting tables, the joy he found in writing a book. He missed Deepak and the satisfaction both of them had had in working a full restaurant. He missed handing over to Sarah Rankin her percentage share of his tips, the bigger the amount the better. There was no fun working at BLG or studying economics at the LSE. Just making more and more money would never make him happy.

Picking up his pace he went across the road between the cars and the taxis to Brigandshaw House and walked into the foyer of the building where his co-workers were waiting for the lift. The lift door opened. They all got in. It was another day at the office.

As usual his mentor had arrived at the office early.

"Good morning, Mr Grimshaw. What's on the menu today?"

"Good morning, Randall... We're going to float off the retail business in our new acquisition and make it into a public company by offering shares to the public. There's a big interest in British retail. With the flotation money we'll be able to pay back the purchase price of the whole acquisition. The shares we then own in the new company will be free. They won't have cost us a penny of our own money... Let me show you how it will work."

"Please do."

"The *Financial Times* 100 index went up two per cent yesterday. Everyone is piling into the stock market. Our IPO will be a great success."

"What's an IPO, Mr Grimshaw?"

"Don't they teach you anything at the London School of Economics? An IPO is an Initial Public Offering. We're going to offer the public through the London Stock Exchange a thirty per cent interest in the new retail company. Of course we'll retain control of the company with our seventy per cent stake until we sell the whole company to one of the retailers' competitors and move onto our next target. The IPO will be many times oversubscribed. For every share we offer to the public, the public will likely bid for ten. We call it oversubscribing. When the company is finally listed on the Exchange the shares will go up fifty per cent. If it does, the lucky buyers of the shares will make a fifty per cent profit on their investment in a matter of days. Everyone wins. Everyone makes money when the stock price goes up."

"What happens if the share market falls?"

"It won't. The world is growing at a pace unrivalled in history. Populations are exploding. More people going to the shops. Everyone is making money. Now sit you down, Randall, and I'll show you exactly how it's going to work. And your uncle wants to see you in his office at eleven. You're a lucky man having an uncle as the boss. Especially an uncle whose children have not come into the business. And how is married life treating you? Sit down, Randall. This is going to be a big one that will make your uncle smile. Money. Lots and lots of lolly. The business world is so exciting. And if I get this one right my bonus will blow my wife's brain out. Sandy always said that if I didn't have money she would never have looked at me. I just hope she was kidding. She wants a new dishwasher. And a new car. Her friend Anne has a new Jaguar. The wives are so competitive. They like to show off to their friends that they married the richest husband."

"Sounds wonderful, Mr Grimshaw. I'm very happy for you... Before we start, do you mind if I make a phone call to my stepmother's brother? He's a senior at the *Daily Mirror*. It's always good to keep in with the media don't you think? His name is Harry Wakefield. He was named after our founder, Harry Brigandshaw. Another one of those family connections."

"You go ahead, Randall. You go ahead."

Instead of sitting down in Mr Grimshaw's office with its glass partition into the general office, Randall went back to his desk in one of the small cubicles where everyone could see everyone's heads. It was time to show Bergit's brother his novel, and hope that Harry Wakefield liked what he read. When they moved into the new flat after Christmas there would be a spare bedroom he could turn into his study. If Amanda wouldn't let him live in Africa there was nothing to stop him writing about it. In his mind he would be in Africa while he sat alone at his desk. The flat they had bought was opposite Holland Park. When he looked up from his writing he could look out into the trees. If Harry Wakefield liked *The Tawny Wilderness* Randall was going to write whenever he could squeeze in the time. The thought made him happy. His day had improved... Picking up the phone, Randall dialled the number of the *Daily Mirror*. Only while the phone was ringing did he think of Judy Collins and the smile she had given him when she got off the train.

"*Daily Mirror*... How can I help you?"

"Mr Harry Wakefield, please."

"Who's calling?"

"Randall Crookshank from Zimbabwe."

"I'm putting you through."

"Randall! I've been expecting your call. When do I get to read your book? How was my sister? Zimbabwe seems to have calmed down under the new government."

"Can I bring it round at lunchtime?"

"Of course you can. I'll make sure I'm here. One o'clock, Randall. I'm a frustrated novelist myself. All journalists are frustrated novelists. The trouble is finding the time."

"Thank you, Mr Wakefield."

"Call me Harry. I'm not sure what I am to you. Step-uncle doesn't sound right."

"The book was rejected by an agent."

"The books of new authors usually are. They prefer writers with a proven name. Or somebody already famous. After I've read your book you and your new wife must come round for supper. I've heard all about you from Bergit. Thank God the bush war is over. They say the Queen is going to give Robert Mugabe an honorary knighthood. All the best universities want to give him honorary degrees. He's the hope of the post-colonial Africa. We can talk more about it when you come to dinner."

With hope in his heart, Randall walked back to the office of Mr Grimshaw, his mind struggling to concentrate on business.

RANDALL AND AMANDA began the move into their new flat on the first of February, four weeks after Randall's twenty-third birthday. Furniture, surplus to the big house in Great Bookham, had been sent up to London by Amanda's parents. When they said goodbye to the landlady there were tears in Mrs Salter's eyes. To add to the pain, Oliver Manningford's play had folded before Christmas leaving Oliver without work and without a girlfriend, the famous Veronica West having moved onto another toy boy. James Tomlin's television series had also reached its end.

"The worst part is having nothing to do," said James as he bade them farewell. "Anyway, at least Oliver and I are in the same boat. It'll be quite like old times. We've both saved up some money so there won't be any panic. You're much better off in a regular job, Randall. The arts suck.

Poor old Mrs Salter. She'd grown rather fond of both of you. So, when's the baby due, Mrs Crookshank? I can't believe you two are going to have a baby. You're far too young to settle down and miss all the fun. But we all move on, Randall. All of us except me and my friend Oliver."

"He'll get another big part. So will you."

"We hope so. Hope springs eternal. Whatever happens in life you have to hope... You get back to your writing. You never know until it happens."

"It's difficult to keep a story in your head when it's being swamped with your work. A complex book full of people is the complete opposite of facts and figures. In my muddled mind at the moment the two hate each other. But I'll try in my new study first thing in the mornings when my mind is fresh. Between writing, BLG and the London School of Economics life should be fun."

"And don't forget me and the baby, Randall. If all goes well the baby will be born in two months' time."

"Everything will be fine, Amanda. You're young and healthy." James, smiling sadly, was looking around the room.

"The doctor says so. Well, this is it. The big move up in our lives. You'll come and visit us, James?"

"It won't be the same."

"No, I suppose it won't. Maybe you and Oliver should look for proper jobs. Move on before life passes you by. We've moved on, haven't we, Randall?"

"Yes, I suppose we have."

Randall, looking around the sparsely furnished room that had been his home since arriving in England from Rhodesia, wasn't sure if he liked the move. He walked across to the window and the desk where he had written *The Tawny Wilderness* with such enthusiasm. Down below in Mrs Salter's small back garden the washing line was empty. Inside himself Randall felt miserable. Standing at the window looking out at nothing, Randall understood: he had lost his youth, the spontaneity, the anything-goes when you are having fun.

"Let's go, Amanda."

"What's the matter, Randall?"

"It feels like I'm leaving part of me behind. The better part of me."

"You can't dream about being a writer all your life despite what Harry

Wakefield had to say. You said so yourself that he is a frustrated novelist. You men can't dream all your lives."

"Part of me would like to. Anyway, that is that. Let's go. So long, James. Nice to have known you. I have a feeling that when we meet again, you, me and Oliver, I will be different. Maybe it's called growing up. Who knows? And Harry did say I wouldn't write a good book until I'm forty. Until I have lived a lot more life. So who knows? With luck I'll make my fortune and with my lovely wife and children move to the countryside and write unpublished books for the rest of my life, as happy as a pig in shit... I'm really going to miss this room. All those people in my book lived with me here. I'll be leaving them behind."

"You're getting sentimental."

"Yes, Mrs Crookshank. Exit the writer. Here comes the successful man of business. Wish me luck, James."

"Look after yourself... Oliver and I are going down to the old Leg of Mutton. You want to come for one last drink?"

"I wish... See you, old friend."

"Give me a hug, you old bastard. Thanks for the friendship. Look after him, Amanda. He's a good man. You're lucky to have him."

2

$\mathcal{A}$manda went into labour eight weeks later, everything normal. Her waters broke on the Saturday morning while Randall was in his new study trying to write, the page in front of him blank, the trees in the park across the street leafless, the buds of spring not yet showing. He had been sitting in complete frustration at his desk for half the morning, the previous week's work at BLG still in control of his mind.

"Randall! My waters have broken."

Jumping up, Randall banged his knee under the desk, his ballpoint pen running off the desk and dropping off onto the floor. Rubbing his right knee he ran to the door, his heart beating, his whole body in high elation.

"Have you ordered a taxi?" he shouted.

"There's water on the floor. Please, Randall."

"Don't be frightened. It's all so wonderful. A miracle. We're going to have a baby."

The phone was in the lounge next to the television. On the pad next to the phone, Amanda had written the number of the nearest taxi company. Randall dialled, spoke quickly to the operator, and ordered the taxi.

"Come on, darling. They'll be waiting downstairs in a couple of minutes. How are you feeling?"

"Frightened. You remember feeling her kicking when we were lying in bed? Now she's really kicking."

"He wants to get out and join the world. That's a real man you've got in there, Amanda. Put your coat on. I've got your bag."

"You know it's going to be a girl... How long will it take for me to have my baby?"

"You'll have to ask the doctor at the hospital."

Everything, as Randall said afterwards, looked perfectly normal. The taxi was waiting, the run to Paddington Hospital took twenty minutes, the elderly nurse booked Amanda in, the doctor came and had a look at her, asked a few questions, smiled knowledgeably, and went off to attend to other business. Amanda, lying in her bed, just looked at Randall, suffering her pains when they came... Hours had passed when the doctor returned to Amanda's room.

"The first one often takes a long time, Mr Crookshank. You go home and get some sleep. We'll look after your wife. When the birth is nearer, the nurse will give you a ring. You've done your work. Nothing more the man of the family can do at this stage."

Half asleep, the man's weak humour washed over Randall.

"She'll be all right?"

"They'll both be fine. Your wife is healthy and she's in a first-class hospital. You get some sleep. Sometimes expectant fathers are better sitting at home. Your wife needs to stay calm."

"Are the contractions getting nearer?"

"They're not actually. Could be hours before your baby is born."

"And if the baby won't come?"

"We'll do a caesarean. Don't you worry, Mr Crookshank. Go home. Get some food. Get some sleep. You'll both need all your strength with a crying baby in the house."

"Why will it cry?"

"They all cry, Mr Crookshank. How a new life begins. You'll get used to it. Eventually. Now, off you go. That's doctor's orders."

Randall kissed Amanda on the forehead, her eyes staring up at the ceiling, the look so far away as if she could see something through the roof.

"You'll be all right?"

"Of course I will, lover. Do as Dr Thompson says."

"I won't be far away."

"Just think of me."

"Yes. Of course. I can stay if you want."

"Get out, Randall."

They laughed briefly and Randall left Amanda's hospital room, the thought of a good sleep not unpleasant.

Back at home, he got into their bed and went to sleep, the door of the bedroom open to the ring of the telephone, the light left on.

WHEN RANDALL WOKE the light was still on, the flat quiet, no sound of traffic. He looked at his watch: he had slept eight hours. He made himself a cup of tea and ate yesterday's leftover macaroni cheese before phoning the taxi company. In the hospital room Amanda was still staring up at the ceiling.

"How are you feeling?"

"I think he said the cervix isn't opening. The contractions are down to every three minutes."

"What does it mean?"

"Dr Thompson is due any minute. Did he phone you?"

"No. Nothing. I woke and came straight back to the hospital."

"I think it means a caesarean operation. They cut the stomach open and take out the baby. The night nurse said it's very common."

Randall sat down and waited. Amanda had closed her eyes. She was deathly pale.

Dr Thompson came into the room half an hour later. After carefully looking at Amanda he was no longer smiling. He left the room and soon after they came for Amanda, put her on a trolley and wheeled her into the operating theatre, Randall left outside looking through the porthole in the door into where the hospital staff began preparing Amanda for the operation. The drugs they had given her at the beginning of her labour to ease the pain had been supplemented. Amanda, away through the small window on the operating table, looked drowsy. Randall waved with no response from Amanda. When they cut the baby out of her stomach Randall was watching. A nurse put the baby on a table behind the operating table. Through the door, Randall could hear them talking amongst themselves. The baby was just lying there, no sound of any crying. Excruciating panic began building in Randall's stomach. The assistant surgeon picked up the baby and put it down again. Amanda was just lying there as the surgeon stitched up her stomach. There was no sign of Dr Thompson. Randall wanted to go in. The newborn baby, lying on its back on the small table, hadn't moved. He looked from the baby to Amanda, unconscious on the operating table. For what seemed like an hour, Randall stood in the corridor and waited.

"I'm sorry, Mr Crookshank."

Randall turned round to look at Dr Thompson.

"What's going on in there, Dr Thompson?"

"Your son was stillborn. We don't know why."

"Is my wife going to be all right?"

"We hope so. She's under sedation. The nurses will take her back to her room. I'm so sorry."

"You said nothing was going to go wrong."

The doctor looked at Randall, saying nothing. Randall had a primal urge to hit the man. The door to the operating theatre opened as they wheeled Amanda out on the trolley. The dead baby was left behind. Randall followed the trolley. When they put Amanda in the bed Randall sat down in the chair next to her and waited.

"When will she wake up from the anaesthetic?" he asked the nurse.

"An hour. Maybe two. Be patient. I'm so sorry."

Two hours later Randall shouted at Amanda to wake up. Her eyes had flickered open and stayed vacant, her eyeballs rolled up. The shout made the eyes focus. She was looking straight at him.

"What happened, Randall?"

"We lost the baby."

"Was it a girl?"

"No, it was a boy."

The next day, when they were shown the dead baby on the slab in the mortuary, was the first time they cried. They turned and clung to each other. Dr Thompson had said it was important for them to see the body as otherwise, later, they wouldn't believe what had happened. The small body was taken away.

Three days later in the church with the bells, Amanda and Randall said goodbye to their son. With them in the church stood James and Oliver. When the short service was over, the undertaker went off with the small coffin to take it to the crematorium, Randall not even knowing the man's name. Everything Randall had done – getting a job, going to night school, getting married – now seemed unimportant.

"Let's all go down to the Leg of Mutton and Cauliflower and get drunk," said Randall. "Right now I don't want to think."

Outside the church the undertaker's hearse was just leaving.

"I wanted that child so much," said Amanda. "Most of me is dead in that coffin. I can't cry anymore. I can't feel. I might as well be dead. You three go and get drunk. I want to be alone."

"I can't leave you."

"Oh yes you can. Please, Randall. Just leave me alone."

"I'm coming home with you."

"Then come home. Who cares? And to make it worse, Dr Thompson says I can't have another baby. No, you three go and get drunk. It's over, Randall. For nine months I had hope. Now I have nothing. I made you marry me because I was pregnant. This is all my fault."

"We'll still get along fine."

"Will we? Maybe. I hope so. But right now I want to be alone. I've been punished. You do something wrong and you get punished."

Randall looked from James to Oliver shaking his head. Amanda had put her hands in her over coat pockets. Randall put his hand into her left pocket and touched her fingers. The fingers were cold and unresponsive. Slowly, aimlessly they both began walking in the direction of Holland Park.

"Look after yourselves," called James.

Putting one foot in front of the other, Randall and Amanda walked on up the road, neither of them knowing where they were going.

BY MIDSUMMER, when the leaves on the trees in the park were dark green, Amanda had put on twenty pounds in weight. They still slept in the same bed but Randall never touched her. She had given up her job with the insurance company a month before she lost the baby, saying she wasn't coming back. She had nothing to do all day but stare out of the window and eat.

The day William Drake paid her an unexpected visit her post-natal depression was at its worst, her mind, body and soul in the depth of misery. Amanda was unable to remember the last time she had left the flat. The front doorbell rang four times before she got off the couch.

"Where's your boyfriend, William?"

"He's left me. Can I come in?"

"As you can see I'm not exactly model material. I'm a mess and I don't care. The worst part is not caring... What do you want, William?"

"Nothing... No, I want company. An old friend. As children we loved each other. I want a friend, Amanda."

"He's having an affair. We haven't had sex for over a year."

"The first thing, young lady, is to smarten you up. You look absolutely terrible. You're not tall enough to put on all that weight."

"It was the baby."

"I know it was. Your mother is worried about you. When she phones you won't talk."

"What's there to talk about? I'm a childless married woman with a husband who doesn't look at me. If I try and have another child the doctors say it will kill me. Do you know I nearly died in that hospital with my baby? I just wish I had... Well, don't stand there. Come in and sit down."

"Don't you want to go for a walk in the park? Walking and exercise make you feel better."

"What happened to Kelvin?"

"He went off with a woman."

"I'll be buggered... I'm so sorry. I didn't mean it that way."

"At least you smiled... Put on some walking shoes."

"When did he leave you?"

"Months ago. Life goes on."

"And the business?"

"Always busy. I have a girl helping me now. You two should meet. You'll like Evelina. She's quite a bit older than us. She has a flare for fashion. Always knows what's coming next... Go and change. We're going for a long walk. Where's Randall on a Sunday?"

"Probably with Judy Collins. He met her on the train. Or I think it's Judy Collins. He's likely cheating on both of us. Who cares?... I'll go and get changed... How does a girl lose weight, William?"

"She stops eating. There were no fat people in the German concentration camps during the war. Body fat is in direct proportion to what you eat and burn off with exercise. Leave it to William. I'll have you back in shape in no time... You remember all those walks we had as kids?"

"Of course I do. They were the happiest times of my life until father caught us behind the raspberry bushes and ruined everything. We were only looking. You don't have sex at ten years old. All he had to do was explain about the birds and the bees. Or get Mother to tell me. It was all so silly when I look back. All that damn loveless upbringing of Father's. He was more worried about a scandal if someone else saw us naked. He was just thinking of himself. Why are we all so damn selfish? So, you don't want me to do any more modelling?"

"Not looking like that."

"Is it that bad?"

"It's worse. Come on. We're going to have a good old natter as we walk. A good talk with a friend is better than any therapist."

"You think I need a therapist!"

"Probably. So do I most likely. If he'd dumped me for another man it wouldn't have been so bad. But for a woman! That really hurts. And he won't be happy. Kelvin is as queer as a coot. We'd had an argument. About money. Why does everything in life have to come down to money? Silly man was worried that when he was older I'd dump him for another man. How stupid can you be? We were partners in every sense of the word. Business and life. I loved him. Still do."

"Poor William. Just talking to you has lifted my spirits. Funny how seeing other people with problems makes you feel better about yourself. There's some kind of satisfaction in watching other people's misery. You don't feel so alone in the world... What are you doing with an umbrella? The sun's shining."

"You never go anywhere in England without an umbrella."

"Have you ever had an affair with a woman, William?"

"Not once in my life."

"You're lying. Weren't we having a love affair as children, except we were too young to know how to have sex? I wonder what would have happened if my father hadn't caught us. I often think about it. As we grew older and our bodies developed we would have taken our love to another stage. Become lovers in the full sense of the word. By now you and I would be a perfectly normal married couple instead of what we are."

"What are we, Amanda?"

"A complete bloody mess. Our lives finished before they started. If I lose weight and make myself attractive can I try and seduce you?"

"You can try. Won't do any good. Sexually, I'm only attracted to men."

"Kelvin most likely thought the same. Now look at him. Don't some women turn you on that teeny weeny little bit?... There we are. Good, solid walking shoes. I can't remember the last time I went for a walk. I don't even go out. Randall comes back late during the week and falls straight into bed. During the weekends he locks himself up in his damn study saying he's writing a book. That's if he doesn't go out. We don't even communicate anymore. The only marriage we have is on that stupid piece of paper they call a marriage certificate. The man I once knew doesn't exist. We're strangers. How can you be so close to someone and then fall apart?"

Outside the block of flats they crossed the road, Amanda looking back up at her window which was still open. There was little traffic on a Sunday afternoon. Inside the park William took her hand, neither of them talking as they walked under the tall trees. Couples were sitting on park benches. A family, a young couple with two children, were having a picnic, the look of their happiness bringing back Amanda's pain.

"Maybe this is our destiny, William. You and I just as friends, never to mate. Some dreadful barrier in between that neither of us will be allowed to penetrate. Father built a brick wall between us, making us stand on tiptoe to look at each other. Never to be normal – What would we ever get out of such a life?"

"Friendship... Your hand's still cold."

"I'm cold. Everything about me is cold."

"Did you love him?"

"I think so. I loved the idea of having a family most of all. Of belonging to people; your own flesh and blood. I was so horribly selfish. Do you believe in God?"

"Sometimes. We all believe in God when it suits us. Usually when we're in trouble and want forgiveness. Even from God we want something."

"I think God punished me for deliberately getting myself pregnant.

You know Randall was a virgin when I seduced him. The poor man didn't know what hit him, he was so young and naïve. There weren't any girls in Rhodesia. Not out on the farms. He was so pent up with sexual frustration he nearly exploded. Now he wants to sow his wild oats. Find out about other women as I found out about other men long before I met Randall. The older men never wanted to stick around so I caught Randall before the poor man found out what life was all about. I caught him in my trap and tried to stop him getting out... Can we sit down on that bench?"

"No we can't. You're going to walk and walk. When we get a little further down the line in your rehabilitation we're going to go for runs. In six months you won't recognise yourself."

"It won't bring Randall back to me. I'd lost my pull over him when I got pregnant. The pregnancy turned off his sexual desire for me. Or maybe he'd had enough and it was time for Randall to move on. Are people ever wilfully monogamous? The church says we should be but the church has many rules that are meant to make us behave ourselves. If society was a free-for-all we'd rip ourselves to pieces. Maybe we already have. The new world has invented so many ways to steal from each other that appear perfectly legal. It's all one big advertising campaign to make us buy buy buy. Most of what we buy we don't want. In a better society, aren't the false desires created by advertising, stealing? These days you can't believe a word anyone says to you. The church was meant to instil self-discipline by teaching us a set of rules... Nowadays nobody does anything unless it suits themselves. They'll tell you any rubbish to get what they want. Do you think the world is falling to pieces?"

"Anything goes. Including men having sex with men."

"I didn't mean it that way."

"No, you probably didn't. No one but gays understand gays. It's how we were built. There's nothing we can do about it."

"You sure it wasn't my father shattering our friendship that turned you off women?"

"I never thought of that."

"What he did to ten-year-olds was a shattering life-changing experience. We were just innocent children when the wrath of God was brought down upon our heads by an angry father."

"We all like to blame someone for our problems."

"But we would have grown up different if my father had understood our innocence."

"Maybe. Who knows? It's all part of the process of going through life."

"I'm enjoying being with you, William."

"Thank God something is going right in my life for a change... Is he happy?"

"Who are you talking about?"

"Your father."

"Probably not. He never seems to enjoy himself."

"Not only do we bring the wrath of God down on other people's heads, we bring it down on our own selves. Anyway, at least our parents are again talking to each other. Even if it is too late to make them friends."

"Why is life so complicated?"

"It makes life interesting."

That night, after a long walk that made Amanda feel a lot better, she went to bed by herself. Randall had not come home. The next day, instead of sitting in the flat eating and feeling sorry for herself, she took a bath, washed her hair and made herself as presentable as possible before taking the Tube to Knightsbridge and William's home that doubled as his workplace. The woman he had called Evelina answered the door. Their eyes met, pulling Amanda towards the older woman, the smile on her face making Amanda feel welcome.

"You must be Amanda. William was telling me all about you. You want some coffee or some tea? We've outsourced the cutting and sewing to a clothes factory in Manchester. It's all got too big for us here. We do the design, cut the patterns and choose the materials and send it all to Manchester which is where William is at the moment. He'll be back in London tomorrow."

"So business is booming?"

"You could say that. We're producing a thousand garments a month. Everything in the rag trade is thought out six months to a year before we show it to the public. Which is where I come in... Let's go sit in the lounge... My job is to work out what we think will sell in next year's spring collection. I look into people's future by following the trends. If I get it right we get lots of orders from the retailers. There's a lot of competition out there. You have to get it right. With the right idea given to William he puts it all together."

"Are you married, Evelina?"

"No, I'm not and never have been. At least not in the conventional sense of a marriage. I'm a lesbian. I prefer women... So, what will it be, Amanda? Tea or coffee? One sugar or two?... No, that's wrong. After what William explained to me he wants you to lose weight. So, no sugar."

"Tea will be nice... What else did William tell you about me?"

"That you lost your baby and your husband is no longer interested in you."

"For the first time he didn't come home last night. Why I'm here to see William. I didn't want to sit at home and mope on my own."

"Will he come home tonight?"

"Who knows? I'm not even sure if I want to go home and sit around waiting to find out... I'm sorry. I must be interrupting your work. I'll come back again when William is at home. We grew up living next door to each other in Great Bookham."

"I know. You sit yourself down while I make the tea. Afterwards, while I'm working in William's sewing room, you can read a book. William has a most interesting little library. After work you and I will have a girls' night out. William's not due back from Manchester until late tomorrow. How does that sound to you?"

"Would you mind?"

"I'd love to spend an evening with you, Amanda."

"Evelina is such a pretty name."

"It's a derivation of Eve. My parents gave me the name of Eve. When I went to senior school I changed it to Evelina. No one wants to be plain, ordinary Eve."

After drinking her tea, and Evelina having gone off to do whatever she did in the sewing room, Amanda picked out a romantic novel she hadn't already read from William's shelves of books and settled down on the couch in the living room. Within minutes she was in a far nicer world. A break for lunch brought Evelina from her workplace and then Amanda went back to her book.

When Evelina appeared at six o'clock she was all dressed up and looked ten years younger. Amanda smiled with surprise.

"Amazing what good clothes and make-up can do for a girl," said Evelina, giving a twirl.

"I feel so underdressed."

"When we've slimmed you down to your old weight I'll get you some new clothes."

"You're being so nice to me, Evelina... Where do you live?"

"I have my own flat just around the corner. You were so engrossed in that book you didn't hear me slip out and get changed. First we are going to my place for cocktails and then I'm taking you out to dinner. There's a lovely Italian in Knightsbridge. The owner is a good friend of mine."

"Is she also a lesbian?"

"Of course she is. Like follows like. Birds of a feather. Call it what you will... You'll enjoy yourself at Camilla's Corner. William and I often go there. Many of our retail clients are gays or lesbians. Not only do like go with like, they do business together. A common bond is a common trust. Works like a charm. Tonight you are going to meet my world and William's... How did you enjoy reading *Marigold Summer*?"

"It was lovely. Everyone so happy."

"It's one of my favourites. You should try reading her *Clover Blossom*. From a long face when you arrived you've come a long way. You're smiling. Life's to be enjoyed. Forget about him. If he wants to stay out screwing other women let him get on with it. But you've got to move on."

"How old are you, Evelina?"

"I'm forty-one."

"You don't look a day over thirty."

"Now that's flattery. I like it."

"I mean it."

"So, are you ready for a good night out?"

"Just lead the way."

"That's pretty much my intention. It's amazing what a few drinks can do for a girl's inhibitions."

"Are you coming onto me?"

"What on earth gives you that impression? William's showed me photographs of you before you were pregnant when you were modelling his clothes, and that's where we're going. Amanda. Trust me. You're going to get out of the dumps and wow the world again."

"I've never been out with a lesbian before."

"There's always a first time for everything."

"You think Randall will come home tonight?"

"Stop thinking about your cheating husband. Put him right out of your mind. You and I are going to have some fun. We can walk to my flat. Being in such close proximity is how I met William. You've got to know people to get on in this life."

Not sure what she was getting herself into and not particularly caring, Amanda walked into the most beautiful flat she had ever seen. It was neither over- or under-furnished, everything right in its place, every shade of colour blending into a perfect whole.

"This is all so beautiful. Is it all your own work?"

"Like clothes on a woman I can see everything before it happens. William is the same. We don't have to piece it together bit by bit. We see everything as it will be before we start the job. Then it's down to every tiny detail... I make a very good Manhattan. Would you like me to make a cocktail? I was working in America some years ago but I missed the antiquity of London. There's so much history in London. I was born in the West End to a rich father. They say there are four ways of getting money: you can work hard for it like William; you can inherit it; you can marry it; or you can steal it. I'm twice blessed in that old adage. With my contacts and William's genius the partnership is making a whole lot of money. I know where to get things and where to sell things. I also know how to make a profit. One of the most difficult jobs in the fashion world is charging the right price. Too low and you don't make the right margin. Too high and you price yourself out of the market... I can pour you a gin and tonic if you prefer. I like to get to Camilla's around eight o'clock. With William in Manchester tomorrow it isn't going to be a big day."

"I'll try that Manhattan."

With two stiff drinks under her belt they took a taxi to the restaurant. Even on a Monday the place was packed. At the back of the room was a small softly lit bar. The woman Amanda presumed was the owner walked them across to the bar.

"You can have a table later. You'll have to sit here at the bar until I've got a free table."

"This is my new friend Amanda. Amanda meet Camilla. The restaurant food is Italian as is Camilla's chef. Camilla is also a Londoner of aristocratic lineage. Her maternal great-grandfather was a baronet.

Very old family. We'll be just fine up at the bar, thank you, darling. Camilla and I go back to when we were at boarding school together. We were each other's first lovers."

"I'll leave you two to enjoy yourselves."

The owner went off having lightly touched Evelina's shoulder, giving her friend a look of sweet understanding. Everywhere Amanda looked were one-sex couples. There was not one man with a woman in the entire restaurant. Feeling relaxed from the Manhattans Amanda sat comfortably up on a barstool as she looked around Camilla's Corner. Evelina, sitting up next to her, smiled, took a small handful of peanuts in her fist and ate them one by one, not taking her eyes off Amanda.

"Are they all gay?" said Amanda, leaning close to Evelina.

"Every one of them. Pedro here is the best barman in London. He's also the chef's boyfriend. Camilla's Corner is a sanctuary for all of us where we don't have to worry about other people. So, do you like the place?"

"It's wonderful."

"Two of my Manhattans, Pedro."

"It will be my pleasure, Evelina."

"This is Amanda. She's new."

"Welcome Amanda."

By the time they sat down at the table to eat their dinner, Amanda no longer cared if Randall was home or not. By the time they had finished a perfect dinner with a bottle of red Chianti, Amanda did not have a care in the world. They left the restaurant, got into a taxi and went back to Evelina's flat.

"Don't worry, Amanda. I never try seduction on the first date."

"Why don't we pretend it's the second?"

"Would you like to try?"

"I haven't had any sex for over a year."

"You poor darling. I was going to put you down in the spare bedroom. It's going to be a life-changing experience. Are you sure?"

"No one is ever sure of anything. If I don't like it we'll stop."

"It's your mouth I find so sexy. Come here, Amanda. Don't think. Don't worry. Just relax."

3

*W*hile Amanda was being romanced by a woman, Randall was sitting at home wondering what had gone wrong in his life: his wife hadn't come home; he hadn't gone to work; the hangover from Sunday's drinking with James and Oliver was the worst he had had in his life; and all because he hadn't told Amanda where he was going on Sunday morning to prevent another argument. There was no note, no phone call. There had not been a sign of Amanda all day.

By the time Randall went to bed he was worried something had happened to Amanda, the fear mingling with his still-rampant hangover making him feel sick, his alcohol-saturated body now screaming for more alcohol as he tossed and turned in his lonely bed. By the time he was due to go to work the next day he couldn't think straight. Again he phoned Mr Grimshaw at the office saying he was still feeling sick.

"I'll tell your uncle, Randall. You stay home until you're well again. No point in spreading germs around the office."

Putting down the phone, Randall wondered what the man's reaction would have been to a junior employee without a doctor's certificate if the junior employee's uncle wasn't the company's managing director.

At eleven o'clock Randall phoned Amanda's parents in Great Bookham to see if Amanda had gone home in a huff after he had not come home on Sunday night.

"Amanda said she might be paying you a visit, Mrs Hanscombe. She gets pretty bored at home on her own. Can I speak to her?"

"She's not here, Randall. How are you?"

"I'm fine. Ask her to ring me at home if she comes."

"What are you doing at home?"

"It's the flu."

"Strange. People mostly get the flu in the winter. Are you two all right?"

"Of course we are."

"Let me know if I can help."

"Thank you, Mrs Hanscombe."

"How is Amanda?"

"Not so good after losing the baby. I don't know what to say to her so I avoid the subject not to hurt her."

"It's the most terrible thing in a woman's life to lose her baby. A miscarriage is bad enough. But carrying that boy to term and then losing him is the worst pain imaginable for a woman. You should talk to her about it. Don't let her keep it bottled up inside."

"I don't know what to say."

"Tell her that men don't feel the same pain as you had no physical contact with the baby. Try and comfort her pain. Say you want another baby."

"She can't. Dr Thompson said another pregnancy could threaten her life."

"I didn't know. I was never close to Amanda like my other children. Something went wrong when she was ten years old. Ever since, she withdrew from me and her father."

"She told me, Mrs Hanscombe. William Drake. Weren't they a bit young to be accused of premarital sex?"

"It wasn't exactly put like that by Mr Hanscombe."

"It's what stayed in Amanda's mind."

"I'm sorry."

"So am I. For both of them."

"Talk to her about the baby, Randall. She won't come and talk it out with me."

"I'll try. I don't have much experience of people. Especially women. Growing up without a proper mother wasn't easy, however hard Bergit tried to fill my mother's shoes. There was me and Phillip. Dad had his own worries what with Rhodesian politics and trying to run a farm. Farming can be very stressful as you never know what is going to happen: too much or too little rain. One year locusts stripped the tobacco leaves and cost us twenty thousand pounds in lost revenue."

"You still love Africa, don't you? Think of Amanda losing her baby in the same way you lost your Africa. How's the job going?"

"If I were truthful I'd say that I hate it. But I won't. Careers in England come with sitting in offices. I'll get used to it. I have to. You can't live on thin air. Everything in England requires lots of money if you want to enjoy yourself. You can enjoy yourself on the banks of an African river that doesn't cost anything once you're there. England's a very material world so I have to make sure I earn a good salary."

"That flat was very expensive."

"I know it was. And I appreciate Mr Hanscombe's generosity."

"Be kind to her, Randall. Where is she?"

"I don't know. Thank you for your advice. I'll do my best."

"I hope your flu gets better soon. Goodbye, Randall."

Before the phone went down he could hear his mother-in-law crying. Randall went to the window and stood staring across the busy road into the park, his mind blank. For the first time since he could remember Randall had no idea what he was going to do.

"Where the hell are you, Amanda?" he asked out loud.

ON THE PREVIOUS SUNDAY NIGHT, all three of them drunk, they had walked back to Mrs Salter's boarding house from the Leg of Mutton and Cauliflower. What had started as a Sunday morning drink in the pub with old friends to relieve Randall's boredom had got out of hand. Neither Oliver nor James had been given another part. One round of drinks led to another. To drown their sorrows they had drunk the day away, not even eating, just one beer after another, the intake slowing as the day went by, none of them wanting to go home, the day too young to sleep. When they got Mrs Salter's front door open, Randall fell through the opening flat on his face. He was still not sure how Oliver and James had got him up the stairs. The next thing he remembered was waking up lying on a floor, the room pitch dark, Randall not knowing where he was.

More than anything he wanted to go to the toilet. He got up off the carpet and tripped over a chair, his bladder involuntarily opening. The light went on.

"Where the fuck am I?"

"Have you just pissed in your pants?"

"James!"

"You're still drunk. Go to the bathroom or you'll be pissing on my carpet."

"Amanda's going to kill me."

"She'd kill you if she saw what you've done to your pants. We had to carry you up the stairs. There was no way you were going home on the Tube to Holland Park."

"I can't go to work today."

"You're not going anywhere until you've sobered up and done something about those trousers. I can smell you from here."

"Sorry, old boy... Where did the blanket come from?"

"You passed out on my carpet after we carried you up the stairs. Oliver covered you... That was quite a drinking session. Now go and piss and get back on your carpet. I want to go back to sleep."

"Have you got a hangover?"

"It's too early for a hangover. I'm still drunk."

"What did we talk about?"

"As Oliver says, the worst thing in life is a drinking companion with a memory. I expect we solved the entire problems of the world."

"I'm sorry, James."

"It was our fault. We're older than you. Our bodies are more used to alcohol saturation."

"She's going to kill me."

"Wives usually do when their husbands don't come home at night. That was quite a drinking session."

"You can say that again."

"I just did."

ALL THROUGH TUESDAY RANDALL'S mind stayed in a fog as he suffered a two-day hangover. The minutes and hours went by as he waited for

Amanda. A key went into the front door lock making Randall look at his watch: it was ten past three in the afternoon.

"Hello, Randall. What are you doing home on a Tuesday afternoon?"

"Waiting for you. I've been worried sick."

"Oh, you shouldn't have been. How was Judy Collins?"

"What are you talking about? And why do you look so happy?"

"You didn't come home on Sunday night," said Amanda, ignoring his question.

"And you didn't come home last night. Where were you?"

"Out enjoying myself. So, how was Judy?"

"I went to see James and Oliver. I was bored. I hate my job and since we barely talk to each other I hate my life."

"Then why won't you make love to me?"

"Because I'm scared stiff of getting you pregnant again and this time killing you."

"You know I'm on the pill."

"You were on the pill when you got pregnant."

"I wasn't."

"You said you were."

"I deliberately got myself pregnant. I'm sorry. I deserve what happened to me. So why didn't you come home on Sunday?"

"We went to the Leg of Mutton."

"And met another girl. How convenient."

"If you must know we all got drunk and I passed out on James's floor and pissed in my pants."

"That's disgusting."

"But it's true. Ask James if you don't believe me."

"So you weren't with a woman?"

"Of course I wasn't."

"And you haven't been having an affair with Judy Collins?"

"Of course I haven't. Ever since we moved into this flat I've caught a different train and not set eyes on the woman."

"I thought an affair was why you wouldn't make love to me. You were getting it somewhere else."

"And you better phone your mother."

"What's she got to do with it?"

"I told her you hadn't come home. I thought you had gone to Great Bookham. So, where were you, Amanda?"

"I spent the night with a friend. A lady friend. When you didn't come home I went round to see William. William was at the factory in Manchester. His new partner was very nice to me. She took me out to dinner."

"Oh, so you were with a woman. My imagination was running riot. I thought you had found another man."

"So, why are you at home on a Tuesday?"

"Two-day hangover. I've never felt so bad in my life... Your mother says we must talk about the baby. That it's much worse for you than me."

"What does my mother know about anything? She's never had to worry about a thing after marrying a much older man who was rich. She's never had an emotion in her life."

"She was crying when she said goodbye to me."

"My mother? Crying? Don't be daft."

"What are you going to do, Amanda?"

"Well, for one thing I'm going to make myself a late lunch. A small late lunch. I'm on a diet. She wants me to get back to modelling."

"Who is this woman?"

"Evelina. She's forty-one and is taking me under her wing so to speak... By the way, you look absolutely terrible."

"Can't be worse than I feel. I'm never drinking alcohol again in my life... Can we stop fighting?"

"Of course we can. What's there to fight about? You got drunk with the boys. I was out with a woman."

"You look so damn cheerful."

"I feel cheerful... You want some food?"

Amanda was humming a tune as Randall watched her walk through to the kitchen. Through Randall's fuddled brain came a picture of Judy Collins's boobs without much point: by now she'd have a regular boyfriend having long forgotten the young man from Rhodesia she had met on the Tube. Coupled with his thoughts of Judy came back his yearning for Rhodesia and the African bush. He was homesick. He wanted to go home: to hear the call of the Cape Turtle dove saying 'where's father, where's father'; the night sound of the crickets and frogs; the dry smell of the African bush; the songs of the kids from the farm as they rode back on a tractor's trailer from winning a football match for their primary school; the clang of the *simby* in the early morning calling the gang in the compound to work; the idling sound of a well-tuned tractor; the call of an owl calling its mate. And with that all the feeling of happiness.

"Do you want some lunch? Don't they say you have to feed a hangover... My mother crying. I don't believe it."

"I want to go home, Amanda."

"You are home."

"No I'm not."

"You're not starting again to harp on about Africa? You've got a good life ahead of you here. What's the matter? That's your trouble, Randall. You don't know when you've got it made. Just look at this beautiful flat and it didn't cost you a penny."

"Don't rub it in... I'm going for a walk to clear my head."

"You could have gone for a walk when I wasn't here."

"No I couldn't. I was worried sick something bad had happened to you."

"You don't have to worry about me. Do you know they sell a thousand upmarket garments a month? She's the business brains."

"Do you want me to meet her?"

"Not particularly... That'll do. I've promised Evelina not to eat so much. She doesn't like fat girls. To quote William: 'Life's a hoot.'"

"How is William?"

"Didn't see him."

"I'm glad you've got a new girlfriend."

"So am I."

WHEREVER HE WALKED there were people. The real problem was Amanda no longer turned him on. Oliver had said it was common for both men and women and called it the two-year syndrome. After years of having sex with the same person they'd both sucked all the lust out of the relationship. After two years Oliver said you had to use your imagination but that it wasn't the same, the myth of man's monogamy blown clean out of the window.

"We say we want to be faithful, Randall, to protect ourselves. To protect our money and our children. To eliminate the thought of growing old on our own. But when it comes down to sex the most violent love affair has dissipated after a couple of years. Some people suck it out of each other in a couple of weeks in an orgy of sex when they can't keep their hands off each other. Then, bam, along comes another woman who turns you on and off you go again. It's all about the evolutionary process of spreading the genes. Who you marry is usually dictated by money. What he or she's got. Or what they are going to inherit from their family. 'I love you' most often means I love what you've got. The rest is lust. We use each other. Look at Veronica West. The moment my acting career went on the skids she left me. Now the newspapers have her pictured with another up-and-coming man. It's image. Publicity. It's good for her career. If that son of yours had lived it would have been different. You'd both have had a lasting common interest. That's life. You have to face up to it. If she's not making you want her she's also probably lost interest in you... Whose name is the flat in?"

"Amanda's. Why, what's the difference? We're married."

"The glory of youth, Randall. All that lovely innocence. If you were to divorce she'd kick you out of the flat. You were better off in Mrs Salter's room when neither of you had anything. When you were both waiting tables. What was the expression you used? 'The laid-back couple.' Those are the times you'll remember. Don't worry about it. You're not the first young man to get bored with a woman."

"But what do I do, Oliver?"

"Find yourself another woman. Go forward with your life. Don't get stuck in a rut... Have you started to argue with each other?"

"All the time. Over silly things. I hate it."

"Have another drink."

"You two are going to get me drunk."

"What are friends for?"

"So marriage with love and happiness is a myth?"

"Happily ever after is a myth. Like a lot of other things we are taught in this life. Welcome to the real world, Randall. Cheers... How's the job going?"

"I've never been more bored in my life. What's the point of making all that money if you're not going to be happy?... What do I say to Amanda?"

"Probably it's best to say nothing. Let your affair run its course. I'd bet my bottom dollar that if she hadn't got pregnant you two would never have got yourselves married. You're far too young to tie yourself down. There's a whole big world out there. And if you want to write books as you say, you'd better get out there and do some living. And anyway, if you get her pregnant again your doctor says it might kill her. It's over, Randall. Your first big love affair is over."

"That's so unbelievably sad... However much I want to, I can't go back to Africa. There's no future for a white boy in Zimbabwe."

"There's more to the world than Africa. Go to America. Go to India. See the world."

"How do I support myself? I haven't any money."

"Waiting tables. You did it in London. And one day, when you've lived enough, you'll write that novel."

"Have you found another part in a play?"

"Not yet. But I will. It's not all bad, Randall. Cheer up. You're young, healthy and the girls find you attractive. What else could you possibly want? Remember Amanda as a beautiful experience. Don't destroy what you had by staying together too long."

"Thank you, Oliver. You're a real friend."

"My pleasure... And James here has an audition on Friday for a new television series, don't you, James? So, there we have it. Oh, and one more thing. Don't take my crap as gospel. Do your own thing. In the end, a man has to work it out for himself. The reverse of what I just said is looking back later after a string of affairs to realise you lost in Amanda the one big love of your life."

"Life is so complicated."

"What keeps life interesting. If everything was plain sailing we'd all die of boredom... So, James. What's the new series about?"

"I have no idea except that it's a drama and not a comedy."

With the early part of their drinking session at the pub still playing through his mind, Randall sifting the words, he sat down on a wooden park bench. Later, when his mind was in neutral from his hangover, an old man sat down at the other end of the bench. The man was very old and all on his own, staring happily away into the trees. He sighed, making Randall look at him. As Randall looked, the old man slowly got up off the bench and walked away into the trees.

Two hours later, the walk having dissipated his two-day hangover,

Randall went home. There was no sign of Amanda. On the coffee table propped against the vase, the vase empty of flowers, was a note from Amanda: 'Gone to see Evelina.'

Smiling, content that his wife had found a friend, Randall picked up his book and began to read. Soon he was deep in the Spanish Civil War in the world of Ernest Hemingway. The afternoon progressed into evening, the twilight fading into a soft summer night. There was still no sign of Amanda.

"What on earth do these women find to talk about?" said Randall as he went to their bedroom. He was tired. Properly tired. No longer worried. With his clothes left on the floor he got into the big double bed. Within seconds he was sound asleep.

When he got up in the morning to bathe and shave there was still no sign of Amanda. Using the same piece of paper he scribbled a note saying he had gone to work.

"That was a quick recovery," said Mr Grimshaw.

"Forty-eight hour flu."

Smiling, feeling so much better after a trouble-free sleep, Randall sat at his desk in cubicle land. Only one head was looking around, the rest were invisible, presumably doing their jobs. With a deep, resigned sigh Randall got down to his work, another day at the office.

That night when they were in bed Randall made a sexual advance to his wife. Instead of turning to him Amanda leaned up on one elbow and turned out the bedside light.

"Goodnight, Randall. Sleep well."

Puzzled at the rejection and the cheerful goodnight, and a little relieved, Randall turned his back to Amanda and was soon sound asleep.

A MONTH later at the end of September when Randall got home from his stint at night school there was another note up against the empty vase.

'Sorry, Randall. I've moved in with Evelina. We're lovers. I've told Dad to sell the flat. Have a good life.'

As the note fell from his hand onto the carpet Randall began to laugh hysterically. When he recovered he picked up the note and read it again.

"Well, I'll be buggered. My wife has left me for a woman."

PART 6

MARCH TO SEPTEMBER 1985 – WELCOME TO AMERICA

1

Three and a half years after the end of his marriage to Amanda and moving out of the Holland Park flat back into his old room at Mrs Salter's, Randall Crookshank received his Bachelor of Economics degree from the London School of Economics, his Uncle Paul, Oliver and James watching the ceremony. The following day at BLG Randall was given his own office on the top floor of Brigandshaw House. At the age of twenty-seven he found himself in the smallest office of the executives' suites, his career pointed in a straight line to the top. LSE had given him a First, the reward for all his painstaking hard work at night school. His suit was new from his tailor, his hair had been cut by a professional, his shoes were the best he could buy. To everyone around Randall his life and future looked perfect. A few in the office were jealous, Mr Grimshaw among them.

His appeal to young women had increased in direct proportion to his salary and his new title of BLG manager of property development. His score rate, when he thought about it, had risen to two 'newies' every month. Like an out of control stallion Randall went from woman to woman, expensive dinners the price of their willingness to have sex. Never once did he take a woman to his own home, the room at Mrs Salter's with the window that looked down on Mrs Salter's washing line, a private place for his other bohemian life with James and Oliver and his memories of Amanda. Ever since the note up against the flowerless vase Randall had not set eyes on Amanda, the only thing left of her being the memories. He was two people. The executive rake in his smart clothes at expensive restaurants, and the dressed-down man in his single room with the burning ambition to one day write a book that would interest a big London publisher so he could leave the false world of business and move to the country and spend the rest of his life as an artist. But it all came down to money. A man needed money to live in a city and reap its material and sexual pleasures, and most of his money went on wide-eyed expectant women who wanted the man of money and future and not the dreamer who wanted to write books.

On the following Sunday after receiving his degree and all the polite hand-clapping that went with it, with neither of them having a date for the evening, umbrellas up in the cold March evening, James and Randall walked from Mrs Salter's to the Leg of Mutton and Cauliflower for a drink, Oliver working at his new successful play at the Savoy Theatre and unable to join them. As always in a Notting Hill pub there were many good-looking young women in search of male company. Apart from his job at BLG most things in Randall's life, especially when it came to women, were temporary. You bought the drinks, ordered a taxi, paid for the expensive dinner and got yourself laid, everyone happy.

"Do you like your new job as property development manager?" asked James when they got up to the bar.

"The only thing I like about my job is the salary. No, that's not quite true. I enjoy getting a good job done. That gives me some satisfaction when everything works out properly... When do you start the new film at Pinewood?"

"Next month, I hope. The producers are finding it difficult to raise the money. It's always the money. The script's good. The director knows what he's doing and except for myself, I suppose, they've got the right actors... There are a couple of good-looking new faces at the table behind you. Don't look round. Plenty of time. They're on their own... And there it goes. One of them has smiled at me. What are you having, Randall? The only thing I don't understand with all your money is why you don't move into a posh flat."

"Because I'm comfortable where I am among old friends... I'll have a pint of bitter to start with... What's the other one like?"

"Not bad at all. It always pays to hunt in pairs."

"Or with Oliver. That man's a magnet for women. You know Veronica West is trying to get back with him after the success of his new play? Women! They either want fame or fortune. Preferably both... Did I tell you – when the new project is complete I'm going to America."

"How long for?"

"Barend Oosthuizen didn't say. You and Oliver could come over. Have a go at Broadway and Hollywood. That would be a new adventure for all of us. Give me something in the end to write about... Cheers, old boy. Is she still looking at you?"

"Not at the moment. We're not the only single men in the pub."

"They'll need the talk of company executive and film actor to get their full attention. Why does there have to be so much bullshit in the mating dance? Most of them don't want me or you, they want what we represent. And all we males really want is a night in the sack. It's all so trivial. So animal. So damn basic. And once you've had her a couple of times you move to the next one, the old sex drive never completely satisfied. And all they want is a man to look after them for the rest of their lives. Does anyone ever tell the truth in this life? It's all take take. You turn a crappy old warehouse near the River Thames into an upmarket apartment block and charge the new proud owner an exorbitant price for looking out of their window at a river. And BLG makes a bloody fortune. If we get the asking price for Westcastle we'll add a nought to what it cost me to put the project together. It's an obscene profit just for buying an old warehouse, getting the land use changed from commercial to residential and bringing in the architect and builders. The world's gone mad. Too much money chasing too little property creating classic asset inflation. One day the whole damn pack of cards will come down. You can't make so much money out of nothing by just changing the colour of the chameleon. And in the end the poor sod who pays quarter of a million quid for a fancy three-bedroom flat is still stuck in a high-rise between four walls, his only escape through the window. They must be out of their minds. The ground and the warehouse only cost us a million. Now we've got forty-eight flats to sell."

"What are you going to do in America?"

"No idea. Exchange ideas. See if Barend has found even better ways to screw people out of their bank's money. And that's the most of it.

Everything is mortgaged. Buy now, pay later, hope the price goes up, everyone gambling. The City of London is turning itself into one big casino."

"I don't understand business."

"You're lucky. In a better world they'd call it swindling. Now they call it free market capitalism with everyone getting rich out of nothing: BLG, the banks and the buyers of the flats. Life in Rhodesia was a lot more simple. When you planted a crop and looked after it you could see what you had grown. There it was in front of you. You didn't wave a wand over something and turn it into something else. A bag of maize was still a bag of maize."

"Have you heard from your family in Zimbabwe?"

"It's actually going rather well. World's View is prospering. Phillip's safari business is flourishing. Long may it last. The black population is exploding so they'll need all the food the farmers can grow. But like everything else in this world there's a snag. Half the whites have left the country, most of the farmers going to Australia taking their farming skills with them. They don't trust Mugabe's government. They still think that after the bush war he'll eventually turn on the whites. That what they have at present is an Indian Summer... Who knows?... Shall we go over and talk to the girls? Bring your drink, James. When we ask to sit in the spare chairs at their table they can always tell us to bugger off. I'll leave you as the actor to start the conversation. I'll pay for the drinks and the dinner."

"You're turning me into a pimp."

"Sorry, old boy. We can do it the other way round if you like."

"You know I don't have much money. I'll open the scene. You follow."

"Let the dance begin."

THE FOLLOWING DAY, after a successful evening with James as his hunting partner, both girls impressed with their bullshit, Randall was called into his uncle's office. For once Uncle Paul wasn't smiling. Fortunately for Randall the wining and dining had been cut short, both girls playing hard to get, saying they had to work in the morning and what were James and Randall doing on Saturday, the second date quickly set. With less than five drinks from the previous evening Randall's brain was clear.

Randall looked from his uncle behind his desk to the portrait of Harry Brigandshaw that hung over the boardroom table, politely waiting.

"We have put up your salary considerably now you have qualified, Randall. But there are conditions. You have a bad quirk which worries me and the other directors. You must make up your mind once and for all as to what you want to be. Your days of living in a bedsitter surrounded by actors and artists must be terminated. You must forget about wanting to be a writer. In life you can't be hitting the wall in two places at once if you want to succeed. Forget about writing, Randall. Forget about the encouragement of Harry Wakefield. Like so many journalists he's a frustrated artist who would like to see you fulfil a dream he couldn't fulfil himself as he's never had the time. Harry knew that he either concentrated on journalism or writing novels. He chose journalism and made a big success out of it... We want you to buy a two-bedroom flat in Westcastle. I've spoken to the bank. With your new salary and your guarantee they were happy to give you a mortgage."

"Whatever for? I'm happy where I am."

"Image, Randall. In life you are what people see you surrounded by. Your future clients and business associates want to feel comfortable doing business with a successful man. They want to see you are successful and not have someone point out you live in one room in Notting Hill Gate. In a better world this wouldn't be necessary. A man would be judged by his intellect and not by his possessions. But in today's material world they want to see your success to feel comfortable and want to do business. If you take a prospective client out to dinner you take them to the best restaurant. Buy the best wine and know what you are buying. Talk about your flat in the West End or on the Thames. Impress them as a successful man so they will want to trust you and want to do business. No one would trust a top executive who lives in a bedsitter."

"Why ever not?"

"Because you don't appear successful. You have a flaw. Appearances mean everything. Like your tailor-made suit which I like by the way. It speaks loudly of money without being vulgar."

"The girls like it." said Randall, giving his uncle a twisted smile.

"No they don't, nephew. They like what it represents. A successful man with money."

"Must I move into a flat and give up my friends?"

"It's not a request, Randall. It's for your own good. And the good of the firm... So, that's settled. Oh, and your grandmother wants to help you choose the curtains."

"So it's an order?"

"If you want to look at it that way. You're being groomed for a seat on the board of directors of BLG, a public company that has to maintain its public image. I'm sure you'll understand. And when you choose a wife this time think how she will enhance your career. It's a hard, nasty world. Get used to it... And as you go out, ask Mrs Walker to come and see me."

"Yes, sir."

"You don't have to call me sir in private."

"I could always resign and go back to writing."

"You could, Randall, but you'd soon run out of money. You've got used to the best restaurants and a suit like the one you've got on. Going back to being an itinerant waiter I don't think would suit you anymore... You can leave the door open. And congratulations. You've done a top-rate job with Westcastle. The highest ratio of profit to investment the company has made so far out of a property development."

"The value of property is surging. We got lucky."

"Long may it last. The trick is knowing when to get in and, sometimes, when to get out. Have you heard from my brother in Rhodesia recently?"

"Not this week."

"Give him my best regards when you speak to him and tell him I still think he should sell the farm while he can and come back to live in England. There are always ways of getting money out of a country. Even Zimbabwe."

"My father will never sell World's View."

"Only a fool falls in love with his share certificate. There's a time to buy and a time to sell. I can't even imagine what his flats in Chelsea are now worth. He could retire to the country and be very comfortable."

"He loves Africa."

"Yes, I suppose he does. Harry Brigandshaw also loved Africa. Luckily for all of us he came back to England which helped us to build up this company. Or you, Randall, wouldn't be about to own a prize piece of property overlooking the Thames. Congratulations. A man's success is judged by his possessions. It makes him who he is. Don't forget that, Randall, if you want to get on in the world."

Remembering not to shake his head and piss off his uncle, Randall walked out of the office telling Mrs Walker she was wanted as he passed by her desk. He would miss James and Oliver on a daily basis but nothing in life was perfect. Like the old, broken-down warehouse that he had changed into a smart block of flats he too had to change. He was now the material man. The man of property. He was going to be rich. Eventually, when he took over BLG from his uncle, he'd buy an estate in the country. Have a summer house in the Bahamas. His own private aeroplane. Everything that money could buy. And with it an ego the size of his worldly wealth. As he sat down in his office, a pile of work in front of him, every small detail requiring his attention, the most fundamental question kept coming back to him: would he be happy? The new flats with all their expensive fixtures were to Randall as cold as charity; impersonal places that he doubted would ever feel like a home where a man and a cat would be comfortable. Instead of getting on with his work, Randall sat back in his chair, his mind going away from the world in which he was living. He was deeply sad, sorry for himself with uncomfortable premonitions, what he was doing with his life simply not working. He wanted to rise up from behind his desk and fly away to a non-material world where people loved each other for who they were and not for what they were worth. Where a man walked in the woods and not down a street. Where the air was full of birdsong and not the sound of traffic. And most of all he wanted to be back home in Africa, back home on World's View with the cats and the dogs and his happy family.

When his secretary came in with the morning's mail and put it on his desk his mind was still only half in the room.

"What's the matter, Randall? Are you all right?"

"Have you ever been homesick for your country?"

"This is my country. How can I be homesick when I'm here?"

"They're buying me one of the flats."

"Lucky you. My boyfriend would kill for one of those flats."

"Are you going to marry him?"

"Don't be silly. He doesn't have any money... There are letters from four more estate agents who want to sell the Westcastle flats. People are clamouring. I wish I had an uncle who owned the business."

"I think it's as much his wife who owns the shares, the daughter of Harry Brigandshaw."

"What's the difference?... Do you want me to shut the door?"

"No, you can leave it open... You're probably right."

"About what?"

"Life. It's all about money. Sad but true."

"What's wrong with money?"

"It has no value."

"Sometimes I just don't understand what you are talking about."

"You're probably lucky. Sorry, Sonia. I'll try and behave."

"You've got everything a man of your age could possibly want. And still you're not satisfied. I just don't understand men. Before you go stark raving bonkers find yourself a wife."

"I had one of those."

"What happened?"

"She left me for a woman. After the baby died at birth. I didn't know how to comfort her."

"I'm sorry. There are so many things about people we don't know. I've worked here a year and no idea you have been married. You must have been very young... What was her name?"

"Amanda. Her name was Amanda. She nearly died having my son."

When Sonia left his office she quietly shut his door. And she was right. People didn't really know about each other. Despite seeing Sonia every day in the office for a year he knew nothing about the girl other than her work and how they both related to their work and life's daily trivialities. They were as impersonal as strangers. With the door again closed Randall sat thinking, most of what he thought about making him feel uncomfortable. And soon he wouldn't have James and Oliver to pull him out of his brown moods. The only concrete thought that came to his mind was the name of the girl he was seeing on Saturday, a girl he was sure would like his new flat.

"You can't fart against thunder, Randall Crookshank, so just get used to it." Reluctantly Randall picked up his pen and got on with his work.

. . .

THREE MONTHS LATER, Randall, with the help of his grandmother's decorating skills, moved into his new flat, the first of the new owners to take up residence. Everything looked and smelt new, the chemical smell of new paint still lingering. To look properly at the river he had to lean out of the window, the view no comparison to the Zambezi – moving barges instead of crocodiles; brick and concrete buildings on either side of trees; the smell of commerce instead of the rich sweet smell of the African bush. For a moment Randall wanted to cry. When he looked back into his new home everything around him was sterile: the new metal furniture in the latest style; the artwork they had made him buy stuck on the pink-tinged walls; the flowing curtains; the one small square of carpet in the middle of the cold dark hard plastic floor with its fancy patterns; the big television without which the world did not exist; and the flowerless vase, the only sign of humanity in the whole damn room. Even that smell of paint had the smell of new money.

Trying his best not to look appalled, he turned to his grandmother and put on a smile. The old girl was happy for once with something to do.

"You don't have to kid me, Randall. You forget I spent much of my life in a cottage covered in climbing roses on the Isle of Wight. I still miss the call of the seagulls. Why I bought you those curtains with seagulls all over them. The small yacht your grandfather went down on at Dunkirk was called the *Seagull*. We sailed together many times on the *Seagull*. Sometimes the seagulls come this far upriver. You'll see. I've so much enjoyed helping you with your flat. When you get old the worst thing in life is boredom. I wish I was back in the Isle of Wight as much as you would like to be back in Africa."

"How did you know?"

"You're my grandson. The same flesh and blood. Some of what I am you are too. Sometimes when I'm watching you without you noticing me you go far away in your mind. Body language often says more than words. I recognised the look of yearning in your eyes. At first I thought you missed Amanda but it wasn't Amanda was it, Randall? Do you know where she is?"

"So long as she's happy it doesn't matter."

"Is she still with the girl?"

"I saw William a couple of years ago. She's still living with her friend.

For some reason William said Amanda is always tired so she doesn't work. The woman is William's business partner. She has plenty of money so Amanda not working doesn't matter."

"Is Amanda not well?"

"I don't know."

"Don't you want to know?"

"Better I leave them alone. If Amanda wanted to talk to me she'd give me a ring. The number in the office hasn't changed."

"I'm sorry... Did you love her very much?"

"I don't think we really loved each other in the romantic meaning of love. I just miss her company. Having her around. We were friends. Maybe convenient friends but friends. Our lives had just moved on together as soon as we met."

"Would you have married if she hadn't got pregnant?"

"Probably not. We were fine as we were just living our lives together. We called ourselves the laid-back couple. I miss her laugh. But life goes on. We all move through life day by day, one day at a time."

"I'll make us some tea. Tea always makes you feel better. When is your trip to America?"

"At the end of the summer. Uncle Paul wanted me to move into the flat first. Thank you for helping me."

"It was my pleasure. New homes are like new shoes. It takes a little time to wear them in. I miss your father, did you know that? When Jeremy went to Rhodesia part of me went with him. It's so far away. A mother wants her children and grandchildren in close proximity so she is part of their lives. Having you in England has been a joy to me... Now look at that. The kettle has boiled."

"Why don't you go visit World's View?"

"I'm too old to travel. I'd worry about what I'd left at home. I'm comfortable the way I am. I don't want to break my daily routines and find myself disconnected when I get back home. No, Jeremy has his own life and his own family. I'm lucky Paul and Beth don't mind my living with them. I don't want to start living in two worlds like you Randall... There's your tea. Just as you like it. Anyway, in this changing world who's to say Jeremy won't be forced to come back to live in England and then we'd all be together again. What's bad for Jeremy would be good for me.

That's how life goes. Count your blessings. I count mine diligently every morning. It helps."

"What was Grandfather like?"

"He was a man. Oh, he was a man."

"That's a lovely compliment."

"Let's go and sit in the new chairs. They look rather exciting but are they comfortable? There's no point in a chair that isn't comfortable."

"It's strange to have had grandfathers and never to have known them."

"Is your mother's mother alive? You never talk of her."

"All I know about my grandmother is she was in the theatre. She died soon after my mother was killed by the lions. Grandfather Crossley had gone his own way by then and we didn't know how to get in touch with him."

"Is he still alive?"

"I have no idea. Whenever I see old men I wonder if they are my grandfather. I fantasise about going up to them and saying 'Excuse me, I'm your grandson from Rhodesia.'"

"I'm sure you could trace him."

"If he wanted to have anything to do with us he would have contacted my father on World's View. There's a reason. There's always a reason. Maybe it's better for me and Phillip not to know the reason. Dad says there are some things you are better off not knowing."

"But aren't you curious?"

"Of course I am. But you know the old saying, Grandma. Curiosity killed the cat. And I lost my cat to a terrorist's bullet... What if he did something terrible and they sent him to jail? Was that the reason he walked out of my grandmother's life? I'm not even sure if he knows my mother is dead."

"You should try and find him."

"Do you think so?... You know what? This chair is remarkably comfortable... I'm frightened most to find out he doesn't want anything to do with me and Phillip. Phillip and I have talked about it. Maybe our paths will just meet. Crossley isn't a very common name in England. And he definitely came from England."

"What did he do?"

"He was an actor too. Obviously not very successful or we'd have heard of him."

"Or he had a stage name."

"We all have so many ancestors going back into history and we never meet any of them. Most people know nothing about their ancestors. All they have is the same name. And now, with everyone moving around the world so much in the new global village, we all lose contact with our families and roots. In the good old days families stayed in the same villages for centuries. Now the average time people stay in the same house is less than seven years. It's all rather impermanent... Thank you for the tea. It's nice. I like tea more than any other drink. It doesn't come back to bite you. I drink too much alcohol. It goes with modern life. Both business and pleasure. So you think Uncle Paul will be satisfied with my behaviour now I've moved into this flat? That I'm more stable? More settled down? That I'll be better at my job? He's quite hard as a boss is Uncle Paul. You don't see that side of him. I suppose I'll get used to this place. Grow to like it. And sometime in the future feel it's my home... It's so strange a man walking out on his family and never coming back again. There has to be a reason, Grandma."

"Did you ever think he might be very short of money and needed some help?"

"No, I never thought of that. I was only thinking about myself. Are we all selfish?"

"We try to give the impression we are anything but selfish but we all think of ourselves. It's how we are made. You can't change the nature of man. You can't change the beast."

"Then we are all horrible. Is that why the world is always in such a mess? Can't we do something about it?"

"Man's been trying to do something about it since he came onto this earth. Why we have so many religions. So many theories as to the right way to govern ourselves. For a short while we succeed and then all hell breaks loose again."

"But why is that?"

"Underneath everything we are only concerned with ourselves. When someone gets rich, or a country gets rich, others are envious and want to bring them down. To find a way to take what they have away and still appear righteous. That's called politics: like-minded selfish people trying to get what they want."

"How do you understand this so well, Grandma?"

"Oh, I don't understand it. I just read a lot. Put what people write together in an attempt to understand the purpose of life. The reason for my own life. If you live long enough you'll find yourself doing the same thing. At the moment you have more important things to worry about like making money."

"Is money so important?"

"Money is very important when you don't have it, Randall. And in a turbulent world you never quite know if you have enough for the future to survive."

"So you think I should try and look for him?"

"Of course you must. He's your grandfather. Without that man you would not have life and I would not be sitting here sipping tea with a grandson. And there you have it. Once again I've brought it back to myself. My own selfish pleasures."

"We might both have a lot of fun with him."

"Now, that selfish motive had never entered my head." She was smiling at him, both of them happy with their conversation.

"I enjoy talking to you. I never realised you understand me so well. Now, tell me everything about Grandfather Crookshank. Right from the first day you met him."

After twenty minutes of listening to his grandmother tell her story, Randall got up and made them a second cup of tea. She looked so happy as she reminisced. It was as if his long-dead grandfather, killed by a German dive bomber, was in the room with them, his grandmother full of smiles, brimming with happiness, making Randall feel happy. Only later did he realise what he was doing, each word of his family's story banked in his memory for future use in his books, all the new flats in the world with all the money unable to suppress his urge to write books.

"I must be boring you, Randall."

"Don't be silly. Please go on. Don't stop. Your life is the most wonderful story... Now why are you giving me that quizzical smile of yours, Grandma?"

"You want the story for yourself. You're still writing books."

"Just don't tell Uncle Paul. He calls it a flaw in my make-up. A quirk that is not good for business... So, where were you?"

"It was 1938 and your grandfather was chief engineer for Short Brothers who were making the Short Sunderland flying boat and they were test flying one of the aircraft. Harry Brigandshaw was the test pilot and they flew to Switzerland and landed on the lake near Romanshorn where they met the von Liebermans, Klaus and Bergit. Harry had shot down and then saved Klaus von Lieberman's life in the First World War and the two had become friends..."

When his grandmother left in a taxi to go back to the town house in Hyde Park where she lived with her son, Randall's uncle, Randall went straight to the small desk under the window where he could just see the River Thames and began writing down the salient points in his grandmother's story. He was smiling. He was happy. One day he was going to turn it all into a novel: the happy family, the small cottage three hundred yards from the beach, everything perfect, everything happy in the life of his grandparents, his father and his Uncle Paul. Only when he was finished taking notes did he sit back and contemplate his trip to America.

2

*A*t the end of September, when Randall flew out of Heathrow for New York, he had still not made contact with Grandfather Crossley. He had found the man's birth certificate at Somerset House and taken a trip by train to the old man's place of birth, the small village of Neston in Cheshire, close to the estuary of the River Dee. In the local pub he asked a group of old men if they had seen Benjamin Crossley, but all of them shook their heads.

"He ain't been in these parts best part of fifty years. Went off to London to become an actor. Didn't do much good as we never saw of him on the telly. Why you ask?"

"I'm his grandson."

"You got a funny accent. Where you from?"

"Rhodesia. They now call it Zimbabwe."

"Do they now?"

"What did my grandfather do in Neston before he went off to go on the stage?"

"A shrimp fisherman. Like his father. And his father before him. The shrimp fisherman from Parkgate just down yonder. You can go down to the mud flats and see where them boats were. None there now. England's changed. Back long time ago Chester was a port like Liverpool... What's Ben done now?"

"Disappeared."

"Has he now?"

"If you ever hear of him could you give me a ring? That's my business card. I work in the City of London."

"Fancy card. Embossed too. So, your mother was a Crossley. Doesn't she know where he is?"

"She was killed by lions soon after I was born. May I buy you all a drink? I know nothing about my grandfather. What was he like?"

"A holy terror. Especially when it came to women. Sit yourself down, lad. Come to think of it, you have a bit of the look of Ben. So, you do all right then with the ladies?"

"I get my fair share."

"Development project manager. Quite grand. The lads will all have pints. Not that we're lads anymore. Ben Crossley. Haven't thought of Ben in years. What you want him for? He never had no money. None of the Crossleys had any money. They were shrimp fishermen in them boats at Parkgate… Where's this place you called Rhodesia? Never heard of it."

"It was a British Crown colony. We declared UDI. Unilateral Declaration of Independence from Britain."

"Did you now? And what happened?"

"You applied economic sanctions which led to a bush war which led to many of us leaving the country. Didn't you hear of it?"

"Don't read them newspapers… Pints all round, gaffer! The lad's paying. He's Ben Crossley's grandson. Can you believe it?"

The owner of the pub came across to the table.

"Ben came in here about a year ago," he said.

"So he's still alive?"

"He was then. Looked healthy enough. Got himself drunk. Old man Sedgewick told me who he was."

"Can you tell me where I can find Mr Sedgewick?"

"In the cemetery. Been dead these last six months."

"Did he have a wife? Any children? Wouldn't they know about Ben Crossley?"

"You can ask Ida. The kids left home long ago. One went to Australia and the other to America. She's all on her own in that old council house. Lived there all her life. It was her dad's house. When her dad and mum died, Ida and Fred took up the lease. She'll like a bit of company. A good natter. I'll write down her address... Pints all round, you say?"

"Please. And thank you."

"You're welcome."

"You're also buying the pints," said the old man smiling, showing a row of black, rotten teeth as he grinned up at the gaffer from his seat hoping for his free beer.

"Where can I find a place to stay the night?"

"Ida will help you. Lets out the spare bedrooms to help her old age pension. She calls it a bed and breakfast."

"So I'll get some breakfast?"

"What she says... When the Conservative government handed over the council houses to the tenants for a song, Ida and Fred got to own the place. Why it's a bed and breakfast."

By the time the evening was over Randall had a strange feeling as if he had come home.

Ida Sedgewick gave him a room, there being no one else in the house. She had heard of Ben Crossley but never met him. The trail had gone cold.

WHEN THE AIRCRAFT landed at New York's Kennedy Airport, Randall was still pondering the whereabouts of his maternal grandfather. Of one thing he was now pretty certain: the old man was still alive.

The surprise at the airport was finding Hayley Oosthuizen had come to meet him. Her brother Barend had been called to Denver at the last moment for a meeting.

"Barend apologises, Randall. How are you? You do remember meeting me at your uncle's townhouse in Hyde Park?"

"Of course I do."

"Is that all the luggage you've got?"

"Barend said a week or two should do it. It's as much a holiday from the office. A small bonus for finishing the Westcastle project. You know we've sold all but two of the flats. Sold like hot cakes. It's so kind of you to come and pick me up. My first time in America. All a bit strange. So nice to find a familiar face."

They were both smiling at each other, both of them liking what they saw.

"Have you ever been married, Hayley? I'm surprised a good-looking woman like you doesn't have a husband. Have a name other than Oosthuizen?"

"You old flatterer. I've been married twice. No children. Each time I went back to my maiden name. I was always good at picking the wrong men... Look, we've booked you into the Fairmont on 59th Street. It's within walking distance of Fifth Avenue. But be careful if you go out walking at night. This is New York. The crime rate is terrible. Always best to take a cab. There's a good restaurant near the hotel. A small band. You've got time to book into your hotel, get changed and go out to dinner. Take it as BLG America's welcome to Randall Crookshank. You've changed since I met you five years ago. You're now quite the man."

"Now who's doing the flattering?" Again they were smiling at each other.

"So dinner it is. I'll wait for you in the bar at the Fairmont while you change in your room. Do I look all right to go out to dinner?"

"You look wonderful."

When Randall got into the company car, whose chauffeur was a black man making Randall feel at home, he was trying to figure out how old Hayley was. Not that it mattered. The girl was beautiful. Then Randall remembered: her mother was Genevieve, the famous actress, the one-time toast of Broadway and Hollywood.

"Once, when I was a small boy in Rhodesia, my stepmother took us to the cinema in Salisbury. We saw *Robin Hood*. Your mother was Maid Marian. It was the first movie I really remember."

"Everyone has seen *Robin Hood and his Merry Men*. Gregory L'Amour played opposite my mother. The film is a classic. Some people say I even look like my mother... You don't mind dining out with an older woman, Randall? Or we can call it strictly business."

"I'm happy calling it whatever you like."

"The older men bore me. They're so full of themselves. Only talk about themselves and how clever they are."

"Then I'll be clever never again to mention the Westcastle project."

They both laughed. They were comfortably seated in the back of the car as the driver threaded his way out of the airport complex.

"Would you like to meet my mother?"

"I'd be honoured, Hayley."

"She still has her feet firmly on the ground. All that fame never went to her head."

"How did she meet your father?"

"They were sweethearts long before mother became famous. Her mother and father never married. Esther, my grandmother, was a barmaid and met my grandfather during the First World War. It's a long story."

"Why don't you tell me?"

"Well, Merlin was the third-eldest son of the 17th Baron St Clair of Purbeck. He's my grandfather and lived at Purbeck Manor in Dorset..."

By the time the car reached the freeway, Randall was concentrating. He had another story. He had the beginnings of another book.

The bath was pleasant, with Randall taking his time and Hayley happily ensconced at the end of the Fairmont's small bar talking to the barman. The room off the small bathroom was comfortable without looking ostentatious. Randall shaved, cleaned his teeth and sprayed his armpits with deodorant before getting dressed. He had put on a clean shirt and underwear, wearing his best suit, the one he had travelled in left on the chair.

"Sorry. Took a bit longer than expected."

"Chuck here was keeping me amused, weren't you, Chuck? Come on then. We're off to the Loeb Boathouse. The place only livens up after ten."

The Loeb Boathouse, the place Hayley had referred to as a restaurant near the hotel with a small band, was full of people. Randall was surprised how easily Hayley was given a table. They had taken a cab from outside the Fairmont, Hayley not wishing to risk walking the streets at night. Randall, no stranger to expensive restaurants, smelt big money whichever way he looked.

"How on earth did you get a table?"

"It helps to have a famous mother. Also BLG have an account with the restaurant. So far as the IRS are concerned you and I tonight are strictly business. Do you like the place, Randall?"

"How could you not when it's right on a lake?"

The food, when it came, was as good as the opulence, the menu he was given having shown no prices: if a man could afford to go to the Loeb Boathouse, the price of the food was irrelevant. The band, a quartet, began playing soon after Randall had finished his steak, a piece of beef as good as anything he had had in Rhodesia. They sat opposite each other at a small table next to the dance floor, a square of open space in front of the band and surrounded by tables. The wine, after the long flight from London, calmed Randall down, giving him the soft feeling of comfort. Deliberately, neither of them had brought up the subject of business. For Randall there was something sophisticated about older women that made him attracted to Hayley.

"You'd dressed for dinner before you came to the airport?"

"Of course I had. Do you mind?"

"This place is quite wonderful."

With the food finished, Randall asked Hayley to dance. There was a magnetism between them that had captivated his attention, his attraction to Hayley growing with the wine and the evening. On the small dance floor, the musicians playing a song of George Gershwin's, they danced close but still not touching, the fraction of distance more sexually exciting than if they were pressed into each other. Close to Hayley he could smell her perfume, he could smell her womanhood.

"This is nice," she said softly, looking straight into his eyes making Randall even more aware of her.

For the first time since Amanda, also a few years older than Randall, had picked him up outside the Leg of Mutton and Cauliflower and walked with him to his room at Mrs Salter's, he was being seduced by a woman. By the end of the dance Randall wanted to make love to Hayley, their age difference no longer mattering.

"Welcome to America, Randall."

"It's nice to be here."

"Is that all you can say?"

"I could say a whole lot more if you let me."

"We'd better go to my place. The Fairmont has ears. We don't want my father or brother knowing what we're up to... Do you like older women, Randall?"

"Always."

"Then let us finish our coffee and go to my apartment. We can pick up your suitcase tomorrow morning if all goes well. Which it will. Won't it, Randall? Isn't it lucky tomorrow is a Saturday and we don't have to go to the office? I can even take you to a Broadway show. Show you a little of our beautiful city. Who knows, like my parents, you may grow to like America."

"Did Barend really go to Denver?"

"No he didn't."

She was smiling straight into his eyes, her eyes not moving, her lips slightly apart. There was definitely something about older women, Randall told himself. No doubt about it. Like a fish who had taken the bait he was hooked. She took his hand as they left the dancefloor to walk the few paces to their table. She was reeling him in, every part of Randall happy to go where she wanted him.

Not for the first time in his life Randall woke up in an unfamiliar bedroom, a woman's room with its dressing table, the mirror reflecting Randall with Hayley in a large double bed, all the bed linen expensive. The only one awake, Randall let his eyes roam round the high-ceilinged room, all tastefully furnished. On the dressing table next to the vertical swing mirror was the photograph of a young, beautiful woman wearing a green velvet hat with a feather. Randall recognised her immediately. It was a photograph of Genevieve as Maid Marian, the feather long, and green like the hat. Like Hayley next to him, Randall was naked. Without too much alcohol to dull their enthusiasm they had made love deep into the night, finally falling asleep, both of them satiated, both of them happy to sleep. From the photograph to Hayley the likeness of mother and daughter was even more remarkable, which set Randall thinking: it was a long way from World's View and a terrorist's bullet through the window to a plush American apartment with the daughter of a famous actress lying next to him. The room was quiet, no sound of outside traffic, the soundproofing in America with its double-glazed windows better than it was in England.

"It's the only photograph I keep in my apartment. She was so young and beautiful when she made *Robin Hood*. It was some time before she married my father. They say there was an affair between my mother and Gregory L'Amour but I've never heard my mother mention it. She only likes to talk of her past life when there is a connection to my father Tinus and us children. I love my mother very much. Far more than I ever loved my husbands. Did you sleep well, Randall?"

"Never better despite the different time zones. We exhausted each other."

"Didn't we just?... Do you want me to open the curtains? Not much of a view I'm afraid. The top apartments have views over New York. Ours looks out to the block of apartments across the street... You want some coffee?"

"I'd love some tea."

"I'd forgotten. You are like my mother. Both our mothers were English. Dad drinks coffee. I'm told the Afrikaners in Rhodesia prefer coffee to tea. Something about the Anglo-Boer war. One of my ancestors, a Boer general, was hanged by the British for treason. What a strange world. All that hatred boiled down in me to a mixture of Afrikaner and English. And I'm American."

"The world has always been nuts."

"So there you have it. An English baron for a grandfather and a Boer general for a great-grandfather."

"So your grandfather inherited the St Clair title?"

"His only child was my mother so the title and Purbeck Manor went to my Uncle Robert when my grandfather died. And when Uncle Robert died – he was Robert St Clair, the novelist – it went to his son who, as an American, couldn't use the title. So Cousin Richard went to live at Purbeck Manor in Dorset and, through his father, took British citizenship so he could use his title and take his seat in the House of Lords. When he gave his maiden speech with his strong American accent they say half the House woke up to listen. He was a sensation. Robert wrote *Keeper of the Legend* and *Holy Knight*, all about my ancestors at the time of Richard the Lionheart and the Holy Crusades. Both books were made into movies."

"I've always wanted to be a writer."

"Stick to business. You can be in control in business. My mother said she was always controlled by the producers. Writers are controlled by their publishers. You have to do what you are told. Anyway, only a fraction of actors and writers make any money."

"Is money so important?"

"Look around you... Tea it is. We make tea in America with tea bags. Not in a pot. My mother never got used to it."

"So your grandfather must have been the 18th Baron St Clair of Purbeck? And Cousin Richard the 19th?"

"Yes, they were. If my mother hadn't been born a bastard she'd be the Honourable Mrs Genevieve Oosthuizen. How about that? And here we are in America. Makes you think."

Randall, now fully awake and smiling, watched Hayley get out of bed and go to the kitchen. She was naked. Her long legs made her move like a deer, the movement so smooth. With his hands behind his head, Randall lay back and waited for his tea. Life wasn't all bad. His friend Oliver Manningford was right: it wasn't all bad.

"Do you know how old I am, Randall?" The mug of tea was on a saucer, the tag from the tea bag hanging over the side. "I put in a spoonful of sugar with the milk. Just as my mother likes it. I'm thirty-eight years old. And that's the problem. In twelve years I'll be fifty and you'll be still a young man. So don't either of us think of getting serious. Enjoy what we have together now."

"You want to make love?"

"Finish your tea. We've got all day."

A half hour later Randall pulled the wet tea bag out of the mug and stirred up the sugar and milk. His tea had gone cold, the cold tea not unpleasant.

When they went out before lunch, the September sun was shining and the streets of New York were full of people. Hand in hand they walked down Fifth Avenue, Randall gobsmacked by what he saw on display through the shops' plate-glass windows, especially the cars, the big American cars on display in the General Motors dealership. He was happier than he had been for a long time. America was so different, so shiny, everything looking so new, the tall buildings imperious, everything the opposite of what he had grown up among in Rhodesia. His homesickness began to dissipate as he walked down the sidewalk with the rush of traffic on the street beside him, everything under control. Randall was smiling as he looked at everything: the confident people, the cars and taxis, the shops and everything in them.

"Would you like to live in New York, Randall?"

"Oh, yes. I can feel the excitement."

"I'm sure my father could arrange a transfer."

"Uncle Paul wouldn't like it. In the end he wants me to take over BLG in the UK."

"A transfer doesn't have to be forever. Anyway, nothing is forever... You want some lunch?"

"I could eat one of those hamburgers."

"Hamburgers it is."

Later, when they reached the waterfront, the whole world in front of Randall again different, they were each licking ice creams like two happy children.

"When am I going to meet your mother?"

"This afternoon. I always like to visit her on a Saturday afternoon if I'm not out of town on business."

"This is the most extraordinary experience of my life."

"Me, my mother or New York?"

"All of it. Everything is so much more exciting when you are part of it. Thank you, Hayley. Thank you for everything."

"You think it might last?"

"I hope so."

"I was just kidding. So, what do you now want to do before we go see Mother?"

"I'd like another ice cream."

THE WOMAN from the photograph looked a lot older than Randall expected, until she smiled. When Hayley's mother smiled the young girl from the photograph shone through. Randall was awestruck being introduced to such a famous actress. The old man next to her put out his hand.

"Well this is a pleasant surprise for a Saturday afternoon. Randall Crookshank from Rhodesia."

To Randall's delight and surprise Tinus Oosthuizen, the president of BLG Inc in America, spoke with a Rhodesian accent, the slight nasal pronunciation still distinct.

"Your accent hasn't changed, sir."

"We don't call people sir in America, Randall. Come on in. Accents and people don't really change. Despite my American citizenship, for which I am eternally grateful, I'm still a Rhodesian at heart. Africa casts a long spell over those who have lived there. Harry Brigandshaw's farm, which was also the farm of his father, Sebastian Brigandshaw, was named Elephant Walk. It was where I grew up. In those early years of Sebastian Brigandshaw, my grandfather, when the white man first got to what they were to call Rhodesia, the elephant had an annual migration that stretched through the bush for miles, passing through what became Elephant Walk. I can still see the open bush and the animals when I close my eyes: Elephants, giraffe and buffalo, buck, you name it. Precious memories. Precious times... So our daughter is looking after you properly?"

"I've seen all the films, Mrs Oosthuizen. I loved every one of them."

"Well thank you kindly, Randall. If they gave you pleasure, it's a joy to me. Making other people happy is more important for me than anything else. How did you come to meet my daughter so quickly?"

"Hayley was good enough to meet me at the airport. We had met each other before in England. She's kindly showing me the sights of New York. Tonight we are going to the theatre."

"What are you going to see?"

"*Cats*."

"It's wonderful. Everyone likes Andrew Lloyd Webber. He started writing music very young, and luckily he came from a good family with money and theatre connections, so he was able to get his early collaborations staged and recorded. Ever since, he has produced his own shows. Made a fortune of course as he cut out all the predators who feed on artists. Not that I can complain. My people were wonderful to me. How old are you, Randall?"

"I'm twenty-seven."

"Do you like your job at BLG?"

"I'd prefer to run a farm in Zimbabwe and write books. But I'm happy where I am. Uncle Paul and BLG have been good to me. Put me through an apprenticeship and night school where I got my economics degree."

The old woman was looking from Randall to Hayley and back again, a knowing look on her face.

"I'm three years older than my husband," she said for what appeared to be no particular reason. Come and sit down and tell me all about yourself, Randall. Hayley, why don't you go into the kitchen and make us all a nice pot of tea?... What kind of books would you like to write?"

"I've written one already. I called it *The Tawny Wilderness*. It's all about Rhodesia. Because it's told from the white farmer's point of view nobody wants to publish it."

"Give it time. People's ideas change. They get a different perspective. Robin Hood was a thief, don't forget. But he robbed the rich to give to the poor and everyone loves him. These days you steal from the rich and the powers-that-be throw you in jail."

"We were giving them jobs. Giving the country food security. We weren't stealing from them. We turned the bush into productive farmland. Dad's still farming. Uncle Paul says he should get out of Zimbabwe. That we should never have gone to Rhodesia in the first place. Sometimes it's difficult to tell what's right and what's wrong. God knows what would happen to the economy if the white farmers stopped farming."

Randall looked away from the old woman to the old man, trying to imagine her as the young woman he had seen up on the screen in the cinema. The expression on the old man's face was one of loss, faraway loss, the loss in his eyes mingled with yearning. Randall knew the look and feeling all too well. In that moment of recollection neither of them was in the room, both of them roaming the African bush in their minds. The old man sighed and sat down. All the wealth of America hadn't removed the yearning for the place of his birth...

Hayley brought the tea tray in from the kitchen, a big brown pot in the middle, and put it down on the coffee table as they made themselves comfortable. Randall, forever curious, looked round the big, comfortable room. On the walls were original paintings. Randall looked from one to the other, not quite understanding the significance of the paintings. Someone had once said artists could either paint with a brush or paint with words. To Randall, the brush strokes were more difficult to understand than the words. In the corner, almost hidden away, was the soapstone carving of an African man's head. The two women were talking animatedly about things that had nothing to do with Randall. Randall got up off the couch and walked over to the carving. It was so good the old man's head was alive: the eyes; the enigmatic smile; the old man's curly hair turning white.

"That was Tembo, Randall. Carved by an itinerant black artist. Harry Brigandshaw gave him the commission. Tembo's ancestors were saved by Sebastian Brigandshaw after a devastating Matabele raid on their village, when the Matabele Zulus were killing most of the indigenous Shonas. My grandfather took the orphaned boy's family back to Elephant Walk where Tembo was born. Tembo and Harry grew up together, Tembo becoming the bossboy or headman on Elephant Walk. Tembo Makoni's son was Josiah Makoni who was head of ZANU in London at the start of the independence struggle from white rule. Josiah Makoni and Josiah Tongogara were killed in a car accident on their way out of Mozambique to Rhodesia after the Lancaster House Agreement was signed in London that ended the bush war. Tongogara was the head of Mugabe's guerrilla army. Some thought he had a bigger following than Mugabe. That he would be made the president in the new Zimbabwe. That the car accident wasn't an accident and Mugabe had them killed. There's another story that to this day Robert Mugabe is haunted by the spirit of Josiah Tongogara. That Mugabe sets a place for him at the dinner table every night. Africans, some of them, are more superstitious than we are. Who knows? Tongogara won the war and now he's in his grave along with Tembo's son, also a contender for the job of president. My own theory is all politicians are crazy or they wouldn't want to be politicians. But in Africa the only way for a man to get rich is to become a politician... I think the tea must have drawn enough by now. Would you like to pour? When those two women get together they talk so much you think their tongues are going to fall out. I can never follow their conversations as they both talk at the same time. I love both of them more than my own life. But oh can they talk."

"Maybe I'd better wait for your wife or Hayley to pour the tea."

The old man was looking at his wife and daughter with a look of deep contentment. Then he looked back at Randall.

"Probably wise... So what do you want to do in the office?"

"Look at your operation in detail and see if there is anything you've done that we haven't that might work in England. I'm looking for new ideas."

"Barend came back with some tips from your office in England. To be successful in business you have to keep your eyes open... Are you two seeing each other?"

"Yes we are."

"I thought so. Even in the natter with her mother she keeps looking across at you."

For a moment the two lapsed into silence, neither of them knowing what to say.

"Do you think Mugabe killed Tongogara?"

"You're changing the subject, Randall... Who knows? It depends upon which side of the political divide you come from. Everyone has their own agenda. We believe what we want to believe. In America they call it spin to make you believe what the politicians want you to believe. Even in a democracy it's all about making the people go with your flow so you get elected. What they really think is not so important. The older I get the more I wonder if any of us know where we are going. In a democracy the man in the middle makes the decisions. Mr average man and woman. That's fine when everything is going right but not so good when it isn't. Then you need a Winston Spencer Churchill or an Ian Douglas Smith. I wonder how Smith is enjoying his life now he is no longer prime minister of Rhodesia... But I must be boring you with an old man's view of life. It's much better to be young. When we are young we are not so cynical. In business you have to make the right decisions or you go out of business. You can't fudge the issue in business. Don't forget that, Randall... How do you like your tea? When did you say you were going back to England?"

"I'm not sure."

"No, I don't suppose you are." The old man looked again at his daughter and back to Randall before getting up to stand over the coffee table and pour the tea.

"Let me do that, Dad."

They drank the tea before Hayley said it was time for them to go.

"It was an honour to meet you, Mrs Oosthuizen."

"Call me Genevieve. Most people do. You see, for the first part of my life I never had a proper surname. Just Genevieve. In those days that's what happened when you were born a bastard."

CATS WAS another amazing experience for Randall, so much piling into his first full day in America. He had gone back to the Fairmont and collected his suitcase, taking the suit he had travelled in from the chair. He told the Fairmont, on Hayley's instructions, that he wasn't coming back again, the billing for the one night passed to BLG. After the musical they went out to dinner, both of them hungry. Randall was floating, everything out of his control, Hayley knowing each time exactly what they both wanted, Randall happy to go with the flow. Growing up without a real mother left Randall making the decisions. Bergit, after she married his father, had helped without imposing her will on either Randall or his brother Phillip. In terms of mothering, the boys were on their own. When someone got disciplined or told what to do it was Myra and Craig, Bergit's children by Randall's father. However hard Bergit tried to be his mother there was always that distance, that hesitancy, that uncertainty. Randall, looking at Hayley eating her food across the table, wondered if the lack of a real mother in his life drew him to older women. First Amanda, and now Hayley, the two-year difference with Amanda five years ago when he was so much younger and innocent, no different to the larger age gap now with Hayley. Life was complicated... He ate his food, enjoying his evening.

"What are you thinking, Randall?"

"That America is amazing. What a day."

THEY STAYED in bed the next day until eleven o'clock, both of them feeling relaxed and lazy. Then they went for a long walk. In one of the big main streets was a parade with a formation of drum majorettes in front of the brass band and a line of floats following. The parade had come up from the waterfront, the traffic diverted, people smiling and mingling on the sidewalks. The mood was festive. In front of the lines of girls was a drum majorette twirling a big shiny stick that she occasionally tossed high up in the air and caught again, not missing a step. The long legs of the young girls caught Randall's attention, their skirts only inches below their nubile bottoms.

"Your eyes are popping, Randall."

"So would yours be if you were a man. Every one of those girls is a ten."

"They pick them carefully. There's a lot of competition in American schools. It's all part of the motivation."

"What's this parade all about?"

"I have no idea. Why don't we walk down that side street and get out of their way?"

"How old are they?"

"Seventeen, going on eighteen. They're schoolgirls."

"Now that's a sight for sore eyes... Oh, I'm sorry. No harm in looking... America is so vibrant. No wonder so many people in the world want to live like Americans. Just listen to that music. It's all so patriotic."

When they walked away from the parade Hayley was looking annoyed, Randall not quite understanding. Once they were out of sight of the parade Hayley took his hand and everything was all right again, the sun shining down through the tall buildings.

"Did you know it's rare for the sun to shine on the pavement in Central New York? We've caught a special day. Are you happy, Randall?"

"I've never been more happy in my life."

"Do you want an ice cream?"

"I thought you'd never ask."

LIFE CAME BACK to normal for Randall on the Monday morning when Hayley took him early into the offices of BLG Inc. She had an early appointment with a client and quickly left him with Barend in Barend's office. Their father had not yet come into the office. Barend put out both of his hands.

"Good to see you, Randall. How are tricks? Is the Fairmont looking after you? Sit yourself down, buddy. My sister picked you up at the airport okay? And picked you up at the Fairmont this morning? You seen Donna St Clair recently? Now there's a girl. What a trip we had with your brother in Rhodesia."

"The last I heard Donna was married with two kids."

"My goodness. The time does fly. That camp on the banks of the Zambezi River seems like yesterday. So, how are you, Randall? Did you find something to do over the weekend?"

"Hayley looked after me."

"Did she now? You watch my sister. She likes young men. She can suck the juice out of a man in a week and throw him on the garbage heap. Watch my sister Hayley. Two marriages. And so many live-in lovers we all lost count."

"We visited your parents on Saturday. It was such an honour to meet your famous mother. And yesterday there was a parade through the streets. Oh, and Hayley took me to see *Cats*."

"Be careful, Randall. She chews them up and spits them out... Must have been the reason she offered to pick you up at the airport... Anyway, let's get down to business. I want to show you what we are up to in America. You finished Westcastle. Make any money?"

"When I left London we'd sold all the flats except for two."

"That's the stuff. We're getting into computers and information technology. Let me show you. We call it venture capitalism. They have a bright idea and we have the capital and business knowledge to turn the idea into money. And when we find the right youngster with the right idea we turn it into lots and lots of money. Take off your jacket. Sit yourself down. It'll get your mind off my sister Hayley."

"She's very sweet. I like older women. Amanda was a bit older than me."

"And look what happened to her. She went off with a woman. I'm sorry, buddy. That wasn't called for."

"Then please stop laughing or you'll get me going again."

"So how was the divorce?"

"We're not divorced. Her father sold the flat we were living in and took back the money. When he bought us the place he put the flat in Amanda's name. For Amanda there isn't any need for a divorce as she can't marry a woman. For myself, whenever the girls ask me to commit to our relationship and think about marrying them I say I'd love to but my wife wouldn't like it. Saved me a whole lot of problems. No, I don't want a divorce."

"Would you take her back?"

"It wasn't love the way people like to think of love. We were best friends. I miss her company. Who knows what happens in the future?"

"Does Hayley know you are still married?"

"No, she doesn't."

"That should be fun. When my sister wants to be she can be a first-class bitch. Don't get me wrong. I love my little sister. We're good friends. Understand each other. And that's the trouble when she gets her claws into one of my friends. I know what's coming. She's quite happy so long as you do what she wants you to do. I'd be careful not to mention you're still married... Are you staying at her apartment?... Enjoy it while it lasts. I've been trying to find her a man that she lets stand up to her since she was eighteen. She's strong-willed. Add the famous mother and rich father and she don't take no shit from no one. How long are you staying?"

"That all depends."

"That all depends on Hayley. But don't get me wrong. She'll show you a good time. One you won't forget in a hurry... Now, see here. We have a twenty-year-old with an idea. He's in his second year at MIT. I'm trying to understand his latest bright idea. When you get home you should spend some time at your old alma mater. See if you can't spot the next computer science genius. Venture capital. That's where the big return is going to be next. You put together a business plan for the young man, give him the start-up capital and let him run. When it works you float an IPO on the stock exchange; an initial public offering. You can turn a hundred thousand into a hundred million before the wet dries behind the young man's ears. Money. Oh how I love making money. Here's the lad's idea on paper. And here are my notes for a business plan to make the money. Make yourself comfortable and think as you read. Concentrate. See how it looks to you. I'd value a second opinion. You'll want to read through his proposal a few times to understand what he's saying. A lot of it is pure mathematics."

"You don't waste time putting a man to work."

"Neither did Hayley by the sound of it."

"You're giggling again, Barend."

"Went off with a woman! That really sucks. Have you met the other woman?"

"Not yet. She's quite a bit older than Amanda."

"Oh, my God!"

In minutes Randall was immersed in the theory of a computer programme that would translate the sound of a person's voice into written words. Randall, who couldn't type, immediately imagined himself talking his next book onto a computer rather than writing it all down in longhand.

"If this works I'll be the happiest writer in the world."

When he looked up he was alone in the room, Barend having left his office. Alone, content, Randall let his mind daydream: he was in a log cabin, far away from the crowd, writing his next book that everyone who read it would fall in love with. Then he read the proposal again. And again. And again. By the time Barend walked back into his office Randall's head was spinning.

"So, what you think, buddy?"

"I think it's brilliant... If it works."

"But will it make money? Won't people still want to type?"

"How fast can you talk? A lot faster than you can type. And most of us men type with two fingers."

"We'll have to see... Dad wants to see you in his office. Apparently Hayley has asked him to give you a job in America. Just be careful she doesn't destroy you. And don't say I didn't warn you. But if you can control my sister you'll make the whole family ecstatically happy. Anyway, she can't make you do anything precipitous as you're still married. Keep that one up your sleeve. Oh, and lunch today is on me."

THE RESTAURANT WAS upmarket as Randall might have expected, the owner gushing over Barend and his lucrative business account. It seemed Barend ate in the restaurant regularly.

"So you think the voice recognition software will work, Randall? The problem is going to be with the hardware. I'm hearing there are going to be personal computers on everyone's desks, the mainframe no longer the only means of computer processing. It'll revolutionise life on earth much like man getting up on a horse all those centuries ago. They say man's knowledge is doubling every thirty years. Can you believe it? How's your food? Best in town I tell my clients. You take them out to lunch, sum each other up and if you think you can trust each other you do business. I always say a good deal has to be equally good for both parties. I like to mentally sit in the other man's chair and see if it works for him. If it does we'll have a deal that lasts. You got to be able to trust people in business. In life. If you can't trust you can't live. You want another glass of this excellent wine? We don't have to rush back to the office. Most of my money is made right at this table."

"It's the pace of everything in America that staggers me."

"You have to keep up."

"What do you want from me, Barend? Why am I here?"

"You youngsters know a lot more about computer science than a man of thirty-nine like me. You just graduated from university. I want you to go through all my projects and give me the younger man's opinion. Of course, when I turn it into money the whole idea will be mine." Barend was grinning, Randall smiling.

"If I can help it will be a pleasure. Just don't forget that at heart I'm just a farm boy... There's something I want to ask you. Your mother's father was the Baron St Clair of Purbeck, Merlin. Donna is a St Clair. From what I remember from Donna her grandfather was the brother of Baron St Clair. You and Donna must be first cousins."

"No not quite. First cousins once removed... There was a lot of uncertainty about the identity of my mother's father at the time. You see, my grandmother was a barmaid who got herself pregnant during the First World War. Merlin's child. To give the child legitimacy she married a semi-literate corporal who was killed in the trenches some weeks later. Merlin had always said she was beneath him, not from his class, and would never marry her. And he knew nothing of her pregnancy. When she married the corporal she wrote to Merlin to tell him, not of the pregnancy but of her marriage, never expecting Merlin to come back from Flanders. Merlin only found out about my mother when my mother was seven years old. Mother became very close to the baron. Did you notice the colour of her eyes? The same as the baron's. Two different colours. There was no doubt as to who my mother's father was. Merlin never had any other children and doted on Genevieve. Spoilt her. But it suited him so he financially looked after my grandmother and my mother. Yet without either the baron or the barmaid, I wouldn't have life. A life that I'm enjoying. People like to think they have important ancestors. But in the end the only important ancestor is the one who gives you life."

"Is your grandmother still alive?"

"No. She was an alcoholic. She drank herself into a comfortable old age on the St Clair money. What more could a girl ever want?"

"Did she ever remarry?"

"Don't be silly. They all had what they wanted. My grandfather had a pretty daughter and my grandmother had enough money to drink and live comfortably... And when it comes to Donna St Clair there's another question mark. Her father Frank started off life as Frank Brigandshaw thinking his father was Harry Brigandshaw. Apparently Harry had gone back from England to Rhodesia on an extended trip and his wife had an affair with her childhood lover who was Barnaby St Clair... Now you know why I've never married. In this crazy life you never know what they are all up to. You want some more wine? We're all potential alcoholics. Both of us will likely cut our lives short by drinking too much booze. Goes with the territory. I say enjoy yourself while you can. Good luck to you and Hayley. Make hay while the sun shines and to hell with the consequences. None of us really know where we came from and none of us really know where we're going. *Carpe diem*, as they say. And that bit of wisdom came from my days in an English boarding school. Cheers, Randall, good to have you in America. Here's to the both of us having a good life. You've only got one so you might as well enjoy it."

"Cheers, Barend."

"And don't forget most good things in life require a lot of money... Have you ever thought that if a maternal ancestor had said in the summer of 2709 BC 'Not tonight thank you, darling' you wouldn't be here? Multiply that a few times back through the labyrinth of the family tree and the chance of being born at all is minimal. Life when you have it is precious. We should all remember that when we think we're being hard done by. My aim is to get as much out of my life as possible. Rip the ring out of it. Make plans for tomorrow but live for today is the motto of one Barend Oosthuizen."

"Did you think of marrying Donna?"

"Don't be nuts. I wouldn't inflict myself on a nice girl like Donna. Married with two kids you say?"

"Don't you want children?"

"The way I behave with women when I'm drunk I've probably got an army of them."

"I meant children of your own to bring up."

"There's still plenty of time. Charlie Chaplin was still fathering children in his seventies. It's the girls who want children young. A man with money can always get married. You like older women. I like them nice and young before they start all their scheming. When they get over thirty and single they plan their snaring of a husband move by move, some of them so damn good at it you have no idea what's happening. Especially if you're like me with money. Rightly, a few women like Hayley are coming into the top echelon of business and can make their own money; but the only way for most of them to get comfortable is to marry it. I'm all for women's lib. Gives them the freedom to make their own lives and leave us men in peace... More wine, Randall?"

"No thanks. I try not to drink during the day. Keep it down to a few after work during the week. Fridays and Saturdays are my days of drinking."

"So many of my clients are married men who have to get back to their wives in the evenings. Why they like to drink during the day. But it's all part of doing business... Hell, that place on the banks of the Zambezi River was beautiful. Hot and beautiful. Showering in the shade of a tree. When I got back to New York I found I'd left a tiny part of me next to the Zambezi River. It will always be a beautiful memory... How's Phillip?"

"He's fine. He and Jacques are doing well with their safari business. Fancy Jacques being your real cousin."

"The world indeed is small. Well Randall, if you're not going to sit here drinking with me we'd better finish our lunch and go back to the office."

"Thanks for the lunch."

"My pleasure. If you can get out of the clutches of my sister maybe you and I can go out on the town on Friday? Rip some of the ring out of New York. A lot of nice American girls just love a British accent."

"Mine's Rhodesian."

"What's the difference?"

Smiling, enjoying each other's company, they finished their lunch.

3

By Friday night, when Barend took Randall out on the town, Randall was exhausted, his mind and body desperate for sleep.

The job offer had come through on the Wednesday, Randall not sure what to do. Hayley had relayed the details from her father, a big smile on her face, the twist in her lips saying clearly it was an offer he could not afford to refuse.

"The future of the world isn't old England, Randall. It's America. What's the matter with you? The old British Empire is as dead as the dodo, never to rise again. Sure, the City of London is a financial hub like Switzerland but it isn't New York. They don't innovate in London like we do in America. It's the new age of American hegemony. The Russians are finished. People kill to get themselves a job in America like the one Dad just offered you. Grab it with both hands. Don't hesitate."

"I have my Uncle Paul to think about. He's been good to me. I was a refugee when I arrived in England waiting tables."

"With the cross shareholdings between BLG Inc and BLG Ltd it doesn't matter. You'll still be making him money."

"And then there's Grandmother. And my quest for finding my maternal grandfather."

"Make up your mind. Chances like this don't come often in life...

There's a fundraiser at the Carlton tonight. Lots of old friends I want you to meet."

"Couldn't we stay home and get an early night?"

"Whatever for? You're young. What's the matter with you? Can't you keep up? No, we have to go."

"How do you get by on four hours' sleep?"

"Easy. It's practice. The body adjusts to it. We'll have fun. And it's good for business to be seen with famous people. With luck we'll get our photographs in the magazines and newspapers."

"I'm used to eight hours' sleep to make my brain function."

"Look, I agreed you could rock and roll with Barend on Friday. Tonight you come with me."

"Yes, mistress."

"You're so cute."

With a tweak under his chin Randall had stood watching as Hayley walked back to her office. They had put Randall in a small room off the main office to read through the literature given him by Barend. He was in three minds and not two: whether to take the job offer in America, go back to his new flat in London, or run for his life back to Zimbabwe and find himself a secluded spot on the banks of the Zambezi River and start writing another book. The idea of writing a book in a tent was particularly appealing.

"Have you made up your mind?" asked Barend as they walked in.

"Not yet. It's all been so sudden."

"If you are lucky in life that's how it happens. Did she complain about you coming with me tonight?... No, you don't have to answer that one. I know my sister. What d'you think of all the young women here tonight? Ever seen so many good-looking broads?"

"The mind boggles."

"I said we would rock and roll tonight. Let's go and have a drink up at the bar. The bar's the best place to pick up women. Trust me."

"She'll kill me if I go with another woman."

"That's the whole idea of bringing you here tonight. Not to get you killed by my sister but to open your eyes to the bigger picture. She hooked you right off the plane for God's sake. You need the chance to look around. And then you can accept our offer. I like your input. So does Dad. We're going to go with the voice recognition software. Put in some seed money. See how it goes. How would you like to head the project? You've finished Westcastle. There's nothing outstanding for you in England."

"What about my new flat?"

"Sell it. I'm sure they gave it to you at a favourable price. Make a quick profit. Build up your personal capital. Put the cash in the New York stock exchange. If you're smart you can borrow from the bank using your cash to leverage your investment in the stock market. A share that goes up ten per cent with ninety per cent of the investment borrowed from the bank can double your money in a week. You pay the bank an annual interest of six per cent and wait for the share to go up. For a week or a month the interest is virtually nothing. It's how an individual gets himself rich."

"But what happens if the share goes down and you owe the bank all that money? You'd end up quickly in debt."

"Good shares in good companies don't go down in America. I have friends. They know what they're doing. Look, you borrowed most of the money from the bank to buy your apartment. What's the difference? If you sell your apartment at ten per cent above what you paid for it, all the profit is yours, not the bank's. Sure, there are expenses when you sell – you also pay commission when you sell shares. You just want the apartment or the share to go up enough and you're in a financial heaven."

"You make it all sound so easy."

"Welcome to America. Five years from now you'll be speaking with an American accent. Mark my words... Now, just look at that. I know one of those girls. We'll go over and join them when we've had a couple of drinks if something better doesn't come along. Take a good look around. The world's our oyster... You like the music?"

"I like everything."

"That's what I wanted to hear. Now we're getting somewhere."

"The only thing I want more than a drink is one good night's sleep."

"I said she'd suck it out of you. You'll be fine, Randall. A couple of drinks and you'll be chirping like one of those crickets you introduced me to in Africa."

Barend waved at the girl sitting with her group of friends before turning to the barman and ordering the drinks.

"Everything goes on the tab. Pay with a credit card at the end of the evening. Saves all the bother. Everything is easy in America, Randall. We got life organised. We work hard and play hard. You got to get everything out of life while you can."

Not surprisingly to Randall, Barend knew the name of the barman, the barman the best friend of a man out on the town hunting for women. Randall had found that knowing the name of the barman made the girls feel safe. They had a point of reference, the strange man they had not met before not so strange, the old way of waiting to be introduced to a girl long passed. With the drinks, the barman had placed bowls of peanuts and potato chips in front of them. There was a shiny metal rail along the bottom of the bar making Randall's feet comfortable sitting up on his barstool. At the back of the big room, furthest from the long plastic bar, a man was sitting alone on a stool playing an electric guitar and singing. No one took much notice. The singer, an older man in his late forties, looked frustrated. Most of the tables were occupied, the waiters and waitresses serving drinks moving around. There was a pulse, the pulse of people searching for a good time, the servers smiling, the tips building up, the givers and takers both happy. When the bill was paid at the end of the evening by credit card, the payer would likely be drunk, the fifteen per cent tip added to the tab no longer significant.

"What happens, Barend, if you walk out at the end of the evening without paying the bill?"

"You see those big men standing by the exit door? That's their job. The waiter wants his tip. If a customer gets up without paying and walks for the exit door, the waiter or the barman tips off those men. The customer is usually drunk, the waiter and bouncer sober. No contest. They grab you. Most people wouldn't dream of leaving without paying as they wouldn't impress the women or their friends... You want a peanut?"

"I'm already through half a bowl of them. They're addictive. You know, I'm waking up."

"I said you would. The booze works."

"That poor singer's being ignored."

"Lounge singers don't get a lot of attention. It's background noise. You have to be famous in America before you get any attention. You want some food before we go hunting women?"

"The peanuts are fine... Don't you ever have a regular girlfriend, Barend?"

"Sometimes. I have a short attention span. I suppose one of these days when the young girls start to ignore me I'll have to settle down with one and start a family. Or just maybe I'll meet that special soul mate I've been searching for all my life. But I wouldn't bet on it. The hope of eternal love and living happily ever after recedes the older you get. You find that romance isn't quite what you expected. Especially after you've been with each other for a while. Sadly, the best time in a relationship is in the beginning when you're getting to know each other. It's all rather sad. When you discover it's the hunt that's the best part, not settling down to an everyday existence and the same old routine... So Donna St Clair is married with a couple of kids. Just shows. And that could have been me... You know the worst fear I have in life, Randall?"

"What's that, Barend?"

"It's boredom... Scottie. Give us another round. And a couple of bowls of peanuts."

"Coming up, Barend. You two have a good evening, now."

"We're trying."

Wondering why Barend was so melancholy, Randall sat thinking, his mind back in the Leg of Mutton and Cauliflower on the night he met Amanda, the night he lost his virginity, the start of the laid-back couple and the long period of his happiness when all they ever wanted was each other. Looking around, Randall hoped he didn't grow into the way of life that was Barend's, going from one girl to the other, never finding what he wanted ever again, left with the memory of those brief sweet months of perfect content that Randall now understood to be happiness. Which made him think again. Had he loved her? Was what they had had a love of two people for each other and not a convenient friendship? Had he lost it forever when he lost Amanda, when Amanda lost their baby, a boy who by now would have been five and talking, a person, not a small dead body on a mortuary slab? That boy had been so close to life, to having a life, to being a living person. Did he really want to stay in America? Or would it be running away, always looking, always searching for his happiness? Was the new woman he had been with for a week going to be more than a delicious sexual experience? Could he and Hayley ever become the laid-back couple that was Randall and Amanda? Or could such moments ever be repeated? And if they were, would they last?

"Did you love Donna St Clair, Barend?"

"Just a little. Maybe more than a little. But whoever really knows? Good to have you here, buddy. I hope you'll stay with us."

"I'm still thinking about it."

"Yes, maybe it's better to think... Two kids. That's something. Do you know who she married?"

"No, I don't."

"I hope they'll be happy."

"That would be nice. Have a peanut, Barend. You want to go and join your friend?"

Randall watched Barend tell the barman they were going to join the girls at the table, that his bar tab should follow him before they walked across to the girl's table. The girls were smiling, everyone was smiling, everyone was happy, even the singer received a spatter of applause as he got down from his stool at the end of his set, a drink in his free hand sent him by one of the few appreciative customers. It was going to be an evening like so many others for Randall, the places, times and people blurring into a haze of distant alcohol, none of the evenings of any importance, just fun, a way to pass the spare time, a way to spend his BLG money that was flowing so richly his way.

"It's good to have a hunting partner, Randall. Always better to hunt in pairs. The girls think the same. Why she's sitting there with her friends... Hello, Mary. This is my friend Randall Crookshank from Rhodesia. He's going to move to America and join my company. I guess I can't remember your surname. I'm sorry. You do remember me? I'm Barend Oosthuizen."

"Of course I do. My surname doesn't matter. Sometimes I can't remember which one I'm meant to be using. How's business?"

"Pretty good."

"Making plenty of money, I hope."

"You can't believe how well we're doing. May we sit down?"

"Of course you can. Why do you think I was waving at you? Hello, Randall. My, you are nice and young. Where's this place called Rhodesia?

Let me introduce you both to my friends. We all work in the same office. Nothing like a Friday night to go out for some drinks with your friends."

The names blurred, most of them were American, unfamiliar to Randall. The rest of the girls were young, all of them pretty. Barend ordered everyone a round of drinks as he sat down. When the drinks came with the table waiter, Barend raised his hand in acknowledgement to Scottie. The singer came back to his lonely barstool and began to sing again. The drinks flowed. The girl called Mary left with one of the girls. There were two girls now at the table. Mary had paid for their previous drinks leaving the rest to Barend. The girls turned out not to be very interesting. Barend was still looking around. At ten o'clock, instead of getting into trouble, Randall excused himself, got up from the table and left. Outside he caught a cab and gave the driver Hayley's address. She had given him a key to her apartment. When he let himself in there was nobody there, Hayley having gone out. Randall's tiredness had come back again. After a few moments in the bathroom Randall got into bed, sleep coming in a wave as he lay down in Hayley's bed.

In the morning when he woke he was still alone. His watch told him it was nine o'clock in the morning, the first good sleep for Randall since he arrived in America. When Hayley let herself into her flat half an hour later he was still in bed.

"Did you sleep well, Randall?"

"Like a baby."

"Now isn't that nice?"

Randall, not really wanting to know, refrained from asking Hayley where she had been. It was her flat. It was her country. In some ways, whatever decision he made it would now be easier for Randall. To Randall's surprise, Hayley took off her clothes and got into bed, quickly all over him. The woman was insatiable.

PART 7

OCTOBER 1985 TO DECEMBER 1986 – IN
PURSUIT OF HAPPINESS

1

Two weeks later, while Randall was still trying to make up his mind about Hayley and America, Amanda Hanscombe, as she now called herself despite not being divorced from Randall Crookshank, was celebrating Evelina's birthday at Camilla's Corner with William Drake. Still perennially tired but happy among friends, she watched them all enjoying themselves, her mind far away, Amanda not sure where her life was going. Largely, her job was keeping house, a housewife without the legal permanence, a family without children, a lesbian's life, like now, always in the present, a life full of material pleasures but little substance. Whether they loved each other as true and permanent soul mates was questionable, as were so many other of the relationships around her: William smiling at his new boyfriend, a young man happy to be entertained by a man with money; Camilla, the owner of the restaurant, pretending to be lesbian when she probably wasn't, her business with its largely gay and lesbian clientele doing well; so many of the others changing their sexual partners, none of them taking their lives seriously as they partied it away. And always, when Amanda brooded, she thought of her son and how her life would have been if the boy had lived. It made her melancholy, her smile changing to sadness.

More than anything in life, Amanda had wanted to have her own children, a proper family she could watch forever. Her lesbian life was sterile as it could only be by its very nature, a nature that required a man and a woman to make a child. As often happened on such occasions, Amanda thought of Randall, of where he was, of what he might be doing, of what they might have been doing together watching over a growing son. And always, with such thoughts, then and now, Amanda felt guilty of not appreciating all the lovely things Evelina brought to their lives: the compassion, the care, the understanding that was so often missing in so many heterosexual relationships. She had a friend and a lover, a good provider, shouldn't that be enough? she asked herself for the umpteenth time. She was, in simple parlance, an ungrateful bitch. With Evelina's guidance she had lost all the excess weight she had put on with her baby. She was modelling some of William and Evelina's clothes, strutting the catwalk with the best of them, feeling good from all the attention. And without Evelina's help she would have eaten herself to the size of a small pig. She was ungrateful, that was her problem.

Immersed in herself, she had not noticed William was talking, the sound of his voice bringing her back to the present where she was sitting at the biggest of Camilla's tables picking at her food, a well of familiar tiredness, physical, not mental, sweeping over her.

"Sorry, William. What did you just say?"

"I saw James Tomlin this morning on the train. Haven't seen him for ages."

"How was James?"

"He was looking well. He asked after you. I told him you were still with Evelina. He's been asked to go to an audition in America. Both of them are going. Oliver Manningford is also resting as they call it in the theatre when they are out of work."

"That's nice for them."

"The point is, Amanda, the invitation came from Randall. He's in America. New York to be precise. He met the famous actress Genevieve. She's the mother of Randall's new boss and used her influence to get James and Oliver their invitations."

"Are they going?"

"James says it all depends on whether Randall stays in America. He's going out with the boss's daughter."

"Genevieve's daughter?"

"That's right. They all want Randall to stay in America but Randall can't make up his mind."

"Is he living with her?"

"I think so. Apparently she's a whole lot older than Randall... Are you all right?"

"Just my tiredness."

"We've both told you to go see a doctor."

"I'm just tired. There's nothing wrong with being tired."

"Happy birthday, Evelina," said William.

"Yes, happy birthday, Evelina. Enough of me... He's nice."

"Thank you, both of you. If you will, please excuse me for moment, I'll be back shortly."

"He is, isn't he, Amanda?... Have some more wine."

"Just a little. When I drink a little too much I'm inclined to drop off at the table. Can't do that at Evelina's birthday party... Randall's in America. That's interesting. When we were together he always had a hankering to go back to Africa. He hates big cities... An audition will be good for James and Oliver. There are so many ups and downs in the theatre."

"Do you miss him?"

"Sometimes... Do you think, William, if my father hadn't caught us naked behind the raspberry bushes I would still be with Randall? Could that experience have sown the seed that made us both homosexual?"

"Maybe. It was a life-wrenching experience being caught with our clothes off at the age of ten. I can laugh at it now. I couldn't then."

"I'm happy with Evelina. It's just we can't have children and be a normal family."

"Nothing is ever perfect. You never get it all... How are your parents?"

"I have no idea. They still won't talk to me. For my father, his daughter living in a sexual relationship with a woman is far worse than when he caught the pair of us naked. He sold the flat, put the money back in his pocket and hasn't spoken a word to me since... Here comes Evelina back from powdering her nose. We'd better change the subject."

"You should go and see a doctor."

"Yes, I probably should. But there are some things in life best left alone. If there is something wrong with me I don't want to know."

"They'll be able to help you."

"Maybe, maybe not."

Evelina, dressed in one of William's creations, sat down at the table between them.

"What are you two talking about?"

"Not much, Evelina. You know William. He's always gossiping. Can I pour you some more wine?"

"Thank you, darling. That would be lovely. Are you enjoying tonight?"

"Of course I am. Thank you. It's your birthday and I want you to be happy. You're always so kind to me."

"I love you, Amanda. Never forget it. Making you happy gives me my greatest pleasure. And here to add to my joy, we are among friends. What more can I want?"

Gently, with everyone watching and smiling, Evelina kissed Amanda on the lips.

THE NEXT DAY, with William's warning compelling her to make the appointment, Amanda visited the doctor. The man was all smiles, his bedside manner perfect: he took her pulse, strapped a band round her arm and took her blood pressure, put a stethoscope to her chest and listened to her heart, made her pee in a pot so he could analyse her urine and sat back in his chair, the tips of his fingers joined together.

"Fit as a fiddle so far as I can see. If you were older I would take a blood test and send it to the laboratory. Your blood pressure is perfect, there is no blood in your urine, and your heart is pumping perfectly. Quite a few people wake up in the mornings feeling tired. There are different levels of sleep, the best level being the one when we are dreaming and remember what we dreamed. You need exercise, Miss Hanscombe. Lots of walking. Make yourself properly tired so when you go to sleep you sleep deeply. I recommend long walks. At least a hundred paces to the minute. You read the second hand of your watch and count the paces so you know what speed you are doing. Half an hour every day, rain or sunshine. Preferably an hour. That should make you sleep better and stop the tiredness. If that doesn't work we'll have another look at you. Do you have any problems, Miss Hanscombe? Worry can be another contributor to tiredness. Some of my friends call it stress. A good walk will make you feel better."

When Amanda left the doctor's rooms it was eleven o'clock in the morning. She went home, changed her shoes to walking shoes and picked up Evelina's umbrella. Outside the sun was shining but in England one never knew. She walked down Kensington High Street, checked her watch as Doctor Kendal had told her to, and put her best foot forward, finding one hundred paces a minute a nice pace to walk. Ten minutes later, still doing her hundred paces a minute, she found she was walking in the direction of her old home in Notting Hill Gate. She felt better. Happier in her mind. Without realising what she was doing she walked all the way to Mrs Salter's boarding house and pulled out her keys, the old key to Mrs Salter's front door still on her keyring. Opening the door, Amanda let herself in and walked up the three flights of stairs. At the top of the house she looked at her old door before knocking on the one next to it.

"Well, this is a nice surprise, Amanda. Come in."

"How are you, James?"

"Never better. With a bit of luck I'm going to America. Films, Amanda. None of this television. Hollywood. Oliver is coming with me."

"I know. You saw William Drake in the tube train the other day. He told me. Did you speak to Randall?"

"He spoke to both of us. It's not what you know but who you know in this life. Come you in. I'll put the kettle on and we'll have a nice cup of tea together like in the old days. We miss you and Randall. We had so much fun together. The theatre has so many ups and downs it takes your breath away. One minute you think you've got something and then it slips away. Oliver says looking for work in the theatre is like eating soup with a fork: as soon as you think you've got something it dribbles away. We'll count our chickens when we get to America."

"Who's paying your airfare?"

"The studio. Can you believe it?... Oh, it's so nice to see you. All this waiting for work had me down in the dumps."

"Is Randall staying in America?"

"We hope so. Sort of a condition for our tickets. If you ask me there's a bit of bribery going on. And Oliver and I are part of the bribe. Why don't you come with us?"

"I'm still living with Evelina."

"Are you happy?"

"I miss my baby."

Bursting into tears, Amanda slumped in a chair, a concerned James kneeling down in front of her.

"Do you think Randall misses our baby, James?" said Amanda after a while, trying to control her tears.

"I'm sure he does. It was so terrible for both of you."

"I'm sorry for crying on you."

"You cry all you want. Get it out of your system."

"That's the trouble, James. I can't. I'm so unhappy. I should never have walked out on Randall. We were both in denial about the baby. I needed Evelina to look after me, the sex not all that important. What can I do? I don't have a profession or any kind of a career. All I've done to make money is type and wait tables. I'm a glorified housekeeper, so that when she comes home the food is on the table. The sex together is mostly a thing of the past. She says she loves me but we all say that when we want something. There's me, Evelina and my old friend William Drake. The rest are party friends. Drinking friends that come and go that don't mean anything. My parents won't have anything to do with me. Life sucks. I've got every comfort in life and life sucks. What's the matter with me? And to compound the problem I'm always tired. Got no energy. No enthusiasm for anything. There's no point to anything anymore."

"You should go and see a doctor."

"I've just seen the doctor. There's nothing wrong with me."

"I meant a psychologist. Someone who would understand what a woman goes through when she loses her baby. I can't even imagine what that must have been like. A man can't. We don't carry the baby inside us for nine months like you did."

"I don't want a shrink. I want a life. A proper life with my own family. I want some kids."

"You poor girl. Why don't we go across and see Oliver? He's much better than me at things like this... Why didn't you come and see us earlier? We're your friends. Not the party crowd. Though there's nothing wrong with a good party. I still remember your parties and those curries. The stews. The fun we had. Artists think. There was more conversation than the usual trivia you get in pubs. No, that's being rude. All people think but they think differently to artists."

"Weren't we just young and uninhibited?"

"Probably... That's better. Let's go and see Oliver. If anyone can pull you out of the dumps it will be Oliver Manningford. He never changes. The odd bit of fame never goes to his head. Money doesn't much interest him. Why he never moved out of the room next door. Oliver's passion is acting. And when he hasn't got a part like now he just sits and waits for one to come along. And it always does. So now we're off to America. Why don't you come with us? I'm sure between myself and Oliver we could come up with your airfare. You must have a passport as you went to Rhodesia."

"What would I do in America?"

"Come and find out. You've lost weight. You're looking good. You know how to model clothes according to what William told me."

"That's just a hobby. Without Evelina and William I'd never be asked to model at a show."

"You don't know that, Amanda."

"But Randall has a girlfriend."

"Things don't last forever. Give Randall a surprise. A good surprise."

"I'm still legally married to him, I suppose."

"There you are, you see. So if Randall has a job in America his wife can join him. The Americans will give you a residence permit; a green card, whatever that is. It's what Oliver and I must get if we want to work in Hollywood."

"You're being so kind to me."

"That's what friends are for. Give me your hand. Dry your eyes. That's better... Now we go see Oliver."

AMANDA GOT home to Knightsbridge just before dark, not once having to use the umbrella, her mind in excited turmoil. She was no longer feeling tired. Evelina was not at home. As quickly as possible, Amanda vacuumed the flat and went into the kitchen to prepare the supper. By the time Evelina came home from work, the food now ready, the tiredness had returned. Soon after they had eaten Amanda excused herself and went to bed, quickly falling asleep. All through the night the dreams, all vague and strange, came and went, the images forgotten by the time Amanda woke with the dawn. Next to her, on the far side of the double bed, Evelina was still asleep. For the first morning in many

Amanda was not feeling tired, the one thought racing through her mind: 'I'm going to America.' Oliver Manningford, in his inimitable way, had cooked up the plan.

"Never burn your boats, Amanda. Always leave yourself an option. Tell your partner you're going to America to persuade Randall to give you a divorce. That you want to finalise your old relationship. Then she won't mind you going. There's nothing like a break in a love affair to let both of you get a better perspective. Think of it as a holiday. Let come what may. Make your life again an adventure. It's not all bad. It's not all bad. We're going to America, everything thrown in the wind."

2

A month later, when Randall opened the door to Hayley's apartment he had the surprise of his life: standing outside the door was his wife. Behind Amanda stood James and Oliver, both of them grinning.

"Who's there, Randall?" Hayley called from the lounge. "Have your friends arrived? Mother said to bring them over for Sunday lunch."

"Yes, it's Oliver and James. And they brought someone with them."

"Who've they brought, Randall?"

"My wife."

"Your what?"

Ignoring the outburst from the lounge, Randall turned back to his friends: both James and Oliver were now giggling.

"Well, this is a surprise, Amanda. I can truthfully say the last person I expected to see when I answered the door was you. Just look at you. You've lost so much weight."

"You don't look too bad yourself."

"What brings you to America?"

"Oliver and James. They kindly paid my airfare."

"How's your lover?"

"She's fine. We all thought I needed a break."

"What's going on, Randall?" said Hayley from right behind him.

"I'm not sure. Hayley, meet my old friends Oliver Manningford and James Tomlin. And this is Amanda."

"You called her your wife."

"We never actually got a divorce."

"So you lied to me?"

"Let's say I didn't tell you the whole truth. I never actually said we were divorced. I just said my wife had left me for a woman." Annoyed at the tone of her voice Randall turned back to his friends.

"Where are you all staying?"

"We hoped with you," said James. "Oliver and I fly to California on Wednesday for Thursday's audition at MGM."

"And Amanda?"

"She is your wife."

"Stop laughing, Oliver. This is serious."

"She's not staying here," snapped Hayley. "This is my apartment. What's she doing here? If you two want to see each other you can do it out of my house. And if she doesn't go straight back to England you can pack your bags and follow her. You and your friends won't be welcome in America. We thought bringing your friends to Hollywood would make up your mind to accept my father's job offer."

"So they can't come in?"

"They can. She can't."

"That's very rude, Hayley."

"Don't you tell me I'm rude. This is my home. If it wasn't for me you'd have no job and no home. You do what I say. Tell this woman to go or you get out."

"Sorry, chaps. Can you wait in the corridor while I pack my bags? Good to see you both. There's a hotel not far away. Where I was meant to spend my first night in New York."

"They won't get their audition! My mother will see to that."

"I think they will, Hayley. Unlike you, your mother isn't a bitch. Your brother did warn me about you."

"Get out of my apartment this minute."

"When I'm packed. It's been nice knowing you, Hayley. Have a nice life. It should be fun in the office tomorrow."

"You'll be fired."

"Again, I don't think so. But this little tantrum of yours has made up my mind. I'm going back to my flat in England."

"Get out!"

Smiling to his friends, Randall gently closed the front door and walked to the bedroom where he packed his things.

By the time he had finished packing, Hayley had calmed down.

"You can't go, Randall."

"Oh yes I can. It was fun while it lasted."

"I love you, Randall."

"I don't think so, Hayley. You just want your way. I'll phone your mother from the hotel and explain."

With his suitcase in one hand, Randall let himself out of the apartment. The others were waiting for him out in the corridor, none of them smiling.

"I'm so sorry, Randall," said Oliver. "It was all my idea."

"It was just as much my idea," said James. "Amanda came to visit me last month. She was so unhappy we persuaded her to come and see you. The whole trip's turned into a mess."

"We'll see. First we book ourselves into the Fairmont. Then I'll phone Genevieve and explain what's happened. Hey, it's good to see you all. You can never make new old friends."

"Is it over with her?"

"Oh, yes, Amanda. Very over."

"That was quite something." This time Oliver was laughing. "Wasn't she a bit old for you, Randall?"

"Probably. It all happened rather quickly. The lady met me at the airport. Her brother, Barend, told me she has a predilection for young men."

"Don't they call them toy boys in America?"

"Something like that... My job now is to make sure I haven't jeopardised your auditions with MGM. Let's get the hell out of here."

Outside in the street they walked arm in arm down the pavement, Oliver humming a tune. At the intersection they flagged down a cab that dropped them off at the Fairmont. It was warm in the cab after the cold of the street. The phone call to Genevieve went as Randall expected. They were all invited to lunch, including Amanda, neither Genevieve nor her husband, Tinus, surprised at their daughter's performance.

"She's done it a few times before," Tinus said after they had eaten lunch. "You can stay in America with BLG if you want, Randall."

"Better not, sir. You'd be able to cut the atmosphere in the office with a knife. Better I go back to England, and I thank you and Barend sincerely for the opportunity of working with you in America. The voice recognition software will work. There are some others in the office who can follow it through. And if my uncle throws me out of the London office for accepting your offer I'll get another job or go back to Zimbabwe. I still have my flat in the Westcastle complex. For the moment, we still have the farm in Zimbabwe. Let's see what happens. Are my friends still all right for their audition on Thursday, Mrs Oosthuizen?"

"Of course they are. My friends at MGM offered Oliver and James the chance to audition from their previous experience. Oliver is a well-known actor on the London stage. Your sitcoms, James, have been seen on American television. I just made the right phone call to set everything in motion. Good luck to the pair of you. And thank you all for visiting with us for lunch. I love talking about films and the theatre. You and your new generation are so exciting. It reminds me of my youth. Now, off you all go and enjoy yourselves. Four days in New York. That should be fun. And when I see you two boys in a movie, when you are both famous, I'll think of this lunch. And Randall please, once again, call me Genevieve. It's the only name I have ever been called by."

For the rest of the day, Randall feeling a great weight lifted from his shoulders, they walked around the streets of New York like children in a toyshop. When they returned to their hotel and picked up the two keys to their rooms, the manager approached them.

"We received a phone call from Mr Oosthuizen confirming his company's wish to pay for your cheque or bill as I think you call it in England. Welcome to the Fairmont, Mr and Mrs Crookshank. If the two gentlemen would prefer separate rooms they are welcome. Enjoy your stay in New York. You will, of course, dine with us tonight in our restaurant. At Mr Oosthuizen's request I have booked you a table. BLG are good customers of the Fairmont. Your table is booked for eight o'clock, if that is convenient."

"Thank you, that's very convenient."

With the key to the extra room – just in case, as Oliver put it – they went up to their rooms.

"It's not that I mind sharing a room with you, James. It's not that I mind you snoring. It's just with so many days in New York we should both keep our options open in case we get lucky."

"How do you know I snore?"

"I just assumed it, old boy."

"Well I don't. Never snored in my life."

"How do you know?"

"By now, someone would have told me. Have I ever told you, Oliver, that you are an idiot?"

"Frequently... What are they going to ask us to read for?"

"We'll soon find out when we get to California... This is all so exciting. I feel like a kid again. And all that walking has made me hungry... Isn't Genevieve just a wonderful woman? This could be the break of our lives. Some of those big stars in Hollywood get paid millions for making one movie."

"Don't let's get ahead of ourselves. One step at a time. And, for me, that's a soak in a hot bath. But you're right. Happy days are here again. And we gave Mrs Salter three months' rent in advance so if anything goes wrong we have our old life to go back to. Which isn't all bad. How long does it take to make a movie? And tomorrow, young James, you and I are going to practise our American accents. Be prepared. I never joined the boy scouts. Only the Cubs. That was where I first learnt to be prepared for every eventuality... We've got an hour before we all dine together. Do you remember that first time we all went to the Leg of Mutton and Cauliflower? Isn't life strange. If we hadn't all gone to the pub that night we wouldn't be here in New York. I think tonight we should celebrate our reunion with a good bottle of champagne. A vintage Heidsieck Dry Monopole would do the trick. Life is truly wonderful. My life is blessed. Friends. Wonderful old friends. Joyful joy. If it wasn't appropriate in a five star hotel I'd suggest we all sing a song of happiness. Sufficient it is to smile."

Holding hands with Amanda, Randall followed his friends into the lift. They got out at the fifteenth floor and went to their separate rooms.

"Do we make love before or after we have dinner, Randall?"

"We've got an hour... But I thought you were a lesbian?"

"We're all a bit kinky when it comes down to it. Doesn't my making love to a woman turn you on?"

"You have no idea how much. It's just so wonderful to see you again, Amanda. What are we going to do?"

"Like Oliver said: 'One step at a time.'"

THEY WERE both relaxed when they went down to supper, both of them sexually replete, the sex better for both of them than ever before. Oliver smiled smugly at them. Amanda, in one of William Drake's creations, looked devastating, her eyes sparkling. Randall felt he was walking on air. In deference to Amanda, Oliver stood up as he greeted them.

"I took the leave to order the champagne. Charles Heidsieck I'm afraid, wine from the cousin's estate not available. Why are you late? You don't have to answer... The menu is mind boggling. Quite up to a top London restaurant even if I have to say so myself. The colonials have learnt a few tricks since they kicked King George out of the country. At least the Americans still speak English. Do you know there are more people in India speaking English than any other country in the world, including the United States of America? Sit yourselves down. Tonight is going to be a party. I have roamed my eyes over a few of the girls. The first one who said 'how are you doing', I thought she was coming onto me. Made a bit of a fool of myself. Different customs. You have to get used to a new country. After just one day I could be happy living in America. Just look at this place. You can feel people's excitement. Everyone is smiling. People laughing. No long faces. And it isn't the climate. Outside it's as cold as charity. And they say in summer it can be boiling hot in New York."

"The best climate in the world is the highveld of Zimbabwe," said Randall, pushing forward Amanda's chair from behind as she sat down.

"You have mentioned that a few times in passing."

"Well it's true. Do you know, in winter it doesn't rain for six months?... Thank you so much. You can pop the cork straight away now we are all together. I won't even ask the price of the champagne. Good old BLG and Harry Brigandshaw. Now there was a Rhodesian. It must have been paradise growing up as a boy in early Rhodesia before the First World War. His father started out as a hunter, hunting elephant for their ivory. Ironically, it was the Great Elephant that killed Sebastian Brigandshaw. The Great Elephant was a legend. They say that animal had the biggest tusks ever seen... Cheers, everyone. It's so wonderful to see you all. Through all the years, however long I may live, I will always remember the four of us together. Good luck to both of you for Thursday."

"You don't have to stand up, Randall."

"Of course I do, Oliver. This is a memorable occasion for all of us. So I lift my glass. First to my wife, Amanda. And then to James and Oliver, may they soon be screamingly famous. I give you all a toast – 'To us'."

Oliver, tall and slim and dressed in his dinner jacket, got to his feet.

"Not every book of yours will be rejected by foolish publishers, Randall. I raise my glass to Randall's future success as an author, his ultimate goal in life. We all need a goal and we all need to pursue that goal, never giving up. So I give you Randall Crookshank, the famous novelist. Long may he live and prosper. And to BLG, our benefactors, and the legendary Harry Brigandshaw, whom none of us had the privilege to meet, but whose shadow still benevolently hangs over us."

By the end of the third course all four of them were tipsy, Amanda having got the giggles. Leaning close to Randall, her hand on his knee under the table, she whispered in his ear: "I'm not on the pill. And don't worry. There's nothing wrong with me."

At the end of the meal they ordered cognacs to go with their coffee before they went up to bed. Right through the night, between bouts of exhausted sleep, they made love. When they woke in the morning they were entwined with each other.

"You don't want any breakfast, Amanda?"

"Don't be silly. I don't want anything. Everything I ever want is right here with me in this bed... Are we going to be happy?"

"I hope so."

"What are we going to do?"

"When the lads fly to their audition I suppose we had better go back to England... What are you going to do about Evelina?"

"Tell her the truth. Tell her I'm going back to my husband, if he'll have me... Do you still want to be a writer?"

"More than anything."

"Then writing it shall be. The laid-back couple. I can still wait tables."

"I have a bit of money saved up. I can make a profit from the flat. Maybe find a place deep in the countryside and grow our own vegetables... Do you really want to chance getting pregnant?"

"More than anything."

"NEVER MISS AN OPPORTUNITY," Oliver told them at breakfast. "Fly with us to Los Angeles. Use some of your hard-earned money. You can come to our audition. Give us your moral support. I'm sure I can persuade MGM to let you through the gate. Who knows, this may be your last time in America. They've booked us into the Airport Marina Hotel where we are to pick up the manuscripts for our auditions. James and I will practise for most of the night. So, will you come with us? Mrs Salter's troupers. Maybe one day they will want to make a film out of one of your books, Randall... Are you going into the office this morning?"

"I think a phone call to Barend and his father might be better. I don't have anything more to say. Hayley will find herself a new boyfriend. I hate arguments. Especially in public. As much as I would like to be your cheerleader I have to think about money. I have some explaining to do with my Uncle Paul. There's such a thing as loyalty. I broke that loyalty by even considering the American offer. My uncle may no longer look at me as his protégé and successor. You make your moves in life and pay the consequences. So let us all enjoy this moment while it lasts and make a memory. There will be plenty of time to reminisce when we're old. Let's make the best of New York. A theatre, a concert, all the art galleries and museums. For two nights and three days we are going to be the consummate tourists. How does that sound to you and James, Oliver?"

"It sounds perfect... Can you believe it? They eat waffles for breakfast covered in maple syrup. When in Rome, do as the Romans. Thank you, kind lady, I'll start with the waffles. But bring me some tea."

THE LETTER from BLG Inc was hand delivered just before lunch. Inside was a cheque for three months' salary and a brief note from Tinus Oosthuizen, the company president: 'Sorry my family caused the hiatus.

Hope this will see you on your way. When you get back to Africa give it my love.' The note was just signed Tinus. Overwhelmed by the man's generosity and understanding, Randall stood silently. They had been about to leave the hotel and do the rounds of the art galleries.

'Like me he can't get Africa out of his blood. Poor Hayley. She's going to mess up her life.' Coming out of his thoughts, Randall caught up with his friends.

"Oliver, we're coming with you to Los Angeles. Mrs Salter's troupers. What a strange life it sometimes is. All the twists and turns. A man has no idea what's going to happen next."

THE FILM TEST on the Thursday went better than any of them could have imagined, the look of Oliver and James on film more important than their accents or their acting. They were both offered second player parts in a major forthcoming movie. Randall, happy for his friends, felt flat: his friends had a future in American film, the excitement bubbling over in both of them. That night they took themselves to Dino's on the Strip, a restaurant recommended by a new acquaintance at MGM and once owned by Dean Martin. They all celebrated late into the night, going back by cab to the Airport Marina Hotel where they were all staying. There had been no sign of Dean Martin or any other member of Frank Sinatra's Rat Pack. Leaving their friends in high elation, Randall and Amanda caught a plane for England. All through the long journey Randall was wondering what he was going to be doing, the dollar-denominated cheque from BLG still in his pocket. At Heathrow Airport it was raining, a cold east wind blowing. At the end of the train ride from the airport they bundled themselves into a taxi for the last leg of the journey to Randall's flat.

"There's an old saying that the British would never have had an empire if they had had a better climate – no one would have wanted to move. The English winter is horrible. Welcome to Westcastle, Amanda. Your new home-to-be until we make up our minds what to do. At least the flat has central heating. Growing up in the Isle of Wight, my father said they didn't have central heating. In winter you stood in front of a roaring fire, one side of you boiling hot while your arse was freezing. Well, here we are, Mrs Crookshank. Home sweet home. If you lean out of the window you can see the Thames. Why people pay fortunes to live cheek by jowl with each other I fail to understand. In England you can never get away from people. Some people like it. I've heard of people who like the sound of traffic. Can you believe it! So, what d'you think? Sparse, modern and very upmarket."

"Evelina would love it."

"You'd better go and see her. It's best to never make enemies. Right now I'm phoning my uncle's secretary to make an appointment. While I'm gone tomorrow you can go see Evelina."

THE INTERVIEW in Brigandshaw house went worse than Randall had expected, the only benevolent smile in the room coming from the portrait of Harry Brigandshaw up on the wall. Randall and his uncle were alone, the door to the office closed.

"I offered you everything, Randall. Quite frankly I'm disgusted. You've thrown everything I've done for you right in my face. I gave you a job, a tertiary education, a flat in one of London's most sought-after locations and a brilliant future. And this is what you do. You go off to New York and join the Americans. Don't you know the meaning of the word loyalty? I thought we were family. I don't have a son so when I retire from the business you would have become chief executive. But not anymore, Randall. No, not anymore. Please clean out your desk. The mortgage company will likely call up the bond on your flat without the company guarantee... I never took you for a fool. I was wrong."

"I'm so sorry."

"I'm sure you are. When people lose out they quickly become sorry. You took advantage of my generosity. So get out, Randall. And don't show your face here again. Can you imagine what the other employees are thinking if I can't control my own nephew? The accounts department have a cheque ready for you."

"I'm so sorry, Uncle Paul. What about Grandmother?"

"We'll see about that later. I might mention your grandmother is equally disappointed in you. We all are."

"Please give her my love."

Randall put out his hand which was not accepted. Feeling the size of an ant, he walked from the room, glancing up at the Livy Johnston portrait of Harry Brigandshaw as he went. In his own office he cleaned out his personal possessions into a cardboard box.

"I hope I haven't jeopardised your job, Sonia," he said to his secretary.

"So do I."

Realising that people's first concern was for themselves, Randall left the BLG offices for the last time. Outside in the street he looked back and up at the building that had been his workplace for so many years. He was clutching the cardboard box in his arms. Then he turned and crossed the road, heading for the railway station. First he had lost Zimbabwe, now he had lost his job and his home in England.

When he got home Amanda was waiting for him in the lounge of his flat.

"They threw me out on my neck."

"She did much the same."

"They're going to force me to sell this flat unless I can replace their guarantee for the mortgage. It's just you and me."

"The laid-back couple. Why don't we just make love and forget about the lot of them?"

"So it didn't go too well with Evelina?"

"It was horrible. People change so quickly."

"Especially when they aren't getting what they want... You know something? I hate this furniture. It's so sparse. So cold. It has no feeling... What the hell are we going to do?"

IT ALL HAPPENED SO QUICKLY. One minute Amanda was a kept woman, the next she was waiting tables. Christmas came and went in suspended animation, their money problems mounting. The property market had changed. The speculators who had bought the Westcastle flats expecting to turn a quick profit were now trying to offload their investments. Randall, unable to pay the mortgage without a salary, was quickly running out of the money he had received as severance pay from BLG Inc and BLG Ltd. By March, Randall was going to be broke, if not insolvent and facing bankruptcy. The stock market had also taken a turn for the worse. The words on everyone's lips in the City of London were 'bear market' and 'recession'. The price of housing had slumped. With the speculators mortgaged up to the hilt and unable to sell and make a profit, many of the mortgages on the flats BLG had sold were in arrears. By the end of June, Randall was in crisis, the possible sale value of his property the same as his mortgage. Randall had put all the money he had saved over five years working for his uncle into the deposit on the flat. Unlike many of the speculators, Randall had paid twenty per cent of the purchase price with his own money. When the one offer finally came, Randall sold, including the furniture. He was unemployed, unable to find a job in the slump and broke.

With James and Oliver still in America, Mrs Salter also finding renting rooms more difficult, they got back their old room with the big window that looked down onto Mrs Salter's washing line. They were finally off the hook, both of them smiling. His old desk, where he had written *The Tawny Wilderness*, was still under the window. Amanda, happier than at any time since the first flush of sexual excitement with Evelina, was still trying to get herself pregnant. When the light came up each morning Randall got out of bed and went to the desk to write his new book. In the evenings they went to their respective restaurants, both of them grateful to the Sarah Rankin temp agency that found them their jobs. When James and Oliver returned to England at the end of August, moving back into the rooms they had kept at Mrs Salter's while they were making the film, the old bohemian life returned for all of them. Once again, Oliver and James were looking for work. Life was normal, the stress and strain of making big money no longer important to them.

"You got to wonder what it's all about," said James. "Hollywood was fun but we're both glad to be out of it. Everyone was chasing their own celebrity. Why people want to show off and live in mansions is beyond my comprehension. You can only eat one meal at a time and sleep in one bed. When you're asleep who cares what luxury is around you?"

"Don't tell me about it," said Randall. "You want a cup of tea? I'll put on the kettle. One minute you see all that wealth and then it's gone. Frankly, I miss neither the job nor the money."

"How's the book going?"

"Not bad... Did you make any money in America?"

"Spent most of it. The more you make the more you spend – you know the old saying. Got enough over to last a while now I'm not spending big bucks. Something will come along. Oliver wants to go back on the stage. Says it's more real than film. I agree with him... What's it about?"

"Life. People. What we think we want out of life. Getting what we want and then not wanting it."

"Sounds familiar. People write about themselves and their friends. Are we in the book?"

"Both of you." Randall was smiling, Amanda watching, James not sure if Randall was pulling his leg.

"Don't make us too obvious. You have changed the names?"

"Of course I have, James."

"Are you working tonight?"

"Neither of us are."

"That's good. Then I'm taking all of us to the pub for a beer... What are you looking so happy about, Amanda?"

"Life. You just never know what's going to happen next."

"You look positively radiant."

"Well thank you, James."

That night, when they got back from the Leg of Mutton and Cauliflower, Amanda told Randall she was pregnant.

"Are you quite sure? Have you been to the doctor?"

"A different doctor this time. He says there is absolutely nothing wrong with me."

"And all of that tiredness you talked about?"

"A thing of the past. Looking back, it was more sadness than tiredness. Being sad makes you listless. Thank God that's all gone... You and I are going to have a family."

"We don't have any money."

"We'll find a way. Where there's a will there's a way. I'm just so happy. Without your own kids life has no point."

"I'd better get a proper job."

"Don't be silly. Finish the book. You've been through a lot of life since you wrote the last one. First finish the book, submit it to publishers and then we'll make up our minds. When do you want me to start typing?"

"When it's finished. I don't want us discussing the book together until it's finished... When's our baby due?"

"In six months' time. Lots of time to finish the book. That was so much fun in the pub. Mrs Salter's troupers. Old friends together. What more could anyone want?"

The following day, when, at Randall's insistence, they went to see Amanda's new doctor, she was feeling full of happiness, Randall as excited as she was at the prospect of the baby. Through the night she had woken twice to find Randall softly feeling her belly.

"Are you sure there is nothing wrong with the health of my wife, Doctor Spencer?"

"Every test I've done is encouraging. Your wife is perfectly healthy."

"Then why did she lose our first baby?"

"You'd better ask the doctor who performed the delivery. There's nothing I can see that will jeopardise your wife having a perfectly healthy baby."

"He told her never to get pregnant again."

"He must have had his reasons."

"Then what were they?"

"Not for me to speculate. Come and see me in a month's time, Mrs Crookshank. Preferably no alcohol and definitely no cigarettes. Eat lots of vegetables. Until your stomach grows too heavy, get plenty of exercise. Plenty of walking in the park. The London parks are so beautiful at this time of the year. Carry on working for as long as you feel up to it. Congratulations to both of you. And what do you do for a living, Mr Crookshank?"

"I wait tables like my wife. I lost my job and can't get another one."

"Many of my patients are suffering. The trick is not to worry, if that is possible. What did you do before the slump?"

"I was project director at BLG."

"My goodness."

"My uncle owns the British end of the business. He fired me."

"My word."

"It's a long story."

"They usually are... Look after your pregnant wife, Mr Crookshank, and have a nice day. I do so love England when the sun is shining."

"So what happened with the other doctor?"

"Not for me to criticise a fellow doctor. But people do lie to protect themselves. Even medical doctors. Something probably went wrong. But whatever you do won't bring back your son, Mrs Crookshank. I'm sure your doctor did the best he could. Things can go wrong in the best of circumstances. Be grateful your wife is alive and healthy. BLG, you say? My goodness. I have shares in the company. How do you think the company will do in the future?"

"I have no idea."

Amanda looked from the doctor to her husband. Both of them were smiling.

Outside in the street, Amanda gave a skip and jump before taking Randall's hand as they started their walk back to the room at Mrs Salter's. She was cooking a stew for lunch for all of them.

"They don't eat properly."

"Who are you talking about?"

"Oliver and James."

"So Dr Thompson was lying through his back teeth to protect them from a lawsuit."

"There's no point in dwelling on it. I've done enough of that already. Let bygones be bygones. Whatever went wrong was most definitely not intentional. It's all right now, Randall. That's what's important. I'm healthy, pregnant and we are going to be parents. We have a normal future ahead of us."

"Except we don't have any money."

"You have a hard-earned degree in economics. They can take away your job and your money but they can't take away your brains without killing you. We'll make out. We have enough to live off at the moment."

"Are you going to tell your parents?"

"Didn't do us any good last time. Do you know my father made a damn good profit when he sold the flat? And still put the money in his pocket to teach me a lesson. They never so much as contacted me when I lived with Evelina. More than once they spoke to William Drake when he visited his parents, so they could have found out where to get hold of me."

"Did you ever phone them?"

"Of course I didn't."

"By now they might have forgiven you."

"There's a point in a relationship when you can't keep mending what has been broken. They have other children. They'll be all right without me. I'm the blot on their lives... Are you going to try and find that grandfather you were talking about?"

"At the moment my head's full of the book... You want to go and walk in Holland Park? How long will it take to make the stew?"

"Better go straight home. After you finish writing tomorrow, if the sun is still shining, we'll go for a stroll in the park... It's going to be a girl."

"How can you tell?"

"I have a feeling."

"A girl. My goodness. She'll probably give us as much trouble as you gave your parents... You know, they say the chance of finding a publisher is the equivalent of being attacked by a great white shark and struck by lightning all at the same time?"

"Don't be so negative."

"I could go to the banks and raise some money on the back of my reputation at Westcastle. This recession won't last forever. They never do. Greed gets the better of fear. I could go into the property development business on my own. Make a fortune. Send the kids to private schools. Have enough to put them through Oxford. Isn't that what it's all about to be a parent?"

"Having a loving home is more important. You'd hate living with the sharks, always having to out-think them. You have to be dishonest to make that kind of living in the modern world. You don't make big money by doing an honest day's work. Wasn't Westcastle a case of telling the buyers that if they bought now they would make a quick profit? And now look at them. Who was more honest? The buyers without money getting loans from the bank when they knew they couldn't keep up the payments, or the bank who loaned them the money at an inflated interest rate hoping their risk was covered by ever rising property prices? Or you as the developer?"

"How do you know all this, Amanda?"

"I do listen to what you say. Whatever you might think. Waiting tables is good honest work."

"Is it? The trick we both know is gushing all over people when they are hopelessly drunk to maximise our tips."

"If you find a publisher, is he going to be honest or make you sign a contract that screws you?"

"I've got your point. The world we live in stinks... How long will the stew take?"

"A couple of hours."

"I'm starving."

Amanda, watching her husband, smiled inwardly. All men thought women were stupid. Especially when it came to business. If women didn't have to bring up a family and keep a house they would be just as successful as men in the workplace, a thought that kept Amanda thinking. Would she really like a man's life? Wasn't being home with children the better part of life's bargain?

"I like being a woman."

"I like being a man."

"Then both of us are lucky."

Back at the room, Amanda got stuck into the cooking. All the old pots and plates they had bought those years ago were still in the room. She had bought the cheapest cut of pork that needed the most cooking. First she fried the meat the butcher had chopped up into pieces, a lot of it bone. Then she fried the onions, with the cooked meat cooling out on a plate. Then she cut the meat from the bones and put it all back with the onions, adding water and her special mix of herbs and spices, turning up the heat. When the water boiled, she turned down the heat and let the mixture simmer. Amanda was perfectly happy, the rich smell of cooking permeating the room. Randall was sitting at the desk by the window reading through what he had written earlier that morning. Without Randall noticing, she slipped out of the room to knock on the doors of Oliver and James to tell them when lunch would be ready. The first door she knocked on was that of James.

"I was hoping you would invite me over. That smell of your cooking has seeped under my door and made my mouth water. Reminds me of my mother's cooking. Why is mother's cooking always the best? All the fancy restaurants can never make a meal that tastes as good as my mother's. Oh, except you of course, Amanda."

"You're turning on the charm, James."

"Usually works. No, but when it comes to your cooking I mean it. You should open your own restaurant instead of both of you waiting tables. When the baby is born you can take it to work with you in a basket. Put the mite in the corner of a nice warm kitchen."

"How did you know I was pregnant?"

"I live in the room next door. It's difficult with the windows open in the summer not to hear what you two are talking about. I'm so happy for you. Even a little jealous."

"You should find a nice girl and get married."

"No nice girl in her right mind would marry a mostly out of work actor."

"Lunch will be ready at one o'clock... I like the idea of the restaurant. We could call it 'Mother's Cooking'. Encourage families to bring their children, including their babies. You rarely see carrycots in the restaurants. Will you tell Oliver his lunch is being cooked for him? And go down and tell Mrs Salter."

Happy with the compliment about her cooking, Amanda returned to her room to cut up the vegetables they had bought cheap on the Saturday morning in the Portobello Road market – the vegetables would go in the pot with the meat in three quarters of an hour's time. Cooking, she told herself, was all about the right ingredients and timing.

"Have you ever thought of getting a restaurant of our own, Randall? Wouldn't your father put up the guarantee for a bank overdraft? He still has his shares in those Chelsea flats with the artist."

"How's the cooking doing?"

"We could call it 'Mother's Cooking'."

"We can think about it. I was going to phone Zimbabwe and tell them you're pregnant. I hate asking Dad for money."

"He won't have to give you money. Just the guarantee."

"What's the difference? Anyway, I have a degree. At some stage I'm going to have to use it, unless I can make a living out of writing."

"Just an idea. One business you always say is much the same as another, that it's all about making money. We could end up with a chain of restaurants with your genius."

"Do you think I'm a genius?"

"Of course you are... How's the book coming?"

"I just never know what the readers are going to think of it. People like so many different kinds of books. Whether mine will suit them I don't know. Whether they will like my characters and my kind of story. The relationship between writers and readers is very personal. The writer is putting his mind, if he's lucky, into the heads of all those readers he will never know or meet, all from different backgrounds. No, I don't know if anyone will like it. I just know I like it myself. It gets it all out of me... That stew smells perfectly delicious."

"James said the same... You know he can hear every word we say? He knows I'm pregnant."

"Then we don't have to tell him. Or Oliver. Or Mrs Salter... Why don't you go down and invite her to lunch? She's as much part of our family. What would Mrs Salter's troupers be without Mrs Salter? She loves talking to James and Oliver about the film they made in America. Her eyes glaze over as the talk takes her back to her youth. Old people are like that. They live in the past, when they were young. When is it being released in England?"

"I'm sure they'll tell us. Who knows, we might all be invited to the London premiere at Leicester Square. They usually have the big studios' first nights at the Odeon in Leicester Square. Part of a long-standing tradition... Are you listening to me, Randall? Oh, and James has gone down to invite Mrs Salter."

Happy with herself, Amanda went on chopping up the vegetables, Randall back in his book, his mind far away.

By the time the stew was cooked perfectly to Amanda's taste, Randall had finished correcting the early-morning writing that he had begun when the sun first came up over the rooftops of London, the pigeons calling, the traffic moving, the life of the city once more begun.

At one o'clock on the dot Oliver knocked, the tall, slim man grinning all over his face when Amanda opened the door. Next to him stood James. Both of them had their hands up in front of their chests, the wrists turned down as if they were begging. Oliver was licking his lips. At each of their feet stood a bottle of wine.

"That smell beats Dino's on the Strip."

"Come in, Oliver. Collect your bowls and spoons. You can make yourselves comfortable on the windowsill, or on the floor with your backs to the bed. Luncheon is served, gentlemen. Mrs Crookshank's famous stew. Oh, how nice of you both to bring some wine."

Five minutes later, Mrs Salter joined them and the party began, the desk clear of Randall's writing, a tablecloth placed instead over it with glasses for the wine and the pot of stew. Under the pot of stew was a cork mat. Amanda served them the stew with a big ladle. They were quickly chattering as everyone enjoyed themselves, Amanda's stew eaten with relish. Only Randall was still far away, his mind in his book. For the first time in months, Amanda stayed in the present, her mind neither wandering back or looking forward. She knew she was happy. She knew she had done the right thing, Evelina and their life with the gays and lesbians a thing of the past; or so she hoped. James sat on the floor, his back against the double bed, a bowl of stew on his lap, spooning the food up to his mouth as he listened to the conversation. With the desk moved forward, Oliver sat on the windowsill, his long legs at an angle to the floor.

"Are you going to tell us what it's about, Randall?" asked Oliver.

"Greed. Profligacy. Excess of every kind. Mind-boggling wastes of money. Showing off at every turn. Being rich and famous."

"And where is it set?"

"In London and New York. The financial centres of the world. Where money is the only passport. They lie, cheat and steal to get what they want. Not a spark of integrity or concern for anyone else but themselves. And at the end, rich and famous, they find they have nothing."

"Sounds like the ingredients for a screaming bestseller."

"I hope so. You see, I'm probably just like the rest of them... How's the stew, Oliver?"

"Never been better. You want some more wine? Plenty more in my room. When the money runs out I'll start to worry. Meantime, let's enjoy ourselves. Life can sometimes be short. Who knows what's going to happen next? But just for the moment it's not all bad. Thanks for inviting me. This is what I call living. We've been lucky, all of us. Never forget, Randall. Never forget the good times. And may we all have many more of them... Mrs Salter, more wine? Oh what luck it is to be alive. To have real and lasting friends."

"When's the movie coming out?" asked Mrs Salter.

"Three weeks before Christmas. You're all invited to the premiere."

"The Odeon, Leicester Square?" asked Randall.

"Of course. Where else? We're all going to walk up that red carpet."

"Why do films take so long to come out?"

"It's all the editing and cutting. Films are made in bits and pieces and put together afterwards. And then there's the marketing. All the build-up. All the leaks to the press. One big marketing operation. Why I prefer doing plays. You go through a play in two hours, always in the part. All those stops and starts of filmmaking made me crazy."

Both Amanda and Randall drank little of the wine, knowing they were working later in the evening. When the party broke up they were the only ones sober.

At half past six they went to work, both of them in a rush. All Amanda could think of as she hurried to work was her baby in a carrycot in the kitchen of their own restaurant with the big sign outside proclaiming 'Mother's Cooking'.

3

*A*ll too quickly the summer came to an end. When Amanda was six months pregnant Randall finished his book and she began the typing. She was sick mostly every morning, none of the nausea mattering. Three days before the première of the movie an old man appeared at the door. He had long white hair down to his shoulders. The beard that covered most of his face was as white as his hair. His clothes were odd, belonging to an earlier century. He was looking over Amanda's shoulder at Randall, his blue eyes sparkling, a smile on his lips. The old man said nothing.

"Can I help you?" Amanda asked.

"Randall Crookshank, I presume?" The old man was still looking over her shoulder at Randall. "The likeness is almost startling. May I come in?"

"What do you want?" asked Amanda, almost rudely.

"I'm Ben Crossley, Randall's grandfather. Ida Sedgewick gave me your address. I believe you have been looking for me. She said when you changed your address you sent her a postcard. I'm in London for the première of a movie. I'm a character actor. Live in America. Been living in America ever since I left my wife. How's your mother, Randall? You are Randall? I've been a terrible father. Never had much to offer your mother. When she married a wealthy Rhodesian tobacco farmer I thought it best to keep out of the way. Didn't want to muck it up for her. They say in-laws are a prime cause of their children's marital problems. How is she, anyway?"

"My mother died soon after I was born," said Randall, moving forward. "You'd better come in."

"How's your brother Phillip? I remember being told you had been born, Randall. It was soon after that I drifted away to America. Your grandmother said she would be better off without me. I wasn't the best of husbands. Bit of a roving eye."

"He's still in Africa. Running a safari company."

"What happened to Carmen?"

"She was eaten by lions."

"And no one told me."

"No one could find you."

Behind the old man, the door to Oliver Manningford's room opened. The old man turned and looked at Oliver.

"Well, bugger me," said Oliver. "It's old Ben Crossley. What a coincidence. You over for the première?"

"Among other things. Randall is my grandson."

"Now, that really is a coincidence. Randall's never mentioned your name to me. If he had, I'd have told him we were all in the same movie. I'll be buggered. Randall, this is one of the best character actors in America. Small parts but all of them gems. Ben Crossley can do every accent in the book. Are you staying with us or going back to America?"

"Now I've found my grandson I'm not in a hurry to fly back to the States. I might just stay for Christmas. How does that sound, Randall?"

"You'd better come in. This is my wife, Amanda."

"Eaten by lions... I had no idea... Do you mind if I sit down?"

"Where are you staying?" asked Randall.

Amanda looked from Randall to the old man and back again.

"At the Dorchester... In Park Lane."

"I know where the Dorchester is. It's one of the most expensive hotels in London."

"You might say you're pleased to see your old grandfather." He was trying to smile, trying to make light of the tension. Amanda was holding both hands over her belly. Oliver, still standing just outside in the hallway, had surprisingly nothing to say.

"I'm in shock, of course. Sit you down. How are you? I'm Randall."

"Did Carmen ever mention me?"

"I was too young to remember."

"My poor daughter. And all these years I thought she was living in luxury. Maybe I'd better go. Don't want to intrude."

"Please come in and sit down. If it were not for you I wouldn't have a life."

"I suppose that's something. In the end, I suppose, that's all it is. Just a link in the chain."

"Would you like a cup of tea?"

"That would be very nice, Amanda. Poor Carmen. Lions, you say?"

"Have the big chair. We live rather sparsely."

"What happened to all my son-in-law's money? Rhodesia going, I suppose, and with it the good life."

"It's a long story. At the moment I'm pretty broke."

"I can help. Saved most of my American money. Is your wife pregnant? I remember that can be rather expensive. One of my wife's bones of contention. When we were living together I never had any money."

"I have a degree in economics."

"And you live in a bedsitter... And you, Oliver?" said the old man as he sat down and faced the open door. "What are you doing in a boarding house? You were going places."

"This is my old home. I like the familiar. You want to see James?... Anyway, I'll leave you alone with your grandson."

Oliver, always the diplomat, quietly shut the door. In the silence, they heard his footsteps cross the small hallway. His door opened and closed. The old man had sunk into the easy chair. Amanda put the kettle on to make the tea. They all waited for the kettle to boil.

"I'm afraid I've made a big mess of my life," said the old man into the silence. "I only ever thought of myself. Selfish. That's the word. I took from people what I wanted and walked away. A lot of my acting was stolen from other people and not only fellow actors. Why they say I am always so inside my characters. So, what do you both do for money?... Thank you, Amanda. Such a pretty name. One spoonful of sugar."

"We both wait tables. I'm writing a book. I wrote one before but it was rejected. Said I was too young to write a good book."

"I could help you. Two of the publishers in America have been after me to write my memoirs. I've worked with most of the famous people in Hollywood. The public like the inside story on celebrities. The last offer was an advance of half a million dollars. I turned them down, of course. I'm seventy-six years old. Far too old to sit at a desk and write a book. Can't remember half of my life, it was such a rollercoaster. Anyway, I don't need the money. Maybe you could come to America and write the book for me."

"I'm a novelist. There's a huge difference in writing a fictional story and reporting."

"Anyway, it probably wouldn't work as there isn't enough time for me to tell you what I remember of my life. The doctors tell me I have another six months to live. Which was why I really came back to England and went up to Neston. The première is a coincidence. I don't often go to premières, even premières of my own movies... When you know you're dying you want to go home. To where you came from... I did know my wife was dead. Five years into my new life in America, when I was finally making money, I had a conscience and came back on a visit to London where I'd spent my adult life. They told me Maureen was dead. There was no mention of your mother, Randall. I presumed your mother was still married to that rich tobacco farmer in Rhodesia. I was going to give Maureen some money. The day after I found out I flew back to America. You see, I couldn't even atone for my sins. Finding you has given me a purpose. What was I going to do with all my money? Quite ironical, don't you think? All that money and no one to leave it to except two grandsons I'd not even taken the time to get to know and a daughter I now find is dead. Rather pathetic... Anyway, the money will enable you to publish your book. You can publish it yourself. Or bribe one of the publishers."

"I'd prefer to think it would publish on its own. By being a good book."

"Yes, I suppose you would... When I die you won't have to worry about money. It's all in my will. You'll have all the freedom in the world to write your books and not have to worry about money. It's money people most worry about in life... The farm is still called World's View? That's what I told the lawyers. When I died it was their job to find Carmen, you and Phillip. They are good at that kind of thing... This tea is very nice, Amanda. Just the right amount of milk... And then they told me in Neston you have been looking for me... Well, I've taken up enough of your time. The cab driver will still be waiting for me down in the street. They always wait for people who stay at the Dorchester. Rich people like to give away big tips. Makes them feel important, I suppose. Or superior... There's just one favour I would like to ask you, Randall. May I borrow a copy of that book you say was rejected? The best way to get to know someone is to read a book they have written... Please give my regards to Oliver and James."

"James lives on the same floor."

"I had the feeling he did... And the book? I promise to bring it back. Who knows, if I think it's any good I can ask one of those publishers to look at it. I've read so many scripts in my life as an actor I think I'll recognise a good story if I see one. Plays, movies and books. They're all stories. If they don't have a good story the movie isn't worth making. Don't tell me what it's about. Whatever my grandson has written I will find interesting. You see, art is in the genes. I always wanted to be a performing artist. You want to be a creative artist. Your wish to write is probably all my fault. Thank you for the tea, Amanda. And look after my grandson."

"It's going to be a girl."

"Then I hope she will be as pretty as you."

Amanda watched Randall pull out the drawer to his desk and take out a copy of *The Tawny Wilderness* and give it to his grandfather.

"What's wrong with you, Grandfather?"

"Cancer. It's terminal, nothing much they can do... Do you have a phone number? When I've finished this book I can give you a ring and we can all go out to dinner... My grandson, a writer. Now, that really is something. Please don't follow me down. I dislike awkward situations. After I've read this book we will have something in common. Then we'll be able to talk."

"Do you have to go back to America?"

"Maybe. Maybe not. But I will. America is where I live. It's my home... Sorry to barge in on you like this... No, I insist. Don't see me down to the cab."

"And if he isn't waiting?"

"I'll walk up the road and flag down another one. One of the benefits of London – you can always find a cab. I can still walk. I rather like to walk. What a strange encounter. Oliver Manningford and James Tomlin, friends of my grandson."

The old man got up and walked out of the door, Randall's telephone number in his pocket.

Amanda took Randall's hand, both of them feeling awkward. They could hear the old man slowly move down the three flights of stairs. The front door opened and closed. Then there was silence. They waited, expecting to hear the door downstairs open. After a while, Amanda closed the door to their room and moved across to the window. Down in the garden, Mrs Salter was sitting in a deck chair. There was no washing on the washing line. Instinctively, she felt her stomach to comfort the baby. Life was so strange. If the old man and the woman he walked out on had not had their daughter Carmen the baby inside of Amanda would not exist.

"They say everyone in the world is only seven steps away from each other," said Randall, joining her at the window. "I know Oliver who knows my grandfather who knows all those film stars. Makes you think. So, when we finally meet, the old man is dying. Makes you question the purpose of life. What it was all about. Maureen. Do you know, I barely know the name of my grandmother? Makes her life seem so pointless. A marriage, a permanent struggle for money, and then they break up, their daughter off in Africa. I should have told him she was buried at the top of the Zambezi escarpment, the grave marked by my father with a wooden cross and the words 'Go well, my darling'. The Africans say 'go well' to their departed. Wishes them well on their journey to the other life. Do you think there's another life, Amanda? Do you think my mother was watching us talking? Was my mother with my grandmother? Were all my ancestors watching? Was one of my ancestors watching a caveman or a monkey up a tree? Some say monkeys and Homo sapiens evolved together and have common ancestors."

"He'll enjoy your book."

"I hope so. That just now was the strangest half hour of my life."

"You want some more tea?"

"Yes, I suppose so... Now I don't feel like writing. I have that empty feeling. I suppose there's a good chance I saw my own grandfather in a movie and didn't know. Do you ever read the names on the credits after you've seen a film? I never do. The leads, maybe. But not the smaller, character parts."

"If he turned down half a million for a book deal we're going to be rich."

"Is that all life is about? Too much inherited money could take away my incentive to write. Take away the passion. You have to have passion to write a book. It gets you motivated."

"But you write because you love writing."

"There was also money in the back of my mind. And recognition. Yes, the writing gets it out of my system instead of arguing about life with other people – arguing about the ethics of the capitalist system I once used to believe in, thinking a man should receive a just reward for his labour and not some politically motivated welfare state that gives the power to politicians... They are probably right. I'll have to wait until I'm forty to get a better understanding of life and people. Now I'm going to be on tenterhooks waiting for him to ring. To find out if all this writing is just a waste of time. He'll know, after all those years in film and theatre. He'll know all right. It's just I didn't want to find out. It was better to go on kidding myself to believe I was doing something important in life. If he says the book is lousy, the purpose of my life will be gone. Nothing will seem important anymore."

"Running your own restaurant can be important."

"Not much point when you're rich."

"Are you going to phone Phillip? Tell him you've found your long-lost grandfather?"

"I'll tell him we've met but not about the will or the money. Take the wind out of his sails. Now I'm talking as if the old man is dead. I should have gone down to see him into the taxi. I feel such a fool."

"How long does it take to read a book?"

"Depends on the reader. And the book... Is an old man who lived in England and America going to be interested in Rhodesia? Interested in Africa? Find our lives in the bush have anything in common with a Hollywood actor?... That was my grandfather. I can't believe it. He was here. Right in this room... What do you want to do now, Amanda?"

"Sit down and think. If what he said about the money is true our lives have been stood on their heads. I was getting all excited about building up our own restaurant together. The only goal in life should be to make a success out of something without the help of outside people. Achieve something on your own. It's the achieving that counts, not the money. My father said that. And he was right. Why when he sold the flat and took back his money it didn't worry me one bit."

"Maybe we should ask my grandfather to leave all his money to Phillip. Phillip can put the money in an offshore trust so that if Zimbabwe goes down the drain he'll have money to fall back on... If you're going to sit and think, I'm going out for a walk. My mind is in turmoil."

"He'll like the book, Randall. Genuinely like the book. He won't have to be complimentary just to be nice to you. It's a good book. I know. You go for a walk. Carrying all this weight in my stomach makes pleasure-walking not quite so pleasant. It's a nice day outside. Go out and get some air. You'll feel better. Brunch will be ready when you return. Eggs, sausage and fried tomatoes just the way you like them. I'll make us a pot of filter coffee."

"I'm so glad we're back together again."

"So am I... Why is your grandfather's opinion so important?"

"Because he's my grandfather."

By Saturday afternoon when they were dressed up for the première of the movie, Amanda in one of William Drake's expensive creations she had managed to let out to go over her extended belly, the phone had still not rung. Amanda felt sorry for Randall as he waited, saying nothing, looking at the phone, willing it to ring. There had been no word from the old man about the book or the première. If it weren't for the book, Randall had said he would have phoned the Dorchester Hotel but didn't want to ask how far the old man was into the book. With a last glance at the telephone, Randall opened the door for her and they left the room. Oliver and James had gone on ahead. Amanda wasn't sure if they would be standing in the crowd or walking with Oliver and James up the red carpet. Oliver had looked impeccably dressed when he left. James, as usual, looked a mess in his old evening dress. Both men were smiling, happy for once in their lives to be in the media's limelight, all of it good for future work. Feeling self-conscious on the Tube in her evening gown, Amanda travelled with Randall beside her on the London underground to Leicester Square station. When they arrived at the Odeon there was a big crowd outside the cinema, no sign of James or Oliver.

"I feel a prize idiot in a dinner jacket," said Randall as they joined the rest of the onlookers waiting for a glimpse of the Hollywood celebrities. They were early, unusual for Randall. He was looking around searching for his grandfather, the old man with the long white hair down to his shoulders nowhere to be seen. After half an hour in the summer afternoon Amanda got a sight of Jack Lemmon and pointed him out to Randall. Randall said nothing. The excitement built up as a few people began walking up the red carpet and into the theatre. James and Oliver followed the first members of the cast. Instead of being excited at the sight of his friends walking the red carpet, and not sure if they should break through the crowd and follow them, Amanda saw Randall was agitated, craning his neck to look over the milling crowd of people.

"It's a good book, Randall."

They both turned round as one. Right behind Randall, in a garment the press were to call medieval, stood Randall's grandfather, a broad grin on his tired face, trying to hide his pain. The old man was using a stick, holding the brass top in both of his hands, leaning on the stick in front of him. Despite the pain on his face, the old man looked imperious as he called to the backs of the crowd to make way. The crowd melted open, letting the old man walk through to the red carpet, Amanda and Randall following his beckoning. Music was playing loudly, the crowd cheering. It seemed to Amanda the people knew more about Ben Crossley than his grandson. Seeming to float, Amanda walked up the red carpet and into the Odeon theatre, Randall smiling with the best of them. An usher showed them to their seats, next to Oliver and James who were already seated. Upfront, the big screen was empty, the house lights still on in the theatre as the cast and their families took their seats.

"Chemotherapy is a bastard, Randall. Why I didn't phone you. I'll be better tomorrow and we can all have lunch. Takes a couple of days to get over the chemo. I've already invited Oliver and James."

"I didn't know you were famous, Grandfather."

"What's fame. But yes, I do have what they call a small cult following."

"Didn't seem small outside."

"Thank you, grandson. I've told both James and Oliver what I think of your book. They both agree with me. All we need is some good marketing. Publicity. You have to push to get anywhere in this brave new world. You can write. That's all that is important. I can see the pictures. Feel and smell the African bush. Empathise with your characters. So, who among your friends and family was born in the back of the truck between two swollen rivers?"

"I was, Grandfather. Your daughter gave birth to me in the back of the farm truck. My dad delivered me. They were on their way into the Salisbury hospital when they got caught by the rising rivers. Happens in Africa. Lucky they didn't get caught in the flash flood of the river or I wouldn't be sitting at the première of a Hollywood movie next to my own grandfather."

"That's lucky for both of us... Here we go. The lights are going down."

"Will I recognise you, Grandfather?"

"I hope so."

With the lights down Amanda sat back to enjoy the movie. The film was the usual Hollywood comedy set in American suburbia, the story the interplay between the neighbours. It didn't require much thinking. Amanda laughed with the rest of the audience, eating the popcorn passed down by Oliver. It was good, light entertainment that made people comfortable as it transported them briefly out of the daily routine of their mundane lives. When Amanda saw Oliver up on the screen for the first time it made her excited. Oliver's character was one of Jack Lemmon's neighbours. At the end, there was a brief scene with James playing a policeman. Amanda was surprised how well they both put on American accents. After Jack Lemmon, despite the smallness of his part, the star of the show was Ben Crossley, the old belligerent neighbour who hated everyone. For the movie, the old man's long white hair had been tied in a ponytail. Like all great expectations, Amanda felt flat when it was over, the excitement gone, the crowd going home. Except for Ben Crossley, they all went home together. The old man said he was too tired to join a celebration. He had gone back to his hotel in a taxi as soon as the film had ended.

"Well, that one's over," said Oliver back in his room. "There's only one thing to do now and that's get drunk... He didn't look well, Randall."

"He's dying. Cancer. Chemotherapy. When he feels better tomorrow, don't forget we're having lunch together. You want to go to the pub?"

"Let's drink to success here. A good bottle of Merlot."

"Don't you have a girlfriend?"

"Not at the moment. When he gets back to the States he's going to find you a publisher for your book."

"Did you know he was rich?"

"Not really. Money doesn't interest me that much. Except when I have enough money to buy a good bottle of red wine."

For once in their lives the party did not get going, the evening an anticlimax. Only Randall looked happy. After two of Oliver's bottles of wine they went to their respective rooms. Amanda was tired, emotionally and physically. Happily, she took off William Drake's gown, displaying her extended belly, and got into bed.

"He liked my book."

"That's wonderful, Randall. Goodnight. We'll talk about it in the morning."

"The film was lousy. There was no story to it."

"It wasn't much good. But it was what people want. Mindless comedy. That's a good movie."

"Who for?"

"The studios. It's all about money."

"How's our baby?"

"She's fine. Goodnight, Randall."

"Goodnight, Amanda. Sleep tight... Wasn't it nice for once not going to work? Good old Sarah Rankin sending in temps."

When Randall switched out the bedside lamp Amanda could see the moon through the window. She had forgotten to draw the curtain. Before she could do anything about it she was sound asleep, awash in the world of her dreams, a place of happiness that stayed with her right through the night. For a long while after waking she lived back in her dream, lying quietly on her back, enjoying her happiness.

PART 8

FEBRUARY TO APRIL 1987 – AND THE GAME GOES ON

*J*ames Oliver Crookshank was born on the twenty-third of February at 127 Lawrence Avenue, Paddington, the most exclusive maternity clinic in London according to Ben Crossley who had arranged and paid for the delivery. Three weeks earlier, Randall had finished writing *Masters of Vanity*, his second novel. They were sitting alone in the waiting room when the news of the birth was brought to them by the gynaecologist.

"Congratulations to both of you. Despite your early worries, Randall, there was nothing wrong with Amanda. I recommend they stay at the clinic for another day. Go on in. You could have watched the delivery but that was your decision. And Mr Crossley, it's been a privilege meeting you. I have always been one of your admirers. You look so much better, by the way. There are always new ways of treating cancer. Are you still in remission?"

"For the moment. I always look at the worst scenario and smile at a better one."

"When are you returning to America?"

"I have taken a flat in the West End to continue the treatment."

"You see, we British are not so far behind the Americans when it comes to cutting-edge medicine."

Relieved and happy, Randall walked down the corridor towards Amanda's room.

"I can't thank you enough, Grandfather."

"One of the few benefits of having a lot of money. You can buy the best. I'm as excited as you are. A great-grandson."

"James and Oliver have agreed to be his godfathers."

Half an hour later, with the baby back in a crib and Amanda asleep, they left the hospital.

"It's the most extraordinary feeling, becoming a father."

"We all get the first rush of excitement. The sad part of life is that many of us walk away from our children later on or the children go their separate ways. Enjoy the feeling now, Randall. You'll want to remember this day. I hope the boy keeps you two together. After leaving Maureen, I drifted from woman to woman, never satisfied. You always hope someone else is going to hold your attention. Looking back, I would have been better staying with your grandmother. Looking after her. She was an alcoholic, like your mother. Life is never easy. People are difficult. Living with someone is difficult. We take our frustrations out on the nearest person. They say you have to work at a marriage. I always thought that if you have to spend half your life trying to be nice to people then what's the point? It's false happiness. What you say and not what you think. If you can't be genuine with someone you shouldn't be with them... You get cynical with age. Youth doesn't know what it is getting itself into when love comes along. That first flush of sexual attraction we so often misguidedly call love. But now, young man, you have responsibilities. You are going to have to educate that boy, guide him through the turmoil of life or he'll end up like one of those greedy bastards in your book."

"Have you finished it?"

"Not quite. I'm savouring it. Sipping to the last."

"Now you're being nice to me."

"Where shall we go? How about the Savoy Grill for lunch? Not every day a man becomes a great-grandfather. So, will he be known as James or Oliver?"

"Probably James. But later, when he's old enough to think for himself, he can change to a less ordinary Oliver. Or Jimmy. Or whatever they will be calling themselves in the twenty-first century."

"Does she ever mention the woman?"

"Not often."

"Have they seen each other?"

"I'm not sure. She wants to show the baby to Evelina."

"Be careful. Amanda's now got what she wants."

"She won't run out on me again. The boy needs both his parents. We're happy."

"I hope so for all of you. Five years with Evelina was a long time. The problem in the gay community is not being able to have children. Men couples have to adopt. In lesbian couples they have the option of one of them getting pregnant. All they have to do is find a donor. She seems a nice enough girl. So it is not for me to judge. But don't forget she walked out on you once to have an affair with a woman... I have a proposition for you, grandson. One that I hope will protect all of you in the future. Sometimes it's better to remove temptation and the influence of another person. The woman in question is a lot older than Amanda, or so I understand. The very thought of my great-grandson being brought up by a lesbian couple makes my skin crawl. It's against the most fundamental principle of nature. Being nurtured by two women sleeping in the same bed and making love to each other will bend his mind. I may be old-fashioned but going against the core principle of evolution is plain stupid. All this new-age 'everything goes' is going to destroy civilisation if we're not careful. In America, half the people who marry will end up divorced. Not that I'm the best example or have the right to criticise. I just think that without a strong family unit we will destroy our society the way I destroyed the lives of my wife and my daughter. All this new liberalism is a by-product of unbridled 'human rights' where politicians, and even the church, agree with what the people think they want in their pursuit of hedonism. People don't really care about principles anymore, they just want to pleasure themselves and call it the right of every individual to do what the hell he or she likes. You've drawn a good picture of modern society in your book where all they want is money and more money, everything in life material. Without real values we become nothing. I don't think *Masters of Vanity* will find a publisher at the moment. You pillory greed. Most people who buy books think affluence is wonderful. By self-publishing you will find a minuscule audience as the bookshop chains won't want your book on their shelves. The book's too good to waste... Taxi!... Got the bugger... Thank you, driver. The Savoy Hotel... Get in, Randall. Now I'm feeling better I get hungry."

"So what do you suggest?"

"I sponsor your writing. Give you an allowance which will give you the freedom to write and not worry about waiting tables. If you have to make a living I don't think you will write. In the end, the right publisher will come along. Or all this new technology will give you a way to get direct to your audience."

"How do you know so much about literature? The process of writing?"

"One of the snags of making a movie is all the sitting around. You never quite know when the director will call you. Mostly, I sit in my caravan and wait to be called. After you've learnt your lines there's nothing much to do but wait. And that's boring. Over the many years I've developed an insatiable appetite for books. All kinds of books. Including books on writers. They all say that to write a good book the mind has to be free from clutter... Why don't you take Amanda and the new baby out to Africa? You could build yourself a house next to the dam on World's View. Have the peace and quiet to write your books and free Amanda from temptation and the greedy clutches of a female predator. Seven years into the new independence, Zimbabwe seems to have settled down. The guns are silent. People are getting on with each other. You white farmers are the backbone of the economy. What I'm suggesting, Randall, is you go home. Take your wife and son and go home. Go back to Africa. Whenever you talk of World's View I see that faraway longing in your eyes. In one book I read they called it being bush-happy. I want you to succeed as a writer. Succeed as a husband, a father. All the things I never did. I suppose if I'm honest I want you to live the life I never had. By giving you some of my money I hope to atone for some of my sins. If my health holds a little longer I'll come and pay you a visit. Go up to the Zambezi escarpment and look at the grave of my daughter. Place a white rose on the wooden cross and pray for her soul and ask her forgiveness. Talk it over with Amanda. In the euphoria of giving birth, she just might go for it. And when you are old together and still happy you can look back and thank your old grandfather."

"You think Zimbabwe might succeed?"

"Who knows? Mostly, luckily, everything succeeds in the end or the world as we know it wouldn't exist. We would have all destroyed each other. You see, Randall, meeting you has given me something to fight for. Why I'm now fighting the cancer. Back in LA, an old man with no family didn't have any purpose. When I was told I had cancer I thought it a blessing. A way out. There's not much to do on your own at the age of seventy-six. And most of my old friends are dead and buried. I still want to meet Phillip. I want to see you published."

"I'll ask Amanda."

"That's my boy. After a good lunch you can go back to the hospital. You can sleep the night in the chair."

The taxi stopped at the door of the restaurant back from the main entrance to the Savoy Hotel. The maître d' recognised Ben Crossley and led them to a small table in the corner of the dining room. The old man, not surprisingly to Randall, had thought ahead and booked a table before they left the clinic. They ate their lunch, Randall's mind in a turmoil, the thought of Amanda taking his son to live with Evelina making him sick. Had the two of them planned the reconciliation to get Amanda pregnant? His mind began running in circles. Then he thought of the book that wasn't going to be published, the thought of another rejection only increasing his nausea. His grandfather was talking, most of the words flowing over Randall he was so immersed in his problems. Could people be so cruel as to steal that boy who had looked up at him from the crib, the bond between them instant?

"I'm going to stay in England. If she wants to leave me for Evelina I'm better finding out now, rather than later. I'm going to start my own business. Become a property developer. Start small and see how it goes. I have the training. I know what I'm doing. Thank you for the offer of an allowance, but no thank you. I want to make my own way in life. And if the new book isn't going to publish maybe I need a break from writing to make my own money. When I have enough I'll go back to my writing with a lot more life to write about. There are plenty of years in the future. We can still go out to Zimbabwe for a visit and show my father his grandson. You can take us all on an African safari if that's all right with you. At the moment I don't have the money for a holiday. Dad will be excited. So will Phillip. I'll get the bank to finance my venture when I get back to London. The main rains will be over in Zimbabwe at the end of next month. It starts cooling down in March. I'll enjoy showing you the farm and Phillip can take us on safari while my stepmother looks after the baby. She'll love that. So will Myra. It will only cost you the two extra airfares. Zimbabwe won't cost you a penny... Thank goodness you're smiling. I'm sorry. I wasn't really listening earlier on."

"It's your choice. Forewarned is forearmed. I know a bit about women. They think differently to men."

"To be paid to write and not publish wouldn't be right."

"Have it your way, Randall... Do you want some pudding?"

"Just some coffee. Then I want to go back to the clinic."

"You can always change your mind when you get to Zimbabwe. They tell me Africa is somewhat addictive once you have lived there."

The old man was smiling at Randall, a soft knowing smile on his face.

"Are you going to make another film, Grandfather?"

"Who knows? Whoever knows in this life? Life is always full of surprises. Some good, some not so good... So, we're going on safari. Sounds good to me. By the end of March I will have finished the new treatment. As Oliver Manningford once said to me, 'It's not all bad.' Why don't you ask your bank if they'll finance your project before we go on safari? Now, finish your coffee. Your wife and son are waiting for you. I will go back to my flat and take a nap, after which I will read the rest of your book. Another generation, Randall. Makes you think about how we got here on that long journey of man's evolution. Father to son or daughter. A process that is neverending. I often wonder how it all started. The Old Testament says God made us in seven days some five thousand years ago. I wonder if that wasn't a metaphor for the millions of years of evolution? All those old skeletons. The dinosaurs before us. It seems all so impossible without divine intervention. Now I'm soon to leave this world, I'm still not sure how we got here. Will man, like the dinosaurs, become extinct? Probably. Every species known to man has a near certainty to become extinct. As Charles Darwin said, 'It's all part of the process of evolution.' Maybe there is a heaven and a hell and I'm about to find out to my detriment. Go and see her, Randall, but watch out for your son. He's your responsibility and don't you forget it. You have my future, my wife's future and my daughter's future back in that little crib. He gave me such a big-eyed look that I thought he recognised me. If only we knew what it was all about."

"Thank you so much for lunch. Thank you so much for everything."

"My pleasure, grandson. My pleasure."

THAT NIGHT, when Randall went to work at the restaurant, he was determined to make his life succeed. Back at the clinic after work he sat in the chair and went to sleep, his wife asleep on one side of him in the hospital bed, his son asleep on the other side in his crib. In the morning, he took his family back to Mrs Salter's, the boy as quiet as a mouse. James and Oliver came to look at him. Mrs Salter walked up the three flights of stairs. At eleven o'clock, having made an appointment, Randall went to see the bank manager in the City who had financed the Westcastle project for BLG, and laid out his proposal.

"Randall, it's so nice to see you again. When you phoned I thought you were back at BLG. I'm afraid the bank can't give you a loan without collateral. If you take the new project to your uncle and he approves, the bank will be most happy to finance your project. You did a first-class job at Westcastle despite the current downturn. Sold your units just in time. If you had a guarantee for the finance we'd be delighted to oblige. The best time to start a new property development that will take a couple of years to come to fruition is in the middle of a slump."

"So you won't lend me any money for an even smaller project?"

"I wouldn't lend you the money to build one house without the right guarantees. I'm so sorry."

"I'll try another bank."

"Try all of them, Randall. And good luck to you."

Frustrated and annoyed, Randall began walking out of the man's office, the smirk on the man's face making Randall want to throw a punch. The man ignored him and went back to the work on his desk, putting on his reading glasses in the final act of dismissal. To the bank manager, Randall no longer existed.

Getting back to the room having walked off some of his frustration in the park, Randall found the place empty. There was no sign of Amanda or the baby. Randall went into panic.

"Where's she gone, James?" he asked next door, barging in without knocking.

"Mrs Salter has bought her a pram. They went for a walk. Not often the sun shines in February. They were all wrapped up. What's all the fuss about?"

"Writing books has given me a too-vivid imagination. I thought she had taken the baby to Evelina."

"Wow. That's a bad thought."

"And the bloody bank won't lend me any money."

"Not surprising, old boy. The banks only lend money to people with money. You haven't got a penny. Join the club... You working tonight?"

"I have to. Every night. I'm going to ask for extra day shifts now Amanda isn't working for a couple of weeks. That kid's going to be expensive."

"Won't your grandfather guarantee the overdraft?"

"I told him I wanted to do it on my own."

"Doesn't work that way. Why we so often need family. It's a rat race out there, Randall. When's the christening? I've never been a godfather before. The good news today is Oliver has been offered a part in a play. They first go on tour and if the play works in the provinces they will bring it back to the West End."

"You got any work in the offing?"

"Not yet. But I'm always hopeful. My American money is getting a bit low."

"When's Oliver going?"

"Soon. I'll miss the old bugger."

"I'm going out to Zimbabwe to take my son to see my family. Grandfather is paying the airfares."

"Then I'll be all alone. Life really can be a bugger."

"We'll christen James when we get back... I really thought the bank would lend me the money on my past track record. Westcastle made a bloody fortune for BLG."

"Better luck next time... Here they come. Your son has a good pair of lungs."

"Will him crying at night keep you awake?"

"He's my godson. It doesn't matter. When I'm all alone up here when you go to Africa I'll have all the time in the world to sleep. I wish I could write a book. Give me something to do. All this sitting around is boring."

That night James Oliver kept the whole house awake. Amanda tried breastfeeding but the baby wouldn't take. They both went into panic.

Back in the crib the boy howled his lungs out. Mrs Salter, bleary-eyed and annoyed when Randall opened the door to her knock, walked into the room and picked up the child, holding him over her shoulder. The baby let out a burp that startled Randall.

"Wind. My niece always had wind. Gives them pain and they howl."

"I'm so sorry, Mrs Salter."

"Don't you worry, Amanda. Now we can all get some sleep. It's quite a learning curve, the first baby. Always burp him before putting him down. If I don't sleep properly I'm irritable in the morning. Goodnight. And, please, remember to burp the young man."

When the door had closed and the sound of Mrs Salter's feet had gone down the staircase, they both got the giggles.

"Can you believe it? He's gone to sleep."

"I didn't tell you earlier on but the bank won't give me a loan."

"What are we going to do? We can't bring up James Oliver waiting tables. Anyway, we need a flat. Somewhere that's a tad more soundproof."

"If you were talking to your mother she'd have warned you what to do with the baby."

"Well I'm not. Can we get back into bed? I need some sleep."

"I want to show James Oliver to my grandmother. If I take him during the day Uncle Paul will be at work."

"He'll have got over it by now."

"I'm not so sure. He was real pissed off with me when we last spoke."

"Why won't they lend you the money?"

"I don't have a guarantee."

"Ask your grandfather. We've got to have money. Real money. And lots of it. Can't bring him up in a bedsitter. You've got a degree in economics. Go and look for a job."

With his frustration rising, Randall could not get back to sleep. Amanda, fast asleep, had turned her back to him. Later, when Randall woke from a bad dream, it was still pitch dark in the room. Outside in the cold of winter the city was almost silent. Randall pulled up the blankets, turned over and away from Amanda, and went back to dreamless sleep.

Like so often with Amanda she had not forgotten the simmering argument in the morning.

"So, what are you going to do? Better get your act together, Randall."

"Where are you going?"

"Out. To see some friends. Best you go and see your rich grandfather. Or go and apologise to your uncle."

"What about my writing?"

"It doesn't work. The old man told you so. You're wasting your time. You got to have money. If the books aren't going to sell, what's the point in writing them?"

"I thought you liked my books."

"Everything's different. We have a baby."

"Which friends?"

"William Drake."

"And Evelina?"

"Probably. As I said, Randall. Get your act together."

When the place went quiet and Randall was all alone, the euphoria had gone, replaced by reality. Randall got dressed for the cold outside to go and see his grandfather. When he got to the rented flat in the poshest part of London, the old man answered the door. Randall walked through to the lounge, following his grandfather.

"Grandfather, I need a guarantee for the project. I'm in a bit of a spot with Amanda. She's gone with the baby to see her friends."

"Not from me, grandson. My deal is simple. An allowance for you to write in Zimbabwe. Right now she's probably showing your son to her girlfriend."

"So you won't help me with my project?"

"The sooner we get all of us on the plane the better."

"You really think she'll go back to Evelina?"

"I'm betting on it if you don't do something. At the moment, you don't have a penny and you don't have any prospects. The book is good. Very good. But you're telling people what they don't want to hear. People should never tell anyone the truth, Randall, if they want to stay friends or sell books."

"She wouldn't do that to me."

"Want a bet? Let's go find ourselves a travel agent. Book the trip for as soon as possible. Give her no option. With a bit of luck she'll still be in two minds and take the easy way out of going for a holiday. In Zimbabwe, you can make up your minds what you want to do with the rest of your lives. Discuss it with her seven thousand miles from her girlfriend."

"Everything's happening so quickly."

"It usually does."

By the time Randall went to work that evening there was still no sign of Amanda and the baby. Nothing was going right. When his grandfather had phoned the gynaecologist to clear them for the trip he was told to wait six weeks before subjecting the baby to cabin pressure and the heat of Africa. The old man said he would book and pay for the flights to travel in the middle of April. With Amanda not in the room when he got back, Randall had made three phone calls to different executive placement agencies, briefly giving them his history. None of them were interested. The property market was flat, no one looking for project managers. When he suggested bringing them his CV all three told him to send it in the post. Randall felt cornered. Amanda was right: if the books would not sell, what was the point in writing them? He had had a dream and the dream wasn't working, the hard facts of life with all of its problems in front of him. Alone, without responsibility, his life as a bohemian didn't matter. For half an hour before going to the restaurant he looked at the phone thinking of phoning his uncle, but did not have the courage to make the call. It was all very well kidding himself that he was a writer, doing something important, when all he was really doing was writing letters to himself.

That night, the restaurant was full. Randall was worked off his feet with no time to think and feel sorry for himself. He was not concentrating on bullshitting his customers, so the tips were not as good as usual. After the West End theatres closed the restaurant filled up again. Randall was tired from running backwards and forwards to the kitchen.

"What on earth are you doing serving tables, Randall?"

"I'm sorry. Do I know you?"

"Of course you do. I live at Westcastle. You people sold me my flat. Just a pity I didn't wait for the drop in house prices. We were next door neighbours but one, before you sold your flat. Weren't you project manager of the whole caboodle? Do you own this place, or something?"

"What do you all want to have? The fish is particularly nice tonight. The chef picked it out himself at the market at five o'clock this morning."

"Are you just a waiter?"

"Yes I am. Look, I'm sorry. The place is a bit full tonight."

"Well, I'll be blowed. See how the mighty have fallen. Looking at you now I don't feel so bad about my flat being worth less than what I paid for it. You chaps were pretty good at pushing up the prices. All that hype."

"So, what will it be?"

"Come back in five minutes."

"As you wish, sir."

As Randall walked away to serve another table he could still hear the man loudly talking to the others at his table.

"If my memory is right, our waiter has a degree in economics. Must have been making a fortune at BLG, the amount they scammed off everyone for the flats. I heard what they originally paid for the land. Downright robbery if you ask me... The bloke's a waiter! Can you believe it?... Now, who wants a really good bottle of wine?"

Not wanting to have an argument and lose his job, Randall swapped the table with Joe, his fellow waiter.

"So-called friends from the past, Joe. Can you take table nine? After a bottle of wine or two the insults will get worse. I owe you. Screw the bugger for the biggest tip of the evening."

"Is he rich?"

"Stinking rich."

"It'll be my pleasure."

Twice, the man at table nine tried to catch his attention and twice Randall ignored him. By the end of the evening the man was drunk. When the bill was presented the man argued. The chef was brought out from the kitchen. Joe, not knowing what to do, stood waiting for the drunk man to hand over his credit card.

"You're not my waiter! Where's Randall? Tell him to pay the bill. Took me for a ride. And the food was lousy."

The manager of the restaurant came out of his office, wringing his hands and smiling at the customer, so obsequious Randall wanted to vomit. The drunk man's guests were looking uncomfortable, the tables around them quiet. Randall, not wanting to be drawn into the argument, took the plate with the bill and the credit card that had settled it back to his last table. The man had added ten per cent when he received the bill, the tip the best of Randall's evening. Taking off his small apron, Randall hung it on the hook. Joe shrugged at him as Randall left the restaurant. The argument at table nine was still going on. It had happened before, customers picking a fight in an attempt to get out of paying the bill.

Randall was smiling as he walked up the cold street on his way to the Tube station. The manager might be a creep, but so far as Randall knew no one had left his restaurant without paying the bill. All the way home he was thinking of Amanda and what he was going to do if she hadn't come home, the memory of the last time now fresh in his mind. When he opened Mrs Salter's front door he could hear the baby crying. The relief was instant. Upstairs when he opened the door Amanda was holding the baby, trying to quieten him. Randall could hear James in the room next door coughing. The child looked hysterical.

"What's wrong with him?"

"I don't know. Babies can't talk."

"You'd better give him to me. Have you burped him?"

"Of course I have."

"He's waking up the whole damn neighbourhood... Grandfather is booking us a flight to Zimbabwe for the middle of April."

"Whatever for?"

"He wants to meet Phillip and take us on a holiday. On the farm, James Oliver can scream his lungs out and only the family will care. They give the babies a sedative when they're on the aircraft."

"I don't want to go."

"Why ever not?"

"I saw Evelina. She says if you don't have the money to bring up the baby she'll do it for me. I can't live like this."

"Give him to me."

"Won't do any good."

"Try me. If we live in Zimbabwe Grandfather will pay me an allowance to go on writing. We can build ourselves a house next to the dam."

"I don't want to bring my son up in Africa."

"I asked three agencies if they had any jobs."

"And did they?"

"No, they didn't. The market is quiet at the moment. Please, give me my son."

The moment Randall took hold of the baby he stopped screaming, letting out a burp: the boy had indigestion.

"How did you do that?"

"Let's go to bed. I'm sick of people arguing. James is awake next door. So is Mrs Salter. If you try and take the boy to live with Evelina I'll get a court order preventing you."

"Don't be damn silly. Where are you going to get the money for a lawyer?"

"From my grandfather. Let's just get through the next six weeks and go out to Africa. Women suffer from postnatal depression."

"I'm not depressed. I'm being realistic."

"You know something, Amanda? I'm not sure what you're up to. Was me getting you pregnant planned by Evelina?"

"Of course it wasn't."

"Then we'll take a month or two in Zimbabwe while we work out what we do. I am going to send *Masters of Vanity* to the publishers. All of them if I have to… Now, can I get some sleep? Look at that. Now I've put him in the carrycot he's gone to sleep. You see, fathers aren't so useless after all. Let's be nice to each other and stop arguing. We have a son. We have each other. Let's be thankful. Count our blessings. You'll enjoy a stay on the farm. You'll be the centre of attention. You and the baby."

"You really think I planned all this?"

"Sometimes I'm not sure what people are up to. Including you, my wife. But he's our son. Not yours. Not mine. Ours. And he always will be… You mind if I turn out the lights?"

The next morning Randall went to the library and made copies of *Masters of Vanity*. The hire for the Photostat machine in the library was cheap. One of the books in the library, the *Writers' & Artists' Yearbook*, gave every publisher and literary agent's address with their literary specialities. All through the long process he was thinking about Amanda and blaming the problem on himself for his own infidelity with Judy Collins. It was all his own fault. Knowing deep inside he was wasting his time and money, he wrote addresses on ten big envelopes to go with the short letters he had written earlier in the morning. At the top of each letter he filled in the name of the publisher. With the manuscripts and letters in the envelopes he walked to the post office.

"You're pissing money up against the wall," he told himself as he walked out into the rain. It was cold and wet, a typical, miserable day in London: the English winters were perfectly horrible. Amanda, thankfully, was at home, the baby awake and smiling. Making himself put a smile on his face, Randall walked across the room and gave her a kiss, telling himself that if he hadn't had that affair with Judy Collins none of this would have happened.

"What was that all about? You're wet. Where've you been?"

"Blue skies and sunshine. By the middle of April the main rains will be over. We can sit round the pool, James Oliver in his pram under a msasa tree. Who needs London in winter? The sunshine will lift your spirits. A good climate for a change will make you less irritable. We can go for walks on our own. Myra will love to watch the baby. My sister is nineteen years old. I can't believe it. Craig turned twenty-one last year. Seems like yesterday they were kids... I've got to go to the restaurant. Lunchtime shift. Two shifts today."

"So what have you been doing all morning?"

"Copying and posting the book direct to publishers."

"Without a preliminary letter explaining what it's about? You're wasting your time!"

"Done a lot of that recently... Are you coming to Zimbabwe?"

"I'm thinking about it... I've got to do the washing. I'll never get it dry. Babies are a lot of work."

"In Zimbabwe we'll have servants."

"That will be nice."

"Why don't you take the washing to the launderette? If we're going to Zimbabwe we can afford it. You won't have to use Mrs Salter's washing line."

"It's raining outside."

"Suit yourself. Just think of a nice, comfortable stay in Zimbabwe with all the pressure from the baby taken away from you."

"That would be nice."

Smiling inwardly, Randall put the original manuscript in the drawer of his desk, kissed Amanda again and left the room for the restaurant.

By the time Joe came on at six o'clock for the evening shift Randall was more hopeful the idea of ease and comfort would persuade Amanda to go to Africa. And if the book did not sell there was always the choice of a job on the farm as an assistant to Vince Ranger. It would be going back to where he left off but anything was better than Evelina getting her hands on his son. Even a little encouragement from a publisher would send him back to writing and accepting his grandfather's offer.

"How did it end last night, Joe?"

"You won't believe it. I got a fifty pound tip out of him. Mr Brindle may look subservient to the customers but underneath he's as hard as nails. When that bastard refused to pay, Brindle leaned close to his ear and whispered he'd call the cops. The man went white as a sheet, pulled a pile of money out of his wallet and left it on the table and walked out. Mr Brindle saw him right to the door. When I added it all up at reception I put fifty pounds and change in my pocket. Anytime you need help again, Randall, call me. So, were you selling houses on commission? That's a tough job. Tried it once. Never sold a damn thing. Why I'm back to waiting tables. Fifty quid. If that happened every time I'd be rich."

Wondering what he was doing with himself, Randall went back to work, the five years of night school and the degree in retrospect seeming ridiculous. The second shift was longer than the lunchtime shift, people staying late into the early hours of the morning, drinking bottle after bottle of expensive wine. Strangely, Randall was not jealous of their money, too many of his own late nights in restaurants still fresh in his memory. Once a man had had a smart flat, a flashy car and an expense account the outward show of money seemed less important. The food, the wine, the chat up was all old hat to Randall. Looking back, as he stood waiting for his first evening customer to come into the restaurant, it all seemed rather pointless. Most of those girls he wined and dined to get them into bed he could barely remember, let alone their names. And he was sure they wouldn't remember him either. It was all a blur of alcohol; why he was happy to settle down with Amanda. Now all the reverse was happening without any money. It made Randall want to write, to try and explain to himself what it had all been about. A rich Evelina would give Amanda security for the future, for herself as much as the boy. Two lesbians couldn't marry each other but Evelina, the older woman, could will her money to Amanda. Was it all about money, he asked himself? A corporate job would make things better but his build-up of capital for a future security would have to start from scratch: a house, furniture, a car, plus all the rest of the trappings that came with wealth. And that, it seemed, was what Amanda now wanted. No longer the bohemian, laid-back couple when they were both so young it didn't matter; when being happy was more important than the appearance of all that money. With the rich Evelina now back in the equation Randall doubted Amanda's idea of the restaurant, called Mother's Cooking or any other damn name, would work... A party of six came and sat at table nine, one of the three tables he served. Putting on his forced smile he went across to serve them.

"Is this your party, sir?"

"Yes it is."

Giving the man the only menu with the prices, Randall left them, standing with his back to the near wall and watching. When the man with the prices raised his head Randall went back to the table.

"What do you recommend? What's your name?"

"My name is Randall."

"Good evening, Randall. You have an odd accent. Where are you from?"

"Rhodesia," said Randall without thinking.

"And what did your family do in Zimbabwe, Randall? They do now call it Zimbabwe?"

"We farmed tobacco."

"Do you still have your farm?"

"For the moment. They want the farmers to sell to the government and the British government to pay the Zimbabwe government in sterling but pay us farmers in Zimbabwe dollars which you can't get out of the country."

"Ah, the Lancaster House Agreement. So, what do you recommend?"

"The fish is good. The chef went to the fish market at five o'clock this morning to pick the halibut."

"Then we'll all start with fish. How big is your family farm?"

"Six thousand acres."

"And when the ten-year readjustment period in the agreement expires so will the willing-seller willing-buyer clause expire and with it the British commitment, and Ian Smith will be out of the parliament. I'm in the tobacco business, Randall. We're able to buy your tobacco again now sanctions have ended. Best Virginia tobacco in the world. Certainly the cheapest. Did you farm yourself?"

"I did."

"What went wrong?"

"They killed my cat... Would everyone like the fish?"

"Thank you. Everyone will have fish... Don't you miss the old life?"

"You can't believe it."

"We'll order the second course after we've eaten the fish. Bring us two bottles of wine."

Randall looked down at the wine list to where the man was pointing before collecting the menus around the table.

"I'll bring them back again."

"Nice talking to you, Randall."

"Thank you, sir."

Feeling drained, Randall went to the kitchen and placed the order before collecting the wine from the cellar. Then he went back to the table, where he opened the bottles, first pouring a small amount in the man's glass for him to taste.

"Very nice. Very nice."

After pouring half-glasses around the table Randall went back to the kitchen to collect the fish. The restaurant was beginning to fill up. By the time the halibut had been eaten Randall was serving all his tables, his mind concentrated on not making a mistake. The tobacco man spread out his evening, ordering each course at a time. The man was obviously rich which was not surprising to Randall: the money in tobacco was not in the farming but in the manufacture and distribution. By the time the evening was over Randall was pleased by the size of the man's tip.

"How big is the crop, Randall?"

"We gross two to three million US dollars depending on the season and the prices you chaps pay us on the auction floors."

"I wish your family luck. When are you going back?"

"The middle of April if all goes well."

"And are you staying?"

"I don't know... Thank you, sir. Enjoy the rest of your evening."

It sounded like a lot of money spoken at the dinner table but most of the money they received on the farm paid the wages and all the rest of the overheads. And what had been left after paying running expenses over the years had gone into the dam and all the new irrigation equipment. Randall's father had always said the farmer was never satisfied, giving real meaning to the term 'ploughing back your profits'.

Apart from the early investment in the Chelsea block of flats in partnership with the artist Livy Johnston, everything they had in Zimbabwe was in the farm, a farm that in three years' time, at the end of the ten-year stabilisation period, would be in jeopardy. And now he was going home... Tired, mentally and physically, his feet hurting from standing up most of the day, Randall left the restaurant, one of the last to leave. The thought kept going through his mind: on his next birthday he would turn thirty with not a penny to show for it.

The whole house was quiet when he reached home, the three flights of stairs more heavy on his legs than usual. Without turning on the lights Randall took off his clothes and got into bed. Amanda did not move. Randall heard the baby gurgle which made him smile, a brief moment of happiness before he fell asleep.

2

A week later the first letter came in the post: Random House were not interested, a brief, short stereotyped letter of rejection. Randall doubted if the publishing house had even had time to read the manuscript. He put the letter at the bottom of the desk drawer under the original manuscript. For the whole week neither of them had mentioned Zimbabwe. There had not been a repeat performance of showing the baby to Evelina so far as he knew. Amanda was strangely quiet. At the end of the week, the day after the first rejection letter that Randall had not mentioned to Amanda, they went to the Hyde Park house of Randall's uncle to show the baby to his grandmother. Politely, everyone, other than his grandmother, was out of the house. Granny Crookshank gushed over her great-grandson, talking about her past to Amanda when she too had had her first baby. There was no mention of his Uncle Paul or BLG. After half an hour they took the baby home. On the floor, inside Mrs Salter's door was a letter to Randall, along with bills for Mrs Salter and a handwritten letter to Oliver Manningford: the name of the publisher was on the outside of the envelope. Randall picked up the letter, put it in his pocket, and took the carrycot up the stairs. He knew there was little point in opening the letter so soon after he had sent them the manuscript. At the top of the stairs he used his key to open the door to their room.

"You'd better open it, Randall."

"Not much point. Had one yesterday. They haven't had time to read."

"Told you to send them a preliminary letter with a synopsis. People are lazy. They don't want to plough through a whole manuscript to find out what the book's about. You've got to make it easy. They get hundreds of books to read every week."

"If I was famous they would read it. Or if I was writing about some popular cause. How the hell do you get someone to read your book?"

"Don't ask me. I told you you were wasting your time writing. We had fun dreaming when it didn't matter... Your grandmother liked the baby."

"Of course she did. It's her great-grandson. Her legacy... You should take him to see your parents. Do they know he was born?"

"I didn't tell them I was pregnant... What you should have done, instead of wasting all that time sending your book to publishers, is write letters to every company in London that might need a man with a degree in economics telling them what you have done. That would have been productive."

"Grandfather Crossley has bought the tickets to Zimbabwe. We're travelling first class."

"That should be fun. Two paupers and a baby travelling first class. I hope he bought us return tickets."

"You could get a job in London as a secretary when we get back."

"I don't want to work in an office," snapped Amanda. "I have a baby to look after. The whole thing's a mess... Why is it so damn cold in here?"

"We could put him in a crèche during the day."

"Over my dead body... Open the bloody letter."

"Are we arguing again?"

"Looks like it."

"It's another rejection."

"Told you so... Put the heater on. Why the hell doesn't Mrs Salter put in proper central heating?"

"Because she can't afford it. And if she did it would add fifty quid to our rent every month."

"I hate being poor. I've never been poor before."

"We were poor when we first met and stayed in this room together. I didn't have a penny."

"That was a game, Randall."

"Oh. So that's what it was. I thought we were the happy-go-lucky laid-back couple without a care in the world enjoying our lives. We don't know how to enjoy ourselves anymore."

"Then make some damn money. How can you enjoy anything without money?... Let me look at that letter... See. It says so right here. They're not interested."

Randall turned his back, bent down and lit the gas fire with the lighter, staying down on his knees to warm his cold hands, grateful the argument hadn't started the baby crying. Next to him on the floor, Amanda had thrown down the letter. For what seemed to Randall an age, neither of them spoke.

"Want a cup of tea?"

"That would be nice, Amanda."

"I'm sorry. That letter must have hurt. I'm a real bitch sometimes. Maybe some of the others are reading the book... First class. Never travelled first class. We'll be travelling with all the posh people."

Each day Randall looked for another letter. For the moment the fight with Amanda seemed to be over. He wrote a draft of a letter making his work at BLG seem as important as possible, the ratio of profit to capital investment in the Westcastle project a highlight of his CV. Where to send the letter was a problem. Most jobs and publishers were found through introduction, not through sending out flyers. But where to start without his uncle's approval? And if they did come back they would ask for a BLG reference, something his uncle had refused. He was out on a limb. With anything new in Randall's life, the problem was always to get started: it wasn't what you knew or did, like writing a good book, but who you knew to get it published, to make money, to compete in the world. And to make it all worse the old man was again looking sick... And then, despite all his worries, they were going, the bags packed, the baby sedated by the doctor, the old man looking stronger and Africa beckoning, Amanda mildly excited by the thought of travelling in the same class as the rich and famous. After half an hour of pampering in the first-class lounge at Heathrow Airport they walked out to the plane, a British Airways direct flight to Harare. Thirteen hours after leaving London, with one stop to refuel in Nairobi, Randall found himself home, the warm smell of Africa once again filling his nostrils, the family reunion quickly becoming a blur of chattering people.

When Randall's father said 'welcome home' there was no doubt about it: Zimbabwe was his home, not England. He was an African, whatever the colour of his skin. Sitting in Phillip's safari bus, the mood of his family was festive, with no one talking of anything but the present. The sun was shining, the bush on both sides of him familiar as the bus, driven by Jacques Oosthuizen, Phillip's business partner, made its way up to the farm. It was just like old times: no thought of wars or terrorist attacks, no thought for Randall of Evelina taking his son, no thought of Mugabe taking the farm. Everyone was happy, everyone laughing, Amanda and the new baby the centre of attention. With everyone high on the family reunion, Jacques started the singing as the bus ran on and on through the vast, empty expanse of the African bush, dotted by the occasional farmhouse with its rows of adjacent tobacco farms and sheds. The old man, his grandsons on either side of him, sat beaming, his pipe in his mouth, his long white hair down to his shoulders blowing in the wind, his blue eyes sparkling, a hand on Phillip's shoulder, not a thought of his cancer visibly troubling his mind. It seemed to Randall the old man was savouring his moment as part of a family for the first time in his life.

The house up on the hill with its view of the world looked perfect to Randall as they reached home just after three o'clock. The dogs went mad. Randall said hello to Silas, the house servant, both of them giving each other big grins. Primrose, married to the head gardener, and Randall's nanny while he was growing up, had come up from the compound. Primrose took the baby out of the carrycot and held him up to the sun.

"I have seven grandchildren, Randall," she said in Shona with a smile. "Is this a boy or a girl?"

"He's a boy. How are you Primrose?" Like Primrose, Randall had spoken in Shona.

"I am here to look after him. Your father asked me to come."

From the direction of the swimming pool, with its *braai* area, came the smell of roasting lamb, a whole sheep turning on the spit. Silas, who had been the cook at World's View ever since Randall could remember, had gone down to the pool to tend the roasting sheep, taking the fat from the catch-tray in a baster and basting the meat. Myra and Craig had gone into the house to change into their swimming costumes. Phillip was in deep conversation with his grandfather, as, arm-in-arm, they walked round the garden beneath the dappled shade of the msasa trees. Bergit, Randall's stepmother, looked radiant as she watched over her family. Silas went into the house and came back with the bowls of salad. The dogs, all of them Alsatians, were chasing each other round the lawn, dashing through the flowerbeds in barking abandon. Randall looked for the cats. One of them was looking at him from the windowsill inside the house, the same window through which a terrorist had fired at Randall killing his cat, the gunshot that had started his odyssey. To Randall's surprise, there was no bullet hole in the windowpane when Randall walked up to see the cat, his father following.

"Eventually the whole window cracked from the heat of the sun. We had to put in a new windowpane. How are you Randall? With all the hullabaloo at the airport, and everyone singing in the bus, I haven't had the chance to speak to you. I know about BLG. My brother told me on the phone. Paul's pretty pissed off. What happened?"

"It's complicated, Dad. There was a woman in America. Anyway, it all turned out for the best as it brought me and Amanda back together again and now we are parents."

"I can't believe he's Carmen's father. Myra said she recognised him straight away when you were coming through the airport building. She's awestruck at meeting a famous Hollywood actor. Carmen thought her father wasn't interested in her or her mother. She never talked about him or her mother. They were thousands of miles away and we were in Africa."

"We all pay for our sins."

"What are you going to do?"

"I'm not sure. Having burned my boats with BLG the market doesn't want anything to do with me. I'm back waiting tables. Two shifts. I do lunch and dinner to make ends meet."

"Do you want any financial help? I have income in England from the Chelsea flats."

"I'm thirty next year. A father. I think I should look after my own family."

"Suit yourself... Any luck with your books?"

"Not yet."

"I'd like to read one of them. Anyway, you have your degree. They can't take that away from you. Not even Paul. He thought you were going to take over running the company when he retired. You were doing so well."

"As I said it's all a bit complicated."

"We'll go down to the pool and have some lunch. We've plenty of time to talk when the family have got used to having you back again."

"How was this year's crop?"

"Not bad. We're still grading. The floors haven't opened yet. The late tobacco wasn't as good as the early plantings... You want a cold beer?"

"I wouldn't mind one."

"Is everything well with you and Amanda?"

"I hope so. The woman is still around."

"I don't understand lesbians."

"Neither do I. And that's what's worrying me... Phillip's so excited to meet his grandfather. Look at them. The old man wants to go up to the escarpment and place a rose on my mother's grave."

"We'll take him. You, me and Phillip. Phillip's doing well with his safari business. Why don't you stay with us, Randall? You can have the assistant's cottage. We don't have an assistant just now. It's me and Vince Ranger."

"How's Vince?"

"Same as ever. Best farm manager in the Centenary block. Totally reliable. Totally loyal."

"He never married?"

"No, he didn't. With the bush war and the aftermath there weren't too many eligible young girls."

"Is he happy? Maybe being a staid bachelor isn't so bad after all."

"Women can be difficult. Your mother was difficult. All that drinking."

"Apparently, my grandmother Crossley was an alcoholic."

"I didn't know. When you're young all these things happen so quickly. It's you and the girl. Nothing else matters."

"How's Bergit?"

"Wonderful. We really love each other. I'm truly blessed... We can have a small ceremony at your mother's grave. I would like the priest to come with us. To bless the grave. The old man will like it. There's a new priest at Bindura. Haven't met him yet... Let's go and find ourselves that beer."

Leaving Randall in the lounge talking to and stroking the cat on its comfortable perch on the windowsill, his father went to the kitchen to get the beers out of the fridge. When Randall looked through the window most of the family had gone down to the swimming pool. Just behind the pool stood the *braai* with the spit and the roasting sheep. Myra and Craig, Randall's half-sister and half-brother, were in the pool swimming. One of the dogs was standing on the edge of the pool barking at Craig who was splashing water up at the dog. The room, far away from the pool, was silent, the purring cat the only sound. Without Randall realising, his father had come into the room; he felt the touch of a cold beer on his bare arm. When he turned from looking out of the window his father was holding out a glass. They both filled their glasses with beer. The cat had stopped purring. They both stood silently side by side looking out of the window. The old man and Phillip walked through the gate into the pool and *braai* area. Silas had put a bucket of ice with beers on the table. They watched Phillip help himself to a beer and take one for his grandfather.

"Cheers, son... So much of the good parts of my life have been round that swimming pool."

"You still haven't taken down the security fence seven years after the war."

"You never know, Randall. Good to have you home... It all seems quiet on the surface but you never know what the politicians have in store for you. Peter Walls stayed in charge of the combined army until Mugabe got full control. Then Walls was retired and one of Mugabe's guerrilla generals put in charge of the army. If you ask me they still hate us but for the moment can't do without us. Or rather, without our skills. Politicians are a different breed to the likes of you and me. They say one thing while they're planning another. Mugabe's first problem was the Matabele, the Zulus who ran this country before we English took over and stopped the tribes fighting with each other. Mugabe sent the Fifth Brigade into Matabeleland. They'd been trained in North Korea. Made a right royal mess of the Matabele by some accounts. Slaughtered twenty thousand of their fellow brothers from the struggle. In those days the Shona needed the Matabele to fight against us. Nkomo gave up fighting Mugabe politically and joined the government instead of getting himself killed. Mugabe doesn't like opposition. Opponents disappear or have accidents, forget about all those poor sods in Matabeleland. No, I kept the fence up. Africa is volatile. The world is volatile. Always was. You know that old saying, Randall? 'Everything changes and everything stays the same.' If you don't have the military power you are not your own master. And we gave up our guns. We'll have to wait and see what Mugabe does to us. But, in the meantime, life is good here on the farm. I sleep a lot better. As you get a bit older you're more inclined to take life as it comes, knowing there's bugger-all as an individual you can do about it anyway... How's that beer?"

"Bloody marvellous. You just have no idea how good it feels to be home. Once an African, always an African."

"Tell me about it. We'd better go down and join them. I want to hold that son of yours. A grandson. When I got to this country I never so much as imagined I'd have my own family. Must be weird for the old man meeting his eldest grandson for the first time. How did you all find each other in the end? Myra thinks it quite bizarre. Said she's seen the old man in the cinema and on the television dozens of times and had no idea he was your grandfather. Life truly does have a way of surprising you... The cat's purring again."

"I'm stroking him... Why do we love cats and dogs so much?"

"They don't answer back, Randall. Other people always have something to say. And sometimes it isn't what you want to hear. That cat just purrs... Here comes Vince Ranger for lunch. You'd better go and say hello. Who knows, you two may be working together again."

"Why do cats close their eyes when they purr?"

"They're content. They get food, a warm place and the occasional tickle. What else can anyone want? I wouldn't mind coming back as a cat."

"It was right here they shot my cat."

"I know it was."

"And now everything looks so normal."

"Do you think she'll want to stay?"

"Who knows? Women are a bit like Robert Mugabe. You never know what they're thinking. If you mention the Fifth Brigade escapades in

Matabeleland she'll freak. For Amanda with her new baby it's all about security. And that woman has a lot of money."

"It's an instinct built into every mother to look after their children. Men are a bit more casual if you think of your grandfather."

"Thanks, Dad."

"I wasn't thinking of you."

"I don't want to lose him. I never want to lose James Oliver. It's quite obscene to imagine my boy being brought up by two women. Goes against the very core of human nature."

"I know nothing about lesbians."

"Neither do I. Sometimes, when it all goes wrong, I don't think much about anything."

"The older you get the less you think you know. Should be the other way round. But it isn't."

"Did Silas crush some oranges into the fat he's basting with?"

"Of course he did. What gives the meat that rich taste."

"Now you're making my mouth water. Lamb on the spit. Nothing better."

"Maybe a buck or a side of beef."

"We're a filthy bunch of carnivores."

"Can't change the nature of the beast. It's how we've survived. It is how we are, as we are... Lunch is about to be served. Let's go get it. And good to have you home. Really good. In the end, the only thing in life is family. Look after your son."

3

*T*wo days later they drove up to the Zambezi escarpment, to the site of his mother's grave. The old man had searched the garden for a white rose. On the dashboard in front of the old man was a white lily. Randall and Phillip were travelling in the back of the farm truck, sitting on an old mattress, their backs to the cab. The priest had been asked to come up from Bindura but was unavailable. Amanda and the baby had stayed on the farm. Earlier that morning Randall had shown Amanda the small cottage, previously lived in by the assistant. Someone had left the flap open above the bathroom window. When Amanda went to the toilet a snake slithered out of the window.

"You must be joking, Randall. I couldn't bring my son to live here."

"It just needs cleaning. Needs living in."

"All the cleaning in the world won't stop the snakes coming in the house. What was it?"

"A green mamba."

"Is it poisonous?"

"Why we have snake-bite kits on the farm. The snakes won't hurt you unless they are cornered."

"He was cornered all right. Lucky the window was open. I couldn't live here."

"You enjoyed the time we had in the Zambezi Valley with Barend Oosthuizen."

"That was business. He was part of your career. A part of your future if you were going to be successful. I was scared stiff last night. At first it was so quiet. Then all those strange noises."

"Didn't you like the frogs and the crickets?"

"What was that barking noise? It wasn't a dog."

"A buck."

"Africa gives me the creeps. I prefer the familiar noise of London's traffic. I'm a town girl, not a farm girl."

"Oh, Amanda, what are we going to do?"

"That's up to you."

Still thinking of Amanda and what he was going to do, Randall tried to enjoy being back in the bush. A pair of fish eagles were circling far over to their right. The birds were high in the sky, their cries just penetrating the engine noise of the truck. Both Randall and Phillip were smiling up at the birds.

"That's the most beautiful sound in the world," said Phillip. "The cry of the fish eagle. They say that once you've heard the cry of the fish eagle you will always want to come back to Africa. The sound is so evocative."

"Don't make it worse, Phillip. She doesn't want to stay in Africa. A green mamba slunk out of the shit-house window when we went to look at the cottage."

"That's a bit of a bugger... What are you going to do?"

"I'm between a rock and a hard place. Trying to make a living in England and that bloody woman."

"I'd love to be married. But every time I look at my friends it scares the shit out of me."

"It's fine when you do what they want."

"Doesn't she want you to be happy?"

"She thinks I'd be a lot happier with a corporate job and a nice salary. Why she helped me to go to night school and get my degree."

"Does seem a bit silly not to use it. Can you get another good job in London?"

"Probably. The recession has peaked. The markets will be on the up again. My trouble is, I want to write but can't make a living out of it... What do you think of Grandfather?"

"He's rich, famous and terribly lonely. I wonder if it was all worth it dumping his wife and ignoring our mother in pursuit of a film career in America."

"The arts. Probably where I got the bug. They say most of what you have is inherited... He's going to leave us his money."

"Too much money can be a curse... I always feel so sad when I go to her grave. Our poor mother. Drunk, drives away from the farm on her own and runs out of petrol in the bush. She must have been terrified as she tried to walk back for help. Our lives would have been so different if the lions hadn't killed her... There they go. Diving down into the valley. Those birds are so free... Do you think she was in a lot of pain?"

"I hope not... She'd have been a grandmother. Dad's changing gears. We're almost there. Let Grandfather get out of the truck first. We'll be able to see the cross from the side of the track. Let him place his flower on the grave of his daughter alone. Then we can all join him and hold hands as we think of our mother."

"You're crying Phillip."

"Yes, I am."

The wooden cross, with the words 'Go well, my darling' burned into the wood, was half blown over by the wind. The brothers watched their father walk first to the grave. Like Phillip, he too was crying. In his right hand he was carrying a spade, in his left a pick. It took Randall's father half an hour to reset the cross. Phillip had climbed out of the truck. Randall sat watching alone thinking that even his mother's gravesite would one day be gone, her life forever invisible. With the cross back in place, the old man placed the white lily on the right of the cross and bent his head, his white hair blowing in the wind that came up the escarpment from the Zambezi Valley. As he stood there, the fish eagles flew back and cried down to him, the pair of birds high up in the clear blue sky. In front of the old man, where the escarpment dropped into the valley, a small river flowed out into the space to drop the thousands of feet down to the floor of the valley. Randall got out of the truck to stretch his legs. His grandfather turned and began to walk back to the truck, his hair out of place from the wind. He was walking slowly. As he walked, the wind blew the white lily from the cross onto the grave. No one talked as they got back into the truck, the handholding ceremony forgotten, everyone too upset. The truck engine started and the car turned round, heading back to the farm. Randall, facing the grave from his seat on the mattress, watched the cross until it was out of sight.

"You know it's a wig," said Phillip. "The chemo destroyed his hair. He puts on the wig every morning to keep up appearances for his fans. The beard is stuck to his chin. The long hair, he told me, is his trademark. Is he going to recover?"

"I don't know. But now with us two and young James, Grandfather says he's going to fight to the end. We've given him something to live for."

"How long are you staying?"

"Not long. We'll probably go back with Grandfather at the end of the week. There's no point in arguing with Amanda. Anyway, with my luck, if we stayed we'd get comfortable and Mugabe would confiscate the farm. We forget, Phillip. They fought the bush war to get back the land. That was the whole point of the argument. Vindictive envy. Call it what you want. When he's ready, he'll kick us off the farms. Especially now we've made the land productive. The sad part is the land will be worthless if it isn't farmed properly; modern, scientific farming. Peasant farming won't produce anything like the crops of commercial farming. A few people will be self-sufficient, back in their old lifestyles from the previous century. There'll be no tobacco exports or maize going into Salisbury. Maybe we asked for it. Who knows? The comparison of our lifestyles and theirs is horrendous... What do Myra and Craig want to do? What have they been up to?"

"They both live in Harare. Craig finishes at university at the end of the year."

"What's he been studying?"

"Social science."

"What's that?"

"The study of how to be a good citizen. How to do good for others."

"How well the theory. How sad it all is when it comes into practice... Myra's turned into a beautiful woman. Extraordinarily beautiful, in fact."

"She's been talking to our grandfather. I hope he isn't putting ideas into her head. You know, Randall, if we are all honest with ourselves there's no future for us here in Zimbabwe. There never was. However much we try and blend in like Craig, we'll always be different: what's he going to do, get a job with an NGO and do charity? Maybe in a few hundred years the white blood will have mingled with the black and you won't see the difference. That's the only future for the descendants of colonialism if they want to stay in Africa. If they don't want that they'll have to go."

"And you, Phillip?"

"I take it one day at a time. I saw a quote from one of those smart philosophers who pepper our history with all those good thoughts: 'the most important day of our lives is today.' The only snag with that one is tomorrow. If you spend what you've got today, and tomorrow you haven't got any money and Mugabe has nicked your farm, some of those days in the future may be just as important but not much fun."

"What are you going to do?"

"Get out, I suppose. I love the bush. I love the safari business. But in the end you have to be practical. Especially if you want a wife and family. So go with your head, younger brother, not with your heart. Go back and live in England and write about Africa. Your books will never disappear like Rhodesia. You know the old saying: 'life's a bitch and then you marry one.' Amanda is probably right. Security is the most important thing in life, not having a good time… But I'll miss all this. Oh, hell, I'll miss it."

"What's Craig going to do with a degree in social science? What's he going to do for a living?"

"As I said, there's always an NGO. Spend his life hoping he is doing some good. What he really wants to be is an actor. Can you believe it? We all have dreams when we're young. Then hard reality comes along and we all have to make a living out of something. Most people with degrees in social science work for the government. And you don't see too many whites working in the Mugabe government."

"Have you talked to him?"

"What's the point? It's his life. You can't tell anyone what to do with their lives. Especially not a brother or sister."

"What's Myra doing in Harare?… Are we all going to the club tonight?"

"Why not?… She's got a job in the bank. Some kind of training programme."

"Is Clay Barry still the member-in-charge?"

"They retired him from the police last year. Put a black man in charge. Clay spends most of his days drinking in the club. He'll be there."

"What's he going to do?"

"Nothing. Just hope his pension lasts and they don't take that away from him. His wife's in hysterics, poor woman."

"Life really has changed."

"Yes it has. This is the new Africa... But life goes on. Always does until the day you die... What's England like to live in?"

"Cold and wet most of the time. And people constantly on top of you. You can never get away from them. But there are lots of gorgeous women."

"That sounds better."

"As my old friend Oliver Manningford says: 'it's not all bad'... Where do they live?"

"They share a flat in the Avenues. Two bedrooms. Dad pays the rent. A second-hand car to get them around. The one who is suffering most is their mother. Bergit gets lonely without them. But that's how it seems to work. Parents put all that work into bringing up their children and then they fly the coop, the world in front of the children, the world behind the parents. Makes you think."

"You've become quite the philosopher."

"Why, with you back and the kids visiting, everyone is trying to have such a good time. The more tourists I get with Jacques the less time I spend on the farm. From the noise and chaos of bringing up four children, they're mostly now alone. Once a week they go to the club for a drink. Evenings they drink a bottle of wine, eat dinner and go to bed."

"Are they still happy?"

"Oh, they're happy with each other. Just lonely. The place is so quiet... You won't be staying to work on the farm which is a pity. And you never know, it may all turn out just fine. A thriving new emerging economy based on farming and tourism, the rising economy slowly eliminating poverty like they did in Malaysia."

"And if we go like Ghana and most of the rest of post-colonial Africa, with one coup after another, or a despot stealing what's left of the money, what then?"

"Then we're stuffed. But you've got to be an optimist. Apartheid can't last much longer in South Africa and that country has a modern economy. It won't be easy to kick out the whites in a high-tech economy. Then the whole way of developing Africa and eliminating poverty will change for the better for all of us."

"I like your optimism but none of it will persuade Amanda. If I want to stay married I have to go back to England and get myself a proper job. Join the rat race. Please Amanda by showing off how rich we are... Don't you meet girls who come on your tours?"

"Some of them treat you like a hunting trophy. Have their fun in the bush and go home. Brag they had a safari hunter on the banks of the Zambezi River. One of them has been back twice to sample the goods. It's just sex. No talk of a future."

"Where's she from?"

"New York."

"What's she do?"

"Works for an investment bank."

"Sounds familiar. Been there, done that myself. How I ended up falling out with Uncle Paul... Is she older than you?"

"I never asked her. Probably. They have all this plastic surgery in America. It's difficult to tell their age. I was just part of the tourist package. Sometimes it's me they go for. Sometimes it's Jacques. One of the perks of running a safari business, I suppose. Short, sharp and sweet. No complications. If they get themselves pregnant they don't write and tell us... Is he worth a lot of money?"

"Grandfather? Millions, by the sound of it."

"I'll be buggered. What the hell are we going to do with it?"

"Let's just wait and see. When I tell him I'm not staying in Africa on his allowance to write books, he may leave it all to the cats' home. He wants me to stay far away from that woman to protect James Oliver from being brought up by a couple of lesbians. Life gets complicated, Phillip. You just got to believe it. The moment your life gets involved with other people, all hell breaks loose. You're probably better off on your own."

"But what's the point? What's the point of life spent on your own?"

"Look. Right over there. Elephant. They must have come up from the valley."

"This part of Africa must have been truly wild when the likes of Sebastian Brigandshaw, FC Selous and William Hartley came out from England at the end of the nineteenth century. You know, without Sebastian Brigandshaw you and I wouldn't be in the back of this truck looking at those elephants."

"I know. Granny Crookshank told me all about the family history and how Harry Brigandshaw, Sebastian's son, and our grandfather met up. They flew together to Switzerland in one of the first flying boats. Landed on the lake. Grandfather was the aeronautical engineer, Harry the test pilot. It was through Harry Brigandshaw that our father came to Africa to learn to grow tobacco and take up a Crown Land farm after the Second World War. The British needed tobacco they could pay for in sterling and not have to buy in dollars from the Americans. I took a whole lot of notes. One day, I'm going to turn it all into a novel... Have you ever seen an elephant in a land of tobacco? Makes one hell of a mess of the tobacco. Yes, those old days must have been wonderful. No people. Just the animals. They say there was less than half a million people in the whole of what is now Zimbabwe."

"How many we got now?"

"Nine million and counting. The white man's medicine. In those days most of the children died before they were five years old. Most of the people who hate us for taking their land owe us their lives. Makes you think. All those twists and turns that give us life and give two brothers the pleasure of chatting to each other in the back of a truck while driving along a dirt road blowing up dust."

"The chance of being alive is very small. I'm so glad I had a brother. And a father. And a grandfather I'd never met a week ago... Aren't you hungry? We'll have to wait until we get to the club. Could you put me up if I had to come to England? Can't imagine what I'd do for a living. I suppose I could fiddle around as a part-time mechanic and odd-job man, I've learnt a lot about engines from Jacques. Growing up on a farm, you learn to fix things."

"You could start a business. Make a fortune."

"You're kidding."

"You'd make a living. And you are always welcome in my house. Whatever the circumstances. What are brothers for? What is family for? Now you mention it, I am hungry. They still do those plate-size steaks at the club?"

"That hasn't changed. Quite a few of the farmers have gone. Mostly to Australia... Our poor mother. Such a short life."

"At least she doesn't have to worry."

"I want to think about her. Do you mind if we don't talk for a while?"

Randall, watching the dust trail stream out behind them, layering the bush on both sides of the road with a white powder, went into his own thoughts. For a while he thought of his mother, the mother he had barely known, wondering what she would have been like. Then his own problems came back to him: if he wasn't careful, his own son would grow up without a father, the boy's life abnormal right from the start.

When the truck drove back onto the farm and up to the house, he could see his wife sitting by the pool in her bathing costume. Despite having only just had the baby her figure was looking good. When the truck stopped at the security gate he jumped out. Phillip had climbed out the other side and opened the gate, climbing back into the truck.

"I'll walk to the pool, Phillip."

They waved at each other as the truck went up the driveway. Randall walked across the lawn to the pool, the four dogs following: the dogs had got up from under a tree when Randall had stepped off the truck. A pigeon was cooing from high up in one of the msasa trees. Randall again waved at his wife, the fear still in the pit of his stomach. First, Randall looked in the pram at his son, the boy sound asleep. Amanda was lying on a chaise longue in the shade of a tree. Randall knelt down on one knee next to her, the grass under his knee gentle and soft.

"Was it bad at your mother's grave?"

"No worse than usual. We're all going to the club. You'd better get dressed. And you're right, we should go back to England with Grandfather... Are you enjoying yourself, Amanda?"

"The club sounds fun. And when we get home it won't be long before summer. I've been talking to Myra and Craig about England. With my connections in the rag trade and Myra's good looks, I think we could start her modelling."

A hand touched Randall's shoulder and when he looked up it was his sister, Myra. They both smiled.

"Randall, it's so exciting. Instead of working in a dreary old bank I could be a London model. With Mum and Dad both born in England, Amanda says I won't have any difficulty getting a work permit to work in England. I'm so excited."

"Good for you. Don't get your hopes up too much."

"Amanda says you two are going to move into a flat and I can come and stay with you. London! I've never been out of Africa. I'm so excited."

When Amanda and Myra went up to the house to change, Randall stayed alone at the pool. The pigeon was still calling from the tree. Randall was sad, the day thinking of his mother not the best in his life. The dogs had gone off. When the girls came out dressed in their best for the club Randall sighed, looked up at the pigeon and walked from the pool. By the time he reached the house, walking over the lawn, the dogs now following, his father and stepmother were ready to go. The old man was nowhere to be seen. Randall went into the house to his old bedroom and changed from his shorts into a pair of long trousers. When the sun went down the temperature would drop, reminding Randall he should take a sweater. Jacques had brought round the small safari bus and was waiting for the others. Vince Ranger, the farm manager, had joined the family on the veranda. Vince and Craig were deep in conversation as they all walked to the bus. The old man had appeared dressed in his best impression of medieval clothing right down to the cloak. Amanda, dressed in one of William Drake's creations, stood out from the rest of the women she looked so different. Myra walked down in a simple dress wearing sandals in contrast to Amanda's high heels. Randall watched his stepmother give Amanda a look from under raised eyebrows.

Ten minutes later, the bus drove up to the Centenary West clubhouse where people were milling on the veranda that stretched the length of the front of the club. The veranda looked out over the cricket field. Most of the people were wearing the clothes they had worn playing tennis. Tennis and squash rackets were stacked on one of the wooden tables. Behind the clubhouse were six tennis courts and two squash courts. Through the inside window of the veranda that looked into the bar, Randall could see Clay Barry sitting up at the long wooden counter. He was alone. Feeling sorry for the man, Randall walked into the bar. To Randall's surprise, Noah was still the barman, the man's tight curly hair now peppered with white: he had been the club barman since before Randall was born. Both Clay Barry and Noah looked old.

"Can I join you for a drink, Mr Barry?"

"Please, call me Clay. And if it isn't young Randall. What brings you here? Didn't you run away to England? Give him a drink, Noah. Make mine a double. What you having, Randall?"

"A beer. How are you, Noah?"

Clay Barry was drunk. The barman gave Randall a smile. When

Randall turned round his father was waving at him from outside on the veranda.

"Sorry, Clay. Got to go. The family want me outside."

"Next time, old boy. Good to see you. How's the old country? Family been here too many generations so they won't let me in. Well, that's my story... How's that drink of mine coming, Noah?"

"Coming, Mr Barry."

"Whatever would I do without Noah? Give him the beer, Noah. Put it on my tab. Still remember the night they killed your cat, Randall. Don't worry about me. I drink on my own with the ghosts. The club's full of ghosts. The dead and the living. You go and join your family. Who's the lady in the fancy clothes?"

"She's my wife. We have a son. He's asleep in his cot."

"Now that does make me feel old... Cheers, old boy. Good to see you again."

"How's your wife?"

"She doesn't like my drinking. Got nothing else to do... Cheers, old boy. Down the old hatch. What would we do without booze?"

Randall walked from the bar without taking a beer, having mouthed 'no' to Noah. According to rumour, Noah had been an informer during the war, listening to the members talking in the bar and passing the information to the terrorists; or freedom fighters as Noah would have put it. Life, Randall thought, was indeed odd: the ex-Rhodesian policeman and the informer alone in the bar, the bush war a bitter part of both of their histories and no longer important. Now, thankfully, there were no loaded FN rifles in the empty racks below the inside of the window that ran the length of the room.

On the veranda, the tall, slim old man with the long white hair down to his shoulders and the white beard was the centre of everyone's attention. Dressed in his trademark clothes, the old man had been recognised. With the baby at her feet in the carrycot, Amanda looked out of it, no one paying her attention, everyone gawping at the man from Hollywood. One of the children was offering the old man a piece of paper and a pencil. Randall's grandfather took his own pen out of the inside of his cloak and signed the piece of paper. The old man was smiling. The boy was smiling. Everyone watching was smiling. Inside the bar Randall could see the lonely back of Clay Barry sitting up on his barstool. Noah, sitting on a barstool on the other side of the bar, had a puzzled look on his face, seeming not to know what the fuss was all about on the veranda. Everything to Randall looked like the end of an era.

A waiter brought him a beer on a tray that had been sent by Randall's father. The world at the Centenary club seemed to be in suspense, the old colonial habits alive but fragile. The old arrogant confidence of colonial Rhodesia had gone, the whites now the subjects, no longer the masters. A shudder, with all its feeling of premonition, made Randall's hands shake as he poured out his beer. He could see clearly it was all an anachronism, that it was all over. Amanda was right: trying to bring up James Oliver in Zimbabwe would be simply ridiculous. He would just have to hope that his pull over Amanda would be stronger than that of her lady lover; that the power of money and lasting comfort would not take his son away from him. Putting the full beer glass and the empty bottle on the table, Randall sat down next to his wife. From the cot, James Oliver was looking up at him, the big eyes wide open. Again Randall felt a shudder of premonition.

"What's all the fuss about, Randall?"

"He's famous. Famous people gather attention. Did you know the hair's a wig?"

"When are we getting supper?"

"The man in the bar was the local chief of police. The barman was an informer for the terrs. Makes you think."

"When are we going home?"

"Soon."

"I'd have thought your father would have been more interested in his grandson. He takes no notice."

"Men are like that. They don't show their emotions. It's so strange being back in the club. They attacked the Centenary East club but never this one."

"Who are you talking about?"

"The terrs... Are you happy, Amanda?"

For a long pause, Randall waited for an answer. The old man, surrounded by so many people, was laughing. Amanda got up, leaving the baby, and crossed the veranda to join them. Inside the bar, Clay

Barry had put his head down on the bar counter. Both of James Oliver's tiny hands were waving at him. When Randall offered the boy a finger the small pudgy hand took hold.

"Don't worry, lad. Whatever happens, I'll look after you."

Looking out over the cricket field, the grass newly cut, Randall began drinking his beer. He was thinking how quickly people's lives could change. Nothing was ever permanent. No one ever secure. All that money in the bank could disappear just as quickly as Rhodesia. Like so many Rhodesians, or Zimbabweans as they now tried to call themselves, he would have to buckle down and start his business life all over again. With luck by now his Uncle Paul's animosity towards him would have simmered down. He had done a good job at Westcastle, made BLG a lot of money, and that had to count for something. Or would the man's pride still make him vindictive? The world of business was small in the global village. People checked up on prospective employees, a phone call made: 'Oh he's good at his job, old boy. Just has other things on his mind. A bit unreliable if you ask me. Wants to be a writer.' Randall caught the eye of the waiter and ordered himself another beer. Randall couldn't move. He was the babysitter. The thought of writing had flipped his stomach, the thought of one of the publishers reading his book flooding his mind with hope. Then the hope receded. Inside the bar, Clay Barry's wife was trying to help her husband off the barstool. Even Noah was looking sad. The waiter came back with the beer.

"Can I pay you cash?"

"Members only, sir. It's on your father's tab."

Smiling, remembering that some things never changed, Randall poured out his beer. The beer tasted good. James Oliver was gurgling happily. Clay Barry had left the bar.

"Now, that's a good wife if ever I saw one. In sickness and in health. In good times and in bad. She's still looking after him. You're a lucky man, Clay Barry. Whatever your problems."

"Talking to yourself is the first sign of madness. Thanks for watching him. The steaks are on the way."

"When I'm old and drunk, Amanda, will you look after me?"

"Maybe. We'll have to see. Depends what you do when we get back to London."

For a while Randall sat still without saying anything before looking up from his son at his wife who had once left him.

"Yes, I suppose it does. As you say, we'll just have to see."

PART 9

NOVEMBER 1987 TO APRIL 1988 – MONEY
MAKES MONEY

1

Amanda was sick of arguing: they were still in one room, the baby was eight months old and Randall was still waiting tables, fiddling around with his stupid books that would never make them any money. Half-heartedly, Randall had looked for a full-time job in what was, in Amanda's eyes, his rightful profession. The man had a degree, for God's sake, she kept telling herself. A degree in economics. Why didn't he use it and look after his family, instead of cooping them up on the top floor of Mrs Salter's boarding house looking down on a line of wet washing. It was nearly Christmas and they had nothing. Evelina was right: she should give her son a proper upbringing and be responsible. The previous night's conversation with Evelina came flooding back through Amanda's mind.

"The whole idea was to have a baby and live together as a family. I want to look after you and James Oliver. I don't know what you're fussing about. We have our baby. Our lives can be full. Leave the fool and come back to me, darling. We'll all have a wonderful life together. I have lots of money, and more and more in the future. Dump the man. You can't bring up a child on a waiter's income. A temp waiter at that. I don't care how many shifts he does every day. He'll never amount to anything. And then what happens to our son? You know inside of you the real reason you went back to Randall was to get yourself pregnant. That trip with your friends to America was a bit of luck. The excuse to get yourself impregnated. We were happy together in this gorgeous flat for years. You like our friends. William Drake has been a friend all your life. Come back to me. I'll give you all the security you crave. With me, you'll be something. Living with Randall in a bedsitter, cooking food on a gas ring, you are nothing. He's never going to get a proper job. The man's obsessed with his damn books. Only a very few writers make money out of writing. In this life you have to have money. The rest is a pipe dream. When you first met Randall you were young and money was not so important. You could afford to dream. Now you have our son."

"He's Randall's son."

"Not after we adopt him. I will make James Oliver my legal heir. He'll have a future. A good boarding school. Influential friends. He'll have a real future. At the moment, as the son of a waiter who can't sell a book, your son, like Randall, is going to end up a failure. Give James Oliver a chance. Give him two doting parents. Two responsible parents who love him and do something about it. You don't love Randall. You love me. You said so last night."

"Last night I came round to see you after an argument with Randall."

"We made love, Amanda. Doesn't that mean something to you?"

"Of course it does."

"So you weren't lying to me? You said you loved me after we made love."

"I was confused. Randall and I had just had an argument. Why can't he get a proper job?"

"Because he can't see the wood for the trees. He's more interested in himself than you and James Oliver."

"His books are good."

"But they don't make money. What's the use of a book if it doesn't make money? And that grandfather never helped him. Got his cancer in remission and went back to America. Only prepared to give his grandson money if Randall went back to Zimbabwe. Zimbabwe, for goodness sake! What kind of future would James Oliver have in Zimbabwe? If the man's so rich why doesn't he give you money now?"

"He wants me far away from you."

"What's the difference? Zimbabwe is less than a day from here by aeroplane."

"I'm so sick of arguing."

"Then dump the man. Come back to a life of luxury. We love each other. I'll give you both a wonderful life. We'll be happy for the rest of our lives. What more could you want? And, most importantly, what more could James Oliver want? You've got to think of the boy. Without me and my money what future can he possibly have? Randall's turning thirty in a few weeks' time. If he gets a job in commerce or industry, he'll have to start all over again. He'll soon be past it. Men are managing directors of companies by the time they are thirty, with years of experience on the job. Is a top company going to take on a man who's been a waiter? Be realistic. The man's screwed up his life with his writing. And if you're not careful he'll take you and the boy down the drain with him. You've got to have money in this life. Everything costs money. Leave him. Move back with me. Please, Amanda. It's for the good of both of you."

"I'll think about it."

"That's better. You only have one life. Make the best of it. I've ordered a babysitter for James Oliver. She'll be here in a few minutes. We're going to dress you up in the best and go out to dinner. Have some fun. Make love when we come home. This is your home, Amanda. Not that dreadful bedsitter."

"It'll break his heart to lose his son."

"Then why doesn't he do something about it? Like getting a job? Being responsible? Being the boy's parent and not fooling around? The man's selfish. He's only thinking of himself. Now, come and look what William and I have made for you. You're going to look gorgeous. I love you, Amanda. I want to look after you. I want to look after both of you. You need a life. At the moment you don't have a life living hand to mouth. You can't spend the rest of your life worrying your guts out over money."

"What restaurant are we going to?"

"Now you're talking. Camilla's Corner. They'll all love to see you."

"I must be home with the baby when Randall gets back from his work."

"We'll see about that."

Which had later brought on another argument. This time with Evelina. With James Oliver bundled into a taxi, paid for by Evelina, the babysitter standing puzzled on the steps outside Evelina's apartment,

Amanda had rushed home just in time to greet Randall on his return from work. Randall, tired out, had fallen into bed, turned over and gone to sleep. All night Amanda had tried to sleep, happy to get up and breastfeed James Oliver, the one pleasure she still had in her life. In the morning, waking from a broken sleep, Randall was up at his desk writing in the first quiet of day. It rained all day, the gas fire burning in the small room they called home. As she stared at the rain, which she could see outside the window in front of Randall bent over at his desk, her mind was in turmoil. One minute she was going back to Evelina, the next she had changed her mind.

"Aren't you going to try looking for a job?"

"Please, Amanda, I'm writing. You know how difficult it is when you break my concentration."

"I was with Evelina last night, and the night before." The words had come blurting out of her mouth.

For a long, tense moment, Randall stayed still at his desk. Then he turned round, the look on his face a mixture of hurt and building rage. Randall did not speak. Amanda got up from where she was sitting on the side of the bed and went to look at the baby. The explosive silence in the room continued.

"I've been a fool, haven't I, Amanda?"

Fussing with the baby, Amanda said nothing, only breaking her silence when she looked up at Randall.

"She wants me to go back to her."

"So it was all planned from the beginning?"

"Not exactly."

"Then what did happen?"

"I don't know. I don't know what I want. All we do now is argue. We don't have anything. No now and no future."

"I thought we had each other."

"Not if we're arguing. I'm thinking of the baby and his future."

"I don't think so, Amanda. You're thinking of yourself. You want the life of ease and luxury. From my experience, it doesn't always bring happiness."

"I'm sick of living in one room with a baby. We're always on top of each other. Which is why we argue. He needs so much."

"Every time I get near to a job it comes down to a BLG reference. My uncle won't give me one. The only way I'm going to get back into the industry is by pleading with my uncle. Begging for my job back. Grandmother calls it tough love. That the only way to make me behave myself in BLG is to make me buckle down and humiliate myself so I won't do again what I did in America. Maybe you are right. Maybe there's nothing I can do to support you both. I'm the one being selfish. A life of love with a couple of lesbians can't be worse than this."

"That's obnoxious."

"Probably. I've tried asking Grandfather for a bank guarantee to start my own business but he'll only support us if we live in Zimbabwe far from Evelina. And from what you just said he was right... Did you two make love?"

"Yes, Randall."

"Then you'd better go back to her."

"Do you mean it?"

"What else can I do? I have no money. No prospects. Just enough income to feed us. I'm out of the competition if you don't love and want me. I'm a perfect idiot... It's five o'clock and I have to get ready for work. The book was going well until you interrupted."

"I'm sorry, Randall."

"No, you're not. But you might be right. I'm a failure. What son needs a father who is a failure?... I'll go and have a bath. Leave you to your own conscience. We're in a mess. One big, bloody mess. And I'm sure it's all my fault."

Amanda watched Randall pick up his towel and leave the room for the bathroom they shared with Oliver and James. Ten minutes later, Randall came back to get dressed. The silence continued. When Randall opened the door to go to work he turned back to her. His eyes were cold, his lips tight.

"Will you both be here when I get back?"

"I don't know."

"Think carefully, Amanda. You've done it once before. This time if you go there will be no coming back. Ever."

"You don't understand. I want the best for James Oliver."

"Don't rationalise, Amanda. It doesn't suit you. Be careful you don't destroy both of your lives. Your own and your son's. There's only so much I can do. I can't force you. I couldn't look after my son on my own however much I might want to. What a shame. With the boy, I thought we were back together permanently. But then nothing in life is permanent. Oh, and I made twenty quid in tips last night. One of my old friends in my BLG days felt sorry for me. Gave me a big lift being felt sorry for. And that's being sarcastic. There's only one thing more silly than being felt sorry for and that's feeling sorry for oneself. Goodnight, Amanda."

"Don't you want to say goodnight to the baby?"

"Not tonight, Amanda. Not tonight."

The door closed. Amanda listened to his footsteps going down the stairs. At the bottom of the house the front door opened and closed. The room fell deathly silent. Outside it was pitch dark. Amanda got up, her legs heavy, and closed the curtains. The baby was still asleep. Feeling perfectly miserable Amanda lay back on the bed. She had nothing to do. She wasn't hungry, didn't want a cup of tea. The gas fire was hissing. She got up and put another coin in the meter, twisting the knob to make the coin register. On the way back she paused at Randall's desk. In the middle of the desk, in front of his chair, neatly stacked and joined with a paperclip, sat the first chapters of Randall's new book. Every day he left it in the same place when he went to work, hoping she would take the typewriter out of the cupboard and start the typing. Her lack of typing was a bone of contention, Amanda not wanting to encourage his writing. Guilt made her pick up the manuscript. She got back on the bed, put pillows against the headboard and made herself comfortable. Next to the bed James Oliver was still asleep in the carrycot. She smiled down at her son and began reading the first page of the manuscript. There was no heading. Just chapter one. They had not discussed the new book, Amanda having no idea what it was all about. Even though she knew Randall read back the previous day's writing there were very few changes. His handwriting was neat and legible. Within minutes Amanda was transported out of the room, out of her misery, far away from her problems, into Randall's fictional world. Later, when she looked at the clock on the wall, two hours had gone by, her time spent in the book feeling like only a few minutes.

"Shit, Randall. You might be a lousy provider but you're one hell of a writer."

Without thinking anymore, Amanda got up from the bed and walked across the small room to the cupboard, taking out the typewriter and walking with it to Randall's desk. The baby was awake, smiling at her. To stop any interruptions she picked him up, took out her right breast that was full of milk and gave it to the baby. The boy latched on and sucked, Amanda smiling down at him as he drank her milk. Satiated, the boy fell back in her arms and let out a burp. Amanda, putting him over her shoulder, burped him again. She was smiling. She was happy. She put him back in the small cot and went to the desk, pulling out the chair. She picked up the manuscript, tapped it on the desk to square the pages, and began to type. Again she was back in the book, back in Randall's world, the world of his people. Still smiling, she let the words flow from the handwritten pages, through the typewriter and onto the paper, her hands flying over the keys as she worked.

All through the evening she typed. There was no thought of Evelina or Randall, just the characters talking from the book. At twelve o'clock, having eaten a sandwich up at the desk, Amanda stopped typing. She put the typewriter back in the cupboard with the typed pages. Back at the desk, she tapped the handwritten manuscript back into place and left it exactly as Randall had left it in the middle of his desk. Only when Randall returned from work, did she come out of the story. Again they were not talking. Randall undressed, got into the double bed next to her, turned over and went to sleep. Amanda turned out the bedside lamp and lay back in the bed. She was smiling. The characters from the book played back in her head... With all three of them quiet, Amanda drifted into a dreamless sleep, woken once by James Oliver when he wanted his feed. Even with all the baby food from the little bottles, the boy was always hungry for her milk. Randall had not woken. She turned out the light and went back to sleep.

In the morning, when Amanda woke, Randall was back at his desk writing. The light was on at the desk, the curtain still drawn. She got up and made the tea, putting his mug down on the desk in front of him. Randall did not notice. The story was still in Amanda's head, the story of Randall's people. Quietly, she took her tea back to bed wondering how on earth so much story could come out of one man's head. There were no notes. No reference books. It all came straight out of the man's head.

Saturday was the day Amanda went shopping late in the afternoon when the stalls in the Portobello market cut their prices on perishable food. It was an old trick from their days as the laid-back couple. With her two hessian shopping bags full of vegetables and fruit, a bag in each hand, the rain still drizzling, the street lights coming up, she began the walk back to the room. Instead of wondering what the hell she was doing, she was thinking of Randall's book. It was set in the post-Mugabe, post Anglo-Saxon world hegemony where one of the last remaining white farmers left in the country had been asked to go back to farming to produce food in a world of hunger and terminal poverty, the Zimbabwean population having been decimated by AIDS and emigration. The main character in Randall's book was made the chief when he gave the people food and protection, the skills from his days as a successful commercial farmer making the land again productive. With the farm and the people prospering came the predators. From a stash of arms the white man had hidden in a cave at the end of the war of liberation that had brought Robert Mugabe to power, the new chief armed his people to protect what they had achieved. Some of the predators gave up fighting and joined the people and helped with the farming. The new chief married a beautiful girl whose father had been the local chief before he fell out with Robert Mugabe's party and was assassinated by the war vets, the same people who had chased the white commercial farmers from his land, along with four thousand others, causing Zimbabwe's economy to collapse. On Saturdays in the kraal, the drums were again playing, the people dancing, their world a refuge in a land ravaged by poverty, destroyed by capitalist greed, a scourge more devastating to the world than any invading army in history.

When Amanda got home with the food, just in time for Randall to go to work, the manuscript was neatly stacked in its place on the front of Randall's desk. First she fed the baby while Randall changed for work. When he had gone, she unpacked the food and made a vegetable soup. With the housework done she went to his desk and picked up the manuscript pages, flipping through to where she had finished reading. There were eight new handwritten pages which she read, her thirst for the story insatiable. With a spoon and a bowl she ate some of the soup. She was smiling: the chief's daughter, married to the new chief, had had a daughter, the parents in love with the child and each other, the difference in their age and skin colour of no significance, the political drama playing out alongside the mutual love of two different people who were blending into one... With the typewriter out of the cupboard, Amanda continued her typing. By the time Randall came back from work, the typescript and the typewriter back in the cupboard, she had typed nearly half of all the pages. Randall, tired and irritable, got into bed, turned over and went to sleep. Smiling, remembering the unfolding happy end to his story, Amanda, the light now out, drifted off into sleep. In her dream she was living in an African kraal with Randall. The sun was shining. Both of them were happy. The people around them were happy. The kraal was an island, a sun-filled island far from the storm.

A week later Randall finished his book. When Amanda went to type the last pages she found a new sheet of paper on top of the first page. On the page was written the book's title: *The White Saviour*. Amanda read the last four handwritten pages of the book. On the last page, at the bottom, was today's date, the sign Amanda knew signified the end of the book. In the book, the outside world had come to an end, the world's cities torn apart by hungry, thieving people, law and order long a thing of the past. Only in the kraal, with no communication with the outside world, was there any sanity; happy, content people living off what was again productive land. Amanda understood the book's message: the real world they all lived in was headed for the cliff.

With the book finished, and Randall bored, they argued. Amanda's life in the cramped room became a living hell. James Oliver developed a colic keeping them both awake at night. During the day the room was intolerable. To add to her woes, Randall had taken to drinking cheap wine soon after he got out of bed, and Amanda grew terrified he was going to lose his job. Many times, when Randall went to work, he was drunk. In desperation, Amanda brought up the subject of Randall's book.

"I typed the book. I think it's wonderful."

"What's the point in showing it to anyone? The economy is in a slump. No publisher is going to take on a new author."

"We must Photostat the typed pages and send it out. It won't do any good sitting in the cupboard. Aren't you glad I did the typing?"

"If I had a gun I'd shoot myself."

"Then what would happen to James Oliver?"

"He'd end up with two mothers and a happy future. I'm sick of waiting tables. I hate this bloody climate. I hate my bloody life."

"You're drunk."

"Not yet. At least when I'm drunk I don't feel anything."

"You can't go to work like this."

"They'll fire me if I do and fire me if I don't. What's the difference? I'm screwed. Life is screwed. The world's screwed and the real shit hasn't yet started. Living in a city without pots of money is like living in a rat hole. One big rat hole full of rats."

"Thanks for the compliment."

The door opened and slammed, leaving Amanda to cry on her own. For the first time in years she thought of calling her parents. Instead, she picked up the phone and called Evelina."

"Can you come and collect me? It's raining and I don't have the fare for a taxi."

"You poor darling. I'll be there in twenty minutes. Have you been crying? Your voice sounds desperate."

"He's drunk and gone to work. It's the end. This afternoon, he looked as if he wanted to hit me."

"Has he ever hit you?"

"Not yet. I am desperate."

"Pack your bags. I'll bring William in case Randall comes back. If he gets to work drunk they'll fire him. I've turned the spare bedroom into a nursery. I knew this would happen."

"Please hurry."

"Let me phone William and then we're on our way. You poor darling. Men can be so horrible. When they can't get their own way they turn to drink and violence."

"He wasn't always like this."

"It's not what they were that matters. It's what they are now that counts."

Alone, expecting Randall back any minute, his mood more foul from losing his job, Amanda waited. She had packed a few things for herself and James Oliver. An hour went by. When the front doorbell rang Amanda rushed out of the room and flew down the three flights of stairs, throwing open the front door. William Drake ran back up to the room and came down again, this time slowly, the cot in his right hand, the suitcase in the other. From the basement flat Mrs Salter was watching them through her window. It was still raining, a fine, cold drizzle, picked out by the street lights. In William's car, sitting on the backseat with her baby, it was warm. When Amanda looked back through the car's rear window she could no longer see Mrs Salter's semi-detached house. The car went out into the main road and turned towards Knightsbridge. No one was talking. The car stopped outside Evelina's block of flats, a place that for so long had been Amanda's home. She tried to tell herself she was home again but kept thinking of Randall. She had left him. She and James Oliver had left him.

William, still looking worried, let her out of the car.

"You'll be all right now, Amanda. I'll leave you two and the baby alone. Your mother was asking after you when I went down this weekend. I said you were fine. Your father isn't very well. He's got so old. You should go down and visit them."

"Now I'm back with Evelina, he'd slam the door in my face."

"They'd like to see their grandson."

"You told them I had a baby?"

"What else was I meant to say?"

"How are my sisters?"

"Much the same, I believe. Suburban housewives using their husbands' money to keep up appearances; how much is mortgaged and how much is theirs, who knows? These days they judge a family by their home and the car they drive, where the kids go to school. And, thank goodness, their clothes, or Evelina and I wouldn't have a business. When you've calmed down, Evelina will bring you over to supper. You'll like my new lover. We're so happy."

"Thank you, William. What would we do without old friends?"

"My pleasure. And without those raspberry bushes who knows what might have happened? Just kidding. Go and see your parents before it's too late. Maybe next time I drive down to see my parents we can all go over and visit the next door neighbours and have a little drinky. Evelina can put on her charm. About time she met your parents. The world's changing. Thinking people are no longer so against us gays. They understand us."

Amanda, her mind in a turmoil, more worried about herself and her baby than her parents, didn't reply. She leaned inside the driver's window and kissed William on the cheek. Evelina had picked up the carrycot with the baby. Amanda picked up her suitcase. The car drove away into the drizzle.

"Welcome home, darling. Don't look so worried. Many women leave their husbands. Or their husbands leave them. It's part of modern life."

As Amanda walked behind Evelina into the building, she was thinking of Randall coming home to a cold, empty room, his wife and baby gone. She was crying. When they reached the front door of the flat, standing in the corridor, she tried to smile. Inside, Evelina put the cot on the dining-room table. James Oliver was gurgling, his big eyes wide open and smiling.

"It's the best thing for him. This is what we always hoped for, Amanda. You, me and our own little baby. I'm so happy. Come, let me show you the new nursery. Don't think about Randall. If he can't support his family properly what can he expect? Now, give me a big kiss. We'll have a cosy dinner, a bottle of wine and make love to each other. Be happy, darling. We have everything we want."

All through supper Amanda's sinking feeling persisted. She fed James Oliver in front of Evelina and still felt terrible. Inside of her, she knew she had done something irreversible and the feeling would not go away. She wondered if it would ever go away; when something bad was done, it stayed. When they got into bed, the same bed she had slept in so many nights next to Evelina, she did not want to make love. Annoyed, Evelina turned out the light. The baby was in the new nursery, all on his own. Amanda preferred having him next to her. She couldn't sleep, lying on her back, Evelina snoring next to her, Amanda listening for any sound coming from her baby through the wall. She began to cry, silently, the tears wetting both sides of the pillow. Outside, far away in the night, she could hear the London traffic. The expensive Knightsbridge block of flats was old, the walls thick, the sounds of London isolated. Amanda drifted off, the transition between being awake and asleep blending, taking her away.

When she woke in the morning there was the desperate feeling of panic when she didn't know where she was. Then she heard James Oliver crying from the next room, the sound only just penetrating the wall. The crying had brought her awake. Evelina, turned away from her under the blankets, was still fast asleep. The room was warm. Amanda got up, walked through to the next room and fed her baby, the whole flat warm from the central heating. Then she thought of Randall and wondered what he was thinking. What he was going to do. Probably, she thought, he would go back to Africa. She was glad she had typed the book. At least that was something. Then she got back into bed next to Evelina, putting her arms round the woman and snuggling up to her, bringing Evelina awake. When Evelina was awake she turned over. They faced each other, both of them smiling. Then they made love, slowly and lovingly. Amanda's new life had begun.

2

William Drake came round three weeks after Christmas with the news. Amanda's father was dead. William's mother had phoned him from Great Bookham and asked him to give Amanda the news. Evelina was working, Amanda alone with James Oliver in the Knightsbridge flat.

"Do you want me to drive you to Great Bookham? The funeral is tomorrow."

"Why didn't my mother phone me?"

"Did they know your phone number?"

"If they wanted it they could have asked you."

"Your mother is sick. She won't eat. Your sister, Gillian phoned me. Douglas and Nigel are in India on business. They're due at Heathrow this afternoon."

"When did he die?"

"A week ago."

"It's my fault they ignored me."

"I'm afraid it is, Amanda."

"Did they invite me to the funeral?"

"Not exactly. You can stand in the back of the church. He is your father."

"Why won't she eat? My poor mother."

"Gillian says your mother no longer wants to live. People do die from sorrow. You must go to your mother. What they think of you doesn't matter. If you don't go you'll never be able to live with yourself. We can stay tonight with my parents. They are going to the funeral. We can all go together. Leave James Oliver with Evelina. Don't complicate it any more."

"Why was I so damn selfish?"

"I did warn you. No, that's silly. What's done is done."

"They think I never went back to Randall. Why are we all so horrible?"

"I've spoken to Evelina and she has employed a nurse for James Oliver to look after him while we are away... Have you heard from Randall?"

"Not a word since I left him. I'm horrible, William. I've screwed up everyone's lives."

"Other people help in the screwing. Self-righteous people who won't understand lesbians? Doesn't help. Men wanting to write books instead of providing for their families? Doesn't help. Your father judging both of us when we were ten years old didn't help. He tore our friendship apart. And that really hurts when you're a child. We didn't know at that age we were doing anything wrong. Don't only blame yourself, Amanda. The nurse will be here shortly. Get yourself ready. This time I'm not taking no for an answer. You've got to talk to them or at least try. If it doesn't work, you won't have to blame yourself. Your father had a good life. Think of him positively. Six children and he only fell out with one of them. And if we go back to the origin of that problem it was probably all my fault. I was curious to see what a girl's body looked like under her knickers."

"My poor mother. She'll be so lost without him. He was her whole life. She always said that without Father she was nothing... And don't forget I wanted to have a look at your willy." The joke went flat, neither of them smiling.

"The family will rally round... Get yourself ready."

"Thank you, William. Sometimes I think you are all I have. The only thing in my life that was ever meant to be permanent."

"What about Evelina?"

"She's got what she wants. A lover, a housekeeper and a mother all rolled into one. It's mostly about Evelina. Everything is fine if I do what I'm told. And the trouble with a lesbian relationship is the lack of security. I don't have any rights. Neither does James Oliver. Now I'm moaning, thinking of myself when I should be thinking of my father and my poor mother. The family will probably kick me in the teeth but who cares? I'll pack an overnight bag... How's the boyfriend?"

"Not too good. He's young and pretty. I don't think I'm the only one."

"Poor William. I'll go and get changed. You think James Oliver will be all right with a stranger?"

"She's a registered nurse. Evelina will be at home at night."

"I want to cry but I can't. Why did we have to be abnormal? We could have been so happy with each other. A normal, loving family. We would never have had to experience all the horrors of life. Childhood sweethearts that spent their entire lives together in harmony. Why did it have to happen otherwise?"

"Maybe life never has a happy ending. Blame the raspberry bushes for not giving us enough cover... Are you still breastfeeding the baby?"

"Not anymore. This is going to be a good one. I haven't seen or heard from my brothers and sisters for years. Always the rebel in the family, that was little Amanda. And yes, you were right. I should have gone down to see him. And now it's too late... Why is it always too late?"

With Evelina staying in the office looking after the fashion business, the registered nurse ensconced in the Knightsbridge flat looking after James Oliver, they drove down to Great Bookham and the house of Amanda's parents.

When they all arrived at eleven o'clock the next morning for the funeral the old Norman Church was packed, the vicar still shaking hands with the mourners at the door of his church. The Drakes went on down the aisle leaving Amanda at the back of the church. The vicar, at first surprised, pretended not to know Amanda. Down the aisle the Drakes had found their seats, William turning round to look back at Amanda before he sat down. The vicar, wearing his best sombre expression, had walked down inside the church to start the ceremony. The coffin, on its stand, pointed at the small curtain behind the altar, was all on its own, its lid covered with flowers. Gritting her teeth, not looking to right or left, Amanda walked down the aisle and placed a single red rose on the coffin before walking back to the rear of the church, the organist playing his sombre music. With her back to everyone in the church, Amanda had mouthed 'I'm sorry' to her father. She was crying silent tears, her face wet with her grief. By the time she looked back the service had begun. When the coffin rolled forward, the curtain opening and closing, making its way to the crematorium, Amanda left the church, the old cedar trees stark in the winter morning looking down upon her from up high. Amanda walked off the path to be on her own. Many of the gravestones were ancient. The Drakes had locked their car. Amanda didn't want to stand next to it looking conspicuous.

"You killed him!"

The voice was a high-pitched choke. Amanda turned and tried to hug her mother.

"Don't you dare touch me! You shamed your own father. Go away from us back to your life of perversion and God help your son."

Behind her mother, on the path that led through the graveyard to the wooden gate at the entrance to the church, stood Amanda's brothers and sisters. They were all looking at her, none of them smiling. A gentle hand touched her shoulder.

"Let's go, Amanda."

"They hate me, William."

"It's called self-righteousness. I get it all the time when people hear I'm gay. You were brave putting your rose on the coffin in front of all of them. Let's go. There's nothing more you can do. We'll drop my parents at the house and drive back to London."

"I thought the coffin would be open; I'd have a last look at him... She hates me."

"She'll get over it. Your mother's upset."

"I'm all on my own, William. All on my own."

"Don't be silly. You have James Oliver and Evelina. We all choose our lives the way we want them. You'll never make them understand."

"Why not?"

"Because they don't want to."

"How can I have killed him? People die of shame when they are shameful. If anyone should have died for my sins it was me."

"She wanted someone to hit out at. Someone to blame. Your father died of a very old age. He was much older than your mother. She'll have to get used to living on her own without your father to fall back on. Marrying a much older man, she had to expect she would end up on her own. It's part of the process of life."

"I never thought of how it would affect them when I went to live with Evelina. How my life would reflect on them."

"We never do. Selfishness is inherent in all of us, despite what we try to portray. They have their own lives. You have yours."

"Do your parents accept your homosexuality?"

"On the surface. Underneath, I don't know."

"Have you asked them?"

"There are some things you ask and some that you don't. That's one of them. For your family and mine it is often all about appearances. To many in this lovely world, what we gays do is a perversion and that perversion reflects badly on our families. They want to be able to boast that their son's a doctor, not a queer who makes women's clothes. It's the same for your brothers and sisters. You are bad for their all-important image."

"Are we wrong?"

"Who knows? Maybe it's better for the gay community to stay on its own. Then no one gets hurt. It's a big world. There's room for everyone."

By the time William dropped her off at the block of flats in Knightsbridge it was dark and raining. Throughout the drive they had stayed mostly silent, both of them deep in their thoughts. Amanda put her hand on William's knee and gave it a squeeze.

"Damn those raspberry bushes for not being bigger."

The smiles they gave each other made Amanda feel better. Then she ran into the building. Upstairs she fumbled for the key. Inside the flat the woman was asleep on the settee. Without waking the nurse, Amanda went into the nursery. In the big new pen, sitting up on the floor mat, James Oliver's face lit up when he saw his mother, the boy struggling to get up on his podgy little feet. Leaning over the wooden railing, Amanda picked up her son. She was smiling. She was happy.

The next day when Evelina went to work and the nurse went home with a week's pay, using some of the skills she had learnt from typing Randall's books, Amanda wrote a long letter to her mother trying to explain. With some of the guilt off her chest she put a postage stamp on the envelope. At the corner of the road, fifty yards from the block of flats, Amanda posted the letter. The big red pillar box was so old it had Queen Victoria's mark on it.

"I'm an unpaid housekeeper but who cares? My son loves me."

For two weeks Amanda watched the mail delivery in the morning hoping for a reply from her mother. The days went by and nothing came. Her days of looking after Evelina were back to what they had been before she went to America with Oliver Manningford and James Tomlin, the trip that had culminated in the birth of her son. She felt bored, frustrated and used, the trivial daily chores in the flat of no importance.

"At least we're not short of money," she told her son when she tried to think positively. And the days went on, Amanda doing her best to live in the present, doing her best to forget the past, and not to contemplate the future.

When a letter did arrive it came from a firm of London solicitors. Amanda had ripped open the typed envelope to be told there was to be a reading of her father's will the following Thursday. The letter invited Amanda to attend.

"What the hell do they want me for?"

The following week at the appointed hour Amanda made her appearance at the offices of Pendleton, Webb and Digby in the City of London. She was the last to arrive, having timed her appearance for exactly eleven o'clock. She had left James Oliver in the care of the same nurse who had previously looked after him. Evelina had more important business with one of her clients to attend to than looking after a baby. The whole family were sitting on chairs looking at Mr Digby behind his desk. The man was dressed in a pinstripe suit and wearing an old Harrovian tie. There was one chair left empty. Amanda, giving the man a brief smile, sat herself down; no one made eye contact.

"As you all know, Mr Hanscombe left a considerable fortune, the money to be placed in a family trust for the life of Mrs Hanscombe when the estate will be split equally among the siblings. Now, be patient, and I will read to you the exact content of the will."

"He can't have included Amanda!" said Gillian.

"Oh, but he did."

The man started reading, the first sentence reaching Amanda's soul.

"I, George Webb Hanscombe, love each of my children equally..."

For Amanda, the rest of the will didn't matter. She got up and slipped out of the room, leaving the man still talking as he read out the content of the will. She was floating. Despite everything she had done to him, her father had loved her. Outside in the street, she flagged down a taxi.

Nothing else in her life mattered at that moment. He loved her. Back at the flat in the nursery, James Oliver gave her a big, wide-eyed smile when she picked him up from his playpen, the nurse letting herself out.

Another letter with its typed envelope arrived the following week, standing Amanda's life on its head. Her father, from his extensive import and export business with India, had left her just short of a million pounds. A part of the income from her portion of the trust was to be given to her mother as part of her mother's allowance. The rest of the income, up to an amount of five per cent of the capital sum, was hers to spend as she wished. She was rich. In her own right she was rich. Picking up James Oliver she danced with him round the nursery. Someone, she wasn't quite sure who, had said that when a person was rich they didn't have to be polite or subservient to anyone.

"Poor Randall. With all that money he could write to his heart's content."

In the moment of her understanding the whole world around her was different; she could do what she wanted; be what she wanted; no longer dependent on anyone. She and James Oliver were free.

When Evelina came home from work and started to boss her around Amanda gave her a smile, ignoring Evelina's instructions for supper.

"Now what's the matter, Amanda? I've had a tiring day. Please do what I say. I haven't got time to argue. And that dress you're wearing looks awful. Running a business is exhausting. You're lucky to be able to sit at home all day doing nothing."

"Well, if cleaning the flat, doing the shopping and preparing your food is nothing, why don't you try it yourself for a couple of days and see how you like it?"

"What's the matter with you today, Amanda? I told you I don't have time to argue. I want my food on time so I can get to bed and be clear-headed in the morning."

"Then why don't you do the cooking for a change?"

"What are you talking about, Amanda? That's your job."

"Most people when they have a job get paid. I'm an unpaid skivvy."

"I feed and clothe both of you," snapped Evelina. "You should be grateful."

"So should you be, Evelina. You have an unpaid housekeeper and a boy that you call your son."

"You'd be out on the street, both of you, if it wasn't for me. And don't tell me you want to go back to that ex-husband waiter of yours. And who paid for the divorce, may I ask? I did. Everything you have I paid for. And all I ask in return is a little civility and supper on the table when I come home after a hard day's work. You don't know when you are well off."

"As a matter of fact, I do."

"Then get my supper."

"Oh, dear. Here we go again."

"What's got into you, Amanda?"

"Just under a million pounds."

"What on earth are you talking about?"

"My portion of my late father's estate."

"Don't talk rubbish. The man despised you."

To Amanda's surprise and delight, Evelina had gone as white as a sheet.

"From his years in the British colonial service in India my father had built up a web of business contacts he turned into a fortune of over five and a half million pounds after death duties. And that does not include the house and antique furniture in Great Bookham which Dad left to Mother with the proviso that when she died the proceeds are to be split equally between us six children. For the moment I am only entitled to the income from my portion of the estate. Only when my mother dies will I receive the capital. But nearly fifty thousand quid a year isn't to be sneezed at... What's the matter, Evelina?"

"Is this true?"

"Every word of it. And if you don't believe me read that letter on the table."

"It makes you independent."

"That's exactly what it does."

"My goodness. I'd better go and make the supper."

"Are you being sarcastic?"

"Not exactly. My word, that is a lot of money. You said your mother told you at the funeral that your father despised you."

"Well, he didn't. He loved me. He really loved me. After all the terrible things I did to him my father still loved me. All of us equally. He said so in his will."

"I'd better go and see if James Oliver needs anything. Would you like a drink? Would you like to go out to supper? I can quickly phone the babysitter."

"Pour the drinks, Evelina, while I get supper and look after my son. My son and Randall's son, however much we try to kid ourselves."

"When do you get all that money?"

"The income right away. I'll tell you what, how about Saturday I take you to Camilla's Corner?"

"I can't believe it."

"While I'm making supper you'd better read the solicitor's letter. Then you'll believe it. So, how was your day?"

"You're not going to leave me are you, Amanda? I'd kill myself if you left me again."

"Don't be dramatic. Just remember from now on we are equals."

"Oh, please, Amanda. I love you. I'd be nothing without you."

Smiling to herself, Amanda walked out of the lounge to the nursery. It felt good being rich which made Amanda realise as she picked up her son that from this day on she was different. Money made people different. And despite all the excitement of getting even with Evelina, Amanda was not sure she liked the feeling it gave of having power over other people.

"Whatever happened to the laid-back woman from all those years ago?" she said to James Oliver as she carried him into the kitchen. With the boy seated in his highchair, Amanda began to prepare their supper.

"Just make sure, Amanda Hanscombe, you don't turn into a nasty person like the rest of them," she said under her breath as she chopped up the vegetables. For a moment she stopped, put the knife down and held onto the edge of the sink, the knuckles of both her hands whitening as she gripped. "You were right, Randall. The best days were the days of the laid-back couple when money and responsibility didn't matter." Slowly, as she went back to cleaning and cutting the vegetables, the tears came down on both sides of her face.

"Can I help you, darling?" came from the lounge.

"No, thanks. I'm just fine."

Wiping the tears away with the back of her hand, she smiled at her son who was bashing his toy bricks together.

"Don't worry, little one," she said softly. "When it comes to you I will always be responsible... You want to chew on a piece of carrot? It's good for young gums. Here, give it a try."

Instead of putting the carrot in his mouth James Oliver threw it across the kitchen.

"Have it your own way."

The boy was happy. And that was all that mattered. He was gurgling and smiling and playing with his toys.

3

At the end of April, two months after Amanda and Evelina celebrated James Oliver's first birthday, the Hanscombe siblings began to fight over the money. Gillian and Amanda's two older sisters began the argument. To keep death duty to a minimum, Douglas and Nigel had valued the family business at a tenth of its market value. Being a private company not quoted on a stock exchange the company was only worth what someone would pay for it. An import-export business relied on the contacts of its directors. Douglas, two months after the funeral, made an offer to the trust to buy out his father's company. Complicit in the deal was Nigel. They argued that without them, the business would be worth a lot less; that the company was Douglas and Nigel and any growth in the future should belong to them. The smiles in the family at undervaluing the company and cheating the British government out of death duty revenue changed to anger among the three older girls. Douglas, they said, wasn't offering them enough. They wanted a true market value. Douglas, a smug smile on his face, said that if the price went above the death duty valuation, the family would be criminally responsible. Gillian, knowing her brothers wanted to take the company public and have it floated on the London Stock Exchange, said the death duty valuation was a premeditated plan by the brothers to cheat not only the government but their sisters. Not only were the three sisters furious, so were their spouses. Gillian's husband, who was charming but not so clever when it came to making his own money, had done his maths. If Hanscombe and Sons made a public offering the value of the shares in the company held by the trust for all six of the siblings would multiply by a factor of ten. Gillian, primed by her husband, said her brothers were stealing from the family trust. The brothers, when Amanda heard the story, said they were doing the work, and had been for years. It made Amanda smile. When Gillian cuddled up to her, the first time they had spoken in years, Amanda said she wanted no part in the argument. The next day she had a visit from Douglas. In the will, each of the siblings had equal voting rights in the trust. But if there were an impasse Douglas had the casting vote. From being the family pariah, Amanda was now the centre of the family attention. No one cared she was a lesbian living with her lover. After Douglas came Nigel, all of them happy to visit the Knightsbridge flat. They were all polite to Evelina. They gushed over their nephew. Amanda, enjoying the feeling of real power for the first time in her life, told each of them she agreed with their side of the story.

"How's the family business going, Nigel?"

"Oh, it's going well."

"Good, then let's keep it going well."

"Will you agree to Douglas and myself buying the business?"

"Not really. Anyway, I don't understand business. As a child you always said I was a bit of a fool. Why don't we leave everything just as it is and then no one will have to make a decision?"

"We could offer you a very lucrative position as a non-executive director of the company."

"Are you trying to bribe me, Nigel?"

"No, of course I'm not. Whatever gave you that impression? I was thinking of James Oliver's future."

"Don't give me that bullshit. At the funeral you wouldn't even look at me."

Amanda, watching her brother squirm, was enjoying herself.

"We would pay you fifty thousand pounds as a director fee."

"For doing what?"

"Attending board meetings."

"And doing what you and Douglas tell me. If anyone is a disgrace to the family, Nigel, it's you and Douglas."

"We could offer Gillian the directorship."

"Then why don't you?... No, I think I know why. She wants that huge amount of capital injected into the trust which she'll get when Mother dies. And in the meantime receive her five per cent of the increased capital which will be more than fifty thousand pounds a year. All of that happens when you take the company public."

"How do you know all this? You were a secretary... Ah, your girlfriend."

"Don't be rude, Nigel. Don't be rude."

"Of course. I'm sorry."

"My husband, in between waiting tables and writing books he couldn't publish, gained a degree in economics from LSE. I typed his papers. He was a senior executive of BLG Ltd. You may have heard of them. They are quoted on the London Stock Exchange. His uncle owned a controlling interest in the company."

"Why on earth would he want to quit?"

"He made a mistake in America. And Randall had an incurable bug. All his life he wanted to write books. Unlike you and Douglas, money wasn't that important to him."

"I had no idea you married a successful man."

"You all cut me dead, remember. You had your own lives to live. You wanted nothing to do with your little sister, before or after I went to live with Evelina and came out of the closet."

"I had no idea. I always knew you as the rebel in the family after Dad caught you naked with William Drake."

"Well, isn't that a shame? As now you need my help and you aren't going to get it."

"What happened to Randall?"

"Last time I heard he was still writing books. In the divorce he gave me full custody of James Oliver. He doesn't visit his son. We never contact each other. And my side of that argument was all about money. Randall's lack of it... You'd better go. Evelina is due home in half an hour. She doesn't exactly like my family."

"So, you won't help us?"

"No, Nigel, I won't. Like so many others in this charming world you and Douglas have become downright greedy... My goodness. Where are my manners? Would you care for a drink?"

"I'd better go."

"Nigel, I was being sarcastic."

With a look of pent-up frustration on his face mixed with anger, her brother left the flat. To rub it in, Amanda saw him down to the parking lot where Nigel had parked his Jaguar. The car looked brand new.

"Is it owned by you or the company, Nigel?"

"The company."

"Not a bad perk. How's the wife?"

"She's the one driving me. She's never satisfied. We have three boys. The school fees are exorbitant."

"We all get what we pay for. Isn't a good old English public school more about the prestige it gives a boy rather than the education? The contacts for the future? Now, with Dad's money I'll be able to send James Oliver to a private school. Not the one your boys are in. That's far too expensive. Have a nice day, as they say in America. And yes, I've been to America. We know so little about each other. Be grateful, Nigel, for what you've got. And remember, both of you, it's Father's contacts that made the business. You two are just employees. If you float the company you will still get one sixth of the proceeds. Think about it. Have a little chat to your wife."

"Would you like to meet her?"

"Not really. Now run along. I have to look after my son."

As he got into his car, Nigel turned round, about to say something rude. His jaw twitched as he tried to control himself. Amanda gave her brother a sweet smile and left him in the parking lot.

"A car in London's a waste of time," she mumbled happily to herself. "Far easier to catch a taxi or the Tube. Image. They all want to show off. What has the world come to?"

Back in the flat, with James Oliver happy in his playpen, she poured herself a glass of South African sherry. The wine was good. The room was quiet. It was pleasant on her own.

"Not bad for a day's work. If they take the company public, whatever that means, it'll double the capital and double my income. Clever girl, Amanda."

The words, spoken out loud, set Amanda to thinking. She would employ a maid. Get someone else to clean the floors and do the washing. She was daydreaming, enjoying her glass of sherry as she waited for Evelina to come home from work. Having money was indeed a pleasant feeling. The only snag she could think of was not having enough to do. Apart from looking after James Oliver she would have to find something else to take up her time. Making love to Evelina wasn't going to bring her any more children any time soon. Her mind, as it did quite often, drifted back to her days with Randall.

"If I learnt a bit about finance typing his papers and listening to Randall talk, maybe he taught me a bit about writing books. How about a small children's book, James Oliver? A little book especially for you. And, as you get older, I'll write books for older children. And if they don't publish it won't matter. My son will read my books... Oh, what fun."

The boy was looking at her as if he understood what she was talking about.

"James Oliver, would you like a glass of sherry? No, better not. You're a bit too young. What shall we write about? What lovely little story will make you smile in a couple of years?"

Happy with the thought, Amanda poured herself a second glass of the sweet sherry. When she heard Evelina put her key in the lock, Amanda smiled.

"Hello, darling. What are you looking so cheerful about?"

"I'm going to write a book. A children's book. And I'm going to employ a cleaner... You want to go out to dinner? Dinner is on me. Have a glass of sherry. Give me a kiss."

The next day, the flat quiet and James Oliver asleep, Amanda got out the typewriter she had used to type Randall's books, there having been no point in leaving it with Randall as he couldn't type. She put in a sheet of paper and rolled it up to the top. She rubbed her hands together. Looked up at the ceiling. Looked out of the window at the block of flats across the street. Got up and walked around the room. Sat on the couch. Went out for a walk. Came back and sat in the chair in front of the typewriter and the clean sheet of white paper. Her mind was blank. Nothing came.

"Randall, how the hell do you do it? Where do you get it from?"

Frustrated, Amanda pulled the sheet of paper out of the machine and put the typewriter back into the cupboard. She told herself she would have to do a lot more thinking before she sat down to write a story.

Counting the hours before Evelina would come home, Amanda picked up a book and tried to read. Bored, she dressed James Oliver, put on a coat and went out.

In the park, the park she had walked so many times with Randall, spring was in the air, the pigeons calling from the trees. Hoping for inspiration, she pushed her son down the path, the midday sun a pleasant change from the winter cold. Vaguely, she wondered if Randall still walked the park. There was no one she recognised. In England, unlike America, strangers never greeted each other. An idea began to dawn. There was a duck and a chicken, the pigeons making her think of birds when James waved his podgy hand at a group of pigeons that were feeding on the ground. An old man sitting on a wooden bench had thrown a handful of grain on the grass. The idea grew. Amanda smiled. As she walked, she had forgotten all about Randall. She would need an illustrator to draw the pictures.

"I've got the money. Why not use it?"

"I'm sorry, madam. Did you say something?"

The old man was talking to her, looking at her hopefully. Amanda pushed the pushchair to the bench, turned it round to face the path and sat down.

"I wasn't. I was talking to myself. But what would you like to talk about?"

≈

LOOK BEFORE YOU LEAP (BOOK TWELVE)

THE BRIGANDSHAW JOURNEY WILL CONTINUE...

Will the lure of fame and fortune be his nemesis?

His life has collapsed, his marriage over, and his son is lost to him. Randall is broke, but with the aid of his two best friends, Randall flies home. Home to Africa. Africa where he can seek solace and a place to heal.

Heading for the Zambezi River with only a vehicle and supplies to last several months, Randall starts to find his inner peace. Finding his rhythm, Africa begins to seep into his soul. His characters are at long last chatting to him. And any thoughts of returning to the world of men are finally gone. Until he hears the noise of a boat beating upstream...

With the sound getting louder, along with shouts of his name, Randall realises his peace is at an end. He's being called back to reality, but why and at what cost?

Look before You Leap is the twelfth book in the Brigandshaw Chronicles, a series that only Peter Rimmer knows how to bring to life with his enduring, complex characters, together with his passion for the places he takes them to.

PRINCIPAL CHARACTERS

∼

Amanda Hanscombe — A girl Randall meets in the Leg of Mutton and Cauliflower

Barend Oosthuizen — Tinus and Genevieve's son who works in BLG Inc, New York

Benjamin Crossley — Phillip and Randall's maternal grandfather

Camilla — Evelina's friend who runs Camilla's Corner

Donna St Clair — Livy Johnston and Frank St Clair's daughter

Evelina — Works with William Drake

George Webb Hanscombe — Amanda's father

Gillian Hanscombe — One of Amanda's older sisters

Hayley Oosthuizen — Tinus and Genevieve's daughter who works in BLG Inc, New York

Jacques Oosthuizen — Phillip Crookshank's safari business partner and cousin to Barend

James Tomlin — Randall's friend and roommate at Mrs Salter's

Judy Collins — A girl Randall meets on the train to Notting Hill Gate

Kelvin Taylor — William Drake's live-in lover

Maureen Crossley — Phillip and Randall's maternal grandmother (deceased)

Mavis Crookshank — Phillip and Randall's paternal grandmother who lives in London

Mrs Hanscombe — Amanda's mother

Mrs Reed — The Hanscombes' housekeeper

Mrs Salter — Randall's landlady in Notting Hill Gate

Myra and Craig Crookshank — Phillip and Randall's younger siblings

Oliver Manningford — Randall's friend and roommate at Mrs Salter's

Paul Crookshank — Phillip and Randall's uncle married to Beth Crookshank

Randall Crookshank — Principal character in *Leopards Never Change Their Spots*

Silas — House servant at World's View

Veronica West — Oliver's girlfriend and an actress

William Drake — Amanda's childhood friend

Minor Characters

Beth Crookshank — Harry Brigandshaw's daughter

Clay Barry — Member-in-charge for Centenary

Deepak — Owner of the Tandoori restaurant in Greek Street

Douglas and Nigel — Amanda Hanscombe's older brothers

Frederick Ponsonby — A literary agent

Genevieve Oosthuizen — An actress and a principal character in *Treason If You Lose*

Happiness and *Moley* — Randall's childhood friends in Rhodesia

Josiah Tongogara — Head of the Zimbabwe African National Liberation Army

Livy Johnston — An artist and principal character in *Lady Come Home*

Mrs Walker — Paul Crookshank's secretary

Noah — The barman at the Centenary West club

Pat Grimshaw — Randall Crookshank's mentor at BLG

Primrose — Moley and Happiness's mother

Sarah Rankin — Temp agency owner in London

Sonia — Randall Crookshank's secretary at BLG Ltd

Tinus Oosthuizen — Harry Brigandshaw's nephew and a principal character in *Treason If You Lose*

Vince Ranger — Jeremy Crookshank's farm assistant

DEAR READER

～

Reviews are the most powerful tools in our kitty when it comes to getting attention for Peter's books. This is where you can come in, as by providing an honest review you will help bring them to the attention of other readers.

If you enjoyed reading *Leopards Never Change Their Spots*, and have five minutes to spare, we would really appreciate a review (it can be as short as you like). Your help in spreading the word and keeping Peter's work alive is gratefully received.

Please post your review on the retailer site where you purchased this book.

Thank you so much.
Heather Stretch (Peter's daughter)

ACKNOWLEDGEMENTS

~

With grateful thanks to our *VIP First Readers* for reading *Leopards Never Change Their Spots* prior to its official launch date. They have been fabulous in picking up errors and typos helping us to ensure that your own reading experience of *Leopards Never Change Their Spots* has been the best possible. Their time and commitment is particularly appreciated.

Hilary Jenkins (South Africa)
Agnes Mihalyfy (United Kingdom)
Daphne Rieck (Australia)

Thank you.

Kamba Publishing

Printed in Great Britain
by Amazon

12915927R00251